BILLY BATHGATE

E. L. DOCTOROW

BILLY BATHGATE

A NOVEL

RANDOM HOUSE NEW YORK

Portions of this work have previously appeared in the following publications:
Granta and *Gentleman's Quarterly.*

Grateful acknowledgment is made to the following for
permission to reprint previously published material:

Fred Ahlert Music Corporation and Henderson Music Company: Excerpts from the
lyrics to "Bye Bye Blackbird," lyrics by Mort Dixon, music by Ray Henderson.
Copyright 1926. Copyright renewed 1953. All rights for the extended term
administered by Fred Ahlert Music Corporation for Olde Clover Leaf Music and
Henderson Music Company, c/o William Krasilovsky, Feinman and Krasilovsky.
Used by permission. All rights reserved.

Bourne Co./New York Music Publishers: Excerpt from the lyrics to
"Me and My Shadow," words by Billy Rose, music by
Al Jolson and Dave Dreyer. Copyright 1927 Bourne Co. Copyright renewed,
International Copyright secured. All rights reserved. Used by permission.

The Songwriters Guild of America and CPP Belwin, Inc.:
Excerpt from the lyrics to "The One I Love Belongs to Somebody Else,"
by Gus Kahn and Isham Jones. Copyright 1924. U.S. rights
renewed 1980 Gilbert Keyes Music and Bantam Music.

Warner/Chappell Music, Inc.: Excerpt from the lyrics to "Limehouse Blues,"
by Philip Braham and Douglas Furber. Copyright 1922 Warner Bros. Inc.
(Renewed).
All rights reserved. Used by permission.

Library of Congress Cataloging-in-Publication Data

Doctorow, E. L.
Billy Bathgate.
I. Title.
PS3554.03B55   1989   843'.54   88-42820
ISBN 0-394-52529-9
ISBN 0-394-57513-X (lim. ed.)

Manufactured in the United States of America
98765432
First Trade Edition
A limited first edition of this book
has been privately printed by the Franklin Library.

BOOK DESIGN BY JO ANNE METSCH

To Jason Epstein

PART

ONE

O N E

He had to have planned it because when we drove onto the dock the boat was there and the engine was running and you could see the water churning up phosphorescence in the river, which was the only light there was because there was no moon, nor no electric light either in the shack where the dockmaster should have been sitting, nor on the boat itself, and certainly not from the car, yet everyone knew where everything was, and when the big Packard came down the ramp Mickey the driver braked it so that the wheels hardly rattled the boards, and when he pulled up alongside the gangway the doors were already open and they hustled Bo and the girl upside before they even made a shadow in all that darkness. And there was no resistance, I saw a movement of black bulk, that was all, and all I heard was maybe the sound someone makes who is frightened and has a hand not his own over his mouth, the doors slammed and the car was humming and gone and the boat was already opening up water between itself and the slip before a thin minute had passed. Nobody said not to so I jumped aboard and stood at the rail, frightened as you might expect, but a capable boy, he had said that himself, a capable boy capable of learning, and I see now capable of adoring worshiping that rudeness of power of which he was a greater student than anybody, oh and that menace of him where it might all be over for anyone in his sight from one instant to the next, that was what it all turned on, it was why I was there, it was why I was thrilled to be judged so by him as a capable boy, the danger he was really a maniac.

Besides, I had that self-assurance of the very young, which was in this case the simple presumption I could get away when I would, anytime I wanted, I could outrun him, outrun his rage or the range of his understanding and the reach of his domain, because I could climb fences and hustle down alleys and jump fire escapes and dance along the roof parapets of all the tenements of the world if it came to that. I was capable, I knew it before he did, although he gave me more than confirmation when he said it, he made me his. But anyway I wasn't thinking of any of this at the time, it was just something I had in me I could use if I had to, not even an idea but an instinct waiting in my brain in case I ever needed it, or else why would I have leapt lightly over the rail as the phosphorescent water widened under me, to stand and watch from the deck as the land withdrew and a wind from the black night of water blew across my eyes and the island of lights rose up before me as if it were a giant ocean liner sailing past and leaving me stranded with the big murdering gangsters of my life and times?

My instructions were simple, when I was not doing something I was specifically told to do, to pay attention, to miss nothing, and though he wouldn't have put it in so many words, to become the person who would always be watching and always be listening no matter what state I was in, love or danger or humiliation or deathly misery—to lose nothing of any fraction of a moment even if it happened to be my last.

So I knew this had to have been planned, though smeared with his characteristic rage that made you think it was just something that he had thought of the moment before he did it as for instance the time he throttled and then for good measure stove in the skull of the fire safety inspector a moment after smiling at him in appreciation for his entrepreneurial flair. I had never seen anything like that, and I suppose there are ways more deft, but however you do it, it is a difficult thing to do: his technique was to have none, he sort of jumped forward screaming with his arms raised and brought his whole weight of assault on the poor fuck, and carried him down in a kind of smothering tackle, landing on top of him with a crash that probably broke his back, who knows? and then with his knees pinning down the outstretched arms, simply grabbing the throat and pressing the balls of his thumbs down on the windpipe, and when the tongue came out and eyes rolled up walloping the head two three times on the floor like it was a coconut he wanted to crack open.

And they were all in dinner clothes too, I had to remember that, black tie and black coat with the persian lamb collar, white silk scarf and his pearl gray homburg blocked down the center of the crown just like the president's, in Mr. Schultz's case. Bo's hat and coat were still in the hatcheck in his case. There had been an anniversary dinner at the Embassy Club, five years of their association in the beer business, so it was all planned, even the menu, but the only thing was Bo had misunderstood the sentiment of the occasion and brought along his latest pretty girl, and I had felt, without even knowing what was going on when the two of them were hustled into the big Packard, that she was not part of the plan. Now she was here on the tugboat and it was entirely dark from the outside, they had curtains over the portholes and I couldn't see what was going on but I could hear the sound of Mr. Schultz's voice and although I couldn't make out the words I could tell he was not happy, and I supposed they would rather not have her witness what was going to happen to a man she might possibly have come to be fond of, and then I heard or felt the sounds of steps on a steel ladder, and I turned my back to the cabin and leaned over the railing just in time to see a lighted pucker of green angry water and then a curtain must have been drawn across a porthole because the water disappeared. A few moments later I heard one returning set of footsteps.

Under these circumstances I could not hold to the conviction that I had done the smart thing by coming aboard without his telling me to. I lived, as we all did, by his moods, I was forever trying to think of ways to elicit the good ones, the impulse to placate was something he brought out in people, and when I was engaged in doing something at his instruction I pressed hard to do my urgent best while at the same time preparing in my mind the things I would say in my defense in any unforeseen event of his displeasure. Not that I believed there was an appeals process. So I rode as a secret rider there at the cold railing through several minutes of my irresolution, and the strings of lights on the bridges behind me made me sentimental for my past. But by then we were coming downriver into the heavier swells of the open water, and the boat began to pitch and roll and I found I had to widen my stance to keep my balance. The wind was picking up too, and spray was flying up from the prow and wetting my face, I was holding the rail and pressing my back against the side of the cabin and beginning to feel the light head that comes with the realization that water is a beast of another planet, and with each passing moment it was drawing in my imagination a portrait of its mysterious powerful and endlessly vast animacy right there under the boat I was riding, and all the other boats of the world as well, which if they lashed themselves together wouldn't cover an inch of its undulant and heaving hide.

So I went in, opening the door a crack and slipping through shoulder first, on the theory that if I was going to die I had rather die indoors.

Here is what I saw in the first instant of my blinking in the harsh light of a work lamp hooked to the deckhouse ceiling: the elegant Bo Weinberg standing beside his pointed patent-leather shoes, with the black silk socks and attached garters lying twisted like dead eels beside them, and his white feet looking very much longer and very much wider than the shoes he had just stepped from. He was staring at his feet, perhaps because feet are inti-mate body parts rarely seen with black tie, and following his gaze, I felt I had to commiserate with what I was sure he was thinking, that for all our civilization we go around on these things that are slit at the front end into five unequal lengths each partially covered with shell.

Kneeling in front of him was the brisk and impassive Irving methodically rolling Bo's pant legs with their black satin side-stripe to the knees. Irving had seen me but chose not to notice me, which was characteristic. He was Mr. Schultz's utility man and did what he was told to do and gave no appearance of thought for anything else. He was rolling up pant legs. A hollow-chested man, with thinning hair, he had the pallor of an alcoholic, that dry paper skin they have, and I knew about drunks on the wagon what they paid for their sobriety, the concentration it demanded, the state of constant mourning it produced. I liked to watch Irving whatever he was doing, even when it was not as it was now something extraordinary. Each fold-up of the pant leg exactly matched the one before. He did everything meticulously and without wasted movement. He was a professional, but since he had no profession other than dealing with the contingencies of his chosen life, he carried himself as if life was a profession, just as, I suppose, in a more conventional employment, a butler would.

And partially obscured by Bo Weinberg and standing as far from him as I was but at the opposite side of the cabin, in his open coat and unevenly draped white scarf and his soft gray homburg tilted back on his head, and one hand in his jacket pocket and the other casually holding a gun at his side that was pointed with no particular emphasis at the deck, was Mr. Schultz.

This scene was so amazing to me I gave it the deference one gives to the event perceived as historical. Everything was moving up and down in unison but the three men didn't seem to notice and even the wind was a distant and chastened sound in here, and the air was close with the smell of tar and diesel oil and there were coils of thick rope stacked like rubber tires, and pulleys and chain tackle, and racks filled with tools and kerosene lamps and cleats and numerous items whose names or purposes I did not know but whose importance to the nautical life I willingly conceded. And the tug's engine vibrations were comfortingly powerful in here and I could feel them running into my hand, which I had put against the door in order to close it.

I caught Mr. Schultz's eye and he suddenly displayed a mouth
of large evenly aligned white teeth, and his face of rude features
creased itself into a smile of generous appreciation. "It's the
Invisible Man," he said. I was as startled by his utterance as I
would have been if someone in a church painting had started to
talk. Then I found myself smiling back. Joy flooded my boyish
breast, or perhaps gratitude to God for granting me at least this
moment in which my fate wasn't in the balance. "Look at that,
Irving, the kid came along for the ride. You like boats, kid?" he
said.

"I don't know yet," I said truthfully and without understanding why this honest answer was so funny. For he was laughing
now loudly and in his hornlike voice, which I thought was terribly careless of the solemn nature of the occasion; the mien of
the other two men seemed preferable to me. And I will say
something more about Mr. Schultz's voice because it was so
much an aspect of his power of domination. It was not that it was
always loud but that it had a substantial body to it, it came out
of his throat with harmonic buzz, and it was very instrumental
actually, so that you understood the throat as a sound box, and
that maybe the chest cavity and the nose bones, too, were all
involved in producing it, and it was a baritone voice that auto-
matically made you pay attention in the way of wanting a horn
voice like that yourself, except when he raised it in anger or
laughed as he was doing now, and then it grated on your ears
and made you dislike it, as I did now—or maybe it was what I'd
said that I disliked because I was joining in some cleverness at
a dying man's expense.

There was a narrow green slat bench or shelf hung from the
cabin wall and I sat down on it. What could Bo Weinberg possibly have done? I had had little acquaintance with him, he was
something of a knight errant, rarely in the office on 149th Street,
never in the cars, certainly not on the trucks, but always in-
timated to be central to the operation, like Mr. Dixie Davis the
lawyer, or Abbadabba Berman the accounting genius—at that
level of executive importance. He was reputed to do Mr.
Schultz's diplomatic work, negotiating with other gangs and

performing necessary business murders. He was one of the giants, and perhaps, in fearsomeness, second only to Mr. Schultz himself. Now not just his feet but his legs to the knees were exposed. Irving rose from his kneeling position and offered his arm, and Bo Weinberg took it, like some princess at a ball, and delicately, gingerly, placed one foot at a time in the laundry tub in front of him that was filled with wet cement. I had of course seen from the moment I had come through the door how the tubbed cement made a slow-witted diagram of the sea outside, the slab of it shifting to and fro as the boat rose and fell on the waves.

I could handle the sudden events, getting baptized as by a thunderstorm, but this was more than I was ready for to tell the truth, I found I was not a self-confident witness here in contemplation of the journey about to be taken by the man sitting before me with his feet being cast in stone. I was working to understand this mysterious evening and the unhappy tolling of a life in its prime that was like the buoys I heard clanking their lonely warnings as we passed out to sea. I felt my witness was my own personal ordeal as Bo Weinberg was invited to sit now in a wooden kitchen chair that had been shoved into place behind him and then to present his hands for their tying. They were crisscrossed to each other at the wrist with fresh and slightly stiff clothesline still showing the loops it came in from the hardware store, and with Irving's perfect knots between the wrists like a section of vertebrae. The joined hands were placed between Bo's thighs and tied to them cat's cradle, over and under, over and under, and then everything together was roped in three or four giant turns to the chair so that he could not lift his knees, and then the chair was twice looped to the laundry tub through the handles and the final knot was pulled tight around a chair leg just as the rope ran out. Quite possibly Bo had at some time in the past seen this scoutcraft displayed on someone else for he looked upon it with a sort of distracted admiration, as if now, too, someone not himself was sitting hunched over in a chair there with his feet entubbed in hardening cement in the deckhouse of a boat running without lights past Coenties Slip across New York Harbor and into the Atlantic.

The deckhouse was shaped like an oval. A railed hatch where the girl had been put below was in the center of the deck at the rear. Toward the front was a bolted metal ladder leading straight up through a hatch to the wheelhouse where I assumed the captain or whatever he was called was duly attending to his business. I had never been on anything bigger than a rowboat so all of this, at least, was good news, that something like a boat could be so much of a construction, all according to the rules of the sea, and that there was a means of making your tenuous way across this world that clearly reflected a long history of thought. Because the swells got higher and longer, and everyone had to anchor himself, Mr. Schultz taking the side bench directly opposite where I sat and Irving gripping the ladder leading upstairs to the wheelhouse as if it were a pole on a subway train. And there was a silence for some time inside the sounds of the running engine and the waves, like the solemnity of people listening to organ music. And now Bo Weinberg was coming to life and beginning to look around him, to see what he could see, and who was here and what could be done; I received the merest glance of his dark eyes, one short segment of arc in their scan, for which I was incredibly relieved, not bearing any responsibility, nor wanting any, for these wheezing shifting seas or for the unbreathable nature of water, or its coldness, or its dark and bottomless craw.

Now there was such intimacy among all of us in this black cabin shining in the almost-green shards of one work light that when anyone moved everyone else noticed, and at this time my eyes were riveted by Mr. Schultz's small action of dropping his gun in his ample coat pocket and removing then from his inside jacket pocket the silver case that held his cigars and extracting a cigar and replacing the case and then biting off the tip of his cigar and spitting it out. Irving came over to him with a cigarette lighter, which he got going with one press of his thumb just a moment before he held it to the tip. And Mr. Schultz leaned slightly forward rotating the cigar to light it evenly, and over the sound of the sea and the grinding engine I heard the *sip sip* of his pull on the cigar and watched the flame flare up on his cheeks and brow, so that the imposition of him was all the more enlarged in the special light of one of his appetites. Then the light went out and Irving retreated and Mr. Schultz sat back on the bench, the cigar glowing in the corner of his mouth and filling the cabin with smoke, which was not really a great thing to be smelling in a boat cabin on the high seas.

"You can crack a window, kid," he said. I did this with alacrity, turning and kneeling on the bench and sticking my hand through the curtains and unlatching the porthole and pushing it open. I could feel the night on my hand and drew it in wet.

"Isn't it a black night though?" Mr. Schultz said. He rose and moved around to Bo, who was sitting facing astern, and hunkered down in front of him like a doctor in front of a patient. "Look at that, the man is shivering. Hey Irving," he said. "How long till it hardens up? Bo is cold."

"Not long," Irving said. "A little while."

"Only a little while longer," Mr. Schultz said, as if Bo needed a translation. He smiled apologetically and stood and put a companionable hand on Bo's shoulder.

At this Bo Weinberg spoke and what he said was genuinely surprising to me. It was not what any apprentice or ordinary person in his situation could have said and more than any remark of Mr. Schultz's to this moment gave me to understand the realm of high audacity these men moved in, like another dimension. Perhaps he was only admitting to his despair or perhaps this was his dangerous way of getting Mr. Schultz's sincere attention; I would not have thought of the possibility that a man in his circumstances would feel he had a measure of control over how and when his death would occur. "You're a cocksucker, Dutch" is what he said.

I held my breath but Mr. Schultz only shook his head and sighed. "First you beg me and now you go calling me names."

"I didn't beg you, I told you to let the girl go. I spoke to you

as if you were still human. But all you are is a cocksucker. And
when you can't find a cock to suck you pick up scumbags off the
floor and suck them. That's what I think of you, Dutch."

As long as he was not looking at me I could look at Bo Weinberg. He certainly had spirit. He was a handsome man, with
smooth shiny black hair combed back without a part from a
widow's peak, and a swarthy Indian sort of face with high cheekbones, and a full well-shaped mouth and a strong chin, all set
on the kind of long neck that a tie and collar dresses very nicely.
Even hunched over in the shame of his helplessness, with his
black tie askew on his wing collar and his satiny black tuxedo
jacket bunched up above his shoulders, so that his posture was
subservient and his gaze necessarily furtive, he suggested to me
the glamour and class of a big-time racketeer.

I wished now in some momentary confusion of loyalties, or
perhaps thinking only as a secret judge that the case had not yet
been made to my satisfaction, that Mr. Schultz could have some
of this quality of elegance of the man in the tub. The truth was
that even in the finest clothes Mr. Schultz seemed badly dressed,
he suffered a sartorial inadequacy, as some people had weak
eyes or rickets, and he must have known this because whatever
else he was up to he would also be hiking up his trousers with
his forearms, or lifting his chin while he pulled at his collar, or
brushing cigar ashes from his vest, or taking off his hat and
blocking the crown with the side of his hand. Without even
thinking about it he tried constantly to correct his relationship
to his clothes, as if he had some sort of palsy of dissatisfaction,
to the point where you thought everything would settle on him
neatly enough if he would stop picking at it.

The trouble may have been in part his build, which was short-
necked and stolid. I think now that the key to grace or elegance
in any body, male or female, is the length of the neck, that when
the neck is long several conclusions follow, such as a proper
proportion of weight to height, a natural pride of posture, a gift
for eye contact, a certain nimbleness of the spine and length of
stride, all in all a kind of physical gladness in movement leading
to athletic competence or a love for dancing. Whereas the short

neck predicts a host of metaphysical afflictions, any one of which brings about the ineptitude for life that creates art, invention, great fortunes, and the murderous rages of the disordered spirit. I am not suggesting this as an absolute law or even a hypothesis that can be proved or disproved; it is not a notion from the scientific world but more like an inkling of a folk truth of the kind that seemed reasonable enough before radio. Maybe it was something that Mr. Schultz himself perceived in the unconscious genius of his judgments because up to now I knew of two murders he had personally committed, both in the region of the neck, the throttling of that Fire Department inspector, and the more viciously expedient destruction of a West Side numbers boss who was unfortunate enough to be tilted back in a chair and having himself shaved in the barbershop of the Maxwell Hotel on West Forty-seventh Street when Mr. Schultz found him.

So I suppose the answer to his regrettable lack of elegance was that he had other ways of impressing you. And after all there was a certain fluent linkage of mind and body, both were rather powerfully blunt and tended not to recognize obstacles that required going around rather than through or over. In fact it was just this quality of Mr. Schultz's that Bo Weinberg now remarked upon. "Think of it," he said, addressing the cabin, "he makes this cheap dago move on Bo Weinberg, can you believe it? Only the guy who took out Vince Coll for him and held Jack Diamond by the ears so he could put the gun in his mouth. Only the guy who did Maranzano and bought him a million dollars of respect from the Unione. Who made the big hits for him and covered his ass for him, and found the Harlem policy he was too dumb to find for himself, who handed him his fortune, made him a goddamn millionaire, made him look like something else than the fucking lowdown gonif he is—this shmuck from the gutter. This bullethead. Listen, what did I expect, pulls me out of a restaurant in front of my fiancée? Women and children, anything, he doesn't care, he doesn't know any better did you see those waiters cringing, Irving, you weren't there you should have seen those waiters trying not to watch him shovel it in sitting there in his Delancey Street suit that he bought from the signboard."

I thought whatever was going to happen now I didn't want to witness; I had scrunched up my eyes and instinctively pressed back into the cold cabin wall. But Mr. Schultz hardly seemed to react, his face was impassive. "Don't talk to Irving," he said by way of reply. "Talk to me."

"Men talk. When there are differences men talk. If there is a misunderstanding they hear each other out. That's what men do. I don't know what you came out of. I don't know what stinking womb of pus and shit and ape scum you came out of. 'Cause you're an ape, Dutch. Hunker down and scratch your ass, Dutch. Swing from a tree. Hoo hoo, Dutch. Hoo hoo."

Mr. Schultz said very quietly: "Bo, you should understand I am past the madness part. I am past the anger. Don't waste your breath." And like a man who has lost interest he returned to his seat along the bulkhead across from me.

And from the slump of Bo Weinberg's shoulders, and the droop of his head, I thought it might be true of a man of rank that he would be naturally defiant, and it might furthermore be true that he would exhibit the brazen courage of a killer of the realm for whom death was such a common daily circumstance of business, like paying bills or making bank deposits, that his own was not that much different from anyone else's, as if they were all a kind of advanced race, these gangsters, trained by their chosen life into some supernatural warrior spirit; but what I had heard had been a song of despair; Bo would know better than anyone there were no appeals; his only hope would be for a death as quick and painless as possible; and my throat went dry from the certainty that came over me that this was exactly what he had been trying to do, effect it, invoke Mr. Schultz's hair-trigger temper to dictate the means and time of his own death.

So I understood of the uncharacteristic controlled response that it was so potent as to be merciless; Mr. Schultz had made his very nature disappear, becoming the silent author of the tugboat, a faceless professional, because he had let Bo's words erase him and had become still and thoughtful and objective in the approved classical manner of his henchman Bo Weinberg, as Bo, swearing and ranting and raving, had seemed to become him.

In my mind it was the first inkling of how a ritual death tampers with the universe, that inversions occur, everything flashes into your eyes backward or inside out, there is some kind of implosive glimpse of the other side, and you smell it too, like crossed wires.

"Men talk, if they are men," Bo Weinberg said now in an entirely different tone of voice. I could barely hear him. "They honor the past, if they are men. They pay their debts. You never paid your debts, your deepest debts, your deepest debts of honor. The more I done for you, the more like a brother I been, the less I have counted to you. I should have known you would do this, and for no more reason than you are a welsher who never paid me what I was worth, who never paid anybody what they are worth. I protected you, I saved your life a dozen times, I did your work and did it like a professional. I should have known this was the way you would make good on your debt, this is the way Dutch Schultz keeps the books, trumping up the wildest cockamamie lie just to chisel, a cheap chiseler chiseling every way he can."

"You always had the words, Bo," Mr. Schultz said. He puffed on his cigar and took his hat off and reblocked it with the side of his hand. "You got more words than me, being having been to high school. On the other hand I got a good head for numbers, so I guess it all evens out."

And then he told Irving to bring up the girl.

And up she came, her marcelled blond head, and then her white neck and shoulders, as if she was rising from the ocean. I had not before in the darkness of the car gotten a really good look at her, she was very slender in her cream white evening gown hanging by two thin straps, and in this dark and oily boat, totally alarming, white with captivity, staring about her in some frightened confusion so that prophecies of an awful evil despoilage filled my chest, not just of sex but of class, and a groan like

a confirmation of my feeling strangled in the throat of Bo Weinberg, who had been cursing a stream of vile oaths at Mr. Schultz
and who now strained at his ropes and shook his chair from side
to side until Mr. Schultz reached in his coat pocket and brought
the grip of his pistol smartly down on Bo's shoulder and the
girl's green eyes went wide as Bo howled and lifted his head in
pain and then said from his squeezed face of pain that she
shouldn't look, that she should turn away and not look at him.

Irving coming up the stairs behind her caught her as she
began to fold and set her down in the corner on a cushion of
piled tarpaulins and leaned her back against cylinders of coiled
line, and she sat on her side with her knees drawn and her head
averted, a beautiful girl, I was able to see now, with a fine profile,
as in the aristocracy of my imagination, with a thin nose and
under it a lovely dimpled crescent curving out downward to a
mouth which from the side was full-lipped in the middle and
carved back to no more than a thin line at the corner, and a firm
jawline and a neck that curved like a waterbird's, and—I dared
to let my eyes go down—a thin fragile chest, with her breasts
unencumbered as far as I could determine by any undergar-
ment, being slight, although apparent at the same time under
the shining white satin of her décolletage. Irving had brought
her fur wrap along and draped it now over her shoulders. And
all of a sudden it was very close in here with all of us, and I
noticed a stain on the lower part of her gown, with some matter
stuck to it.

"Threw up all over the place," Irving said.

"Oh Miss Lola, I am so sorry," Mr. Schultz said. "There is
never enough air on a boat. Irving, perhaps a drink." From his
coat pocket he withdrew a flask encased in leather. "Pour Miss
Lola out a bit of this."

Irving stood with his legs planted against the rock of the boat
and unscrewed from the flask a metal cap and precisely poured
into it a shot of neat and held it out to the woman. "Go ahead,
missy," Mr. Schultz said. "It's good malt whiskey. It will settle
your stomach."

I couldn't understand why they didn't see she had fainted but they knew more than I did, the head stirred, the eyes opened and all at once in their struggle to come to focus betrayed my boy's romance: She reached out for the drink and held it and studied it and raised it and tossed it back.

"Bravo, sweetheart," Mr. Schultz said. "You know what you're doing, don't you? I bet you know how to do just about everything, don't you. What? Did you say something, Bo?"

"For God's sake, Dutch," Bo whispered. "It's over, it's done."

"No, no, don't worry, Bo. No harm will come to the lady. I give you my word. Now Miss Lola," he said, "you can see the trouble Bo is in. You been together how long?"

She would not look at him or say a word. The hand in her lap went slack. The metal screw cap rolled off her knee and lodged in a crack of the decking. Immediately Irving picked it up.

"I had not the pleasure of meeting you before this evening, he never brought you around, though it was clear Bo had fallen in love, my bachelor Bo, my lady-killer, it was clear he had gone head over heels. And I see why, I do most certainly see why. But he calls you Lola and I am sure that is not your name. I know all the girls named Lola."

Irving passed forward, handing the flask to Mr. Schultz, and continuing, and it was at this moment an uphill walk, the boat riding a run of wave prow up, and he reached the forward ladder and turned to wait with all of us, watching the girl, who would not answer as the boat dropped under us, but sat now with two streams of tears silently coursing down her cheeks, and all the world was water, inside and out, while she didn't speak.

"But be that as it may," Mr. Schultz went on, "whoever you are you can see the trouble your Bo is in. Right, Bo? Show her how you can't do certain things anymore in your life, Bo. Show her how the simplest thing, crossing your legs, scratching your nose, it can't be done anymore by you. Oh yeah, he can scream, he can shout. But he can't lift his foot, he can't open his fly or unbuckle his belt, he can't do much of anything, Miss Lola. Little by little he is taking leave of his life. So answer me now, sweetheart. I'm just curious. Where did you two meet? How long you been lovebirds?"

"Don't answer him!" Bo shouted. "It's nothing to do with her! Hey Dutch, you're looking for reasons? I can give you all the reasons in the world and they all add up to you're an asshole."

"Aah that is such bad talk," Mr. Schultz said. "In front of this woman. And this boy. There are women and children here, Bo."

"You know what they call him? Shortpail. Shortpail Schultz." Bo cackled with laughter. "Everyone has a name and that's his. Shortpail. Deals in this brewed catpiss he calls beer and doesn't even pay for it. Chintzes on payoffs, has more money than he knows what to do with and still nickels-and-dimes his associates. An operation this size, beer, unions, policy, runs it like some fucking candy store. Am I right, Shortpail?"

Mr. Schultz nodded thoughtfully. "But look, Bo," he said. "I'm standing here and you're sitting there and you're all finished, and who would you rather be at this moment, Mr. class-act Bo Weinberg? Moves on the man he works for? That's class?"

"May you fuck your mother flying through the air," Bo said. "May your father lick the shit of horses off the street. May your baby be served to you boiled on a platter with an apple in its mouth."

"Oh Bo." Mr. Schultz rolled his eyes upward. He lifted his arms out and his palms up and made mute appeal to the heavens. Then he looked back at Bo and let his arms fall to his sides with a slap. "I give up," he muttered. "All bets off. Irving, is there another cabin down there that has not been occupied?"

"Cabin aft," Irving said. "The back end," he said in explanation.

"Thank you. Now Miss Lola, would you be so kind?" Mr. Schultz reached out to the seated woman as if they were at a dance. She gasped and folded herself back away from his hand, bringing her knees up in the gown and pressing back, which made Mr. Schultz look for a moment at his hand as if he was trying to see what about it was so repugnant to her. We all looked at his hand, Bo from under his lowering brow while at the same time making strange strangling noises, his ears and neck turning red with the effort to burst Irving's ropes. Mr. Schultz had stubby fingers, a plump meaty rise where the thumb and forefinger joined. His nails needed a manicure. Sparse colonies of black hair grew behind each knuckle. He yanked the woman to her feet so that she cried out and held her by the wrist while he turned to face Bo.

"You see, missy," he said, though he was not looking at her, "since he won't make it easier we'll have to do it for him. So he couldn't care less when the time comes. So he'll be only too happy."

Pushing the girl in front of him, Mr. Schultz descended to the deck below. I heard her slip on the stairs and cry out, and then Mr. Schultz telling her to shut up, and then a thin, extended wail, and then a door slamming, and then only the wind and the plash of water.

I didn't know what to do. I was still sitting on the side bench, I was bent over and gripping the bench with my hands and feeling the engine reverberate in my bones. Irving cleared his throat and climbed the ladder into the wheelhouse. I was now alone with Bo Weinberg, whose head had slumped forward in the privacy of his torment, and I didn't want to be alone with him so took Irving's place at the bottom of the ladder and started to climb it, rung by rung, but with my back to it, climbing the ladder backward by my heels and then coming to a halt halfway up between the deck and the hatch, and entwining myself there because Irving had begun to talk with the pilot of the boat. It was dark up there when I peered up, or maybe as dark as the light from a compass or some other dashboard instrument, and I could picture them staring over the prow from that height as they spoke, looking out to sea as the boat rode to its impenetrable destination.

"You know," Irving said in his dry gravelly voice, "I started out on the water. I ran speedboats for Big Bill."

"That right?"

"Oh sure. What is it, ten years now? He had good boats. Liberty motors in 'em, do thirty-five knots loaded."

"Sure," the pilot said, "I knew those boats. I remember the *Mary B.* I remember the *Bettina.*"

"That's right," Irving said. "The *King Fisher.* The *Galway.*"

"Irving," Bo Weinberg said from his tub.

"Come out here to the Row," Irving said, "load the cases, be back on the Brooklyn side or off Canal Street in no time at all."

"Sure," the pilot said. "We had names and numbers. We knew which boats were Bill's and which boats we could go after."

"What?" Irving said, and the word seemed conditioned by a wan smile I imagined up there in the dark.

"Sure," the pilot said. "I ran a cutter in those days, the C.G. two-eight-two."

"I'll be damned," Irving said.

"Saw you go by. Well, hell, even a lieutenant senior grade only got a hundred and change a month."

"Irving!" Bo shouted. "For God's sake!"

"He covered everything," Irving said. "That's what I liked about Bill. Nothing left to chance. After the first year we didn't even have to carry cash. Everything on credit, like gentlemen. Yes, Bo?" I heard Irving say from the top of the ladder.

"Put me out, Irving. I'm begging you, put a muzzle to my head."

"Bo, you know I can't do that," Irving said.

"He's a madman, he's a maniac. He's torturing me."

"I'm sorry," Irving said in his soft voice.

"The Mick did him worse. I took the Mick out for him. How do you think I did it, hanging him by his thumbs, like this? You think I held him for contemplation? I did it, bang, it was done. I did it mercifully," Bo Weinberg said. "I did it merci-ful-ly," he said, the word breaking out of him on a sob.

"I could give you a drink, Bo," Irving called down. "You want a drink?"

But Bo was sobbing and didn't seem to hear, and in a moment Irving was gone from the hatch.

The pilot had turned on the radio, twisting the knob through static till some voices came in. He kept it low, like music. People talked. Other people answered. They warranted their positions. They were not on this boat.

"It was clean work," Irving was saying to the pilot. "It was good work. Weather never bothered me. I liked it all. I liked making my landing just where and when I'd figured to."

"Sure," the pilot said.

"I grew up on City Island," Irving said. "I was born next to a boatyard. If I didn't catch on when I did I would have joined the navy."

Bo Weinberg was moaning the word *Mama.* Over and over again, *Mama, Mama.*

"I used to like it at the end of a night's work," Irving said. "We kept the boats there in the marine garage on a Hundred and Thirty-second Street."

"Sure," the pilot said.

"You'd come up the East River just before dawn. City fast asleep. First you'd see the sun on the gulls, they'd turn white. Then the top of the Hell Gate turned to gold."

T W O

It was juggling that had got me where I was. All the time we hung around the warehouse on Park Avenue, and I don't mean the Park Avenue of wealth and legend, but the Bronx's Park Avenue, a weird characterless street of garages and one-story machine shops and stonecutter yards and the occasional frame house covered in asphalt siding that was supposed to look like brick, a boulevard of uneven Belgian block with a wide trench dividing the uptown and downtown sides, at the bottom of which the trains of the New York Central tore past thirty feet below street level, making a screeching racket we were so used to, and sometimes a wind that shook the bent and bowed iron-spear fence along the edge, that we stopped our conversation and continued it from mid-sentence when the noise lifted—all the time that we hung out there for a glimpse of the beer trucks, the other guys pitched pennies against the wall, or played skelly on the sidewalk with bottle caps, or smoked the cigarettes they bought three for a cent at the candy store on Washington Avenue, or generally wasted their time speculating what they would do if Mr. Schultz ever noticed them, how they would prove themselves as gang members, how they would catch on and toss the crisp one-hundred-dollar bills on the kitchen tables of their mothers who had yelled at them and the fathers who had beat their ass—all this time I practiced my juggling. I juggled anything, Spaldeens, stones, oranges, empty green Coca-Cola bottles, I juggled rolls we stole hot from the bins in the Pechter Bakery wagons, and since I juggled so constantly nobody bothered me about it, except once in a while just because it was something nobody else could do, to try to interrupt my rhythm by giving me a shove, or to grab one of the oranges out of the air and run with it, because it was what I was known to do, along the lines of having a nervous tic, something that marked me but after all wasn't my fault. And when I wasn't juggling I was doing sleight of hand, trying to make coins disappear and reappear in their dirty ears, or doing card tricks of trick shuffles and folded aces, so their name for me was Mandrake, after the Hearst *New York American* comics magician, a mustached fellow in a tuxedo and top hat who was of no interest to me any more than magic was, magic was not the point, it was never the point, dexterity was to me the point, the same exercise as walking like a tightrope walker on the spear fence points while the trains made their windy rush under me, or doing backflips or handstands or cartwheels or whatever else arose to my mind of nimble compulsion. I was double-jointed, I could run like the wind, I had keen vision and could hear silence and could smell the truant officer before he even came around the corner, and what they should have called me was Phantom, after that other Hearst *New York American* comics hero, who wore a one-piece helmet mask and purple skintight rubberized body garment and had only a wolf for a companion, but they were dumb kids for the most part and didn't even think of calling me Phantom even after I had disappeared into the Realm, the only one of all of them who had dreamed about it.

The Park Avenue warehouse was one of several maintained by the Schultz gang for the storage of the green beer they trucked over from Union City New Jersey and points west. When a truck arrived it didn't even have to blow its horn the warehouse doors would fold open and receive it as if they had an intelligence of their own. The trucks were from the Great War, and still the original army khaki color, with beveled hoods and double rear wheels and chain-wheel drives that sounded like bones being ground up; the beds had stakes around the sides to which homemade slats were affixed, and tarpaulin was lashed down with peculiar and even gallant discretion over the cargo as if nobody would know then what it was. But when a truck came around the corner the whole street reeked of beer, they carried their gamy smell like the elephants in the Bronx Zoo. And the men who got down from the cab were not ordinary truck drivers in soft caps and mackinaws but men in overcoats and fedoras with a way of lighting their cigarettes in their cupped hands while the teamsters on inside duty backed the trucks into the black depths we were desperate to see into, that made me think of officers returned from a patrol across no-man's-land. It was the sense of all this purveyed lawless might and military self-sufficiency that was so thrilling to boys, we hung around there like a flock of filthy messenger pigeons, cooing and clucking and fluttering up from the ground the minute we heard the chains grinding and saw the sneering Mack hood nosing around the corner.

Of course this was just one of Mr. Schultz's beer drops, and we didn't know how many he had though we knew it was a fair number, and the truth was none of us had ever seen him though we never stopped hoping, and in the meantime we were honored to know that our neighborhood was good enough for one of his places, we were proud we enjoyed his confidence, and in our rare sentimental moments when we weren't sassing each other for our pretensions, we thought that we were part of something noble and surely had a superior standing among other kids from ordinary neighborhoods that could not boast a beer drop or the rich culture it brought with it of menacingly glancing men who needed shaves and a precinct house of cops whose honor it was never if they could help it to breathe the air out-of-doors.

Of particular interest to me was that Mr. Schultz maintained this business in all its prohibitional trappings even though Repeal had come. I thought that this meant beer like gold was by nature dangerous to handle however legal it might have become, or that people would buy better beer than his if he didn't continue to frighten them, which meant, breathtakingly, that in Mr. Schultz's mind his enterprise was an independent kingdom of his own law, not society's, and that it was all the same to him whatever was legal or illegal, he would run things the way he thought they ought to be run, and fuck woe to anybody who got in his way.

So there you see the heart and soul of what we were, in that moment in the history of the Bronx, and you would never know from these dirty skinny boys of encrusted noses and green teeth that there were such things as school and books and a whole civilization of attendant adults paling into insubstance under the bright light of the Depression. Least of all from me. And then one day, I remember it was particularly steamy, so hot in July that the weeds along the spear fence pointed to the ground and visible heat waves rose from the cobblestone, all the boys were sitting in an indolent row along the warehouse wall and I stood across the narrow street in the weeds and rocks overlooking the tracks and demonstrated my latest accomplishment, the juggling of a set of objects of unequal weight, a Galilean maneuver involving two rubber balls, a navel orange, an egg, and a black stone, wherein the art of the thing is in creating a flow nevertheless, maintaining the apogee from a kind of rhythm of compensating throws, and it is a trick of such consummate discipline that the better it is done the easier and less remarkable it looks to the uninitiated. So I knew that I was not only the juggler but the only one to appreciate what the juggler was doing, and after a while I forgot those boys and stood looking into the hot gray sky while assorted objects rose and fell through my line of vision like a system of orbiting planets. I was juggling my own self as well in a kind of matching spiritual feat, performer and performed for, and so, entranced, had no mind for the rest of the world as for instance the LaSalle coupé that came around the corner of 177th

Street and Park Avenue and immediately pulled up to the curb in front of a hydrant and sat there with its motor running, nor of the Buick Roadmaster with three men that came next around the corner and drove past the warehouse doors and pulled up at the corner of 178th Street nor finally of the big Packard that came around the corner and rolled to a stop directly in front of the warehouse to block from my view, if I had been looking, all the boys slowly standing now and brushing the backs of their pants, while a man got out from the front right-hand door and then opened, from the outside, the right rear door, through which emerged in a white linen double-breasted suit somewhat wilted, with the jacket misbuttoned, and a tie pulled down from his shirt collar and a big handkerchief in his hand mopping his face, once a boy known to the neighborhood as Arthur Flegen-heimer, the man known to the world as Dutch Schultz.

Of course I am lying that I did not see it happening because I saw it all, being gifted with extraordinary peripheral vision, but I pretended I was not aware he stood there with his elbows on the car roof and watched with a smile on his face a juggling kid with mouth slightly open and eyes rolled skyward like a beatific boy angel in adoration of his Lord. And then I did something brilliant, I glanced out of my orbit across the hot street and let my face register ordinary human astonishment, to the effect of omigod it's him standing there in the flesh and watching *me,* and at the same time continued the pistonlike movement of my arms, while one by one my miniature planets, the two balls, the navel orange, the egg, and the stone, after a farewell orbit, plumed out into space, and went soaring in equidistant intervals over the fence to disappear down into the New York Central chute of railroad tracks behind me. And there I stood with my palms up and empty and my gaze transfixed in theatrical awe, which to tell the truth was a good part of what I felt, while the great man laughed and applauded, and glanced at the henchman beside him to encourage his appreciation, which duly came, and then Mr. Schultz beckoned me with his finger, and I ran across the street with alacrity, and around the car, and there, in a private court chamber composed of my gang of boys watching on one quarter, and the open Packard door on another, and the darkness of the warehouse depths on the third, I faced my king and saw his hand remove from his pocket a wad of new bills as thick as a half a loaf of rye bread. He stripped off a ten and slapped it in my hand. And while I stared at calm Alexander Hamilton enshrined in his steel-pointed eighteenth-century oval I heard for the first time the resonant rasp of the Schultz voice, but thinking for one stunned instant it was Mr. Hamilton talking, like a comic come to life, until my senses righted themselves and I realized I was hearing the great gangster of my dreams. "A capable boy," he said, by way of conclusion, either to his associate or to me, or to himself, or perhaps to all three, and then the meaty killer's hand came down, like a scepter, and gently held for a moment my cheek and jaw and neck on its hot pads, and then was lifted, and then the back of Dutch Schultz was disappearing into the dark depths of the beer drop and the big doors flattened out with a screech and locked with a loud boom behind him.

What happened now showed me all at once the consequences of a revolutionary destiny: I was immediately surrounded by the other boys all of them staring, as I was, at the mint ten-dollar bill lying flat in my palm. It dawned upon me that I had half a minute at most before I became a tribal sacrifice. Someone would make a remark, someone else would jab the heel of his hand against my shoulder, and the rage and resentment would flare, and a collective rationale would arise for sharing the treasure and administering a punitive lesson—probably to the effect that I was an asslicking brownnose whose head was going to be broken for thinking he was better than anyone else. "Watch this," I said, holding forth the bill but really extending my arms to hold the circle, because before the attack comes there is a kind of crowding movement, an encroachment on the natural territorial rights of the body; and taking the crisp bill in my fingers I folded it once lengthwise, and once again, and then tightly twice more to the size of a postage stamp and then I did a hocus-pocus

pass of the hands over each other, snapped my fingers, and the
ten-dollar bill was gone. Oh you miserable fucking louts, that I
ever needed to attach my orphan self to your wretched company, you thieves of the five-and-ten, you poking predators of
your own little brothers and sisters, you dumbbells, that you
could aspire to a genius life of crime, with your dead witless
eyes, your slack chins, and the simian slouch of your spines—
fuck you forever, I consign you to tenement rooms and bawling
infants, and sluggish wives and a slow death of incredible subju-
gation, I condemn you to petty crimes and mean rewards and
vistas of cell block to the end of your days. "Look!" I cried,
pointing up, and they tracked my hand, expecting to see me
pluck the bill out of the air, as I had so often their coins and
steelies and rabbits' feet, and in the instant of their credulity, as
they stared upward at nothing, I ducked under the circle and ran
like hell.

Once I was running no one could catch me, though they tried,
I cut down 177th to Washington Avenue, and then turned right
and ran south, with some of them right behind me and some
chasing me in parallel on the other side of the street, and some
of them fanning out down side streets behind me in anticipation
of my cutting back toward them, but I ran a straight course, I was
really getting out of there, and one by one they pulled up pant-
ing, and I made one more change of direction for insurance and
finally I was truly alone. I was in the valley of the Third Avenue
El. I stopped in the doorway of a pawnshop, unlaced my sneaker,
flattened the bill, and slid it down as far as it would go. Then
I laced up and resumed running, I ran for the joy of it, flickering
like a movie in the alternations of sun and shadow under the
elevated tracks, and feeling each warm stripe of sun, its quick
dazzle in my eyes, as Mr. Schultz's hand.

For days after I was my uncharacteristic self, quiet and cooper-
ative with the authorities. I actually went to school. One night
I tried to do my homework, and Mama looked up from her table
of glass tumblers which held not water but fire, this being the
condition of mourning, that the elements of life transform, and

you pour a glass of water and hocus-pocus it is a candle burning, and she said Billy, my name, Billy, something's wrong, what have you done? That was an interesting moment and I wondered if it would hold, but it was only a moment and then the candles caught her attention again and she turned back to her enameled kitchen table of lights. She stared into the lights as if she was reading them, as if each dancing flame made up a momentary letter of her religion. Day and night winter and summer she read the lights, of which she had a tableful, you only needed one once every year but she had all the remembrance she needed, she wanted illumination.

I sat out on the fire escape to wait for the night breeze and continued with my uncharacteristic thought. I had not intended anything by juggling outside the beer drop. The quality of my longing was no more specific than anyone else's, it was a neighborhood thing, if I had lived down near Yankee Stadium I would have known where the players went in through the side door, or if I lived in Riverdale maybe the mayor would have passed by and waved from his police car on the way home from work, it was the culture of where you lived, and for any of us it was never more than that, and very often less, as, for instance, if one Saturday night years before we were born, Gene Autry came to the Fox Theatre on Tremont Avenue to sing with his Western band between showings of his picture—well that was ours and we had it, and it didn't matter what it was as long as it was ours, so that it satisfied your idea of fame, which was simple registry in the world, that you were known, or that your vistas were the same that had been seen by the great and near-great. That they knew about your street. And that's all it was, or so I had believed, and I couldn't have been planning to juggle continuously every day of my idling life until Mr. Schultz arrived, it had just happened. But now that it had I saw it as destiny. The world worked by chance but every chance had a prophetic heft to it. I sat with my ass on the windowsill and my feet on the rusted iron slats and to the flowerpots of dry stalks I unfolded my ten-dollar bill and folded it and made it disappear all over again, but it kept reappearing for me to unfold.

Right across the street was the Max and Dora Diamond
Home for Children, which everyone knew as the orphanage. It
was a red stone building with granite trim around the windows
and along the roofline; it had a grand curving double front
stoop, wider at the bottom than at the top and the two halves
of it joined at the front doors one floor above the basement
level. Flocks of kids were sitting and sprawling all up and down
both sets of stairs and they made a birdlike chatter and moved
in a constant shifting of relationships up and down the steps,
and some of them on the railings too, just like birds, city birds,
sparrows or grackles. They clustered on the stone steps or
hung on the railings like the building was Max and Dora themselves, out with their children for some evening air. I didn't
know where they put them all. The building was too small to
be a school and not tall enough to be an apartment house and
assumed in its design that it had the land to set it apart, which
you just didn't get in the Bronx even if you were the Diamond
family of benefactors; but it did have a kind of hidden volume
to it and a run-down majesty all its own, and it had provided
me most of the friends of my childhood as well as several
formative sexual experiences. And I saw now coming down the
street one of the orphan incorrigibles, my old pal Arnold Garbage. He was pushing his baby carriage in front of him and it
was piled with the day's mysterious treasures. He worked long
hours, Garbage. I watched him bounce the carriage heavily
down the basement steps under the big curved stoop. He ignored the smaller children. His door opened on darkness, and
then he disappeared.

When I was younger I'd spent a lot of time at the orphanage.
I spent so much time there that I came to move around their
wards like one of them, living as they lived with the orphan's
patrimony of tender bruises. And I never looked out the windows to my house. It was very peculiar how I came to feel one
of them, because at the time I still had a mother who went in and
out of our house like other mothers, and in fact I enjoyed some-

thing like a semblance of family life complete with door pound-
ings by the landlord and weepings unto dawn.

Now when I looked behind me into the kitchen it was illuminated with my mother's memory candles, this one room
glittering like an opera house in all the falling darkness of the
apartment and the darkening street, and I wondered if my big
chance hadn't a longer history than I thought in the proximity
of this orphans' home, with its eerie powers, as if some sort of
slow-moving lava of disaster had poured its way across the street
and was rising year after year to mold my house in the shape of
another Max and Dora Diamond benefaction.

Of course I had long since ceased to play there, having taken
to wandering away down the hill to the other side of Webster
Avenue, where there were gangs of boys more my own age,
because I had come to see the orphanage as a place for children,
as indeed it was. But I still kept in touch with one or two of the
incorrigible girls, and I still liked to visit Arnold Garbage. I don't
know what his real name was but what did it matter? Every day
of his life he wandered through the Bronx and lifted the lids of
ashcans and found things. He poked about in the streets and
down the alleys and in the front halls under the stairs and in the
empty lots and in the backyards and behind the stores and in the
basements. It was not easy work because in these days of our life
trash was a commodity and there was competition for it. Junk-
men patrolled with their two-wheeled carts, and the peddlers
with their packs, and organ-grinders and hobos and drunks, but
also people who weren't particularly looking for scavenge until
they saw it. But Garbage was a genius, he found things that other
junkers discarded, he saw value in stuff the lowest most down-
and-out and desperate street bum wouldn't touch. He had some
sort of innate mapping facility, different days of the month attracted him to different neighborhoods, and I think his mere
presence on a street was enough to cause people to start flinging
things down the stairs and out the windows. And his years of
collecting had accustomed everyone to respect it, he never went

to school, he never did his chores, he lived as if he were alone and it all worked beautifully for this fat intelligent almost speechless boy who had found this way to live with such mysterious single-minded and insane purpose that it seemed natural, and logical, and you wondered why you didn't live that way yourself. To love what was broken, torn, peeling. To love what didn't work. To love what was twisted and cracked and missing its parts. To love what smelled and what nobody else would scrape away the filth of to identify. To love what was indistinct in shape and indecipherable in purpose and indeterminate in function. To love it and hold on to it. I made up my mind of uncharacteristic thought and left my mother with her lights and swung myself over the fire escape railing and climbed down the ladder going past the open windows of people in their summer underwear, to swing for a minute from the last rung before dropping to the sidewalk, which I hit running. And dodging my way across the street and ducking under the grand granite steps of the Max and Dora Diamond Home for Children I went down into the basement, where Arnold Garbage maintained his office. Here the smell was of ashes, and in all seasons there was a warmth of ash and bitter dry air with suspensions of coal dust and also attars of rotting potatoes or onions that I preferred without question to the moist tang upstairs in the halls and lofts of generations of urinating children. And here Garbage was busy adding his new acquisitions to the great inventory of his life. And I told him I wanted a gun. There was no question in my mind that he could supply it.

As Mr. Schultz told me later in a moment of reminiscence the first time is breathtaking, you have this weight in your hand and you think in your calculating mind if they only believe me I will be able to bring this thing off, you are still your old self, you see, you are the punk with the punk's mind, you are relying on them to help you, to teach you how to do it, and that is how it begins, that badly, and maybe it's in your eyes or your trembling hand, and so the moment poses itself, like a prize to be taken by any of you, hanging up there like the bride's bouquet. Because the gun means nothing until it's really yours. And then what happens, you understand that if you don't make it yours you are dead, you have created the circumstance, but it has its own free-standing rage, available to anyone, and this is what you take into yourself, like an anger that they've done this to you, the people who are staring at your gun, that it's their intolerable crime to be the people you are waving this gun at. And at that moment you are no longer a punk, you have found the anger that was really in you all the time, and you are transformed, you are not playacting, you are angrier than you have ever been in your entire life, and this great wail of fury rises in your chest and fills your throat and in this moment you are no longer a punk, and the gun is yours and the rage is in you where it belongs and the fuckers know they are dead men if they don't give you what you want, I mean you are so crazy jerking-off mad at this point you don't even know yourself, as why should you because you are a new man, a Dutch Schultz if ever there was one. And after that everything works as it should, it is all surprisingly easy, and that is the breathtaking part, like that first moment a little shitter is born, coming out into the air and taking a moment before he can call out his name and breathe the good sweet fresh air of life on earth.

Of course I did not at the moment understand this in any detail, but the weight in my hand did give me intimations of a fellow I might become; just holding the thing bestowed a new adulthood, I had no immediate plans for it, I thought maybe Mr. Schultz could use me and I wanted to be ready with what I imagined he was looking for, but it was a kind of investiture nevertheless, it had no bullets and badly needed cleaning and oiling, but I could hold it at arm's length and remove the magazine, and shove it back in the handle grip with a satisfying snap, and I could assure myself that the serial number was filed off, which meant that it was a weapon of the brotherhood, which Garbage confirmed by telling me where he found it, in a wet marsh off Pelham Bay, in the far reaches of the North Bronx, at low tide, with its snub nose stuck in the muck like a mumbly-peg knife.

And the name of it was most thrilling of all, it was an Automatic, a very modern piece of equipment, heavy yet compact, and Garbage said he thought it would work if I could find a bullet for it, he himself having none, and quietly without dickering he accepted my suggested price of three dollars, and he took my ten into the depths of one of his piled bins where he kept hidden his El Corona cigar box with all his money, and brought me back seven very wrinkled worn neighborhood dollar bills, and the deal was done.

I was in a wonderful generous and expansive mood that night with the weight of my secret ambition in the right pocket of my knickers where I had discovered, in a confirmation of the rightness of my intuition, that the hole there allowed the gun to be slung down discreetly, the short barrel along my outer thigh, the grip transverse in the pocket, everything neat and accommodated as if by design. I went back to my apartment and gave my mother five of the singles, which was about half her week's wages from the industrial steam laundry on Webster Avenue. "Where did you get this?" she said, crumpling the bills in her fist and smiling at me her vague smile, before turning back to her latest chapter in the table of lights. And then, my gun stowed, I went back in the street, where the adults had taken possession of the sidewalks, having changed places with the children, who were now in the houses, there being some order in this teeming tenement life, some principle of the responsibility of mothers and fathers, and now there were card games on the stoops and cigar smoke drifted through the summer night, and the women in their housedresses sat like girls with their knees pointing up from the stone steps and couples strolled in and out of the streetlights and I was very moved by the sullen idyll of all this impoverishment. Sure enough when I looked up the sky was clear and a section of inexplicable firmament was winkling between the rooflines. All this romance put me in mind of my friend Rebecca.

She was a nimble little girl with black hair and dark eyes and a delicate thin black down above her pronounced upper lip. The orphans were inside now, the lights blazing in the windows of diamond-mesh translucence, and I stood outside and heard the din, louder on the boys' side, and then one of the signal bells, and I went down the alley to the small backyard and waited there in the corner of their broken-down little ball yard with my back against their chain-link fence, and in about an hour most of the upper-story lights were out, and I rose and stood under the fire escape ladder and leapt up, catching the bottom rung, and hoisted myself onto the ladder and so, hand over hand and foot over foot, rose on the black ladder of my love and at the top, swung out to a window ledge without a net below me and entered the open hallway window on the top floor, where the oldest girls slept, eleven to fourteen, and found there in her bed my witchy little friend, whose dark eyes were open when I looked into them, and absolutely unsurprised to see me. Nor did her wardmates find anything remarkable enough to speak of. I led her through the aisle of their eyes to the door that led up a half flight of stairs to the roof, a kind of games park with ruled lines of skelly and shuffleboard glowing darkly in the summer night, and in the nook made by the roof screen and the kiosk of the stair door, stood and kissed Rebecca ardently, and stuck my hand in the neck of her nightdress to brush her breastbuds with the backs of my fingers and then held in my hands her hard little ass that gave its contours to my touch under the rub of her white cotton shift, and then, before I became too far gone beside myself, when I knew her bargaining position was at its strongest, I negotiated a fair price and peeled a one-dollar bill off my depleted fold, which she took and crumpled in her fist as she first hunkered and then sat on the ground, totally without ceremony, and waited, while I stood on one leg and then the other, to remove my sneakers and everything to the waist, with some trembling awkwardness for a wizard, reflecting how odd it was that whereas men like Mr. Schultz and me folded our money

neatly, no matter if our wad was thin or thick, women like my
mother and little Rebecca squeezed theirs in a ball and held it,
forgetting to let go, whether they sat in a distraction of candled
grief with a shawl over their heads or lay on the ground and were
fucked two times for a dollar.

T H R E E

When the boat came into the slip there were two cars waiting in the rain with their motors running. I would have
liked instruction, but Mr. Schultz bundled the girl whose name
wasn't Lola into the back of the first car and got in beside her
and slammed the door, and not knowing what to do I followed
Irving to the second car and climbed in after him. I was fortunate
there was a jump seat. On the other hand I found myself riding
backward facing three of the gang sitting shoulder-to-shoulder
in their bulk, Irving now in an overcoat and fedora like the
others, while they sat and stared forward, looking through the
front window at the lead car over the shoulders of the driver and
the man next to him. It was not a good feeling riding sandwiched
in all of this serious armed intent. I really wanted either to be
where Mr. Schultz could see me or off by myself, maybe on the
Third Avenue El, alone in a railcar and reading the ads in the
flicker of the bulbs while it rocked its way over the streets to
the far ends of the Bronx. Mr. Schultz did impulsive and unwise
things, and I worried that I was one of them. I had been more
readily accepted by the executives of the organization than by
the rank and file. I liked to think of myself as a kind of associate
gang member, and if it was true, I was the only one, it might have
been because the position had been created just for me, which

should have said something to these deadheads though it didn't. I wondered if it all had to do with age. Mr. Schultz was in his thirties and Mr. Berman even older than that, but with the exception of Irving most of the men were in their twenties, and for someone with a good job and the possibility for advancement who was only twenty-one, say, a fifteen-year-old was a punk, whose presence in business situations was inappropriate to say the least, and if not unwise, certainly an affront to everyone's dignity. One of the bouncers at the Embassy Club was Jimmy Joio, who came from Weeks Avenue just around the corner from my house and whose kid brother was in fifth grade with me although it was true he was taking it for the third year when I came along; but the couple of times I'd seen Jimmy he looked right through me although he had to know who I was. With all these gunmen I could be made to feel from one moment to the next some kind of brash freak, not even a boy but a midget, or some small jester of deformity just agile enough to get out of the way of the king's big dogs. What Mr. Schultz liked lived by his protection, but I knew I needed to improve my standing with them all, although when or how that would be possible I had no idea. Sitting on a jump seat trying to keep my knees from bumping into theirs was not the circumstance I was looking for. Nobody said anything but I knew in the practical common sense of such things that I was witness to yet another of Mr. Schultz's murders, and the most intimate of them, certainly the most carefully planned, and whether it added to my credit as a trustworthy associate or put me in serious jeopardy, I was thinking now riding backward up First Avenue at two o'clock in the morning, I didn't like it and could have done without it and was a fucking dope to have exposed myself to it. I had caught on by Mr. Schultz's whim. My God. I felt weak in the legs, queasy, as if I was still on the boat. I thought of Bo perhaps even now continuing his descent with his eyes open and his arms over his head. To the extent that I could think rationally I wanted to know what was going to happen to this Miss Lola because she had been a witness too, and killers were not supposed to like outside witnesses, and I felt peculiarly of her status in this, and

I needed intelligence of her. On the other hand I mustn't panic. She was still alive, wasn't she?

I didn't like the state of my mind and stared out the window to bring into myself the structure of the city, the solidity of the dark buildings, and the colors of traffic lights reflected in the black shining street. The city has always given me assurances, whenever I have asked for them. I recalled to myself my own imperial intentions. If I could not trust my own impulses to direct me, I was not in Mr. Schultz's class. He operated without sufficient thought and so must I. We were directed beings, and to the extent that I trusted myself I should trust him. What I was in was a thrilling state of three-dimensional danger, I was in danger of myself, and in danger of my mentor, and in danger of what he was in danger of, which was a business life of murdering danger; and out beyond all that were the cops. Four dimensions. I cracked a window and smelled the fresh night air and relaxed.

The cars were heading uptown. We went along Fourth Avenue, and then through the tunnel which brought us up on the ramp that curved around Grand Central Terminal and then we rolled onto Park Avenue, the real Park Avenue, going past the new Waldorf-Astoria Towers, with its famous Peacock Alley and its equally famous host the irrepressible Oscar, as I knew from my reading of the *Mirror,* an invaluable source of information; and then we turned left on Fifty-ninth Street and bumped along behind a streetcar whose bell sounded in my ears like the gong at a prizefight, and then we swerved and pulled up to the curb at the corner of Central Park in the shadow of General Tecumseh Sherman on his horse slogging up there through the rain, which fell also from the fountain of tiered basins across the plaza into the shallow pool he would have to have the horse step through if he was going to get the woman with the basket of fruit standing up there on top of everything, assuming it was a piece of fruit he wanted. I have never liked public monuments, they are ghostly foreign things in the city of New York, quite beside the point, if not actually stupid lies, and for all you can say about the Bronx you won't find generals on rearing horses or dames carrying baskets of fruit or soldiers standing in aesthetic hills of dying comrades and lifting their arms and holding their rifles up to the sky. To my astonishment the door opened and Mr. Schultz was standing there. "Okay, kid," he said and in he reached and yanked me by the arm and all at once I was standing there in Grand Army Plaza being rained on and thinking, in this world of water, that that was it for the phantom wizard juggler of the rackets, I would be found face down in a mud puddle under a bush in Central Park, and if dying depth was a measure of achievement I was worth whatever was of value to some dog snout rooting me up from an inch of water and licking the mud off my dead eyes. But he said walking me quickly to the first car: "Take the lady to her apartment. She is not to make any phone calls under no circumstances, although I don't think she will try. She will pack some things. You are to wait with her until I get back. Not long. Just stay with her and someone will call you on the house phone to bring her down. You got it?"

I nodded I did. We came up to his car, and though water was dripping off his hat brim, he only now reached in to the back seat and withdrew a black umbrella and after he opened it he bent into the car and brought her out and handed me the girl and the umbrella; it was a lovely moment, the three of us under the one umbrella, and she was looking at him with some slight and cryptic smile and he was gently stroking her cheek and smiling at her; then he dove into the car and was still pulling the door closed as it gunned away from the sidewalk with a screech of tires, the second car close behind.

We stood in a huge blowing rainstorm. It occurred to me I had no idea where Miss Lola maintained her apartment. For some reason I assumed everything was up to me, and that she would lack all volition and simply wait to be led. But she took my arm with both her hands, and huddling close to me under this great black umbrella rattling like a snare drum, she pulled me along at a half-walk half-run across Fifth Avenue so shining with rain that the rain splashed up at us after it came down. She seemed to be heading for the Savoy-Plaza Hotel. Sure enough, a door-man came out of the swinging doors with his own umbrella and

rushed toward us uselessly except as he demonstrated solici-
tousness, and a moment later we whooshed into the carpeted,
brightly lit but intimate lobby where some fellow in tails and
striped pants relieved us of ours. And a flush of excitement was
on Miss Lola's beautiful face, and she laughed looking down at
the damp wreckage of her costume and ran her hand fetchingly
through her wet hair and then shook her wrists at the carpet and
received the greetings of the reception clerk as her just due—
Good evening, Miss Drew, Good evening, Charles—as well as
the polite salute of the policeman standing there with his hotel-
staff friends as he liked to do in the warmth of the friendly lobby
on inclement nights of his beat, while I, not daring to look at
him, waited with a dry throat for what her explanation would be
for me, a clear punk in any cop's eyes, and tried not to look back
at the revolving door which was no good anyway and deciding
on the curving staircase beyond the elevators which even though
it led up could find me a way down. I prayed Mr. Schultz knew
what he was doing, I prayed for understanding if not resource-
fulness from Miss Lola, Miss Drew, whoever she was and whatever she had been through this night of the death of a man of
whom she was presumably fond enough to be going to dinner
and to bed with. But she made no explanations as she took her
key, as if every night of the year she came in like this with strange
boys in cheap scuffed imitation suede jackets and army-navy
workpants and Bronx pompadour haircuts, and took my arm
and walked with me into the elevator as if I was the normal
companion of her nights, whereupon the doors closed, and the
man took us up without having to inquire as to the floor, and I
rose simultaneously in my thought to the truth that explanations
are required of everyone but the people at the top, and to the
terrible shadow of a revelation that for this Miss Drew glancing
at me now with her cruel green eyes it had been one hell of an
exciting ride on a tugboat.

Here is the kind of hotel this was: When the elevator door
opened we were already in the apartment. The floor was bare
and very highly shellacked and there was a rug or tapestry hang-

ing on the opposite wall, something going on with ranks of
armored knights with lances on rearing horses, each horse
standing on its hind legs at the same angle as the others, like the
Rockettes, and the reason there was no furniture in this room
is that it was the entrance foyer, except if you wanted to sink
down into either of the two waist-high urns in the corners and
put yourself in the middle of a circle of walking Greek philoso-
phers holding wrapped sheets around themselves, or shrouds,
given the mood I was in. But I preferred to follow the new Miss
Drew grandly throwing open the double ceiling-high doors on
our left and striding forward down a short hall hung with brownish oil paintings with fine cracks in them. And hoving up on the
left was an open door from which, as she passed, a man's voice
called out "Drew?"

"I have to pee, Harvey," she said in a quite matter-of-fact
voice, and kept going around a corner and I heard another door
open and close. And I was left standing in this doorway looking
into a room that was a private library with glass-enclosed book-
cases and a tall leaning ladder that rolled on rails and an immense globe in its own polished wood framework, and light that
came from two brass table lamps with green shades at either end
of a soft sofa, on which were sitting two men side by side, one
somewhat older than the other. What I found remarkable, the
older was holding the younger's erect cock in his hand.

I'm afraid I stared at them. "I thought you were out for the
evening!" the older man called out, looking at me but listening
somewhere else. He released his hold, rose from the sofa, and
straightened his bow tie. He was a tall handsome man, this
Harvey, very well groomed in a tweed suit with a vest into the
pocket of which he inserted his hand as if he had some sort of
pain under the cloth, except that as he came toward me he didn't
appear to be in pain, and in fact looked quite healthy and like
a man who took care of himself. Not only that but he com-
manded respect, because without thinking I stepped out of his
way. As he went by me he said, "Are you all right?" loudly in
my ear, and I noticed the tracks of the comb in his hair as it came
back from his temples, this Harvey.

It made things so much easier, living on an explanationless planet. The air was somewhat rarefied, a bit thinner than I was used to, but then there didn't seem to be any need for exertion. With thumb and forefinger the fellow on the couch removed an antimacassar from the sofa and dropped it over himself. He looked up and laughed in a way that suggested we were complicitors, and I realized he was working-class, like me. I had not at first glance understood this. He appeared to be wearing mascara on his eyes, they were certainly bold and black eyes, and his black hair was slicked down flat without a part, and his bony wide shoulders were draped with the tied sleeves of a collegiate sweater with an argyle pattern of light maroon and gray.

Mr. Schultz was responsible for all this stunning experience so I thought I'd better attend to his business. I wandered down the hall and around some corners and found Harvey in a big padded gray-and-white bedroom, bigger than three Bronx bedrooms put together, and a mirrored bathroom door was open on a field of white tile, and Drew was in there with bathwater running and this caused him to speak loudly over the sound of it while he sat on a corner of an enormous double bed with his legs crossed and held a cigarette in his hand.

"Darling?" he shouted. "Tell me what you've gone and done. You didn't ditch him."

"I didn't, my dearest. But he's no longer a presence in my life."

"And what did he do! I mean you were so gaga about him," Harvey said with a wry and rueful smile to himself.

"Well if you must know, he died."

Harvey's back straightened and he lifted his head as if wondering if he'd heard correctly. But he said nothing. And then he turned and looked at me sitting in the far corner on a side chair that had gray napped upholstery, a boy as out-of-place here as in the library, but now visible, in this new intelligence, and I sort of straightened my own back for his benefit and stared just as rudely at him.

He immediately rose and went into the bathroom and closed the door. I picked up the phone at the bedside table and listened for a moment until the hotel operator came on the line and said Yes, please, and then I hung up. It was a white phone. I had never seen a white phone before. Even the cord was wound in white fabric. The big bed had a white upholstered headboard and big fluffy pillows, about a half dozen of them, with little lace skirts, and all the furniture was gray and the thick carpet was gray and the lights were hidden and shone out of a cornice onto the walls and ceiling. Two people used this room because there were books and magazines on both end tables, and two immense cabinets with white doors and curving white legs that were closets inside, his and hers, and two matching dressers with his shirts and her underwear, and until now I only knew about wealth what I read in the tabloids, and I had thought I could imagine, but the detailed wealth in this room was amazing, to think what people really needed when they were wealthy, like long sticks with shoehorns at the end of them, and sweaters of every color of the rainbow, and dozens of shoes of every style and purpose, and sets of combs and brushes, and carved boxes with handfuls of rings and bracelets, and gold table clocks with pendulum balls that spun one way, paused, and then spun the other way.

The bathroom door opened and Harvey came out holding Miss Drew's dress and underwear and hose and shoes all in a bundle in his two hands out in front of him, and he dropped the whole shebang into a wastebasket and then brushed his hands off, you could see he was not happy. He went to some far corner of the room and opened another door and disappeared there and a light went on, it was a walk-in closet and he came out with a piece of luggage which he threw on the bed. And then he sat down beside it and crossed his legs again and then crossed his arms over his knee and waited. And I waited back in my chair. And then the lady came out of the bathroom with a big towel around her and tucked in under the clavicle, and another towel wrapped around her head like a turban.

The argument was about her behavior. He said it was becoming erratic and disruptive. She herself had insisted they accept that dinner invitation for tomorrow evening. To say nothing of the regatta weekend. Did she want to lose every friend they had?

He was entirely reasonable but he was losing me, because Miss Lola Miss Drew conducted her side of the argument while getting dressed. She stood at the armoire and let the big towel fall, and she was altogether taller and longer-waisted and maybe her ass was a little softer and flatter, but there was the prominent spinal column of tender girl bones of my dirty little Rebecca, and all the parts were as Rebecca's parts and the sum was the familiar body of a woman, I don't know what I'd been expecting but she was a mortal being with flesh pinkened by the hot bathwater, she hooked on her garter belt and stood on each thin white leg while she gently but efficiently raised the other to receive its sheer stocking, which she pulled and smoothed upward taking care to keep the seam straight till she could lower her toe-wiggling foot and sling her hip and attach the stocking to the metal clips hanging from the garter belt, and then she raised one foot and stepped in her white satin step-ins and then the other, and yanked them up and snapped the waistband, and it was the practiced efficiency of the race of women dressing, from that assumption they had always made that a G-string was their armor in the world, and that it would do against wars, riots, famines, floods, droughts, and the flames of the arctic night. As I watched, more and more of her was covered, a skirt was dropped over the hips and zipped along the side, two high-heeled shoes were wiggled into, and then, dressed only from the waist down and with the towel still on her head, she commenced to pack, going from drawers and armoire to valise and back, making her decisions quickly and acting on them energetically, all the while saying that she didn't give a hoot in hell what her friends thought, what had that to do with anything, she was going to see whomever she damned pleased surely he knew that and so what was the point of making a fuss, all this whining of his was beginning to bore her. And then she brought the lid down on her leather valise and snapped shut the two brass locks. I had I thought heard just about everything that went on between Miss Lola and Mr. Schultz in the hold of that tugboat but clearly I hadn't, there was some pact between them she was determined to honor.

"I speak of order, of the need for some order," the fellow
Harvey said, although clearly without hope of prevailing.
"You're going to destroy us all," he muttered. "I mean a bit of
scandal is not the point, is it? You're a very clever, very naughty
little hellion, but there are limits, my darling, there really are.
You're going to get in over your head and then what will you do?
Wait for me to come to the rescue?"

"That is a laugh and a half."

And then she sat nude to the waist at her dressing-table mirror
and unwrapped the towel on her head and ran a comb a few
times through her short helmet of hair, and painted on some
lipstick, then found a camisole and shrugged it over her torso
and pulled a blouse on over that, and tucked it in, and then a
jacket over the blouse, and a bracelet or two, a necklace, and she
stood and looked at me for the first time, a new woman, Miss
Lola Miss Drew, a formidable intention in her eyes, and when
had I seen a woman dress herself so, all in cream and aqua, to
run away with the killer of her dreams?

So there we are, three o'clock in the morning and tearing up
Route 22 out of the city, miles into the mountains where I have
never been before, I am sitting up front next to Mickey the
driver, and Mr. Schultz and the lady are in the back with glasses
of champagne in their hands. He is telling her the story of his
life. A steady hundred yards behind is a car with Irving and Lulu
Rosenkrantz, and Mr. Abbadabba Berman. It has been a long
night in my education, but there is more to come, I am going
into mountains, Mr. Schultz is showing me the world, he is like
a subscription to the *National Geographic Magazine* except the only
tits I've seen are white, I've seen the contours of the ocean bed
and the contours of the white Miss Drew and now I see the
contours of the black mountains. I understand for the first time
the place of the city in the world, it should have been obvious
but I had never realized it, I had never been out of it before,
never had the distance, it is a station on the amphibian journey,
it is where we come out sliming, it is where we bask and feed and
make our tracks and do our dances and leave our coprolitic

spires, before moving on into the black mountains of high winds and no rain. And what I hear as my eyes begin to droop is the soft whistle of the wind in the half window I've left open a crack with a turn of the knob, not a whistle entirely but the kind of almost-whistle a person makes who is whistling to himself; and the soundplow of the eight-cylinder car in its bassoing, and the resonant rasp of Mr. Schultz telling how he robbed crap games as a lad, and the tires' humslick on the damp highway, all of it really the protesting circuitry of my brain as I wrap my arms around myself and let my chin drop to my chest, I hear one last laugh but I can't help it, it is three o'clock in the morning of the awesome morning of my life and I haven't even been to sleep yet.

F O U R

I knew from Walter Winchell's column Mr. Schultz was a lammister: the federal government was looking for him because
he had not paid taxes on all the money he had earned. The
police one day had raided his headquarters on East 149th Street
with axes and found there incriminating records from his beer
business. Yet I had seen him with my own eyes and felt his hand
on my face. It is spectacular enough to see someone in the flesh
whom you've only known in the newspapers, but to see someone
the newspapers have said is on the lam definitely has a touch of
magic to it. If the papers said Mr. Schultz was on the lam then
it was true; but "the lam" suggested to most people someone
running by night and hiding by day when really what it is is the
state of being invisible; if you don't run and you don't hide and
you are on the lam then you are there all the time, you are simply
controlling people's ability to see you and that is a very potent
magic. Of course you do it by waving dollars over the air, you
wave a dollar and you are invisible. But it is still a difficult and
dangerous trick that may not always work when you want it to.
It would not work in Manhattan, I decided, because that's where
the federal attorneys were who were planning to try Mr. Schultz
for tax evasion. It would work better in the Bronx, as for instance in the Bronx neighborhood of a beer drop. It might work

best of all, I decided, in the very gang headquarters that had been raided and cleaned out by the police at the insistence of the federal attorneys.

And that is how it happened one summer day the boy Billy came to be clinging to the back of a Webster Avenue trolley as it hummed its way south toward 149th Street. It was not easy traveling this way, your fingers had only the narrowest purchase on the outer sill of the rear window, which was of course the front window when the trolley was going in the other direction, which meant it was a big window and that therefore you had to crouch while you clung so that your head didn't appear in it: when the motorman spotted you in his rearview mirror he could make the car buck, throw it into some sort of electrical braking stutter so that you had to drop off, whether there was traffic behind you or not, which was a real son of a bitch. Not only that, but your feet had only the narrowest fender to toe, so that really you attached yourself for passage more by whole-body adhesion than anything else. And therefore when the trolley made a stop the correct procedure was to drop off until it started up again, not only because you were really vulnerable clinging to a trolley car at rest when any cop could come along and whap you across the ass with his billy club, but so that you would have the strength to hang there till the next stop. You didn't want to fall off while the damn thing was moving along at a clip, especially on Webster which is an industrial street of warehouses and garages and machine shops and lumberyards all of which make for long blocks and a fast-moving trolley enjoying its run between distant stops, going fast enough to rock along side to side on its wheel carriages, banging the hell out of them and sending up sparks up there where the pole scrapes the power from the wire. It is a fact that more than one boy has died riding the back of a streetcar. Nevertheless this was my preferred mode of travel even when, as now, I had two dollars in my pocket and could easily afford the nickel fare.

I hugged the great machine and got there and jumped off, running, just shy of my stop. But I didn't have the address of the East 149th Street headquarters so for a couple of wearying hours I trudged up and down over the hills, going as far west as the Concourse and then doubling back east, and never knowing what I was looking for in that simmering heat, but coming into luck when I saw two cars, a LaSalle coupé and a Buick sedan, sitting side by side in the lot of a closed-down White Castle hamburger joint not far from the junction with Southern Boulevard. By themselves neither car would have caught my eye but together they looked familiar. Next to the White Castle was a narrow four-story office building of indiscriminate color and large dirt-encrusted windows. When I went in the place smelled of piss and wood rot. Had there been a business directory on the wall you couldn't have seen it. I was elated. I removed myself and crossed the street and sat down on the curb between two parked trucks and waited to see what I would see.

And it was very interesting. It was about noon I'd say, the sunlight flashing down the power lines, the smoke of truck exhausts puffing up white as flowers, heat shimmering over the asphalt, and the street surface giving way to my sneaker heel and leaving an indentation like a crescent moon, so that a good detective could point out This is where he sat, right here where he banged his heel down, and from the depth of the indentation I'd say it was probably noon. And every once in a while someone would come along, some guy in shirtsleeves mostly, and he'd duck into that building. And one got off the corner bus, and one came out of a car that waited at the curb with its motor running, and one pulled up in a yellow cab, but all them were in a hurry, they were urgent, and with anxious expressions on their faces, white or black, and some of them strode and some of them scurried and one of them limped, but the thing was they all carried brown paper bags going in and when they came out they had nothing.

Now you would think it was easy to find a paper bag lying around on the sidewalk or down an alley or in a trash can, but for some reason this was not so on 149th Street, to get my hands on one I actually had to locate a grocery store and go in and spend money to buy something. And then I curled the mouth of the bag closed just like they did, folded it over a couple of

times so that it looked wrinkled, and then I took a deep breath
and though I was a block away, just to get into the mood of it
I loped along like all those guys and got up a good sweat and
pushed my way through the doors of the building into the dark
urinal of a lobby and bounded up wooden stairs that you could
hear a cockroach walk on, and I knew they would be at the very
top, it was what made sense, and the higher I got the lighter it
got, and at the top floor was a skylight covered by a rusty grat-
ing, and at the end of the landing was a plain steel door that had
a number of peculiar gashes and dents in it, and the knob had
been chopped off so I just nudged it with my finger and it swung
open and in I went.

I don't know what I was expecting but I found a short empty
corridor with splintery floor and another door, a brand-new
unpainted steel door this time with a little peephole and it did
not give way to the touch so I knocked and stood back a foot or
so so the guy could see my bag and I waited. Could they hear
my heart banging to be let in, louder than a sledgehammer,
louder than an ax on steel, louder than a dozen cops rushing up
four flights of wooden stairs?

And then the door unclicked and swung open an inch or two
so what the hell, I found myself in a pleasant large room with
several old beat-up desks and a man at each desk counting slips
of paper, or stacks of bills, and they all lick their thumbs when
they do this, and a phone was ringing, and I stood at a counter
that came up to my chest looking in at all of this with my bag
proffered and tried not to mind the guy who had opened the
door standing behind me six feet tall and noisy of breath, the
kind of person who snore-breathes, and I could smell the garlic,
and I didn't yet know his name but it was Lulu Rosenkrantz, and
he had this oversized head with unkempt black hair in need of
a cutting, and little eyes practically hidden by his shaggy brows
and a nose broken into blossom and blue cheeks all sunken in
on their pockmarks, and each wave of garlic he exhaled I imagined as fire coming out of his throat. I didn't see Mr. Schultz
anywhere, the fellow who came over to the counter was a bald
man with rubber bands billowing his shirtsleeves above the

elbow and he looked at me for a second curiously and took the bag and turned it over and emptied it out. I remember the look on his face when a dozen or so packages of cellophane-wrapped Dugan's cupcakes, two to a package, poured out on the counter: suddenly pale and alarmed in the eyes he was, and stupid with the effort to comprehend, all in the second before he held the bag upside down and shook it to see if anything would flutter out and then for good measure looked up inside it to see the trick hidden there. "What the fuck is this?" he shouted. "What the fuck are you bringing me!"

People stopped working and grew quiet and one or two rose and came over to look. Lulu Rosenkrantz moved up behind me. We all stood there in silence looking at these cupcakes. And it was nothing I had intended, I wouldn't have bought them if I'd found a bag in the street, I'd have blown up the bag with air, so that it looked as if I was carrying something, and then when you do that to paper bags you know you can pop them, hit them like a guy playing the cymbals, you hold the neck with one hand and punch out the bottom, and supposing I had done that, exploded the bag in front of this guy, I mean with a wild boy you can't tell what he might do, and that would have been the end of me, a dozen guys would have hit the floor and Lulu Rosenkrantz would have clubbed me on the top of my head with his fist and then when I was down on the floor he would have put his foot in my back to hold me still and executed me with one shot in the base of the skull, I know that now, you don't ever want to make sudden loud sounds when you're with these people. But because I'd had to buy something to get the bag I'd chosen cupcakes, chocolate with vanilla icing, which I happen to like, maybe I figured they would heft like packs of policy slips and stacks of bills in rubber bands, but I had just swept them off the bakery rack with my two arms and dumped them on the grocery man's counter, I didn't think about it, I had paid my money and come down the street and up the stairs and run cupcakes through a steel door and under the eyes of one of the deadliest gunmen in New York right into the heart of Mr. Schultz's policy racket. And it was unerring, like my juggling had been when with aplomb I'd tossed the navel orange, the stone, the two rubber balls, and the egg into a kind of pulsing fountain over the fence behind me to the tracks of the New York Central, at this time everything I was doing was working, I could do no wrong, it was really mysterious to me, I had known without knowing that whatever my life was going to be in this world it would have something to do with Mr. Schultz, but I was beginning to suspect it now, and with the faintest intimation that I might be empowered. That is the feeling you get, that your life is charmed, which means among other things that it is out of your hands.

At this precise moment while these heavyweight brains stood in their contemplation of the Idea of the Cupcake, Mr. Schultz came out of a back office preceded by the sound of his voice and then by a man in a gray pinstripe suit walking backward while trying to stuff some papers into his briefcase. "Goddammit counselor what do I pay you for!" Mr. Schultz shouted. "All you have to do is make the deal, it's very simple isn't it, a simple deal, all this legal bullshit you're giving me, why can't you just do what you're supposed to do and stop dicking me, I'm dying here, I could go to law school myself and pass the bar in every state of the union waiting for you to move your ass."

Mr. Schultz was in his shirtsleeves and he wore suspenders and no tie, and he had a handkerchief crumpled up in his hand, and he was mopping his neck and ears as he advanced on the lawyer. It was my first clear look at him when the sun wasn't in my eyes: thinning black hair slicked back, a lot of forehead, heavy eyelids with pink rims, a reddened nose, as if he had a cold or suffered from some allergy, a bowl of a jaw, and a wide and disturbingly undulant mouth for a voice so much like a horn in timbre: "Stop with the papers a minute and listen to me," he said and leapt forward and with a swinging backhand knocked the briefcase flying. "You see what I got here? I got twenty desks. You see the men sitting at these desks, I got ten men. Doesn't empty desks mean anything to you? They are niching me, you stupid fuckingass lawyer, every week I'm under cover I lose bets, I lose banks, I lose my men to those motherfucking dago scungili. I've been out of it for eighteen goddamn months you Ivy League dickhead, and while you are having your after-noon teatime with the D.A. they're taking everything I got!"

The lawyer was flustered but also he was red in the face with anger about that briefcase, and pursued it now and the papers as well, hunkering down and shoveling everything back in. He was one of those fair-skinned people who flush up with their dignity. I noticed his shoes, shiny black wing-tips with rows of tiny decorative holes. "Dutch," he said, "you don't seem to appreciate you do not hold the cards in this situation. I went to our friend in the state senate and you see what he accomplished. I've gone through three of the best lawyers in Washington, I have a top man working on it now, a very important and re-spected litigator, knows everybody, and even he's hedging. This is a tough one, these are Feds and they are impervious, and it's unfortunate but it takes time and you're just going to have to live with it."

"Live with it!" Mr. Schultz shouted. "Live with it?" I thought if he was going to kill he would do it now. He let go a string of curses that was in his voice almost a kind of litany, he strode back and forth ranting and raving, and this was really my first experi-ence of his temper and I was transfixed, I watched the raised veins of his neck and wondered why the lawyer was not cowering in front of him, I had nothing to compare this to, the vehemence seemed to me ultimate, I could not understand as the others did that this was not new anger, but one worn down somewhat by usage, as in a family argument, which is to say running, and therefore with a necessarily ceremonial aspect to it. So I was astonished to see Mr. Schultz drift over to the counter right in front of me, where he noticed all these cupcakes, and in the midst of his harangue grab one of the packages and break it open and peel off the browned pleated paper they bake each one in and drift back into the argument while consuming a chocolate cupcake with vanilla icing, but without quite being aware of it, as if eating was a distracted form of rage, and both were the function of a generic appetite that was nameless. And this was good enough for the guy holding the empty paper bag, the Riddle of the Sphinx was cracked, he went back to his work and the others turned away and went back to their desks, and Lulu Rosenkrantz returned to his place by the door and sat down and leaned his bent-cane chair against the wall, and shook an Old Gold out of his pack and lit himself a cigarette.

And I was still here and still alive and for all anyone knew I belonged here, at least for another moment or two. Mr. Schultz had not even seen me, but one pair of shrewd and amused eyes had seen and understood everything, including I suppose the brazen genius of my ambition, and their direct and unblinking gaze now made me aware of a man sitting at a desk near the window on the far wall, and he was talking on the phone as he looked at me, he was conducting what appeared to be an intimate and quiet conversation that did not seem at all inconvenienced by the shouting and screaming of Mr. Schultz. In a flash I knew for a certainty this was the great Abbadabba Berman, Mr. Schultz's financial brain, perhaps because his slow smile at me through all the noise and over the heads of everyone else even as he spoke on the phone was the distributed concentration of a mind superior to its surroundings. He turned slightly and raised his arm and drew a figure in the air and immediately a man on the right side of the room got up and wrote the figure 6 on a blackboard. And all at once the men at the desks in unison began to strip pieces of paper off their stacks of policy pads and rain them on the floor as if a sort of abstract Lindbergh parade was passing by. As he was to tell me later, the six was the final digit before the decimal point of the total odds of the first three races of the day according to the pari-mutuel machines at the Tropical Park in Miami Florida. And it was the first element of what would be the day's winning number. The second element of the number would come the same way from the second two races. And the last digit would most of the time come from the day's final two races. I say most of the time because if the winning number happened to have been played heavily, if for instance it had been touted by the astrological dream books the players liked to consult, Mr. Berman put in a last-minute call to an associate who was an official at the track and placed a bet, thus making a minute change in the odds on the pari-mutuel machines, thus changing the last digit of the winning number to one not so heavily played, thus protecting Mr. Schultz's overall profits for the day and bringing honor to the rackets. This legerdemain had been of Mr. Berman's devising and was the sort of thing that caused him to be known as Abbadabba.

I immediately granted him all the powers of his reputation because of the way he wrote a number in the air and it passed through all the noise and shouting to become visible on a blackboard. When he finished his call and arose from his desk, he rose only a short distance; he wore a summer yellow double-breasted suit and a panama hat, which was pushed back on his head, and the suit jacket was open and hanging down at an angle which suggested to me that he had something of a humpback. He walked with a rocking lurch from side to side. His shirt was a darker yellow silk, and a pale blue silk tie was clipped to it with a silver tiepin. It surprised me that someone that physically unfortunate would want to dress sharply. His trousers were pulled up so high by his suspenders that he seemed not to have any chest. When he came up to the counter not much more of him was showing from his side than was showing of me from mine. His brown eyes were encircled by steel-rim spectacles. I did not feel menaced by their gaze, which seemed to have originated in a realm of pure abstraction. Each brown pupil had a milky blue rim. His nose was sharp with little tufts of hair curling out of each nostril and his chin was pointed, and he had a sly V-shaped mouth in the corner of which the stub of a cigarette moved up and down as he spoke. He rested a clawlike hand over a package of cupcakes. "So kid, where's the coffee?" he said squinting at me through smoke.

F I V E

A minute later I was tearing down the stairs saying over in my mind how many black, how many black with sugar, how many with cream, how many with cream and sugar, I ran down 149th Street in the direction of the Boulevard Diner, I ran faster than the cars were moving, and the horns of the buses and trucks, and the grinding gears, and the clop and rattle of horse-drawn wagons, the sound of all the traffic driving its way fiercely into the high hours of the business day, sounded like choir music in my breast. I did a cartwheel, I did two in-the-air somersaults, I did not know in that moment how otherwise to praise God for giving me my first assignment for the Dutch Schultz gang.

Of course and as usual I was in advance of the actual facts. For several days I lived on the edge of everyone's patience and was consigned for the most part to the same curbstone of my observation across the street where I had begun. Mr. Schultz had not even noticed me, and when he finally did, as I swept up policy slips from the floor, he didn't remember the juggler, he asked Abbadabba Berman who the fuck I was and what I was doing there. "He's just some kid," Mr. Berman said. "He's our good-luck kid." For some reason that answer satisfied Mr. Schultz. "We could use some," he muttered and disappeared into his office. And so I rode the Webster Avenue streetcar every morning like a fellow going to work, and if I was given a job to do, if I brought coffee, or swept up the floor, I counted the day a success. Most of the time Mr. Schultz was not present, it was Mr. Berman who seemed to run things. I had plenty of time to begin to appreciate that it was he who had made a decision. Mr. Schultz had made a judgment, but Abbadabba Berman had engaged me. And then, the day when he chose to describe the details of the numbers game to me, the concept of apprenticeship rose in my mind, and I found a dignity in myself here as a kid operator sitting on a curb that quieted me down and gave me patience.

When Mr. Schultz was not present the life was tiresome, the runners came by in the mornings with their paper bags and by noon they had all delivered, and the first race of the day's card went off at one P.M. and the numbers went up on the blackboard every hour and a half or so, and the magical numeric construction was completed by five o'clock, and by six the shop was closed and everyone had gone home. When crime was working as it was supposed to it was very dull. Very lucrative and very dull. Mr. Berman was usually the last to leave and he carried a leather briefcase that I assumed held the day's take, and just as he came scuttling out of the office building a sedan pulled up and he got in and was gone, usually glancing at me sitting there across the street and giving me a knowing nod through the window, and I wouldn't count my day over until he had, I tried to learn something from every small sign and infinitesimal clue, and that face in the small triangle of rear window, sometimes obscured further by a cloud of cigarette smoke, was my cryptic instruction for the night. Mr. Berman was like the other side of Mr. Schultz, the two poles of my world, and the one's rage of power was the other's calm administration of numbers, they couldn't be more unlike as men, for instance Mr. Berman never raised his voice but spoke out of the corner of his mouth that was not employed with his perpetual cigarette, and the smoke smoked up his voice and made it hoarse, so that it came fragmented, as a line broken into dots, and I found I had to listen closely to hear what he said, because not only did he not shout, he never repeated himself. And he had the aura of mild deformity about him, his hunch, his stiff-kneed walk, that suggested a frailness, a physical grayness that he painted over with his neat and color-matching clothing style, whereas Mr. Schultz was all brute health, moving about in a disorder of moods and excessive feelings that nothing like clothing could really fit on or augment.

One day I found some slips on the floor near Mr. Berman's desk that looked different and when I was sure no one was looking I picked them up and shoved them in my pocket. In the evening back on my block I looked at them, there were three scraps of paper and each was drawn with a square divided into sixteen boxes, and all the sixteen boxes of each square were filled with different numbers, and I looked at them for a while and began to see something, the numbers added up to the same sum no matter which line you added, the horizontal line or the vertical or the diagonal. And each square was totally different, he had figured out sets of numbers in each case that worked that way and he hadn't repeated himself. The next day when I had the chance I observed him and saw that what I had assumed was his work was a kind of doodling idleness, he sat there all day and did calculations at his desk, and I had assumed they had to do with the business, but really the business didn't demand that much of him, there was nothing to it, the numbers that interested him were the puzzling kind. Mr. Schultz was never idle that I was able to tell, he did not have that quality of thinking about anything but business, but I saw that Abbadabba Berman lived and dreamed numbers, and that he couldn't help himself, he was as helpless with his numbers and everything they could do for him as Mr. Schultz was in the grip of his ambitions.

Not once in that first week of my hanging around did Mr. Berman ask my name or where I lived or how old I was, or anything like that. I was prepared to lie in any case but it never came up. If he spoke to me he called me kid. He said one afternoon, "Hey, kid, how many months in the year?" I answered twelve. "Okay, now suppose you give each month its number, like January is the first month and so on, you got it?" I said I did. "Okay, now you don't tell me your birthday but take the number of the month, and then add the number of the month following, you got it?" I had it, I was thrilled he was talking to me. "Okay, now product that sum by five, you got it?" I thought a moment and then said I had it. "Okay, now you product by ten and add the number of your birthday to the result, you got it?" All right, yes, I had it. "Now give me the number you come up with." I did—nine hundred and fifty-nine. "Okay," he said, "thanks for telling me, your birthday is September nine."

This was of course correct and I grinned with appreciation. But he pressed on. "I'm gonna tell you how much change you got in your pocket. If I do that and I'm right, I win it, okay? If I'm wrong, I'll match the sum and you will have double what you had before, okay? Turn around and count it, but don't let me see." I told him I didn't have to count it, I knew how much I had. "Okay, double the sum in your mind, you got it?" I had: the amount was twenty-seven cents and I doubled it, fifty-four. "Okay, add three, you got it?" Fifty-seven. "Okay, now product it by five, you got it?" Two eighty-five. "Okay, subtract the number six, you got it? Now tell me the result." I told him, two hundred seventy-nine. "Okay, you've just lost twenty-seven cents, am I right?" He was right.

I shook my head in admiration and smiled though I was smarting, and the smile felt false on my face. I handed over my twenty-seven cents. Maybe I had the sneaking hope he would give it back, but he pocketed it and turned back to his desk and left me to my broom. It occurred to me then that with his sort of mind if he needed to know my birthday, or the amount of money I had, this is the way he would go about it. What if he wanted my street address. Or the number of my public school. Everything could be translated into numbers, even names if you assigned a number to each letter as in code. What I thought was idleness was a system of understanding, and it made me uneasy. They both knew how to get what they wanted. Even a stranger who knew nothing about him, neither his name nor his reputation, would perceive in a flash Mr. Schultz's willingness to maim or kill anyone who stood in his way. But Abbadabba Berman cal-

culated everything, he figured the odds, he couldn't walk that
well but he was lightning quick, so that all events and outcomes,
all desires and means of satisfying them, were translated as
numerical values in his mind, which meant he never did anything unless he knew how it was going to turn out. I wondered
which of them was more of a dangerous study to a simple boy
just trying to get ahead and make something of himself. There
was an implacable adult will in both of them. "And see if you can
work out one a those number squares for yourself, it ain't so
hard once you get the ruling idea," Mr. Berman said giving a dry
little hack through the cigarette smoke.

A week or two later there was some sort of emergency, Mr.
Berman was dispatching people in the office and over the phone,
and then he must have run out of people, he beckoned to me
and wrote something on a piece of paper and it was an address
on 125th Street, and also a name, George. I understood immediately this was a break for me. I asked no questions, not even how
to get there, although I had never been to Harlem. I decided to
go in a yellow taxi and let the driver find the way, I had built up
a stake of four dollars from my tips from sweeping and running
errands and I figured a cab ride was a good investment also
because it would allow me to show how fast and reliable I was.
But I had never flagged a taxicab before and I was half surprised
when one stopped. I read out the address as if I'd been riding
in cabs all my life and hopped in and slammed the door, I knew
the proper deportment of dealing with cabs from the movies, I
showed nothing on my face of the excitement I felt, but we
hadn't gone a block with me sitting in the middle of the back seat
with all the room in the world on the cracked red leather before
I decided this was my new preferred mode of travel.

We proceeded down the Grand Concourse and across the
138th Street Bridge. The address I had was a candy store near
the corner of 125th Street and Lenox Avenue. I told the driver
to wait, like people in the movies did, but he said he would wait
only if I paid him as much of the fare as was on the meter. This
I did. When I walked in the store I knew it was George standing

there behind the counter with a big puffy eye and a red bruise on the side of his face, he was holding a piece of ice under his eye and the melting ice was running through his fingers like tears, he was a light-complected Negro man with gray hair and a trim gray mustache, and he was shaken, ashen actually, two or three other men who looked not so much like customers as friends of his were there sitting at the counter, and they were black too and wore their wool working caps though it was the hot summer, they were not joyful to see me. I stayed calm and tried to act like a true business representative. I looked through the window at the black passersby on the street looking in at me as they passed, and I saw then the plate-glass window was cracked diagonally in half, and there were shards of glass on the worn linoleum floor near the newspapers, and the taxi at the curb looked as if it wasn't joined properly in the middle, nothing was joined, nothing went together, this dark little candy store had broken off from Mr. Schultz like a piece of the continent into the sea, George reached down into one of the ice-cream containers under the fountain and came up with a brown paper bag rolled tight at the top the way they did it and he dropped it on the Belgian marble counter. "Ain't nothing I can do, I work for them now," he said holding the ice cake up to his face. "You tell him that, hear? You see what happen I try to do right. You tell him. All go to hell far as I concern, you tell him that too. All the white mens together."

And back to the Bronx I went, the paper bag clutched in my two hands, and I didn't even look inside, I knew there were hundreds of dollars there but I wouldn't look, I was happy enough to have this official standing as a runner, I wondered what had happened to George's man but didn't really care that much, I felt too good about handling the thing without a hitch, and without feeling afraid, and that this George did not question my credentials or make a personal remark about me, as angry as he was, but simply treated me as another of Mr. Schultz's men, a professional, one whose face showed no emotion in the presence of pain or misfortune but who had come for the money and gone with it, period, and who was now bumping over the bridge over the Harlem River, his heart pumping with happy gratitude for the beauty and excitement of his existence, and the river flowing with industrial muck, and the welding torches of riverside machine shops like sparklers in the July morning.

S I X

Of course as happy as I was to be catching on with them, things were not going well at that time for the Dutch Schultz gang and they wouldn't until Dixie Davis, that was the name of the lawyer Mr. Schultz shouted at all the time, was able to work out a plan for Mr. Schultz's surrender to the U.S. District Attorney's Office. If you did not know the arcane nature of these matters it would not make sense that Mr. Schultz was hoping to turn himself in for arraignment but he paced up and down dreaming of nothing but that, once actually trying to tear the hair from his head in a fury of frustration that he couldn't yet do that, for the truth of the matter was until he was booked and out on bail he wasn't free to attend to business. But he couldn't turn himself in until he had some legal guarantees that would improve his chances in a trial, as for instance that it should be held out of New York City, where, because of certain unfortunate publicity having to do with his activities, the public from which any jury would be composed tended not to see him in a good light. And that was at the core of the endless negotiations between his lawyer and the D.A.'s office, he wanted some guarantees before he turned himself in and until he had them he could not be arrested and therefore free.

He told me the crime business like any other needs the constant attention of the owner to keep it going, because nobody cares about the business like the owner and it's his burden to keep the profits flowing, to keep everyone on their toes, and most of all to keep the business growing, because as he explained it to me an enterprise can't maintain itself today just by repeating what it did yesterday, if it doesn't grow it dries up, it is like something living, when it stops growing it starts dying, to say nothing of the special nature of his particular enterprise, a very complex enterprise not only of supply and demand but of subtle executive details and diplomatic skills, the payoffs alone deserved a special department of controllers, the people you needed to rely on were vampires, they needed their blood money, and if you weren't there to give it to them they folded up on you, went numb, faded into the mist, you had to be a public presence in criminal enterprise or it would get away from you, and whatever you built up could be taken away from you, in fact the better you were, the more successful you were, the surer the fuckers would try to take it away from you, and by that he didn't only mean the law he meant the competition, this was a highly competitive field that did not attract gentlemen, and if they found a weakness in the armor, they went after it, and even if you had one pissant sentry sleeping on his post say, or some gonfalong foot soldier who could be lured off guard duty, not to speak of your own absence from the command post not even to speak of that, why then you were finished because they drove their tanks in through that opening whatever it was and that was the end of you, they had no fear of you, and without their fear of you, you were a dead man in no-man's-land, and there would not be enough recognizably left of you to put in a coffin.

I took these concerns for my own, as how could I not, sitting on the screened back porch of the two-story red brick house on City Island with the great man confiding his thoughts his worries to orphan Billy, the good-luck kid, the amazed beneficiary of this sudden and unpredictable intimacy. He had gone from not recognizing me to remembering the first moment he saw me across the street capably juggling, how could I not take on the dark troubles of his heart and feel them inside myself as a matter that would not go away, the nagging fear of loss, the dry inner sob of unjust circumstance, and the heroic satisfaction of enduring, of seeing things through? So this was the secret place where he stayed when he was not temporarily present in his protected precincts, this red brick private house just like the flat-roofed private houses you saw all over the borough except way out here it was the only one on a short street of bungalows, on this island that was still in the Bronx, and now I was one of the few people who knew, Irving knew of course because it was his mother's house, and his elderly mother knew because she cooked and kept things going normally—a woman who walked around with her hands always wet—on this quiet side street with a few hardy ailanthus trees like the ones planted in all the city parks, and Mr. Berman knew it because it was he who one day allowed me to come for the ride that he took each afternoon to bring Mr. Schultz the receipts and go over the figures. And as I sat out in the fenced backyard while they were doing this I reasoned that all the neighbors on the street and perhaps for a few blocks around must know it too because how can you not know when a famous visitor is on your street, and a dark car with two men in it sits outside at the curb night and day, this was a small place, a waterfront town really, if of a New York style, but having not really that much in common with the endless paved hills and valleys of Bronx tenements and stores and elevated trains and trolleys and peddlers' carts, it was an island that got sun, and the people on it must feel special, apart from everything, as I did now, relishing my connection with the good life of space, of this view of the Sound, which looked to me like an ocean, a deep horizon of gray sea sliding and shifting about in a leisurely way, the way slate and stone would shift if not fixed to the land, with the stateliness of a monumental body too big to have enemies. Right next door on the other side of the chain-link fence was a boatyard, with sailboats and motorboats of all kinds propped up on blocks or tilting over in the sand, and there were a few sailboats moored in the water off the boatyard wharves. But the boat I had my eye on was tied up at the wharf looking sleek and ready to go, a varnished mahogany speedboat with grooved tan

leather seats built in and bright brass trim on the windshield and
a steering wheel like a car's and a little American flag flying from
the stern. And I saw a gap in the chain-link fence between the
house and the boatyard just at the waterline, and then a path to
the wharf where that boat waited, and I knew this had to be the
craft of Mr. Schultz's getaway, if it ever came to that. How I
admired the life of taking pains, of living in defiance of a government that did not like you and did not want you and wanted to
destroy you so that you had to build out protections for yourself
with money and men, deploying armament, buying alliances,
patrolling borders, as in a state of secession, by your will and
wit and warrior spirit living smack in the eye of the monster, his
very eye.

But beyond that, contriving a life from its property of danger,
putting it together in the constant contemplation of death, that
was what thrilled me, that was why the people on this island
street would never rat, his presence honored them and allowed
them to live in their consciousness of him as in a kind of light
of life and death, with the moments of superior awareness or
illumination the best of them might get in church or in the first
moments of romantic love.

"Christ, I had to earn everything I got, nobody gave me a
thing, I came out of nowhere and everything I done I done by
myself," Mr. Schultz said. He sat in reflection upon this truth
and pulled on his cigar. "Sure I made mistakes, that's the way
you learn, the only time I ever served was when I was seventeen,
I got sent to Blackwell's Island for heisting, I didn't have a
lawyer and they gave me an indeterminate, meaning when I got
out depended on how I acted, and that was fair enough. I tell
you if I had some of these hotshot lawyers I have now probably
I'd have gotten life. Hey Otto?" he said laughing, but Mr. Berman had fallen asleep in his chair with his panama over his face,
I suppose he had heard Mr. Schultz complain once or twice
before about how hard his life was.

"Anyways I was damned if I'd kiss ass just to be let out of
there, I raised hell instead, and I was such a tough son of a bitch
they couldn't take me and sent me upstate to reform school, a

work farm with cows and all that shit. You ever been in reform
school?"

"No sir."

"Well it wasn't no picnic. I wasn't a big guy, I was about your
size, a skinny little punk, and there was a lot of bad boys there.
I knew you gotta make your reputation early, where it matters,
where the word can get around. So I was mean enough for ten.
I didn't take any shit. I looked for fights. I took on the biggest
guys I could find. God help the fucker who messed with me, as
one or two did to their regret. I even escaped from the goddamn
place, it wasn't hard, I went over the wire, and I was out in the
bushes a day and a night before they caught me, and they added
a couple of months for that, and I got poison ivy all the hell over
me for good measure, and I was walking around all that time in
calamine lotion like a mad zombie. When I finally got out they
were glad to see me go, let me tell you. You in a gang?"

"No sir."

"Well how you expect to get anywhere, how you expect to
learn anything? I hire from gangs. That's the training ground.
You ever hear of the Frog Hollow gang?"

"No sir."

"Jesus. That was the most famous of all the old Bronx gangs.
What's the matter with this generation? That was the gang of the
first Dutch Schultz, don't you know that? The toughest street
fighter who ever lived. He'd bite your nose off. He'd pull your
balls out by the root. My gang named me after him I got back
from the reform. It was a honorary thing. It showed I'd done
my time and gone through it, and come out of my training a
son of a bitch in spades. So ever since that's why I'm called the
Dutchman."

I cleared my throat and looked out through the screen over
the privet hedges to the water, where a small boat with a triangu-
lar white sail seemed to be sailing the shimmering mesh. "There
are some gangs now," I said, "but they are dumb fucking kids,
mostly. I don't want to pay for no one's mistakes but my own.
I think these days for the real training you got to go right to
the top."

I held my breath. I didn't dare look at him, I looked at my feet. I could feel his gaze on me. I could smell his cigar.

"Hey Otto," he said, "wake the hell up, you're really missing something."

"Oh? That's what you think," Mr. Berman said from under his hat.

It didn't all happen at once but it happened night and day, there seemed to be no rule of time, no plan except the possible moment and whatever it was we drove to it in a car, and when you look out the window at the life you're going through to get to this moment it takes on an odd cast, so that if the sun is shining it's shining too brightly, or if it is night it is too black, all the organization of the world seems part of the conspiracy of your attention, and whatever is naturally around you becomes unnatural by the peculiarly absolute moral demand of what you are doing. This was my wish, I was training at the top. I remember for instance being dropped off at the corner of Broadway and Forty-ninth Street and told to hang around and keep my eyes open. That was all that was said, but it was momentous. One of the cars sped off and I didn't see it again, the other, the one with Mr. Berman, kept coming around the block every few minutes, a single black squarish Chevrolet sedan inconspicuous in the traffic of black cars and the yellow checker cabs cruising for fares and the double-decker buses and streetcars, relatively empty, and neither Mickey the driver nor Mr. Berman looked at me as they passed, and I derived from that not to look particularly at them. I stood in the doorway of Jack Dempsey's restaurant that had not yet opened for the day, it must have been nine or nine-thirty in the morning, and Broadway was fairly fresh, the newsstands and coconut-drink and hotdog stands were open and a couple of the stores that sold little lead Statues of Liberty but not much else. There was a second-floor dance studio across Forty-ninth Street and the big window was tilted open and someone was playing "Bye, Bye, Blackbird" on the piano. There is a local Broadway, a community of Broadway that you see in the morning before the penny arcades and bars open for the day, the people who live upstairs in the tenements above the movie marquees, who come out with their dogs on the leash to get the *Racing Form* and the *Mirror* and buy a bottle of milk. And the bakery delivery men who pull up and carry the racks of breads and big bags of rolls into the groceries, or the butcher trucks with the guys loading big raw sides of beef on their shoulders and dumping them on the roller chutes leading down to the basements underneath the restaurants. I kept watching and saw the street sweeper with his big broom and his summer white with the khaki-and-orange trim on his hat load up the horse manure and paper and crap and trash of a Broadway night on his wide-blade shovel and dump it all into the big ashcan on his two-wheel cart as if he was a housewife tidying up her kitchen. A while later the tanked water wagon came along spraying the street so that it looked shining and fresh and almost simultaneously I saw the string of electric lights go on around the Loew's State Theatre a few blocks below where Broadway ran into Seventh Avenue. In the sun it was not entirely possible to read the headlines riding in lights around the Times Building on Times Square. The black Chevrolet came around again and this time Mr. Berman glanced at me and I began to feel anxious, I wanted to see whatever it was I was supposed to see but the traffic was ordinary, not particularly heavy, and the people on the sidewalk were going about their business with no great urgency, a man in a suit and tie came along with a crate of apples on his shoulder and set it up on the corner with his APPLES 5¢ sign, the morning was warming up and I wondered if what I needed was in the window behind me where Jack Dempsey was shown in a big blowup photo of the ring in Manila with thousands watching, and there were other photos of the great man shaking hands with famous people, show people like Jimmy Durante and Fanny Brice and Rudy Vallee, but then in the reflection of the restaurant glass I saw the office building across the street, and I turned around to look, up on the fifth or sixth floor a man climbed out on a ledge with a pail and sponge and affixed his safety belt to the hooks imbedded in the brick and leaned back against the belt and began to make wide arcs with his soapy sponge on the window, and then I saw another man on another window ledge on the floor above him coming out to do the same thing. I watched these men washing the windows and then for some reason I knew this was what I was supposed to see, these window washers doing the morning's work high above the street. And on the sidewalk below them was a sign, the kind that supports itself like an *A,* advising passersby that work was going on overhead and to take care, and it was the sign the window washers had set up in the name of their union. I had by now crossed Broadway and stood on the southwest corner of Forty-ninth Street and Seventh Avenue and I watched these guys working up there, two of them were on a scaffold hanging from the roof parapet maybe fifteen stories above the street and I saw this was the expedient for the extra large windows at the top that were too wide for a safety belt to span. And it was this scaffold with the two men and their sponges and pails and rags which suddenly lurched, the rope on one side snapping up into the air like a whip, and the two men flinging their arms back and spilling down the scaffold. One of them came down the side of the building wheeling. I don't know if I shouted, or who else saw it happen or heard it, but while he was still several stories up, some seconds above his death, the whole street knew. The traffic was stopped as if every vehicle had been pulled up taut on the same string. There was a collective screech, a total apprehension of disaster on the part of every pedestrian for blocks around, as if we had all been aware all along of what was going on above our heads in the sky, so that the moment the composition was disturbed everyone knew instantly. Then the body at a point of flat and horizontal extension hit the roof of a car parked in front of the building and the sound it made was as a cannon going off, a terrible explosion of the force of bone and flesh, and what made me gasp was that he moved, the guy moved in that concavity of metal he had made, a sinuosity of bone-smashed inching, as if it was a worm there curling for a moment on the hot metal before even that degree of incredible life trembled out through the fingers.

A cop on a horse was now galloping past me on Forty-ninth

Street. The other window washer was still up there hanging from the unhinged end of the vertical scaffold and kicking his legs to find purchase where there was none, screaming up there as the platform swayed from side to side in the way least calculated to ensure his survival. What does a man have in his arms eight ten stories above the ground, what does he have in his fingers, in the muscles of his fingertips, what do we hold to in this world of unholy depth which presents for us its bottomless possibilities in air in water in the paved soil that opens up under us, cracking like a thunderstorm of the most specific density? Green-and-white police cars were converging from all directions. Up at Fifty-seventh Street a hook-and-ladder fire engine was turning into Broadway. I was breathless with the fascination of disaster.

"Hey kid!"

Behind me on Broadway was Mr. Berman's Chevrolet, which was pulled up to the curb. The door opened. I ran back the short block and got in and slammed the door behind me and Mickey the driver took off. "Don't gawk, kid, you leave that to hicks," Mr. Berman said. He was put out with me. "You are not in the sightseeing business. You're told to stay somewhere you stay there."

At this I forbore to look back out the window, which I would otherwise have done even knowing that the progress of the car down Broadway would have blocked the scene from my sight. But I felt the will in myself in not moving but sitting back silently and staring ahead.

Mickey the driver had both hands on the wheel when he didn't reach down to shift. If the wheel was a clock he held it at ten and two. He drove moderately but not slowly, he did not contend with the traffic but used it to his advantage without ever seeming to speed or cut anyone off. He did not try to make a changing light, or upon a light's turning green to speed off with it. Mickey was the driver and that's all he was, but that was everything; you knew watching him and feeling the movement of the car under you that there was a difference between driving a car and running it with the authority of a professional. I myself did not know how to drive, how could I, but I knew that Mickey would drive a car as calmly and safely at a hundred miles an hour as at thirty, that whatever he called upon a car to do it would do, and now with the vision in my mind of the helpless window washer falling to his death, Mickey's competence stood in my mind as a silent rebuke in confirmation of Mr. Berman's remark.

I don't think in all the time I knew him while he was alive I ever exchanged a word with Mickey. I think he was ashamed of his speech. His intelligence was all in his meaty hands and in his eyes, which you sometimes saw flick back for a professional second in the rearview mirror. They were light blue. He was totally hairless, with fat ridges at the back of his neck which I got to know well. His ears bulbed out in back. He had been a prize-fighter who never got further than the preliminaries in club fights. His greatest distinction was having been TKO'd by Kid Chocolate in one of his earliest fights when the Kid was coming up, one night in the Jerome Arena just across the street from Yankee Stadium. Or so I had heard. I don't know why but I wanted to cry for us all. Mickey drove us over to the West Side into some truck garage, and while Mr. Berman and I went across the street to a diner for coffee, the Chevrolet was exchanged for another car, which appeared with Mickey at the wheel maybe twenty minutes later. It was a Nash with totally different black-and-orange license plates. "Nobody dies who doesn't sin," Mr. Berman had said to me in the diner. "And since that covers everybody, it's something we can all look forward to." Then he tossed one of those little number-square games on the table for me to amuse myself with: the one with sixteen squares and fifteen little numbered tiles which you have to put in order by shoving them around until they're in sequence. The point is you have only that one space to use to get everything around where it belongs; one space usually in the wrong place to put every-thing in the order in which it belongs.

But as I say it was a kind of enlistment, I had walked in and signed up. And the first thing you learn is there are no ordinary rules of the night and day, there are just different kinds of light, granules of degree, and so no reason to have more or less to do in one than in another. The blackest quietest hour was only a kind of light.

There was no attempt on anyone's part to provide explanations for why things were being done and no one sought to justify anything. I knew better than to ask questions. What I did understand is that a strong ethic prevailed, all the normal umbrages and hurts were in operation, all the outraged sensibilities of justice, all the convictions of right and wrong, once you accepted the first pure inverted premise. But it was the premise I had to work on. I found it was easiest when Mr. Schultz talked to me; at these times for a few moments things were clear. I decided I had so far the idea of it but not the feeling, it was the feeling that made for the genius of the idea as anyone could tell just being in Mr. Schultz's presence.

In the meantime I could figure out things were being done at a level of intensity that perhaps had been anticipated in the quiet afternoons on the back porch of the City Island house. I will tell here about Mr. Schultz's Embassy Club. It was a place he owned, one of his properties, and it was quite publicly visible with a fancy canopy with its name in scripted letters on East Fifty-sixth Street between Park and Lexington avenues. I knew all about nightclubs from the gossip columns, and the customers who went there and the fancy names some of them had, from high society, and how they all seemed to know each other, movie stars and actors and actresses coming in after work, and ball players and writers and senators, I knew there were sometimes floor shows with bands and chorus girls or black women who sang the blues, and I knew each place had bouncers for the unruly and the girls selling cigarettes on trays while they walked around in net stockings and cute little pillbox hats, I knew all that though I had never seen it.

So I was excited when they sent me to work there as a busboy. Imagine me, a kid, working downtown in a nightclub! But in the week I worked there it was nothing like I expected. There was first of all not one single famous person I saw while I was there. There were people who came and ate and drank and listened to the little orchestra and danced, but they were unimportant. I knew that because they kept looking around for the important people they had come to see. Most nights the place was half empty except toward eleven o'clock when the floor show went on. The whole place was lit in blue light with banquettes around the walls and tables with blue tablecloths around a small dance floor, and a small stage with no curtain where the band played, not a great band, two saxophones and a trumpet and a piano and guitar and drums, and there was a hatcheck girl but no cigarette girls and no midnight reporters come to get dirt from the famous, no Walter Winchell or Damon Runyon, the place was dead, and it was dead because Mr. Schultz couldn't show up there. He was the attraction. People liked to be where things happened or could happen. They liked power. The bartender stood behind the bar with his arms folded and yawned. At the worst possible table, by the door where it was drafty, every night two assistant United States attorneys sat with lime rickeys they did not touch and filled the ashtrays which I emptied conscientiously. They did not look at me. Nobody looked at me in my short maroon jacket and bow tie, I was so low-down as to be supposed legitimate. I was making good in the nightclub world and took a sort of scintillating pride in the fact that as a busboy I was beneath even the notice of the old-time waiters. That made me valuable. Because I had been put there by Mr. Berman with the usual admonition to keep my eyes open. And I did, and I learned what idiots people could make of themselves who came to nightclubs, and how they loved it if a bottle of champagne cost them twenty-five dollars, and the headwaiter gave them a table when they pressed a twenty-dollar bill in his hand though there were so many empty tables they could have asked for the one they wanted and he would have led them to it for nothing. It was a narrow room, an empty scene, and between sets the band stood out in the alley and every one of them was a viper, even the girl singer, and on the third or fourth night she turned her hand upside down to me and handed me a roach and I sucked on it like I had seen them doing and sipped it in, that harsh bitter tea, like a scatter of embers going down my throat, and of course I coughed and they laughed, but the laughter was kindly; except for the singer they were white musicians not much older than I was and I don't know what they took me for, maybe someone working his way through college, and I let them think it, whatever it was, all I needed was a pair of Harold Lloyd horn-rim glasses and the act would have been perfect. In the kitchen though that was a different story, the chef there was a Negro who was in charge, he smoked cigarettes, the ashes of which dropped onto the steaks he was frying, and he had a cleaver with which he threatened waiters or underlings who offended him. He was a perpetually angry man who blew into flares of rage like the flames that flew up in the fat drippings. The only one who wasn't afraid of him was the dishwasher, an old gray-haired Negro man with a limp who seemed to be able to stick his bare arms in tubs of scalding soapy water with no feeling. We were close because I brought him the dishes. He appreciated the way I scraped them. We were professionals together. You had to be careful in the kitchen because the floor was as greasy as a garage's. Cockroaches were in leisurely residence on the wall almost as if they were stuck there, and the flypaper that hung from the light-bulb strings was black, and sometimes on the counters themselves a mouse or two scurried from one food bin to another. This was all behind the padded swinging doors with the oval windows of the blue-lit Embassy Club.

Yet I stopped to listen to the girl singer when I could. She had a sweet thin voice and seemed to look far away when she sang. They would always get up to dance when she sang because the women liked her songs of loss and loneliness and loving men who didn't love them back. *The one I love belongs to somebody else. He means his tender songs for somebody else.* She stood in front of the microphone and sang with very little gesture, perhaps because of all the tea she smoked, and every once in a while, at really inappropriate moments of the lyrics, she hiked up her strapless satin gown as if she was afraid even her listless gestures would expose her breasts.

Then every morning at about four or four-thirty Mr. Berman

arrived looking as fresh as the morning in some artful combination of pastel colors. At this point everyone would have left, the
U.S. District Attorney's men, the waiters, the band, the place was
only ostensibly open, with maybe the beat cop with his hat on
the bar having one on the house. And it was my job to go pull
all the tablecloths off the tables, and stack the chairs on them so
that the two cleaning women who came in in the morning would
be able to vacuum the carpet under the tables and mop and wax
the dance floor. After this I was summoned to the basement,
where a small paneled office was maintained just down the hall
from a fire door leading to a kind of culvert that led up a flight
of iron stairs to an alley. And in this office Mr. Berman would
go over the night's receipts and ask me what I had seen. I would
of course have seen nothing except what for me was the new life
of Manhattan, a life of the night, where in one short week everything was inverted and I finished work at dawn and went to sleep
in the daytime. What I had seen was the life of the big time and
a certain fluency of money not as it was earned and collected,
as on 149th Street, but as it was spent and as it was turned into
blue light and fancy clothes and indifferently delivered love
songs. I had seen that the hatcheck girl paid Mr. Berman for her
job, rather than the other way around, but that this seemed to
be profitable to her as she went off duty each night with a
different man waiting under the canopy outside. But this was not
what he meant when he asked the question. I had seen my witchy
little friend Rebecca in my mind dressed in high heels and some
kind of black lacy gown dancing with me there to the songs of
the girl singer. I thought she would even be impressed with me
in my waistcoat busboy jacket. I slept in that same office after Mr.
Berman left, and there I dreamed of making love to Rebecca and
not having to pay for it. In my dream I was in the rackets and
this made her love me enough to enjoy what I was doing to her.
But certainly this was not what Mr. Berman had in mind. Half
the time I awoke in the morning all gummed up in my sleep,
which created laundry problems, and I solved these too like a
denizen of Broadway, finding a Chinese laundry on Lexington
Avenue, but also buying myself socks and underwear and shirts

and pants over on Third Avenue under the El. It was like my Third Avenue. I was not unhappy this week. I found I was really comfortable in the city, it was no different from the Bronx, it was only what the Bronx wanted to be, it was streets and they could be learned and I had a job which paid twelve dollars a week now, dispensed from Mr. Berman's pockets just for me to haul dishes around and keep my eyes open though I did not know for what. And after the third or fourth day of this I rarely saw in my mind the cartwheeling body of the window washer in the sun coming down alongside the office building on Seventh Avenue. It was almost as if the East Side was a different behavior even for the rackets. I slept below ground in that office on a fold-out cot and, along about noon, came up the iron stairs into the alley and walked around the corner and a few blocks down and found a cafeteria on Lexington Avenue where the cab drivers had their lunch while I had my breakfast. I ate big breakfasts. I bought rolls and buns for old men the cafeteria owner was trying to kick out the revolving door. I reflected on my competence for life and could find nothing to criticize except perhaps not going uptown to see my mother. I called her once to the phone at the candy store on the corner of our block and told her I would be away for a while but I didn't know if she would remember. It had taken fifteen minutes on an open line for someone to find her and bring her downstairs.

I mention all this as an interlude of peace and reflection.

Then one night I was able to tell Mr. Berman that Bo Wein-berg had come in with a party and had dinner and paid the band to do a couple of numbers of his choice. Not that I had recognized him, but the waiters had all come alive. Mr. Berman did not seem surprised. "Bo will be in again," he said. "Never mind who he sits with. See who sits at the bar near the door." And so I did, a couple of nights later, when Bo reappeared with a pretty blond woman and another good-looking couple, a well-dressed man with a blond pompadour and a brunette. They took the best banquette, near the bandstand. And all those customers who had come there that evening looking for the peculiar excitement seemed now to believe it was their good fortune to have found it. It wasn't merely that Bo looked good, although undeniably he did, a tall, rugged, swarthy man impeccably groomed and with teeth that seemed to shine, but that he seemed to drink up the available light, so that blue light turned red and everyone else in the room seemed dim and small by comparison. He and his party were wearing formal clothes as if they had come from someplace important, like the opera or a Broadway show. He greeted this one and that one, he acted as if he owned the joint. The musicians came out earlier than they might have and the dancing started. And soon the Embassy Club was what I had imagined a nightclub should be. From one minute to the next the place was packed, as if all of New York City had come running. People kept coming up to Bo's table to introduce themselves. The man Bo was with was a famous golfer, but I didn't recognize the name. Golf was not my sport. The women laughed and smoked a puff or two of a cigarette and as soon as it was mushed out I changed the ashtray. It was odd, the more people there were and the noisier the place got with music and laughter, the bigger the Embassy Club seemed to be, until it seemed the only place that there was, I mean with nothing outside, no street, no city, no country. My ears were ringing, I was a busboy but I felt it was my personal triumph when Walter Winchell himself appeared and sat for a few minutes at Bo's table, although I hardly saw him, because I was working my ass off. Later Bo Weinberg actually addressed me, telling me to tell the waiter to refresh the drinks of the assistant U.S. attorneys who were sitting at the drafty table by the door. This caused great merriment. Well after midnight, when they decided to have something to eat, and I went up to the table to place the little hard rolls in their little plates with my silver tongs, as I by now knew how to do with aplomb, I had to restrain the urge to pick up three or four of the rolls and juggle them in time to the music, which at the moment happened to be "Limehouse Blues," which the band did in a very stately and deliberate rhythm. *Oh Limehouse kid, Oh Oh Limehouse kid, going the way that the rest of them did.*

But for all of that I never forgot my instruction from Mr. Berman. The man who had come in just before Bo Weinberg and sat at the end of the bar was not Lulu Rosenkrantz with the ridged brow, and not Mickey with the floret ears, and it wasn't anyone I had ever seen on any of the trucks or in the office on 149th Street, and in fact no one at all that I recognized from the organization. It was a small, pudgy man in a double-breasted pearl gray suit with big lapels and a green satin tie and a white-on-white shirt and he didn't stay that long, smoking just a cigarette or two and drinking a mineral water. He seemed to enjoy the music in a quiet and private way. He didn't talk to anyone and minded his own business and kept his porkpie hat on the bar beside him.

Later when the morning rose in the basement office in the culvert off the alley, Mr. Berman lifted his eyes from the stacks of cashier slips and said "So?" his brown eyes with the pale blue rims looking at me through his spectacles. I had noticed the man used his own matches and left the book in the ashtray and I picked it out of the trash behind the bar after he left. But this was not the moment to give my proof. It was necessary only to make the essential attribution. "An out-of-towner," I said. "A goombah from Cleveland."

There was no sleep for me that morning. Mr. Berman sent me out to a phone booth and I dialed the number he gave me, let it ring three times and hung up. I brought back coffee and rolls. The cleaning women came in and did up the club. It was now nice and peaceful in there with all the lights out except one light over the bar and whatever silt of the morning sun managed to drift in through the curtains on the front doors. Part of what I was learning was when to be on hand and visible, as opposed to being on hand and invisible. The second was the expedient I chose now, perhaps from no more evidence than Mr. Berman's disinclination at this time to talk to me. I sat upstairs at the bar all alone in the dusk of the morning tired as hell and not without pride in myself for having made what I knew was a useful identi-

fication. But then all of a sudden there was Irving, which meant
Mr. Schultz was somewhere nearby. Irving stood behind the bar
and put some ice in a glass, then he cut a lime in quarters and
with his fingers squeezed lime juice into the glass, and then filled
the glass with a spritz from the seltzer bottle. When all this was
meticulously done, with not so much as a ring left on the bar
surface, Irving drank off his lime soda in one draft. He then
washed the glass and dried it with a bar towel and replaced it
under the counter. At this moment it occurred to me that my
self-satisfaction was inane. It consisted in believing I was the
subject of my experience. And then when Irving went to the
front door, where someone had been knocking on the glass for
some minutes, and admitted the improvident city fire inspector
who had picked just this time, and why, except that the words
in the air of the great stone city go softly whispering in the
lambent morning that this sachem is dead and that one is dying,
as if we were some desert blooming in the smallest flowers with
the prophecies of ancient tribes, I saw even before it happened
what an error of thought could lead to, that presumption was
dangerous, that the confidence of imperception was deadly, that
this man had forgotten what a fire inspector was, his place in the
theory of inspections, his lesser place in the system of fires.
Irving was ready with money from his own pocket and would
have had the guy out of there in another minute but that Mr.
Schultz happened to come upstairs from the office with the
morning's news. At another time Mr. Schultz might have genuinely admired the man's gall and peeled off a few dollars. Or he
might have said you dumb fuck you know better than to walk in
here with this shit. He might have said you got a complaint you
talk to your department. He might have said I'll make one phone
call and have your ass you stupid son of a bitch. But as it happened he gave this roar of rage, took him down and mashed his
windpipe and used the dance floor to make an eggshell of his
skull. A young man with a head of curly hair is what I saw of him
alive in that light, maybe a few years older than me, a wife and
kid in Queens, who knows? who like me had ambitions for his

life. I had never seen anyone being killed close up like that. I can't tell even now how long it took. It seemed like a long time. And what is most unnatural is the sounds. They are the sounds of ultimate emotion, as sexual sounds can sometimes seem to be, except they are shameful and degrading to the idea of life, that it can be so humiliated so eternally humiliated. Mr. Schultz arose from the floor and brushed his pants knees. There was not a spot of blood on him although it was webbed out in strings and matter all around the head on the floor. He hitched up his pants and smoothed his hair with his hands and straightened his tie. He was drawing great gasping breaths. He looked as if he was about to cry. "Get this load of shit out of here," he said, including me in the instruction. Then he went back downstairs.

I couldn't seem to move. Irving told me to bring an empty garbage can from the kitchen. When I got back he had folded the body and tied it head to ankles with the guy's jacket. I think now he must have had to crack the guy's spine to get him doubled so tight. The jacket was over the head. That was a great relief to me. The torso still had heat. We inserted the folded body ass-down in the galvanized-iron garbage can and stuffed the space around with wooden straw of the kind that protects French bottles of wine in their cases, hammered the lid on with our fists and put the can out with the night's refuse just as the carter came along on Fifty-sixth Street. Irving had a word with the driver. They are private companies that take away commercial refuse, the city only does citizen garbage. Two guys stand on the sidewalk and heave the can up to the fellow standing in the truck on top of all the garbage. That fellow dumps out the contents and tosses the empty can back over the side to the guys in the street. All the cans came back except one, and if a crowd had been standing around, which there wasn't, for who in the fresh world of the morning wants to watch the cleanup of the night before, the truck motors grinding, the ashcans hitting the sidewalk with that tympanic carelessness of the profession, nobody would have noticed that the truck drove away with one packed garbage can imbedded in all that odorous crap of the

glamorous night, or dreamed that in an hour or two it would be
shoveled by tractor deep below the anguished yearnings of the
flights of seagulls wheeling over the Flushing Meadow landfill.

What depressed Irving, what depressed Abbadabba Berman,
was that this had not been part of the plan. I saw it in their faces.
It was not so much a fear that there could be unforeseen com-
plications, that was not a professional worry. It was that such
poor slobs who on their own get high-and-mighty ideas, which
are in fact low ideas of what high-and-mighty is, are unnecessary
to kill. Essentially the guy was not in the business. After a while
even Mr. Schultz looked depressed. It was still morning and he
had a couple of Cherry Heerings served to him by Irving at the
bar. He looked glum, as if he understood he was getting to be
a cross they all, himself included, had to bear. There was this
interesting separation he made now from his own temperament.
"I can't deal with it when it's all over the street," he said.
"Irving, you remember that Norma Floy, that gash who took me
for thirty-five thousand dollars? She run out on me with that
fucking horseback-riding instructor? What did I do? What did
I do? I laughed. More power to her. Of course I ever find her
little blond head I'll break every tooth in it. But maybe I won't.
And that's the point. These guys are putting it out on the street.
I mean the fucking fire inspectors? What next, I mean the mail-
men?"

"We still got time," Mr. Berman said.

"Sure, sure. But anything is better than this. I can't take this
no more. I'm finished with this. I've been listening to too many
lawyers. Otto, you know the Feds are not going to let me pay the
taxes I owe them."

"That is correct."

"I want one more meeting with Dixie. And I want to make
things really clear to Hines. After that we will confront what we
must confront."

"We are not without resources," Mr. Berman said.

"That's right. We will do the one or two essential things it

appears now we must do. And then it's on to Shangri-la. I'll
show those fuckhead sons of bitches. All of them. I'm still the
Dutchman.''

Mr. Berman told me to come outside and we stood beside the
empty garbage cans by the curb. He said the following: "Supposing you have numbers to the number one hundred, how
much is each number worth? It is true that one number might
be the value one, and another number the value ninety-nine,
which is ninety-nine ones, but each of them in the row of one
hundred is only worth a hundredth of the hundred, you get it?''
I said I got it. "All right," he said, "now knock off ninety of those
numbers and say all you got left is ten of them, it doesn't matter
which ten, say the first five and the last five, how much is each
number worth? It doesn't matter what it says its number is, it's
its share in the total that matters, you get it?'' I said I got it. "So
the fewer the numbers the more each one is worth, am I right?
And it doesn't matter what it says it is as a number, it's worth
its weight in gold is what it's worth compared to what it was
surrounded by all the other numbers. You unnerstan the
point?'' I said I did. "Good, good, you think about these things
then. How a number can look like one thing but mean another.
How a number can look like one thing, but have the worth of
another. After all, you'd think a number was a number and that's
all it was. But here is a simple example how that is not so. Come
take a walk with me. You look terrible. You look green. You
need some fresh air.''

We turned east, came to Lexington, crossed, and headed for
Third. We walked slowly as you had to do with Mr. Berman. He
walked slightly sideways. He said, "I'll tell you my favorite number, but I want you to guess what it might be.'' I said, "I don't
know, Mr. Berman. I can't guess. Maybe the number that you
can make all the other numbers from.'' "That is not bad,'' he
said, "except that you can do that with any number. No, my
favorite number is ten, you know why? It has an equal number
of odd and even numbers in it. It has the unit number, and the

absence of the unit number which is mistakenly called zero. It has the first odd number and the first even number and the first square. And it has the first four numbers which when you add them up add up to itself. Ten is my lucky number. You have a lucky number?"

I shook my head. "You might consider ten," he said. "I want you to go home." He took out a wad of bills from his pocket. "Here's your salary for the busing job, twelve dollars, plus eight dollars severance pay, you are hereby fired."

Before I could react he said, "And here's twenty dollars just for the hell of it because you can read the names of Italian restaurants on matchbooks. And that's your money."

I took the money and folded it and put it in my pocket. "Thank you."

"Now," he said, "here's fifty dollars I'm giving to you, five tens, but this is my money. You unnerstan how I can give it to you but it is still mine?"

"You want me to buy you something?"

"That is correct. My directions for it are I want you to buy me yourself a new pair of pants or two and a nice jacket, and a shirt and a tie and a pair of shoes with laces. You see those sneakers you're wearing? It was a personal embarrassment to me to come in the morning and to see that a busboy at the elegant Embassy Club was walking around all night in his Nat Holman basketball sneakers with the laces so far gone the tongue hanging out of the mouth, and a big toe showing for the final insult. You are lucky few people look at feet. I happen to notice such things. I want you to burn those sneakers. I want you to get a haircut so you don't look like Ish Kabibble on a rainy night. I want you to buy a valise and into the valise put some nice new underwear and socks and a book to read. I want you to buy a real book from a bookstore, not a magazine, not a comic book, a real book, and put that in the valise too. I want you to buy a pair of glasses to read the book if it comes to that. See? Glasses, like I wear."

"I don't use glasses," I said. "I got perfect eyesight."

"You go to the pawnshop and you'll find they have glasses

with plain glass. Just do what I say, all right? And do this. Take
a few days. Take it easy, try to enjoy yourself. There's time.
When we need you we'll send for you."

We were by now standing at the foot of the stairs to the Third
Avenue Elevated. It was going to be another hot summer day.
I had mentally counted the money in my pocket, ninety dollars.
At this moment Mr. Berman unpeeled another ten. "And buy
something nice for your mother," he said, the one remark that
rang in my head all the way home on the train.

SEVEN

The train to the Bronx was empty at that hour of the morning, I was alone in the car staring into people's windows as we went by. I caught glimpses of people's rooms as if I was taking snapshots, a white enamel bed against a wall, a round oak table with an open bottle of milk and a plate, a standing lamp with a pleated shade protected with cellophane with the bulb still on in the morning over a stuffed green chair. People leaned with their arms on their windowsill and stared at the train going by as if they didn't see them every five or ten minutes. What was it like with the sound filling those rooms and shaking the plaster off the walls? These crazy women hung their family laundry on clotheslines between the windows, and their drawers flapped as the train went by. It had never occurred to me before how everything in New York was stacked, one thing on top of another, even the railroads had to be put over the street, like apartments over other apartments, and there were train tracks under the streets too. Everything in New York was on levels, the whole city was rock and you could do anything with rock, build skyscrapers into it, scallop it out for subway tunnels, poke steel beams into it and run railroads in the air right through people's apartments.

I sat with my hands in my pants pockets. I had distributed my money half and half and held on to it with both hands. For some reason it was a long trip back to the Bronx. How long had I been away? I had no idea, I felt I was coming home on a furlough, like a doughboy who'd been in France for a year. Everything looked strange to me. I got off a stop early and walked a block west to Bathgate Avenue. This was the market street, everyone did their shopping here. I walked along on the crowded sidewalks be- tween the pushcarts on the curb and the open stalls in the tenements, every one of the merchants competing with the same oranges and apples and tangerines and peaches and plums for the same prices, eight cents a pound, ten cents a pound, a nickel each, three for a dime. They wrote their prices on paper bags which they hung like flags on wooden slats behind each crate of fruit or vegetables. But that wasn't enough. They shouted out their prices. They called Missus, look, I got the best, feel this grapefruit, fresh Georgia peaches just in. They talked they cajoled and the women shopping talked back. I felt a little better now in all this innocent, urgent, only slightly larcenous life. There was chatter and in the street the horns of trucks blowing and kids darting from one side to another and overhead from the fire escapes men who were out of work sat in their pants and ribbed undershirts and read the papers. The aristocracy of the business had the real stores where you walked in and bought your chickens still in their feathers, or your fresh fish, or your flank steak, or milk and butter and cheese, or lox and smoked whitefish and pickles. In front of the army-navy stores suits hung on hangers from the awning bars or dresses hung from racks wheeled out the front doors, and clothes were bargains too on Bathgate, where for five dollars or seven dollars or twelve dol- lars you got two pairs of pants with the jacket. I was fifteen years old and I had a hundred dollars in my pockets. I knew without question that in that precise moment of the daily life of subsis- tence I was the richest person on Bathgate Avenue.

There was a florist on the corner and I went in and I bought my mother a potted geranium because it was the only flower whose name I knew. It didn't have much of a smell, it smelled

more like earth or a vegetable than a flower, but it was the kind
of plant she herself bought and then forgot to water until it
withered on the fire escape outside the kitchen window. The
leaves were full and green and there were small red blossoms
that hadn't opened. I knew that a geranium was not a propor-
tionate gift but it was sincerely from me and not from Abbadabba
Berman speaking for the Schultz gang. I felt somewhat shaky
now walking home to my street. But when I turned the corner
by the candy store there before my eyes were the Max and Dora
Diamond kids running around in their underwear under the
sprinkler attached to the fire hydrant. The street was closed off,
it was maybe ten in the morning, and they were all running
around in wet underwear, the little ones, screeching, with their
shiny little bodies so beautifully fast and quick. Of course the few
older children wore real woolen bathing suits, dark blue trunks
and connected tops with shoulder straps for both boys and girls,
the uniform orphan-blue wool, and not a few suits had holes
where the flesh peeked through. And there were regular kids
from the tenements all mixed in with their individual colors and
their mothers watching and wishing they could run under the
water too except for their dignity. The water made a rainbow
umbrella over the shining black street. I looked for my witchy
friend Becky but I knew she wouldn't be there, I knew she
wouldn't be caught dead running under a sprinkler any more
than any of the other incorrigibles, it was not what they could
allow themselves to do no matter how hot it might be, it was
their dignity no less than the parents' to make distinctions, in
fact so it was with all of us, not excepting me, I the most rigid
of all, passing into the dark courtyard of my house, stepping out
of the light, climbing through the dark halls of chipped octagonal tile to the apartments where I had grown into my life.

My mother was at work as I knew she would be. I could look
into all the rooms in the world, there was no house like my
house. There had been a fire in the kitchen, the enamel on the
table was burned in a big egg shape and around the edges the
paint was blistered. Nevertheless the candles were lit and lined

up in their tumblers. Sometimes in cold weather, when the wind came through the cracks around the windows and under the door and up through the dumbwaiter shaft, they leaned one way and then the other and swayed and shifted dissynchronously as in a kind of dance. Now they burned evenly although there seemed to be more than I remembered, the effect on me was of looking into a chandelier, that although I was upright I might just as well be lying on the floor and looking up into a grand imperial firmament. There was something majestic about my mother. She was a tall woman, she was taller than I was. She had been taller than my father as I reminded myself now looking at the wedding photo on the bureau in the sitting room which served also as her bedroom when she made up the couch. She had years ago run a crayon over the glass in a big X across his figure. This was after she had scraped away the face. She did things like that. When I was little I thought all rugs were in the shape of men's suits and trousers. She had nailed his suit to the floor as if it was the fur of some game animal, a bearskin, a tigerskin. The house had always smelled of burning wax, of candles gone out, of the smoke of wicks.

A water closet was off the kitchen, a dark cubicle with just a toilet, whereas the bathtub was in the kitchen, covered with a heavy wooden hinged lid. I put the geranium here so that she would see it.

In the little bedroom where I slept I found something new, a battered but once-elegant brown wicker baby carriage. It seemed to take up the whole room. The wheel rims were dented so that it wobbled as I pushed it back and forth. But the tires had been washed until they were white. And the top was up, that hinged part that can be put up against the weather and snapped into place with decorative stanchions on the sides. And a series of splintered holes ran diagonally down through it, so that the light from the bedroom window lit them up. An old rag doll lay askew in the carriage; perhaps she had found them together in the street, or bought them from Arnold Garbage separately and put them together herself, the carriage and the doll, and pulled them up the stairs and into the apartment and into my room for me to find when I came home.

She didn't ask too many questions and seemed happy enough to see me. My arrival split her attention, if the lights were a phone it would have been as if she maintained two conversations simultaneously, she half listened to me, half turned to the lights. We ate our dinner as always sitting beside the bathtub lid and my flowers made a kind of centerpiece and seemed more than anything to give her to understand that I had gotten a job. I told her I was working as a busboy with duties also as a kind of night watchman. I told her it was good work because there were lots of tips. That's what I told her and that's what she appeared to believe. "But just for the summer, of course, because you have to go back to school in September" is what she said, rising to adjust the position of one of the lights. I agreed. But I told her I had to dress properly for the job or I couldn't keep it, so on Saturday afternoon when she got home from work we rode the Webster Avenue trolley up to Fordham Road and went shopping for my suit at I. Cohen's, which was her choice, it was where, she said, my father had found good value in the old days, and she had good taste, she was suddenly an efficient and capable mother in the outside world, and I was very relieved on several grounds, just one of them being that I didn't know how to buy clothes for myself. But she looked reasonably normal too, she wore her best dress of large violet flowers on a white background and combed her hair up under her hat so that it did not show itself as long. One of the things that bothered me about my mother was that she never cut her hair. The fashion was for short hair but hers was long and in the morning, when she was preparing to leave for her job with the industrial laundry, she plaited it in one long braid which she coiled up on the top of her head and then stuck a lot of long pins in. She had a sour-cream jar of these long decorative pins on her bureau. But after she took her bath in the kitchen at night and prepared for bed, sometimes I couldn't help seeing all that straight long gray-black hair combed out on the couch pillow, some of it even falling off the side and touching the floor, some of it getting caught in the pages of her Bible. Her shoes bothered me too, she had bad feet from standing all day at her job, and her solution was to wear men's shoes, white ones which she put white polish on every night, summer or winter, claiming they were nurse's shoes if I happened to be in a bad enough mood to mention them. When we argued my criticism made her smile. It drove her further into herself. She never criticized me, however, being too distracted, only asking an occasional question whose anxiety was dispelled by her own wandering attention almost before she came to the end of the sentence. But on this Saturday afternoon when we went up to Fordham Road she looked very fine and acted almost all the time as if she was in the day together with me. She picked out a light gray single-breasted summer suit with two pairs of trousers and an Arrow shirt with little tabs sewn into the tips of the collar so that it would not curl up, and a red knit tie with a square bottom. We were a long time at I. Cohen's and the old gentleman who took care of us pretended not to see how poor we were, the condition of my sneakers, my mother's white men's shoes, taking us on faith, this little plump man with a tapemeasure hanging around his neck like a prayer shawl perhaps he had reason to know of the pride of poor people. But when my mother opened her purse and displayed the cash I had given her I thought I did detect a look of relief on his face, if not curiosity for this handsome tall woman who brought in this kid in rags and bought him an eighteen-dollar suit and accompaniments like it was nothing. Perhaps he thought she was a wealthy eccentric who had picked me out of the street as a charity case. I knew that night he would tell his wife that his job made a philosopher out of him because every day he saw that human nature was full of surprises and all you could say about life was that it was past understanding.

I. Cohen's did the alterations and put up the cuffs of the trousers while you waited, but we said we'd be back and I walked with my mother up the winding hill toward the Grand Concourse. I found an Adler shoe store and bought a new pair of black sneakers with nice thick soles and then I chose shoes, black wing-tips with secretly heightening leather heels of the style I had seen on the feet of Dixie Davis, Mr. Schultz's lawyer. All of this set us back another nine dollars. I carried the shoes in a box and wore the new sneakers and we continued our way up Fordham until we found a Schrafft's. And there we joined for their afternoon tea all the fine people of the Bronx. We ordered little chicken-salad sandwiches with the crusts cut off the bread, actual tea for my mother and a chocolate ice-cream soda for me, all of it set down on paper place mats in open lace patterns and served by waitresses in black uniforms with white lace aprons that matched the place mats. I was very happy to be doing something like this with my mother. I wanted her to be having a good time. I enjoyed the ceramic clatter of the restaurant, the fussy self-important waitresses balancing their trays, the afternoon sun coming through the front window and shining on the red carpet. I liked the big-bladed silent ceiling fans turning slowly as befitted the dignity of the diners. I had told my mother that I had money in my pocket to buy her some new clothes too, lots of them, and new shoes too that were better for her feet, and that we could go right now two minutes up the street to the Alexander's Department Store if she wanted, right at Fordham Road and the Grand Concourse, the main intersection of the Bronx. But she had become interested in the paper lace of the place mat and was tracing the design with her fingers, feeling the embossing with her fingertips and then closing her eyes as if she was blind and was reading it in Braille. And then she said something I wasn't sure I heard properly but was afraid to ask her to repeat. "I hope he knows what he's doing" were the words she said. It was as if someone else was at the table, the voice was not quite hers. I didn't know whether she had said it speaking for herself or had read it off the dots of the embossed place mat.

But anyway I put forty dollars in her pocketbook that night, which left me with a little over twenty-five. I found I was getting used to these big sums, handling these bills as if I was to the manner born. It is true that you get accustomed to money very quickly, that the miraculousness of the idea of it wears away and it becomes unremarkable. Yet my mother's salary at the laundry was twelve dollars a week and that money remained miraculous in my mind, which is to say valuable in the old way, as my own earnings by their profligacy were not. It was an Abbadabba Berman idea. I hoped the dollars I put in her purse would take on the quality of the dollars in her pay envelope. Around the neighborhood it became clear that I had money. I bought whole packs of Wings cigarettes and not only smoked them continually but was generous with them. In the pawnshop on Third Avenue where I went for the glasses I found a reversible satin team jacket, black on one side, and then you could turn everything inside out and presto it was a white jacket, and I bought that and strutted in the evenings in it. The team name was The Shadows, not a name I recognized as local, and it was stitched in fancy white script on the black side and in black on the white side. So I was wearing that and with my cigarettes and new sneakers and I suppose my attitude, which I might not be able to discern in myself but which must have been quite clear to others, I represented another kind of arithmetic to everyone on my street, not just the kids but the grown-ups too, and it was peculiar because I wanted everyone to know what they figured out easily enough, that it was just not given to a punk to find easy money except one way, but at the same time I didn't want them to know, I didn't want to be changed from what I was, which was a boy alive in the suspension of judgment of childhood, that I was the wild kid of a well-known crazy woman, but there was something in me that might earn out, that might grow into the lineaments of honor, so that a discerning teacher or some other act of God, might turn up the voltage of this one brain to a power of future life that everyone in the Bronx could be proud of. I mean that to the more discerning adult, the man I didn't know and didn't know ever noticed me who might live in my building or see me in the candy store, or in the schoolyard, I would be one of the possibilities of redemption, that there was some wit in the way

I moved, some lovely intelligence in an unconscious gesture of the game, that would give him this objective sense of hope for a moment, quite unattached to any loyalty of his own, that there was always a chance, that as bad as things were, America was a big juggling act and that we could all be kept up in the air somehow, and go around not from hand to hand, but from light to dark, from night to day, in the universe of God after all.

But anyway it was a palpable change, no matter what I wished, you do feel special and there are numerous discreet kinds of recognition granted to you on the street, as if you had entered a seminary or something like that, small registrations in the eyes of people, where now they see you and are sure they don't want to have anything to do with you, or they see you and give you a moment of their serious attention, depending on what their own ideas of the religious life might be, or perhaps political life, but in any event they see you and wonder how you can hurt them or be of use to them, and now and henceforth, you're another name in the system.

At the same time nobody knew anything, you understand, who I was with and where I worked, all of this was secondary to the mythological change of my station, except of course to those who were in the business, who for their part, as a matter of principle, would not show the least interest because these things come out in due course, first of all, and because I was to the professional eye so clearly still a punk, second of all. So this was a very subtle spirit event of my street that I speak of, and except in the public life of summer might hardly have found the currency it did; I mean never in my self-consciousness of my return did I have the illusion that anyone knew the magnitude of what had happened to me, how I had been living in the very pulsebeat of the tabloids, distributed in printer's ink and hidden like the fox in the tree leaves on the puzzle page except that I was right in the middle of the centrally important news of our time.

But one night I was sitting on the orphans' stoop in the white side of my Shadows jacket with my two friends Rebecca the Witch and Arnold Garbage and we had it mostly to ourselves, the younger kids having been herded inside because it was their curfew, and it was that moment of summer night when it is still light blue in the sky but lamppost dark in the street and it was noisy enough with everyone's window open and the radios playing and the arguments going, and there came around the corner the green-and-white prowl car of the local precinct house and when it reached us it stopped at the curb and the motor ran quietly there and I stared at the cop in the car and he looked up the steps at me, and the appraisal was keen and measured, and it seemed to me everything grew immediately quiet, although of course this was not so, and I felt my white jacket glowing in the last light coming down from the sky, I felt levitated by that light and the cop car too seemed to float away, from its dark green bottom to its upper half in white suspension over the tires, and then the head in the window turned away and said something to the cop I couldn't see, the driver, and they laughed and the headlights went on like gunshots in the street and they drove away.

This was the moment of my awareness, in this strange light, of that first anger Mr. Schultz had told me about, how it comes to you as a benefit, as an endowment. I felt the defining criminal rage, I recognized it, except that it had come to me as I sat in contentment with other strange half-children there on the steps of the Max and Dora Diamond Home. Clearly what I had sought and didn't want at the same time, that peculiar notoriety of a kid's dreams, was now official, I was another kind of citizen, there was no longer any question. I was angry because I still thought it was up to me to decide what I was, not fucking cops. I was angry because nothing in this world is provisional. I was angry because Mr. Berman had sent me home with money in my pocket for no other reason than to teach me what money costs and I hadn't realized it.

Now I remembered what he had said, that I should just take it easy and when they wanted me they would find me. I was standing at the foot of the stairs to the El. I hadn't really heard him, why don't we hear the things said to us? A minute later I had bounded up the stairs and dropped my nickel in the turnstile with its thick magnifying glass showing you under light how big an American buffalo is.

So that night I did something I had never done before, I threw a party. It seemed to me properly defiant. I found a bar on Third Avenue that sold beer to minors for the right price and bought a pony and rented the tapping equipment to go with it and Garbage wheeled it all covered up in one of his carriages and we bumped it down the steps to his cellar and that's where I threw the party. The big work was clearing enough of his storehouse of shit out of the way so that we had something like an old couch or two to sit on and some floor space to dance on. On the other hand it was Garbage who supplied the tall dusty glasses we drank the beer from and the old Victor Talking Machine with the sound horn curled like a seashell and the pack of steel needles and the box of race records that gave us our dance music. I told him I would pay rent for everything he supplied. I was determined that night to pay everybody for everything, even God for the air I breathed. And I threw the party for the incorrigibles of the Max and Dora Diamond Home after everyone else including the floor wardens and the custodial supervisor had gone to sleep. Eventually there were maybe ten or twelve kids altogether including my friend Rebecca, who arrived like some of the other girls in a nightgown, but she had earrings on too and some lipstick. All the girls wore lipstick, all the same color all obviously from the same tube. And there we were making a big deal over this beer that must have come from Mr. Schultz's drop because it was really piss water but because it was beer gave us the requisite taste of adult corruption. Someone had raided the house kitchen and come away with three salamis and several loaves of white bread in wax paper and Garbage poked around in one of his bins till he found a kitchen knife and a broken coffee table, and sandwiches were made and beer was poured and I had cigarettes for those who wanted them, and in the dry and ashen air of the basement, with suspensions of coal dust lit in the yellow light of an old standing lamp, we smoked Wings and

drank our foamless beer and ate and danced to the old black
voices of the 1920s singing their slow songs of doubled lines of
love and bitter one-line resolutions, of pig's feet and jelly rolls
and buggy rides and papas who did wrong and mamas who did
wrong and people who were waiting for trains that had already
gone, and though none of us knew how to dance except the
square dancing they taught upstairs, the music taught us how.
Garbage sat by the Victrola and cranked it up and took a record
out of its blank paper jacket and put it on, he sat cross-legged
on a table with a pillow under him and did this, neither dancing
himself nor talking to anyone for that matter but giving by his
assent to everything going on in his basement the best measure
of impassive sociability of which he was capable, neither drinking beer nor smoking but only eating and engrossing himself
with the endless supply of scratchy music, the cornets and clari-
nets and tubas and pianos and drums of sorrowful passion, and
the girls danced with each other and then pulled the boys in to
dance with them, and it was a very solemn party we were having,
white Bronx kids holding on to each other in the sweet black
music, full of the intent to live life as it should be lived, there
in the orphans' home. But little by little it began to look different
because some of the girls found collections of clothing in big
cardboard boxes in the recesses of Arnold Garbage's bins, and
he didn't seem to mind, so they dressed themselves in this and
that over their nightclothes, trying and choosing different hats
and dresses and high-heeled shoes of bygone times, till everyone was satisfied, and my little Rebecca wore a kind of Spanish
black lace affair down to her ankles, and a gauzy shawl of rose
with great looping tears in it, but continued to dance with me
in her bare feet, and some of the boys had found suit jackets
whose shoulders were like football pads on them, and pointed
patent-leather shoes, and big wide ties they looped around their
bare throats, and so by and by in the smoke and jazz we were
all just the way we wanted to be, dancing in the dust of the
Embassy Club of our futures, in the costumes of shy children's
love, and learning as only the fortunate do that God is not only

the instruction of the mind but of the hips in their found rolling rhythm.

Much later Rebecca and I were sitting on one of the couches and she had her legs crossed at the knees and one dirty foot swinging and her nightgown showing below the hem of her black lace dress. She was the last kid there. She raised her arms and she pulled her black hair back behind her head and did something deft back there the way girls do with their hair so that it stays the way they fix it without any visible reason to and despite the law of gravity. Maybe I was a little drunk by then, maybe we both were. Also the dancing had been warm and close. I was smoking a cigarette and she took it out of my fingers and drew on it, one puff, and blew out the smoke without inhaling and put the cigarette back in my fingers. I saw now she was wearing mascara on her eyelashes and eyelids and had on that communal red lipstick, paled somewhat since its application, and was glancing at me sideways with her foot swinging, and those eyes dark as black grapes, and her white neck draped in that torn shawl of dusty pink—I had no warning or preparation from one moment to the next, I was swimming in a realm of intimacy, as if I had just met her, or as if I had just lost her, but surely as if I had never roof-fucked her. My mouth went dry she was so incredibly childishly beautiful. Until this moment I had been the party-giver and big boss of the evening, dispensing his largesse and granting his favors. All those dances—oh I knew everyone knew I favored her on my randy forays up the fire escape, but it was athletics, I paid her, for christsake, I must have been staring at her because she turned away and lowered her eyes, her foot going madly—all those dances I had danced with her and only her were the exacting ceremonies of possession. And this ancient witch child understood before I did that everything was now up in the heart, as if my rise in the world had lifted us to an immensity of consequence, which we were now allowed to see, like a distance ahead of us, like a horizon. They must all have understood, every fucking kid there, while I thought what I had been feeling was only a sweetly mellow good time.

So when everyone else had gone we lay for the first time together without any clothes on that same couch, everyone else asleep, even Garbage in some inner bin of his privacy. We lay in the dark cellar of dust and ash, and I was passive and on my back and Rebecca lay on top of me and cleaved herself on me letting herself down with a long intake of her breath which I felt as a cool flute of air on my neck, and slowly awkwardly she learned her rhythm upon me as I was patient to allow her to do. My hands were on her back for a while and then on her buttocks, I followed the soft down with my fingers, I knew it was as black as her hair, it went from the bottom of her spine down into the crack between her ass, and then I put my finger on her small ring of an asshole and as she raised her hips I touched it, and as she lowered her hips I lost it in the clamp of her hard buttocks. Her hair fell forward as she raised herself and it brushed my face, and when she lowered herself it fell around my ears, and I kissed her cheeks as she rested and I felt her lips on my neck and her hard little nipples against my chest and her wet thighs on my thighs, and then I didn't remember when it started she was making little discoveries which she voiced in private almost soundless whimperings in my ear and then she moved into some arrhythmic panic and went stiff and I felt around my cock the grasp of her inner musculature and when I reached down with my finger and touched the asshole it clamped around my finger-tip and released and contracted and released in the same rhythm as her interior self was squeezing and unsqueezing my cock and I couldn't stand it anymore I arched myself into her and pulled back, raising myself and lowering myself with her dead body-weight as vehemently as if I were on top, pretty soon going so fast she was being bounced on my chest and thighs with little grunts until she found my rhythm and went stuttering and im-perfectly and finally workingly, smoothly against it, meeting me when I was to be met, leaving me when I was leaving to be left, and that was so unendurably exquisite I shot into her and held her down against me with my hands while I came pulsing up into

her milkingly lovely little being as far as I could go. And she held
her arms around me to get me through that, and then there was
peace between us, and we lay as we were with such great trust
as to require no words or kisses, but only the gentlest slowest
and most coordinate drift into sleep.

E I G H T

What woke me was the chill of empty air on my skin, and the degree of ashen gray light that represented morning in the basement of the Max and Dora Diamond Home for Children. A mound of black and rose lace lay on the floor beside the couch as if the witch had disembodied: My lover had gone back upstairs to her childhood. Institutional orphans know with a basic workaday cunning how not to get caught, and it occurred to me that that was not bad training for a gangster's girl. I wondered what age people had to be before they could marry. I reflected as I lay there that my life was changing more quickly and in more ways than I could keep up with. Or was it all just one thing, as if everything had the same charge to it, so that if I was remade to Mr. Schultz's touch, Becky was remade to mine, and there was only one infinitely extending flash of conformation. She had never come before, with me anyway, and I felt pretty sure with nobody else either. Her cunt barely had hair. She was growing herself up to match me.

Oh my God what I felt right then for this mysterious parentless little girl, this Mediterranean olive, this nimble nipply witchling, with her arching backbone, her downy ass, as hard-living dumb as a female could be. She liked me! I wanted to race her, I knew she could run, I would give her a head start because I was older, and I bet she could make a good race of it. I had seen her jump rope, inexhaustibly, with lots of tricks, on one foot, or with a quick two-step, or skipping through the snapping arcs, hip-hopping through a double rope, the left and right coming from opposite directions, and do it faster and longer than anyone else. She could walk on her hands too, totally careless of her falling inversion of skirt and her white panties for all the boys to see, her swarthy legs waving in the air, as she paraded the street upside down. She was an athlete, a gymnast: I would teach her to juggle, I would teach her and myself at the same time to throw-juggle till we had six bowling pins flying in the air between us.

But first I wanted to buy her something. I tried to think of what it should be. I listened. I knew the orphans' home as well as I knew my own, I could lie there, and even hung over, and with every signal sense refracted in an atmosphere fetid with stale beer, I could tell by the degree of vibration of the building what time of day it was: they were barely beginning to get going in the kitchen. It was just dawn. I roused myself, grabbed my clothes, and sneaking up a back stairs I made it to the Boys Showers and ten minutes later was out in the new morning, the hair of my recent haircut wet and shining, my Shadows jacket turned out in satin white, and the breakfast to hand a fresh bagel lifted from the big bread bag left before light on the delivery platform by the Pechter's Bakery truck.

It was so early nobody was up yet, not even my mother. The streets were empty, the lamppost lights were still on under the white sky. I had the idea, going to Third Avenue, that I would look in the pawnshop windows for something and just wait around for the day to begin to buy it. I wanted to buy Becky a piece of jewelry, maybe even a ring.

At this hour not even the newsstand at the foot of the El station had opened. The morning papers lay baled in twine where they'd been tossed from the trucks. I knew the headline in the *Mirror* was meant for me before I looked at it, I felt the attraction of the words before I read them: GRISLY GANG MURDER. Underneath was a murky photo of a dead man in a barber chair who I thought was headless until I read the caption explaining that his head was swathed in bloodied barbers' hot towels. Some West Side numbers boss. I was so distracted, I actually put my three cents on the ground by the stack of papers before I pulled one out to get the story.

I read with a proprietary interest, I read first in the shadow of the El and then not sure I'd gotten it all I stepped into a stripe of light cast by the space between the overhead tracks, I held my arms out and I read again in the pacific glare of the morning the *Mirror* gang murder of the day, while nothing moved on any of the levels, neither train nor trolley, except the pattern of darkness striped with light up and down the cobbled avenue like a jail guard running his stick along the bars of the cells, my head beginning to hurt through the eyes, and the recognition of darkness alternating with light in the black print on the white paper as the personal message for me in this news.

For of course I knew whose work this was, there wasn't much more to the story than there was in the headline and the picture, but I read with intense concentration, not merely as one who was in the same trade, but of the same shop, I was reading of my mentor, and the proof was I didn't need any proof, I knew to the point of looking for Mr. Schultz's name in the story, and wondering why it wasn't there, numb and not thinking properly after my first night on earth of love, as if everybody in the world would know something because I did, as if I didn't know anything nobody else knew, especially the papers. I went back and pulled out a *News,* which had almost the same picture and no more information, and then I took a *Herald Tribune,* one of those hifalutin rags, and they didn't know anything more than the others, although they used more words. None of them knew. Gangsters were killed every day in the week and why and by whom was a matter of public confusion. Lines of power crossed in secret, allies became enemies, partnerships split up, any one man could be killed by just about anybody else in the business on any given day, and the press, the cops, they needed eyewitnesses, testimony, documentation, to make their tracings and figure things out. They might have their theories but it took them a while to get up an authoritative version, as with all historians going through the wreckage after the silence has set in. By contrast I immediately knew, as if I had been there. He had used whatever was to hand. He had improvised something from his rage, I mean you don't sit someone down in a barber chair to murder him, you find him there and you grab a razor. He had gone totally out of his mind the way he did with the fire inspector, I had caught on with the great Dutch Schultz in his decline of empire, he was losing control, it was a bloody maniac's portrait there on the front page, and now what the fuck was I going to do? I had this sense of being implicated in a way that wasn't fair to me, as if he had broken a trust and there was nothing after all to learn from him except self-destruction.

I broke into a clammy sweat and that most dreaded and unendurable of feelings, nausea, rose in me. At such times you just want to fling yourself on the ground and clutch it, nothing else is possible. I looked around and dropped the papers in an ashcan, as if I could be arrested for holding them, as if they were evidence of my complicity.

I sat in a doorway and put my head between my knees and waited for the awful nausea to go away. After a few minutes I felt better, the sweat turns to a chill and you're all right, you can breathe again. Perhaps this was the moment when I germinated my secret conviction that I could always get out, that they could come looking but they'd never find me, that I knew more escapes than they dreamed of. But consciously all I could think was that Mr. Schultz was a greater danger to me when I was not in his presence than when I was. He'd do another one of these things that I wouldn't know about and I'd be picked up. All of them, Mr. Berman too, the less I saw of them the more vulnerable I became. It was a most contrary proposition but as a feeling it was indisputable. If I didn't have him where I could see him, how could I get away if I didn't know when to run? Then and there I knew I had to be back with the gang, it was my empowerment, my protection. I felt, sitting there under the El, that not being with them was a luxury I couldn't afford. It wasn't safe not to be around them.

I told myself I wasn't thinking clearly. To calm down I started walking. I walked and walked, and by and by like some assurance to me that the world could take whatever happened to it, the El came along thundering overhead, cars and trucks appeared in the streets, the people who had jobs were going to them, the streetcars rang their gongs, shopkeepers opened their doors, and I found a diner and went in and sat at the counter shoulder-to-shoulder with my fellow citizens of the world and drank tomato juice and coffee and feeling somewhat better ordered two eggs sunny-side up and toast and bacon and a doughnut and more coffee, and topped everything off with a reflective cigarette, and by then the outlook wasn't so bad. He had said to Mr. Berman in my presence: There are one or two essential things it appears we must do. The window washers falling twelve stories down the side of a building was one of these things and this was another. This was a planned business murder as concise and to the point as a Western Union telegram. The victim after all had been in the business. He was the competition. Therefore his murder was symbolically meaningful for the few people with whom Mr. Schultz wanted to communicate. But at the same time because it was done with a razor it would more probably suggest to the D.A.'s office and to every crime reporter certainly, and to the cops in the know and to the top Tammany people, and in fact to everybody in the industry except the competition, that it must be someone else's work because it didn't have the Dutchman's signature—it was a Negro's type of murder, or a Sicilian's in its vindictiveness, but in any event there was enough of everything in it to be anyone's work.

So all of this was very consoling except now I began to resent that I had been sent away when all these important matters were being adjudicated. I worried that my position had been changed without my knowing it, or worse, that I had overestimated it to begin with. So I walked back up Third Avenue beginning to feel as uneasy as I had originally and with the identical need to be back with Mr. Schultz. I was in a very strange state. I had looked green after the morning murder in the Embassy Club. Maybe I shouldn't have looked so green. Maybe they thought I didn't have what it took. Soon I was running. I was running home in shadow and light. I ran up the stairs two at a time in case a message had come for me while I was gone.

But there was no message. My mother stood twirling up her hair. She glanced at me curiously with her arms raised and her hands behind her head and two of those long jeweled pins crosswise between her teeth. I could hardly wait for her to leave for work. She had an infuriating slowness about her, as if each of her minutes was longer than anyone else's, it was a kind of stately time she moved in of her own weird invention. Finally the door closed behind her. I grabbed my new secondhand valise from the back of the closet, a leather number that folded in at the top like a very large doctor's instrument bag, and I packed my I. Cohen suit and wing-tip shoes and shirt and tie, and my plain glass steel-rim spectacles that looked like Mr. Berman's and some underwear and socks. I packed my toothbrush and hairbrush. I had still not bought a book from a bookstore but I could do that downtown. I had to wheel the terrible baby carriage of my mother's affection out of the way in order to get under the bed where I had hidden my Automatic. I put that in at the bottom, underneath everything else, snapped the hasps, buckled the straps and put the valise by the front door, and I put myself on watch at the fire escape window. I was convinced they would come and get me this very morning. It was now a matter of great urgency to me that they should. It was not possible that they wouldn't. Why would Mr. Berman insist that I get new clothes if they were just going to abandon me? Besides I knew too much. And I was smart, I knew what was going on. I knew more than what was going on, I knew what was going to happen next.

The only thing I didn't know and couldn't anticipate was how they would come and get me, how they would know where I was. Then I saw the precinct prowl car come slowly up the street and stop in front my house. I thought: That's it, it's too late, it's all over, they're rounding up everyone, he's done it, he's killed us all. And when the same wiseass cop who had looked me over a few nights before got out, I experienced the meaning of the law, the power of uniform, and a desperate sense of exclusion from the future. Adept wily and swift though you may be, if the moment stuns you with its terror you are made as helpless, as transfixed by the vision of disaster, as an animal caught in headlights. I didn't know what to do. He disappeared below me into the building and came up the dark stairwell, I could hear his footsteps, but in the street when I looked the other cop was out of the car now and standing leaning against the driver's door with his arms folded right under my fire escape. They had me. I stood behind the front door and heard the footsteps. Then I heard his breathing. Oh Jesus! Then he was knocking on my door with his fist, the fucker. When I opened it he stood there filling the doorway in the darkness, a big fat cop mopping his gray hair with a handkerchief and then wiping the inside rim of his cap. "All right, punk," he said, he was all blue and bulky, the way cops are with everything they hang on themselves under their tunics—pieces and nightsticks and ticket books and bullets—"don't ask me why, but you're wanted. Get a move on."

And here I will summarize what Mr. Schultz told me about this murder, because I could not even begin to render it word for word, try to understand how it was to be in his presence and his confidence when he spoke of these most intimate matters, there is horrified elation, you sometimes don't hear the details just looking at the face that speaks, you wonder at your own great recklessness to have put yourself in his line of vision, you hope he won't see that it is your deepest desire to conform your mind to his, to speak in your own mind with his voice, which means that you cannot. But listening to these confidences, dumb with pride to be receiving them, and remembering my panic of that early morning, I did feel foolish and a bit disloyal ever to have doubted him or his regard for me, because, as he said, despite the honestly improvised nature of the barbershop occasion it had that feeling about it of being right, as right as if it had been planned, except that things planned so often go wrong that it was better than planned, and he knew immediately it was a

genius hit because it did so many different things at the same
time, all of them dovetailing with one another, so like any good
piece of business it was part luck, part inspiration, but in any
event an act of mastery that was both correct as business and poet-
ically effective, in addition of course to being solidly grounded
in the only sound motive, which is simple and just retribution.
He was very proud of the job. I think it eased the embarrassment
of his loss of control with the fire inspector. And there was no
sadness to it, he said, no lingering hurt, nothing mournful as
with Bo, it was nothing that personal, it just so happened Irving
fingered the guy while Mr. Schultz was availing himself of the
pleasures of a cathouse not two minutes from the Maxwell
Hotel. He was celebrating his return from Syracuse, where he
had surrendered to the law, put up bail and walked out of the
courtroom a lammister no longer, he was celebrating part one
of the new plan and was having a preliminary glass of wine with
the fancy girls and, I was to tell him, could anything in life be
greater than that? as if I would know, to reappear and retake
your old life, to be the Dutchman of old from your unshined
shoes to your slightly dirty pearl gray fedora, and so, this was
true luck, a good sign, he was able to get over there and work
things out while the regular barber was still trimming the
fucker's hair. And he was all ready by the time the chair was
tilted back for the shave. The numbers boss held his piece on
his lap under the striped barber sheet, as lots of guys tend to do,
and two of his henchmen sat in the lobby reading the evening
papers by the potted palms just outside the glass barbershop
door. Those were the conditions. One henchman happening to
glance over the top edge of his paper, and seeing there Lulu
Rosenkrantz standing and smiling at him with his broken-
toothed smile under that protuberant and bushy brow, and next
to him Irving holding up his index finger to his lips, he quietly
cleared his throat to capture his colleague's attention and together, with the briefest of glances between them, they folded
their papers and stood, in hopes that their immediate and unani-
mous decision to fuck loyalty would find favor with these two
well-known and formidable personages. Which it did, they were

allowed to disappear through the revolving door of the hotel
with no hard feelings, but only after surrendering their newspapers, which Irving and Lulu sat down to read in the vacated
chairs beside the potted palms, although if the truth be known,
Mr. Schultz said, Lulu couldn't read. At the same time the regular barber, who took only very special people after hours, having
seen and understood the meaning of the ceremony outside his
shop while applying the hot towel to his customer's face, wrap-
ping it the way they do like a custard swirl, so that only the tip
of the nose is visible, quietly excused himself forever from the
profession by means of a mirrored side door leading to a supply
room and to an alley leading to the street, passing with mur-
mured apologies another barber in a white short-sleeve tunic
who was just entering, Mr. Schultz himself with his thick but not
muscular arms showing black hair, and a thick short neck and a
blue-black shadow on his own tormentedly twice daily shaven
cheeks. The Dutchman came up to the recumbent customer and
applied additional hot towels in mimicry of the attentive minis-
trations of a barber, dripping on them especially about the nos-
trils a potion from a small unlabeled bottle he had had the
foresight but not the detailed reasoning to borrow from the
cathouse madam. And hovering about the chair and making
small administrative sounds until he was satisfied that all was
well, he felt under the sheet, took the piece from the slack
fingers, daintily put it aside, lifted the towels where they draped
over the chin, carefully folded them back from the throat,
and choosing an already opened straight razor from the shelf
under the mirror and satisfying himself that it was impeccably
sharpened, he drew it with no hesitation across the exposed
neck just below the jawline. And as the thread-thin lip of blood
slowly widened into a smile and the victim made a small half-
questioning movement in his chair, a slight rise of the shoulders
and lift of the knees, more inquisitive than accusatory, he held
him down with his elbow on his mummied mouth and wrapped
layer after layer of wet hot toweling that was to hand in the
chromed steamer behind the chair over his chest and throat and
head, until only a seeping pinkness, the color of a slow and

tentative sunset, suffused the wadding, so that he was able with unhurried insolence to wipe clean the twelve-inch razor, fold it, and drop it in his breast pocket next to the comb, and after a glance of vindication to the lobby as if there was there, watching, an audience of numbers-industry bankers, controllers, collectors, and runners, rubbed the grip of the Smith & Wesson with the striped sheet, and placed it back in the victim's hand, and placed the hand back in the lap, and smoothed the striped sheet over the body, and withdrew through the mirrored door, which closed on the scene with a click, leaving two barber chairs, two bodies, and two trickles of blood spattering the tile floor.

"There wasn't nothing grisly about it," Mr. Schultz told me, referring to the very headline that had caught my attention. "That was newspaper bullshit. You never get a break from those guys, it was as beautiful and professional as could be. Anyway, probably the knockout drops was what killed the son of a bitch. I mean he moved but so does a chicken after you cut its throat. Chickens run around after they're dead did you know that, kid? I seen that in the country."

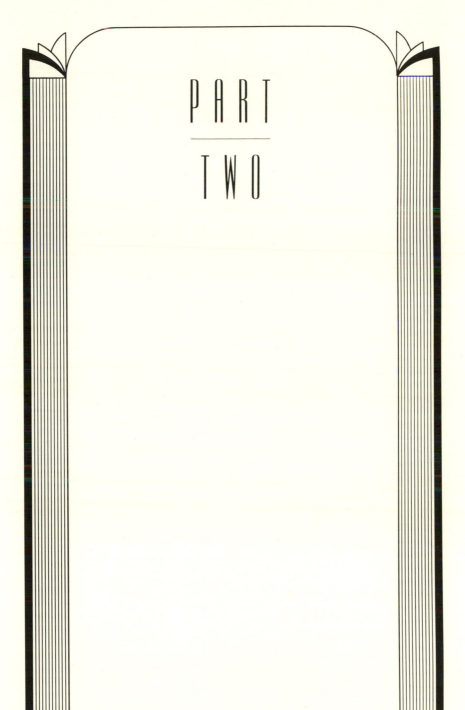

PART

TWO

N I N E

We stood the first morning on the courthouse steps and looked over the town past a bridged mountain stream to the fields and pastures and hills around us, everything green and lilac on the hillsides and the field crops a darker green, the sun was shining in a deeply blue sky, and there was a lowing cow at some distance that sounded to me like a song of the great unconscious gladness of nature, and Lulu Rosenkrantz muttered, "I don't know about this, what do you do when you wanna go for a walk?"

I had never been in the country before except if you counted Van Cortlandt Park, but I liked the smell of it and the light, I liked the peace of all that sky. Also I was instructed in the purposefulness of human settlement. Out there in the distance they grew what was needed, they farmed and kept dairy herds, and this town, Onondaga, the county seat, was their market. It was built onto the side of the hills overlooking the farmland and the stream came down from the mountains right through it. Nobody told me not to so I made an excursion to the old rattly wooden bridge and watched the water flowing fast and shallow over the rocks. It was wider when you were right on top of it, more like a river than a stream. Then a few blocks up along the river I found an abandoned lumber mill, the sheds leaning over like a good wind would flatten them, the place was long since closed but showed clearly someone's past ambition and an enterprise with natural resources that I had read about in school geographies but never fully appreciated. I mean you don't really appreciate a phrase like *natural resources,* you have to see the trees on the mountains, and the stream, and the lumberyard beside the stream to begin to get the idea, to see the sense everything made. Not that I would want such a life for myself.

A lot of people had lived and died in Onondaga and what they left behind was their houses, I could tell immediately the houses had been around for a long time, they were of wood, people in the country lived in wooden houses, one next to another, big boxy things stained dark brown or peeling gray paint and with pitched roofs and gables and porches loaded up with firewood, and there was an occasional weird house with a corner tower topped with a kind of dunce cap roof and with curved windows and shingles nailed on in different patterns and iron grillwork decorating the roof edges, as if they had a pigeon problem. Anyway this was America too I said to Lulu Rosenkrantz, though he was dubious. At least the public buildings were of stone, the courthouse was made of blocks of red stone with granite trim that reminded me of the Max and Dora Diamond Home except it was bigger and had arched windows and doors and was rounded at the corners as justice sometimes is, and the four-story Onondaga District School, the same ugly red stone as the courthouse, and also the Onondaga Public Library, a tiny one-room affair faced over in stone blocks to make it look as if people took their reading matter more seriously than they really did. Then the gray stone gothic church, modestly named the Church of the Holy Spirit, and so far the only thing in town I had found not named after this Onondaga, this Indian, who had apparently made quite an impression. There was a statue of him on the lawn in front of the courthouse shading his eyes and looking west. When Miss Lola Miss Drew came outside for the first time and saw that statue she seemed quite taken with it, she stared at it till Mr. Schultz grew irritated and pulled her away.

The grandest structure in town was the hotel, The Onondaga,

of course, six stories of red brick, right in the heart of the commercial district if it could be called that, because many of the stores were closed with FOR LET signs in the windows, and the few cars parked front wheels into the curb were old black tin lizzies, Model A's and T's or farm trucks with chain drives and no doors, there was not much going on in Onondaga, in fact with our arrival we were what was going on, which came home to me when the old colored man who was the bellboy carried my bag with genuine delight to my very own private room on the top floor and didn't even wait for the tip I was figuring out to give him. This was where we were all to stay, on the sixth floor, which Mr. Schultz rented in its entirety. Each person had at least one room to himself, otherwise it wouldn't look right, Mr. Schultz said glancing at Miss Lola Miss Drew, so she had her own suite, and he had his own suite, and the rest of us had single rooms except that Mr. Berman had a second room for which he ordered a special direct phone line not using the hotel switch-board.

The morning of our arrival I bounced on my bed. I opened a door and lo! there was a bathroom with an enormous tub and several thin white towels hanging on the bar and a full-length mirror on the inside of the door. The bathroom was as big as our kitchen at home. The floor was small white octagonal tiles, just like our halls in the Bronx, except a lot cleaner. My bed was soft and wide and the headboard was like half of a big spoked wheel of maple wood. There was a reading chair with a lamp sticking out of a table right beside it, and a bureau with a mirror, and in the top drawer were little concave sections for pocket change and small items that might otherwise get lost. There were gauzy white curtains that could be drawn with a string and behind them black shades, the same as at my school, where you pulled them tight to watch slide shows or movies, with a little pulley wheel attached to the sill. Next to the bed was a table radio which crackled a bit but didn't seem to bring in any stations.

I loved this luxury. I lay back on my bed, which had two pillows and a white bedspread with a pattern of tufts, rows of little cotton nipples, each one under my fingertip making me think of Becky. I lay with my hands behind my head and poked my pelvis into the air a few times imagining she was there on top of me. Private hotel rooms were sexy places. I had noticed in the lobby downstairs a writing table with hotel stationery free for the taking and I thought in a day or two I would write her a letter. I started to think what I would say, whether to apologize or not for leaving her without saying goodbye, and so on, but was interrupted by the stillness. I sat up. Everything was very hushed, unnaturally quiet, which at first felt like part of the luxury, but then seemed to me like another presence which was making itself known. I don't mean that I felt I was being watched, nothing like that, more like there were certain expectations of the society that were trying to represent themselves to me, in the pattern of the wallpaper, for example, endless rows of little corsages of buttercups, or the pieces of maple furniture standing there so silently like elements of a mysterious rite waiting for me to perform it correctly. I sat up. I found a Bible in the drawer of the bedside table and thought someone had left it there by accident. Then I realized from the resolute neatness and orderliness of the room that it must be there as a furnishing. I looked out the window, my room was at the rear, I had a good view of the flat roofs of stores and warehouses. Nothing was moving in Onondaga. Up behind the hotel was a hillside of pine trees that managed to block out the sky.

I understood what Lulu Rosenkrantz must be feeling, the absence of life as we knew it, raucous and loud and mechanically driven, with horns and bell gongs, and grinding wheel flanges, and screeches of brakes, all that rude variousness of too many people in too small a space, where you could really be selfish and free. But he at least had Irving or Mickey, and years of loyalty to the gang to comfort him, whereas none of them had any particular fondness for me. At this moment nobody had told me what I was supposed to be doing in Onondaga. I thought I was past the point of going for coffee, but I wasn't sure. I knew things that it was deadly to know if you were not trusted. I found myself not for the first time measuring my reasons for confi-

dence against the depth of the danger I was in. It would always
be this way, every time I felt good about the way things were
going and that I was living my charmed life unerringly, all I had
to remember was how small a mistake was sufficient to change
my fortune, maybe even without my knowing it. I was an habitual
accomplice to murder. I could be arrested, tried, and sentenced
to death. But that was not enough to ensure me my place. I
thought of Bo Weinberg and opened the door to the dimly lit
wide carpeted hall and looked up and down for a sign of life. All
the doors were closed. I went back to my room and closed my
own door so as not to disturb the quiet and this so oppressed
me that I decided to do something so I unpacked my new
I. Cohen suit with the two pairs of pants and hung it in the big
dusty closet and put my shirts and things and gun away in the
bureau drawer and then put the empty suitcase in the closet and
then sat on the side of the bed and felt worse than ever. Part of
it may have been that when you're going somewhere it is always
mysterious when you arrive. Or perhaps, as I told myself, I was
not used to living alone, I had only been living alone for five or
ten minutes and I was not yet used to it. In any case my optimism
of the early part of the day had now totally deserted me. The
only thing that cheered me up was the sight of a cockroach
walking up the wall between the sprays of buttercups, because
then I knew The Onondaga Hotel was not all it was cracked up
to be.

The first couple of days I was mostly by myself, Mr. Berman
gave me fifty dollars in small bills and told me to spend it in as
many different places as I could. This was not as easy as it
sounded, Onondaga was not rich in the fruits of the earth like
Bathgate Avenue. The stores were unnaturally quiet dark estab-
lishments with bare shelves and they were separated from one
another by stores that were closed up and boarded. I went into
the Ben Franklin five-and-ten and it was pathetic, I had stolen
from some of the best five-and-ten-cent stores in New York and
knew what they should be and this little place was so dismal and
poor the owner kept only one light bulb on in the back and the

country kids who came in barefoot got splinters from the rotted-out floor. There was hardly any stock. I bought a handful of metal toy cars and motorcycles with policemen molded to them and gave them away. I found a clothing store for women and bought a straw hat with a big brim for my mother and then I took the hatbox to the post office and had them send it the most expensive way. I found a jewelry store and bought a pocket watch for a dollar.

Through the window of the drugstore I saw Lulu and Mickey the driver sitting at the fountain drinking malted milks through straws. They would take sips and then look at the glass to see how much more had to be swallowed before their ordeal was over. I was very pleased to see they had gotten the same assignment from Mr. Berman as I had. When they left the drugstore I shadowed them for practice. They stood irresolutely in front of a window where a tractor was on display. They found a news store and went in but I could have told them there were no New York papers. They came out and lit cigars that were so stale they flared up like torches. Lulu was disgusted, Mickey had to calm him down. They bought a fifty-pound sack of onions and left it in a trash can. They went into the army-navy store and through the window I saw them choose shirts and hats and then lace-up work boots that I knew I would never see on their feet.

By the second day of this spending spree my imagination was taxed. Then it occurred to me something of the same purpose was served by making friends, so I bought ice-cream cones for some kids who were following me, and then in a little park across from the courthouse I did some juggling with three pink rubber balls. Kids were everywhere in Onondaga, they were the only human beings I saw in the afternoons, the only ones out in the sun with nothing to do in their overalls with no shirt underneath and bare feet and squinty faces of freckles, they made me think of my street and the homeful of orphans there, but there was less humor in them, they were not inclined to smile or jump around, they took their pleasures stolidly, giving my juggling feats the most serious attention, but hanging back when I offered to show them how to do it.

In the meantime of all the people not to be seen Mr. Schultz and Miss Lola Miss Drew were the most prominent, day and night there was a running route of room service to his suite. I wondered what she did to make her own suite look occupied. Then I wondered if she bothered. I tried to keep from thinking about her but it was difficult, especially at night in my room as I lay on the bed and smoked my Wings and listened to the faintest dance band music from the crackling radio. I was sorry I had seen her nude, I knew too much to be imagining her in my mind at this particular time, in fact it made me queasy to think of her. Then I became angry. She had certainly taught me how little I knew about women, I had thought first she was this fine innocent blue-blood victim of a terrible cross fire of gang life, then up in her Savoy-Plaza apartment it was clear she had flung her ass around with the best of them, I had thought only women from the wrong side of the tracks were tramps, but there were rich tramps too and she was one of them, she had some kind of marriage that was so advanced in sophisticated license as to be degenerate, she was entirely wild, she liked a kind of primordial action, I mean sitting in a Packard in the early hours of the morning and being driven you don't know the hell where while drinking champagne with the man who's just murdered your boyfriend might be considered by some to be a sordid situation with a degree of risk attached to it, but that was not the thought I saw in her eyes in the privacy of her bedroom when as you know a woman preparing to go out is her true self in shrewd preparation of her commodity, without the need to sit with her knees pressed together or stand with one foot slightly forward of the other and pointing outward.

They were in there together two whole full days without coming up for air. Late the third morning I happened to see them emerge from the hotel lobby. They were holding hands. I was worried that Mr. Schultz would notice me standing around juggling for a bunch of hick kids on the sidewalk. But he noticed nothing except her, he handed her past Mickey, who was holding open the door of the Packard, and ducked in himself. The expression on his face suggested that Mr. Schultz's two days and nights in bed with Miss Drew had somewhat elevated her in his regard. After they drove off I thought, well, if she was going to survive her deadly knowledge of that boat ride, this was indeed the way to do it, which was a laugh because she was clearly so heedless as to make mere survival the last possible thing on her mind.

But I was cheered at the end of the second day by an invitation to dinner at a big round table in the hotel dining room, and everyone was there, Mr. Schultz with Miss Lola Miss Drew on his right, and Abbadabba Berman on his left, and the rest of us, Lulu, Mickey the driver, Irving, and I fanned out facing him. Mr. Schultz was in excellent spirits and it seemed to me everyone in the gang was glad to be together, that maybe I wasn't the only one a little homesick.

There were elderly couples at two or three of the tables who kept glancing at us and then leaning toward each other to talk, the faces of passersby framed themselves in the dining-room windows and were replaced by other faces, and appearing in the doorway every other minute to smile and watch us and maybe make sure we were still there were the man from the front desk and the elderly colored bellboy. Mr. Schultz loved all this. "Sweetheart," he called to the waitress, "tell me about your cellar," which I thought was a bizarre request until she said all they carried was Taylor New York State in screw-cap bottles, which made him laugh as if he had known it all along, she was a plump young girl with blotchy skin and wore a uniform like the waitresses I had seen in the Schrafft's on Fordham Road, black with white trim, and a little starched cap on her head, but despite this she was so nervous she kept dropping things, pouring the water in our glasses to the brim, things like that, and I thought any minute she would rush out of the room crying. Mr. Schultz didn't mind, he ordered two bottles of Taylor's New York State red. I could tell Lulu and Mickey would have preferred beer if they couldn't have the hard stuff but they didn't say anything. They were not comfortable in neckties, either. "To justice," Mr. Schultz said lifting his glass, and touched the glass of Miss Lola Miss Drew, who looked at him and laughed a lovely throaty

laugh, as if he was kidding, then we all clicked glasses, even I
with my milk.

Our table was in the middle of the room, right under a chandelier of clear glass light bulbs that made things dim and glary
at the same time so that it was hard to tell how anyone looked,
I wanted to see what people looked like who had spent forty-
eight hours screwing each other silly, I wanted some evidence,
something tangible that I could use for my imaginative life of
abstract jealousies, but it was not to be had, at least in this light,
it was particularly difficult to see Miss Lola Miss Drew's face, she
was so blindingly beautiful under that cut gold hair, her eyes
were so green and her skin was so white, it was like trying to look
into the sun, you couldn't see her through the brilliance and it
hurt to try for more than an instant. She was totally attentive to
Mr. Schultz and stared at him every time he opened his mouth,
as if she was deaf and had to read lips.

Dinner was meat loaf with string beans and mashed potatoes
and a basket of packaged white bread and a hunk of butter and
a bottle of ketchup in the middle of the table. It was good hot
food and I was hungry. I ate fast, we all did, we went at it with
a vengeance, Mr. Schultz asked the girl to bring another platter
of the meat loaf, and it wasn't till the first edge of my hunger was
rounded off that I noticed Miss Lola Miss Drew hadn't touched
her dinner but was leaning with her elbows on the table and
intently regarding the wolfish crew of us holding our forks in our
fists, chewing with our mouths open, and reaching out to spear
slices of bread. She seemed quite fascinated. When I looked
again she had lifted her own fork and folded her hand over it till
she had made a fist around the shank. She held it one way and
then another to see how it felt, and then forked the slab of meat
loaf on her plate and hoisted it slowly into the air to her eye
level. At this point everyone grew quite still, she had the attention of the entire table, although she no longer seemed to be
aware of us. She lowered the fork and left it standing upright in
the portion of meat and as if she was quite alone and thinking
about something far away took her napkin from the place setting, unfolded it, and laid it across her lap. Then she looked at

Mr. Schultz with a sweet distracted smile and then down at her glass, which he hurriedly refilled. Then she proceeded to dine, taking the fork in her left hand and her knife in her right, and cutting and accepting in her mouth from the fork tines, after she had laid the knife down and switched the fork to her right hand, small bites of the meat loaf and tiny dabs of mashed potato. It was an operation of pronounced gentility performed at ritual speed, just as teachers in school write words across the blackboard while enunciating them syllable by syllable. As we all watched, she took her wineglass and put it to her lips and drank without making any sound, though I listened hard, not a sip or slurp or gulp or gurgle, so that when she replaced her glass on the table I wondered if any wine had gotten into her at all. I had to conclude this was one of the most depressing displays of daintiness I had ever seen, as beautiful as she was, she momentarily forfeited her allure as far as I was concerned. Lulu Rosenkrantz frowned the frown that could terrify a hit man, and then exchanged glances with Mickey the driver, and Abbadabba stared at the tablecloth with a sad expression on his face, and even the impassive Irving lowered his eyes, but Mr. Schultz was nodding his head with his lips pouted as if a necessary point was being made. He leaned forward and, looking around the table, said in his idea of a modulated voice, "Thank you, Miss Drew, for your thoughtful comments, which I believe are offered in the best interests of watching our asses for our own good."

I knew immediately something momentous had occurred but I didn't trust myself to think what it was until later, when I was alone in my room again in bed with the lights out and the crickets in the fields of Onondaga beating away like the night's loud pulse, as if night were an enormous body, like the sea, with things living in it, making love in it, and lying dead in it. Miss Lola Miss Drew disdained memories. Technically she was a captive, her life was at risk. But she had no intention of being a captive. She had something to contribute. Of course what Mr. Schultz had said was correct in that we did have to watch our asses up here, like travelers in some dictator's foreign country. But what stunned everyone at the table was that he had sided with her, she had done this crazy pantomime, presuming to act in that way of privilege of instructing those less fortunate than she, and instead of whacking her across the face, which is probably what everyone else there would have done, he had accepted it and found value in it. It was as if they felt an announcement was being made, that she was being cut in in some way and that was how it was going to be.

Of course, I didn't know if I was right, if that was what everyone thought, but I knew from my own career with him that Mr. Schultz liked to be pursued, he was vulnerable to people who were attracted to him, followers, admirers, acolytes, and the otherwise dependent, whether show-off kids, or women whose men he killed. She was a spoil of war, after all, she had been given her delicious value by Bo Weinberg's love for her. I had to wonder if when he took her to bed Mr. Schultz enjoyed the hard-on of triumph, making love to the lady but giving it to the dead Bo.

The next morning bright and early, Mr. Berman knocked on my door and told me to get dressed in my new suit and to wear my glasses and meet Mr. Schultz down in the lobby in fifteen minutes. I did it in ten, which was enough time to run around the corner for a doughnut and a cup of coffee. I got back as everyone was coming outside. Mickey was there with the Packard, Lulu Rosenkrantz was getting in beside him, and Mr. Schultz and Miss Drew were seated in the back. I jumped in.

It was a short trip, in fact only around the corner to the Onondaga National Bank, which was a narrow limestone building with two long skinny barred windows and columns holding up the stone triangle roof over the front doors. Mickey pulled up across the street and we all sat there looking at it with the motor running.

"I once't chanced to meet that Alvin Pincus who ran with Pretty Boy Floyd," Lulu said. "A very excellent safecracker."

"Yeah, and where is he now," Mr. Schultz said.

"Well they did good for a while."

"Think about it, Lulu," Mr. Schultz said. "Going for the

dough the one place it's under lock and key. You gotta be stupid. That outlaw shit ain't in the economic mainstream," he said patting the briefcase on his lap. "Okay, ladies and gents," he said, and he got out of the car and held the door for Miss Drew and me.

I didn't know what I was supposed to do. When I got out of the car Miss Drew said, "Wait a minute," and straightened my clip-on tie. I instinctively drew back.

"Just be a nice boy," Mr. Schultz said. "I know it's hard."

I could tell my black wing-tips were already raising a blister on my heel, and the wire hooks of my plain glass steel-rim glasses were pinching me behind the ears. I had of course forgotten to buy a book as Mr. Berman had told me and so as a last resort carried the Bible from my room in my left hand. My right hand was held by Miss Drew, which she squeezed as we crossed the street behind Mr. Schultz. "You look handsome," she said. I resented it that even when I wore my Elevator Shoes she was the taller of us. "That's a compliment," she said, "it doesn't call for a scowl." She was very gay.

We were shown right past the tellers' barred cages to the back office, where the president came from behind his desk and shook Mr. Schultz's hand heartily, though his eyes flicked over us all with cool appraisal. He was a portly man with a fleshy tubular underchin that looked like a hydraulic pump under his jaw when his mouth moved. Behind him was this open door and steel gate, and an inner room that was really a big safe with its thick door open and lots of drawers inside the room like mailboxes in a post office. "Well, well," he said after the introductions were made, Mr. Schultz having described me as his prodigy, and Miss Drew as my governess, "please sit down, everyone, we don't often have famous people in our little town. I hope you're finding it to your liking."

"Oh yes," Mr. Schultz said, beginning to undo the straps on his briefcase. "This is a summer in the country for us."

"Well, country is what we can offer. Swimming holes, trout streams, virgin forest," at this his eyes darted for a moment to Miss Drew's crossed legs. "Some pretty fair vistas from up the

top of the hills, if you like hiking. Good fresh air, all you can
breathe," he said, laughing as if he'd said something funny, and
he went on with this mindless booster small talk his eyes coming
back again and again to the briefcase which Mr. Schultz now
leaned forward to place on his desk, the top flap folded back, so
that when it was given a quick shove and then pulled back, packs
of greenbacks slid out on the big green blotter. And with that,
words abruptly ceased to come from the banker's mouth although the hydraulic pump didn't lift it shut for another moment or two.

It was a lot of money, more than I had ever seen, but I showed
more restraint than the banker, giving no indication that I saw
anything out of the ordinary. Mr. Schultz said he wanted to open
a checking account for five thousand and put the balance in a
safe deposit box. A moment later the banker's old secretary was
summoned in and in a fluster of attentions she and the banker
went off to count the haul while Mr. Schultz sat back and lit a
cigar fresh from the humidor on the banker's desk.

"Kid," he said, "you notice how many tellers' cages are open
for business?"

"One?"

"Yeah. One teller with gray hair sitting there reading the
paper. Lulu's friends walk in they won't even find a bank dick at
the door. You know what this guy's reserves must be? Holding
a lot of dirt-farm mortgages? Spends his days foreclosing and
selling off the county of Onondaga for ten cents on the dollar.
I'm telling you. He'll lay awake at night thinking of all that cash
in my safe deposit box. What it represents. Give him a week, ten
days. I will get a call."

"And you will go in on whatever it is," Miss Drew said.

"Goddamn right. You're looking at the patron sweetheart of
the boondocks." He buttoned the jacket of his dark suit, and
brushed imaginary dust off the sleeves. He put the cigar in his
mouth and leaned over and pulled up his socks. "Get through
here I could run for Congress."

"I would like to mention something on a different subject but
not if you're going to get all pouty and sulk," Miss Drew said.

"What. No. My words again?"

"Protégé, like proto-jay."

"What did I say?"

"You said prodigy. That's something else, like a child genius." At this moment the banker returned all happy and hand-rubbing and put out some forms for Mr. Schultz to sign and took the cap off his fountain pen and slipped it on the end and handed the pen across the desk chattering all the meanwhile. But upon the scratching of the signature he went quiet and the documents were duly executed in a hush, as if a state treaty were coming into effect. Then the old lady secretary came in with her receipts and a book of blank checks and there was more fussing and heartiness, and in a few moments we were standing for the goodbyes and thank-yous and let-me-know-if-there's-anything-I-can-dos, it is a fact that money exhilarates people, it puts them in hysterias of good cheer, they suddenly care about you and want the best for you. The banker had hardly taken notice of anyone but Mr. Schultz but now he said, "Hey, young fellow, what's the younger generation reading these days?" as if it was really important to him. He turned the book up in my hand so he could read the title, I don't know what he had expected, a French novel maybe, but he was genuinely surprised. "Well good for you, son," he said. He gripped my shoulder and looking at my governess said, "My respects, Miss Drew, I'm a scout-master myself, we don't really have to worry about the future of the country, do we, with youngsters like this?"

He walked us to the front entrance, all our heels ringing on the marble floor, it was like a procession, with the single teller standing up in his cage as we passed. "Goodbye, bless you," the banker said, waving at us from the steps.

Lulu held the car door open and we settled into the back and after he took his seat up front, Mickey started the engine and put it in gear, and we drove off. Only then did Mr. Schultz say, "What the fuck was that all about?" and reach over Miss Drew to grab the Onondaga Hotel's Holy Bible out of my hands.

There was absolute silence in the car except for the flipping of pages. I stared out the window. We were going slowly down-hill now along the nearly deserted main street. Here in the country they had things like feed stores. I was sitting in a new suit with long pants and my Elevator Shoes and my thigh touch-ing the thigh of the beautiful Miss Drew right in the back seat of the luxurious personal car of the man who had existed for me only as an awesome dream a few weeks before and I couldn't have been more unhappy. I rolled the window all the way down to let out the cigar smoke. There was no question in my mind that something unimaginably terrible was about to happen.

"Hey Mickey," Mr. Schultz said.

Mickey the driver's pale blue eyes appeared in the rearview mirror.

"Stop at the church up the hill there where you see the spire," Mr. Schultz said. He began to chuckle. "The one thing we didn't think of," he said. He put his hand on Miss Drew's knee. "May I add my respects to the guy's back there?"

"Don't look at me, boss," she said, "I didn't have anything to do with it."

Mr. Schultz leaned forward so he could see me on the other side of Miss Drew. He was smiling broadly, with enormous teeth, a very big mouth of them. "Is that right? This was your brain-storm?"

I didn't have the chance to explain. "You see," he said to Miss Drew, "I know what words I'm talking about when I pick my words. The kid's my fucking prodigy."

And that was how I came to be enrolled in the Sunday Bible study class of the Church of the Holy Spirit, in Onondaga New York the interminable summer of the year 1935. To undergo orations on the subject of the desert gangs, their troubles with the law, their hustles and scams, the ways they worked each other over, and the grandiose claims they made for them-selves—that was my sacred fate in the church basement with sweat dripping from the stone walls and the snivels of summer colds dripping from the noses of my fellow students in their overalls or their faded flowered dresses, always a size too big, and their feet swinging under the benches, shoed or bare, every

goddamn Sunday. For all I had accomplished and as far as I had
come, I might just as well have been back in the orphans' home.

But Sunday was only the worst of the days, all week we went
at it, there was nothing to do but good. We made visits to the
hospital and brought magazines and candy to the wards. Wherever there was a store open with something to sell, as long as
it wasn't tractor parts, we went in and bought whatever it was
selling. A mile out of town was a broken-down miniature golf
course, I drove out there with Mickey and Lulu on several occa-
sions and the three of us putted the ball through little wooden
chutes and barrels and pipes and I got pretty good at it and took
a few dollars from them but decided not to go out there anymore
the day Lulu in a fit of bad sportsmanship broke his club over
his knee. In town a small crowd of little hick kids collected
whenever I set foot out of doors, they followed me down the
street and I bought them candy and whirligigs and ice cream
while Mr. Schultz was having receptions for their fathers and
mothers under the auspices of the American Legion, or taking
over the church socials, buying up all the homemade cakes and
then throwing a party for everyone to come have cake and coffee. Of all of us, he was the one who seemed actually to enjoy
these long boring days. Miss Drew found a stable with riding
horses and she took Mr. Schultz out horseback riding every
morning and I could see them from the sixth-floor corridor
window trotting down the country roads to the fallow fields
where she was giving him instruction. The post office delivered
things she had ordered by phone from a fancy store in Boston,
riding outfits for both of them with tweed coats with leather
patches on the elbows and silk neck scarves and dark green felt
hats with little feathers stuck in the brim and sleek soft leather
boots and jodhpurs, those peculiar lavender pants that bloomed
out at the hips, which was fine in her case since she tended in
her long-waisted way to be a bit flat back there, but not really
suited to the stolid build of Mr. Schultz, who appeared unath-
letic in them, to say the least, not that any of us, even Mr.
Berman, wanted to bring this to his attention.

The only time I enjoyed was the very early morning. I was always the first one up and I took to buying the *Onondaga Signal* from the news store so that I could read it with my breakfast at a little tea shop kind of luncheonette I had found down a side street. The woman there did her own baking and made very good breakfasts but I kept this intelligence to myself. I think I was the only one of us who read the *Signal,* it was undeniably dull with farm news and almanac wisdom and home canning advice and so on, but they carried *The Phantom* comic strip and *Abbie and Slats,* and that gave me some small connection to real life. One morning the front page had a story about Mr. Schultz buying a local farm from the bank and giving it back to the family that had lost it. When I got back to the hotel there were more old cars parked with their wheels against the curb than usual, and sitting and hunkering all over the little lobby were men in overalls and women in housedresses. And from then on, there was a constant watch at the hotel, inside or outside, one or two farmers and farmers' wives or as many as a dozen, depending on the time of day. I noticed about these people that when they were skinny they were very skinny and when they were fat they were very fat. Mr. Schultz was always courteous when he came through and would take a couple of them to a corner table in the hotel dining room as if it was his office, and listen to them for a few minutes and ask a few questions. I don't know how many foreclosed mortgages he recovered, probably none, more likely he gave them the monthly payment money or a few dollars to keep the wolf from the door, as he put it. The way it worked, for the sake of their feelings, he would maintain a businesslike pretense, take their names and tell them to come back the next day, and then it would be Abbadabba Berman who issued the actual cash in a little brown envelope from his office room on the sixth floor. Mr. Schultz didn't want to be lordish about it, he showed great tact that way.

It was very mysterious to me how a countryside could be so beautiful and yet so invisibly in trouble. I wandered down to the river and across the bridge and out on the country roads every now and then, a little farther each time as I got used to it and discovered no harm would come to me from an empty sky, from hills of wildflowers, from the occasional appearance back from the road of a house and a barn and an animal or two standing around. It was clear here upstate that every city came to an end and an empty road began that required faith to travel. Encouraging were the evenly spaced telegraph poles with electricity wires dipping from pole to pole, I was happy to see also the painted white line going assiduously down the middle of the road over every little rise and fall of the land. I got used to the strawy smell of the fields and the occasional inexplicable whiff of dung coming up out of a roadside patch of heat, and what I first heard as silence turned out to be an air of natural sounds, winds and breezes, startled whirrs, slitherings through brush, pipey yelps, bugbuzz, clops, kerplunks, and croaks, none of which seemed to have any visible origin. So that it occurred to me as I made more of these excursions how you hear the life and smell it before you learn to see it, as if sight is the clumsiest of perceptions in the natural world. There was a lot to learn from the mysteriously unfolding landscape, it offered no intervening comfort between unadorned earth and a large and potent sky, so the last thing I would have expected of it was that it would suffer the same ordinary rat shames of tenements and slums. But I had by now taken to venturing off the paved roads and down this or that dirt lane and one day I was kicking along a wide rocky path when I heard an uncountrylike sound with an alarming breadth to it, and as I walked it became identifiable as a continuous rumble, like a motorized army, and I came over a rise to see a cloud of earthen dust rising from the distant fields and then saw in front of me, parked by the roadside, the black cars and trucks of the country poor, what must have been a good part of the population of Onondaga was walking out across the land in the plumes of dust made by a battery of tractors and harvest machines and trucks taking up acres and acres of potato plants, the machines pouring the potatoes down these moving belts into the truck beds, and the people following, bending down to cull the potatoes missed by the machines and putting them in burlap sacks they dragged along behind them, some even hurrying on all fours through the furrows in the urgency of destitution, men women and children, one or two of whom I recognized from Sunday school at the Church of the Holy Spirit.

And now the scope of Mr. Schultz's strategy became apparent to me. I had wondered how anyone could be fooled, because what he was doing was so obvious, but he wasn't trying to fool anybody, he didn't have to, it didn't matter that these people knew he was a big-time New York gangster, nobody here had any love for New York anyway and what he did down there was his business if up here he showed his good faith, it didn't even matter that they knew why he was doing what he was doing as long as he did it on a scale equal to his reputation. Of course he was obvious, but that's what you had to be when the fix was in with the masses, everything had to be done large, like skywriting, so that it could be seen for miles around.

He said at dinner in the hotel one night, "You know, Otto, I was paying the Chairman of the Board as much a week as all this is costing. There's no middleman up here to jack up the price on you," he said enjoying the thought. "Am I right, Otto? We're dealing direct, eggs fresh from the farm." He laughed, everything seemed to be going off in Onondaga just as he hoped it would.

But I could tell Abbadabba Berman was feeling less sanguine. "Chairman of the Board" was the code name for Mr. Hines, the Tammany man. Until the Feds had messed things up Mr. Hines got cops who were too smart for their own good assigned to Staten Island and magistrates who didn't understand their job retired from the bench and, for icing on the cake, bought the election of the gentlest and most peaceable district attorney in the history of the City of New York. It had been a wonderful way to do business. Here, the reality was that they were trying to extricate themselves from a grave situation. Also, the gang was out of its element, they lacked experience in legitimacy and could not be counted upon always to do what was right. And the other thing was Miss Drew. Mr. Berman had never been consulted about Miss Drew. There was no denying she was classing-up the act and thinking of things which her background had taught her, how to work charity, the forms it took, the dos and don'ts of it. And she seemed to be good at giving the Dutchman a little touch of style, so that it was harder for the people up here to think of him as without the shadow of a doubt a man of the rackets. But she was an X. In mathematics, Mr. Berman had told me, when you don't know what something is worth, not even if it is plus or minus, you call it X. Instead of a number you assign a letter. Mr. Berman had no great regard for letters. He was looking at her now as with a dead pan Miss Drew picked at her salad with her right hand and with her left out of sight under the table touched Mr. Schultz's privates which couldn't have been more apparent because Mr. Schultz started up from his seat and knocked over his wine and coughing into his napkin and turning red told her as he started to laugh that she was a crazy fucking broad.

Sitting at the far end of the dining room, in a corner by themselves, were Irving, Lulu, and Mickey the driver. They were not happy men. When Mr. Schultz cried out Lulu had not been looking in that direction and was so taken aback he rose to his feet and reached into his jacket staring around wildly before Irving put a hand on his arm. Miss Drew had split the gang, there was a hierarchy now, the four of us sat at one table each night and Lulu, Irving, and Mickey sat at another. Given the demands of life in Onondaga Mr. Schultz spent much of his time with Miss Drew and me but mostly Miss Drew, and I know I felt ill-used and muscled out so I could imagine how the men felt. Mr. Berman had to have understood all of this.

Of course once the New York press got wind of what Dutch Schultz was doing here, our situation would change rapidly, like a fever breaking, but I couldn't know that, everything seemed very weird and dizzying to me, as for instance that Miss Drew could be my mother and Mr. Schultz my father, a thought that came to me, no not even a thought worse than a thought, a feeling, when we attended a mass at the St. Barnabas Catholic Church one Sunday nice and early so I wouldn't miss Protestant Sunday school at the Church of the Holy Spirit. And he took off

his hat and she pulled a white lace shawl over her head and we
sat all solemn and shining in our rear pew listening to the organ,
an instrument I hate and detest, the way it blurs the ears with
intimidating chordblasts of righteousness, or worms inside the
ear canal with little pipey slynesses of piety, and that father in
silken robes swinging a smokepot up there under a poor painted
plaster bleeding Christ on a golden cross, oh I tell you this was
not my idea of the life of crime, but that there were things even
worse than I knew, because afterward in this church at a table
near the door Mr. Schultz lit a candle in a little glass for Bo
Weinberg, saying what the hell, and then on the sidewalk the
father came after us, I hadn't thought priests on the pulpit in
their colored silks saw who was in the audience, but they do, they
see everything, and his name was Father Montaine, he spoke
with an accent, he said he was hoppee to see us and shook my
hand vigorously, and then he and Miss Lola Miss Drew spoke
French, he was a French Canadian with a limited amount of wiry
black hair which he combed sideways over his head so that he
wouldn't look bald, which of course he did. I felt dumb, thick-
tongued, I was getting fat eating pancake breakfasts on the
expense account and ham steak and applesauce dinners, I wore
my fake glasses and went calling on churches and combed my
hair and kept clean and neat in outfits Miss Lola Miss Drew had
found for me, and that was another thing, she had taken to
ordering clothes in my size from Boston, I was becoming a
project of hers, as if she really was responsible for me, it was
weird, when she turned her intense gaze in my direction I saw
no depth of assignable character, she seemed incapable of dis-
tinguishing pretense from reality, or perhaps she was rich
enough to think everything she pretended was true, but me, I
didn't know what it was to flat-out run anymore, I felt I was not
reliably myself, I was smiling too much and talking like a sissy
and I was reduced to devious practices, doing things I would
never have imagined myself doing in my Shadows jacket, like
eavesdropping, listening in to conversations like some cop on a
wiretap just to try to get some intelligence of what was going on.

For instance one night in my room I smelled cigar smoke and heard voices, so I went into the corridor and stood in the hall just outside the slightly open door of Mr. Berman's room that he had turned into an office and I peeked in. Mr. Schultz was in there in his bathrobe and slippers, it was very late and they were talking softly, if he'd caught me there was no telling what he would do but I didn't care, I was one of the gang now, I was running with them, I told myself what was the point of living on the same hotel floor with Dutch Schultz if I didn't take advantage of it. At least my senses were still sharp, and that was something, I stepped back out of sight and I listened.

"Arthur," Mr. Berman was saying, "you know these boys would go to the wall for you."

"They don't have to go to the wall. They don't have to do nothing but keep their eyes open tip their hats to the ladies and don't goose the chambermaid. Is that too much to ask? I'm paying them, ain't I? It's a goddamn paid vacation, so what are they complaining about."

"No one has said a word. But I'm telling you what I know. It's hard to explain. All these table-manners kinds of things are getting to their self-respect. There's a roadhouse about twenty miles north of here. Maybe you should let them blow off steam once in a while."

"Are you out of your mind? All this work, what do you think happens they get into a goddamn bar fight over some whore? That's all we need, a run-in with the state troopers."

"Irving wouldn't let that happen."

"No, I'm sorry, we're talking about my future, Otto."

"That is correct."

There was silence for a few moments. Mr. Schultz said, "You mean Drew Preston."

"Until now I had not been introduced to the lady's full name."

"I'll tell you what, call Cooney, tell him to get hold of some stag films and a projector and he can drive them up."

"Arthur, how shall I say this. These are serious grown men, they are not deep thinkers but they can think and they can worry about their futures no less than you worry about yours."

I heard Mr. Schultz pacing. Then he stopped. "Jesus Christ," he said.

"Nevertheless," Mr. Berman said.

"I'm telling you, Otto, it doesn't even take money she's got more money than I'll ever have, this one is different, I'll grant you she's a bit spoiled, those kind always are, but when the time comes I'll slap her around a little and that is all it will take, I promise you."

"They remember Bo."

"What does that mean? I remember too, I am upset too, I am more upset than anyone. Because I don't go around talking about it?"

"Just don't fall in love, Arthur," Mr. Berman said.

I went very quietly back to my room and got into bed. Drew Preston was in fact very beautiful, slender and with a clearly unconscious loveliness of movement when she was thoughtless of herself as she would be when we went out into the countryside, like the drawn young women in the children's books in the Diamond Home broken-down library of books no newer than from the previous century, kind and in communication with the little animals of the forest, I mean you'd see that on her exquisite face in moments of her reflection when she forgot where she was and who she was with, and that raised generous mouth curved back like the prow of a boat, and the clear large green eyes that could be so rude with intense curiosity or wickedly impertinent lowered under a profound modesty of lashes. All of us were subject to her even the philosophical Mr. Berman, a man older than the rest of us and with a physical impairment that he would have long since learned to live with and forgotten except in the presence of such fine-boned beauty. But all of this made her very dangerous, she was unstable, she took on the coloration of the moment, slipping into the role suggested to her by her surroundings. And as I thought about this I thought too that we were all of us very lax with our names, when the pastor had asked my name to enroll me in Sunday school I gave it as Billy Bathgate and watched him write it that way in the book, hardly realizing at the time I was baptizing myself into the gang because then I had an extra name too to use when I felt like it, like Arthur Flegenheimer could change himself into Dutch Schultz and Otto Berman was in some circles Abbadabba, so insofar as names went they could be like license plates you could switch on cars, not welded into their construction but only tagged on for the temporary purposes of identification. And then who I thought was Miss Lola on the tugboat and then Miss Drew in the hotel was now Mrs. Preston in Onondaga, so she was one up on everyone, although I had to admit I had probably gotten the wrong impression when I took her back to the Savoy-Plaza and the lobby clerk had greeted her as Miss Drew not necessarily because that was her maiden name, although for all I know in that walk of life the married women keep their maiden names, but because as an older man in professional service he might have known her since her childhood and though she was now too grown-up to be called simply by her first name, she was too fondly known for too long a time to be called by her last. Perhaps it wasn't necessary to get anything straight, not even monickers, maybe that was my trouble that I needed to know things definitely and expected them not to change. I myself was changing, look where I was, look what I was doing, every morning I put on glasses that magnified nothing and every night I took them off at bedtime like someone who couldn't do without them except to sleep. I was apprenticed to a gangster and so was being educated in Bible studies. I was a street kid from the Bronx living in the country like Little Lord Fauntleroy. None of these things made sense except as I was contingent to a situation. And when the situation changed, would I change with it? Yes, the answer was yes. And that gave me the idea that maybe all identification is temporary because you went through a life of changing situations. I found this a very satisfying idea to consider. I decided it was my license-plate theory of identification. As a theory it would apply to everyone, mad or sane, not just me. And now that I had it I found myself less worried about Lola Miss Drew Mrs. Preston than Mr. Otto Abbadabba Berman appeared to be. I had a new bathrobe, maybe I should put it on and after

Mr. Arthur Flegenheimer Schultz went back to bed I would go knock on the Abbadabba's door and tell him what X meant. All I had to remember was what had gotten me to this point in the first place, the innermost resolve of my secret endowment. That must never change.

TEN

I slept to an unaccustomed late hour, which I realized at once when I woke and saw the room filled with light and the white curtains on the windows like movie screens with the picture about to start. The chambermaid was running a vacuum cleaner in the corridor and I heard a chain-drive truck coming around the back of the hotel to make a delivery. I got out of bed and felt very heavy in the limbs, but I did my ablutions and dressed, and inside of ten minutes I was on my way to breakfast. When I got back to the hotel Abbadabba Berman was out front with the Buick Roadmaster at the curb, he was waiting for me. "Hey kid," he said, "come on we'll go for a ride."

I got in the back and found the only available seat was in the middle, between Irving and Lulu Rosenkrantz. It was not a comfortable place to be, after Mr. Berman got in the front and Mickey started the engine, Lulu leaned forward and I could feel the tension in him as he said, "Why does this little shit have to go with us?" Mr. Berman didn't bother to answer but looked straight ahead and Lulu banged back into the seat beside me, giving me a murderous look but clearly talking to everyone else as he said, "I'm fed up with all this crap, I don't give a pig's fuck for any of this."

Mr. Berman knew that, he understood, he did not have to be told. We drove past the county courthouse and as we did an Onondaga police car backed away from the curb and swung out behind us. I glanced back to make sure and was about to say something when my instinct told me not to. Mickey's pale blue eyes appeared regularly in the rearview mirror. Mr. Berman's shoulders barely rose above the front seat, his panama hat was horizontally forward of where it should have been because of his humpback, but to me this was the deportment of canniness and wisdom, I knew somehow the police car behind us was something else he knew and didn't have to be told.

Mickey drove across the rattly boards of the Onondaga bridge and out into the country. Everything looked baked and bleached in the high noon and it was hot in the car. After ten or fifteen minutes, he turned off the paved road into a farmyard and nudged through a protesting squawking flutter of chickens and past a gamboling goat or two and around a barn and a silo and then picked up speed down a long bumpy dirt road, with rocks making a popping against the tires and a big plume of dust billowing out behind us. He pulled up in front of a hut fenced in with chain link. A moment later I heard the brakes of the police car and a slamming door, and a policeman walked past us and unlocked the fence gate with its sign that said KEEP OUT and swung it open and we drove in.

What I'd thought was a hut was in fact a long barracks sort of structure where the Onondaga police took their pistol practice, the floor was dirt and at the far end the wall was earth, a big pile of it having been shoveled up into a sort of hill or berm, and there were overhead wires attached to pulleys at either end of the building like clotheslines. The cop pulled some paper targets out of a bin and clipped them to the lines and ran them to the berm and then he sat by the door leaning his chair back on two legs and rolling himself a cigarette, and Lulu Rosenkrantz stepped up to the railing without ceremony, unpacked his forty-five and began blasting away. I felt as if my head had burst, I looked around and saw that everyone else was wearing leather earmuffs, and only then noticed a clump of them on a table and quickly availed myself of them, clutching my hands over them for good measure while crazy Lulu shot that target into smithereens and left a smell of burning powder in the air and the echo of high-caliber concussions that seemed to press the sides of the building outward and suck them back in.

Lulu hauled the target back and didn't bother to study it but pulled it off and clipped on a new one and yanked it back down to the end and proceeded to load his pistol hurriedly, even dropping cartridges in his haste, he was so eager to go at it again, and again he shot off his rounds one after another like he was in an argument and jabbing his pointed finger for emphasis, so that a continuous roar filled the shed, it was all too much for me, I went out the door and stood in the sun leaning against the car fender and listened to my head ringing, it rang in several different notes simultaneously, like the horn of Mr. Schultz's Packard.

The firing stopped for a few minutes and when it began again I heard the discreet shots of careful aim, a shot and a pause and another shot. After this had gone on for a while Mr. Berman came outside holding up two of the white target sheets and he came over and laid them out side by side on the hood of the Buick.

The targets were printed in black ink in the shape of a man's head and torso, and one of them was peppered with holes both inside and outside the target area with the biggest a kind of jagged shell hole in the middle of the chest, so that I could see the sun reflected in the car hood underneath. The other target had small precise holes arranged almost like a design, one in the middle of the forehead, one where each eye would be, one in each shoulder, one in the middle of the chest and two in the stomach region just above the waistline. None of the shots had missed the target area.

"Who is the better shooter?" Mr. Berman asked me.

I replied without hesitation, pointing to the second target with its unerring carefully placed holes: "Irving."

"You know that's Irving?"

"He does everything this way, very neat, and with nothing wasted."

"Irving has never killed a man," Mr. Berman said.

"I wouldn't like to have to kill a man," I said, "but if I did I would want to know how like that," I said, pointing to Irving's target.

Mr. Berman leaned back against the fender and shook an Old Gold out of his pack and put it in his mouth. He shook out another one and offered it to me and I took it and he gave me his matchbook and I lit both cigarettes.

"If you were in a tight situation you would want Lulu standing up for you and emptying his barrel at everything in sight," he said. "You would know that in such a circumstance it is all decided in a matter of seconds." He flipped out his hand with one finger pointing, then flipped it again with two fingers pointing, and so on, till the whole claw was extended: "*Boom boom boom boom boom,* it's over," he said. "Like that. You couldn't dial a phone number in that time. You couldn't pick up your change from the Automat."

I felt chastened, but stubborn in my opinion too. I looked at the ground at my feet. He said, "We are not speaking of ladies' embroidery, kid. It don't have to be neat."

We stood there and he didn't say anything for a while. It was hot. I saw way up a single bird circling, way up high in the whiteness of this hot sunless day, it dipped around like a model glider, and it had a red or rust tone to it, lazing about up there drifting one way and then another. I listened to the *pop pop* of the pistol fire.

"Of course," Mr. Berman said, "the times change and looking at you I see what's in the cards, you're the upcoming generation and it's possible what is required of you will be different, you would need different skills. It is possible everything will be smooth and streamlined, people will work things out quietly, with not so much fire in the streets. We will need fewer Lulus. And if that comes to pass you may not ever have to kill no one."

I glanced at him and he gave me a little smile with his *V*-shaped mouth. "You think that's possible?" he said.

"I don't know. From what I can see it don't seem too likely."

"At a certain point everyone looks at the books. The numbers don't lie. They read the numbers, they see what only makes sense. It's like numbers are language, like all the letters in the language are turned into numbers, and so it's something that everyone understands the same way. You lose the sounds of the letters and whether they click or pop or touch the palate, or go *ooh* or *aah,* and anything that can be misread or con you with its music or the pictures it puts in your mind, all of that is gone, along with the accent, and you have a new understanding entirely, a language of numbers, and everything becomes as clear to everyone as the writing on the wall. So as I say there comes a certain time for the reading of the numbers. Do you see what I'm getting at?"

"Cooperation," I said.

"Exactly. What happened in the railroad business is a perfect example, you look at the railroads, they used to be a hundred railroad companies cutting each other's throats. Now how many are there? One to each section of the country. And on top of that they got a trade association to smooth their way in Washington. Everything nice and quiet, everything streamlined."

I inhaled the cigarette smoke and there was an undeniable opening-out of excitement through my chest and into my throat like the looming of my own power. What I was hearing was prophecy but of an inevitable event or of a planned betrayal I wasn't sure. And why did it matter as long as I knew that I was valued?

"But anyway, whatever is going to happen you must learn the basics," Mr. Berman said. "Whatever happens you have to know how to handle yourself. I already told Irving he should show you. As soon as they're through you'll take your turn."

I said, "What, you mean shoot?"

He was holding out in his palm the Automatic I had bought from Arnold Garbage. It was all cleaned and oiled, not a speck of rust, and when I took it I saw the cartridge clip was locked into place and I knew from the heft it was loaded.

"If you're going to carry it, carry it," Mr. Berman said. "If not, put it somewhere else than the bureau drawer under the underwear. You're a smart kid but like all kids you do dumb things."

I will never forget how it felt to hold a loaded gun for the first time and lift it and fire it, the scare of its animate kick up the bone of your arm, you are empowered there is no question about it, it is an investiture, like knighthood, and even though you didn't invent it or design it or tool it the credit is yours because it is in your hand, you don't even have to know how it works, the credit is all yours, with the slightest squeeze of your finger a hole appears in a piece of paper sixty feet away, and how can you not be impressed with yourself, how can you not love this coiled and sprung causation, I was awed, I was thrilled, the thing is guns come alive when you fire them, they move, I hadn't realized that. I tried to remember my instruction, I tried to breathe properly and plant myself in the sidearm stance and sight down my arm, but it took all that day and in fact the rest of the week of daily practice and a lot of sprays of earthclots brittle as crockery before I brought it around and turned that piece into the familiar of my own hand's warmth and got it to hit where I looked, and my natural athletic genius of coordination, the spring of my juggler's arm and the strength of my legs and my keen eyesight asserted themselves to their natural levels of achievement and I was hitting the target to kill whoever it was with every little pressure of my index finger. In a few short afternoons I could take aim and place the shot in the center of the forehead, either eye, the shoulders, the heart, or the belly, as I chose, Irving would pull the target back and take it down and put it down measuredly on the table over the previous target and the holes would match up. He never praised me but never did he seem to get bored with instructing me. Lulu didn't deign to watch. He didn't know my plan, which was to have Irving's techniques of accuracy so governed by my skills that I could lose

the form, drop my arm, snap point like Lulu in the punishment
of his blasting rage, and make the same holes in the same places.
I also knew what he would say if I did this, that shooting at paper
targets didn't mean shit, let me go out on a job with someone
rising from his chair in the restaurant and people's guns coming
round in my direction looking big as field eighty-eights, looking
in their barrels as wide and deep as a big bertha on a railroad
flatbed, let me see what I could do then.

Oddly enough, I detected this same attitude in the cop who
came every day to open the gate and sit back on the two rear legs
of his tilted chair and roll his cigarettes, it was only after my
second day shooting I realized he was the chief, he had this braid
on his cap none of the others in town had, not even the ser-
geants, and the arms in his short-sleeved shirt were an older
man's arms of former muscle, and his abdomen slumped, I had
thought a police chief would have something better to do than
personally unlock the gate of the firing range for the city folks
who'd paid him off and hang around to enjoy the show, but in
Onondaga he had all the time in the world and it had nothing
to do with the responsibilities of his office, he was watching a
boy, and even as I fired my clips, I thought of the chief behind
me with the slight smile on his lips, another man imbedded in
his institutional job out in the country, like Father Montaine,
with a very low visibility in the world but quite comfortable even
so and satisfied with the rewards of his life, the smoke from his
shag cigarette keeping me in mind of his presence like some
farmer's on his porch sitting for his amusement to watch the
passing parade.

But for the first time since coming to Onondaga County I felt
I was doing proper work, those few days of squeezing off
rounds, I could hardly wait to get out there, and in the evenings
I came to dinner hungry, with my ears still ringing and memo-
rial pungencies of burned gunpowder sputtering in my brain.
Clearly they were bringing me along, and I could reflect how
organized everything really was in the apparent chaos of Mr.
Schultz's life, how patiently they were dealing with everything,
from the present exigencies of the law to the anticipated needs

of the future, they were managing their business interests from a distance, establishing a presence in this county seat of the north country, adjudicating their own internal problems in their own way, and also he had brought along someone pretty for the ride. It was a kind of juggling, wasn't it, keeping everything in the air. I really liked pistol-shooting, I thought I was probably the youngest expert marksman in the history of the rackets, I'm not sure I went so far as to swagger, but at night in bed I thought of neighborhood louts chasing me down Washington Avenue, how if that happened now I would stop in my tracks and turn with my gun in my hand and my arm pointed and watch them skid, brake, and tumble all over themselves even crawling under cars to get out of my sights, and the picture of that made me smile in the dark.

But nothing else I could think of doing with that gun was anything to smile about.

I should say here that there were things going on behind the life I am describing, business things that I wasn't directly involved in. Mr. Schultz was still collecting on policy, he was still selling beer and running the window washers' and the waiters' unions, once or twice he disappeared for a day or two and went down to New York but by and large he ran things long-distance, which couldn't have been a terribly comfortable way to do business if you happened to be by nature suspicious as he was and distrustful of all but your closest associates, and of them too when they were not where you could keep your eye on them. A lot of time I could hear him screaming on Mr. Berman's special phone, the walls were too thick for the words to be heard but the pitch and timbre and intonation came through clearly and like the man who woke up when the train didn't go past his window I would have been startled if one day passed not carrying his raised voice.

Mickey was gone a lot making the long drive to New York and back in a night and a day, and sometimes other men in other cars appeared whom everyone seemed to know but me, they would take their dinner with Irving and Lulu at the other table, I would

say I saw two or three new faces a week. From all of this I began
to appreciate the size of the operation, that the weekly payroll
alone must be considerable, and from my vantage point Mr.
Schultz would have to be now holding his own after the losses
he had suffered as a lammister. It was difficult to judge these
things because he portrayed himself so consistently as someone
wronged, or double-crossed, or taken for a chump. Mr. Berman
pored over the books constantly, and sometimes Mr. Schultz
joined him, they really put in the time, usually late at night, and
on one occasion I passed the open door of Mr. Berman's office
and saw there for the first time a safe, and some deflated canvas
mail bags lying on the floor beside it, and it came to me that all
the money was ending up right here across the hall from me, a
reality that I found unsettling. Apart from the token sums he had
deposited that day for political purposes, Mr. Schultz did not
keep a bank account, because bank records could be subpoenaed and assets confiscated and tax cases made against him, it
was a simple precaution, the case the Feds had now was based
on adding-machine slips and policy records taken in a raid on
the 149th Street office, which was bad enough. So it was essential accounting practice that everything was done in cash, cash
for the payouts, cash for the payoffs, cash for the payroll, it was
a cash business and the profits to Mr. Schultz were in pure cash
and I dreamed one night of a great tide of cash coming in and
going out and what was left on the beach Mr. Schultz ran along
and scooped up in packets, which he stuffed into a burlap bag
like potatoes, knowing it was a dream as I dreamed it because
it put the country at the seashore but realizing in the dream,
which is to say reading it for the truth of the matter, that he had
been doing this for some time and he had to have accumulated
many many burlap bags of culled cash, or cold cash, and then
it turned into a gold cache, but I didn't know in the dream where
it was hidden, any more than I knew when I awakened.

Around this time, Mr. Schultz's lawyer, Dixie Davis, whom I
had seen that time in the numbers office, came up from New

York and arrived at the Hotel Onondaga in a Nash sedan driven by a member of the gang I didn't know. Dixie Davis was my model for a good dresser, I had gotten my wing-tip shoes from seeing his and now I noticed his country summer shoes, which had a kind of mesh on top, they were brown with this cream-colored mesh going from the laces to the tip and I was not crazy about them although they were probably cool on the feet. He was wearing a double-breasted very light tan suit, which I liked, and a striped tie of cotton colored pale shades of blue and gray and pink, which I thought was smart, but best of all was the straw skimmer on his head, which he put on as he emerged in a crouch from the car. I happened to have been coming downstairs and so I saw Mr. Berman, himself no slouch at color combinations, greet him just outside the revolving door. Dixie Davis had his briefcase with him and it looked fat with the mysterious problems of legal life. He was somehow different from what I remembered, perhaps in anticipation of meeting Mr. Schultz he seemed to lose his self-assurance the moment he pushed into the lobby, he took off his straw hat and looked around somewhat nervously and held his briefcase in both arms, and though he was smiling and being jolly I saw that he was city pale, not handsome as I remembered under that pompadour haircomb, but somewhat toothy, and unctuous in his deportment, he had one of those smiles that went down at the corners of his mouth, what we in the Bronx called a shit-eating smile, and it was on his face as he passed with Mr. Berman into the elevator.

Mr. Schultz was going to be tied up for the afternoon so he told Drew Preston to put in the time acting like my governess. She and I had a conference standing outside the little Indian museum that they had in the red stone courthouse around the back down some basement steps. "Look," she said, "it's just a few headdresses and spears and such and there's no one there anyway to see what a good governess I am. Let's go for a picnic instead, is that all right with you?"

I said anything was all right with me as long as it didn't involve

education. I took her down the side street to where my secret
tea shop lady made up such good things, and we bought chicken
salad sandwiches and fruit and napoleons, and then she bought
a bottle of wine at the liquor store, and we set out uphill through
the east side of the town into the mountains. This was a longer
hike than I expected, I had done most of my exploring north and
west into the farmlands, but hills always look closer than they
are, and we were well beyond the end of the paved streets and
still going up in wide spirals on a dirt road with the big hill
behind the Onondaga Hotel looking just the way it did from my
window, close enough to touch but just as far away, even when
I turned around and looked down at the roofs of the city and saw
what progress we had made.

She strode out ahead of me, which ordinarily would have
brought out my competitive spirit, except I enjoyed watching
the flex of the muscles in her long white calves. The minute we
were out of the town limits, she had unwrapped and removed
her governess's skirt and flung it over her shoulder, which
stopped my heart beating for a moment, but she had a pair of
walking shorts underneath, the hippy kind of shorts girls wear,
and she was walking with a very attractive leggy stride, a smart
practiced walk, head down, her free arm swinging, each buttock
of her shorts rising and falling in a way that very quickly became
reliably familiar to me, she was making good time uphill, her
long legs her little feet pointing in their low-heeled shoes and
white anklets, and then the road leveled and we were out of the
sun into the shade of pines, and here the road petered out into
a path and we struck off into woods, an entirely new world, very
soft underfoot with a thick cushion of dried brown pine needles,
and dry twigs cracking in the stillness, a brownish world with the
sun breaking up high above us in the high-topped evergreens so
that only speckles of it or small patches managed to reach the
forest floor. I had never been in woods of such extent before,
I mean there were dirt lots in the Bronx with weeds growing like
trees all twisted and jungly but there wasn't enough extension
of them to get lost in them, not even the wilder parts of the

Bronx Zoo gave me the sense I had now, of being inside something, as in a cavern or a cave, I had not realized that about forests that you would be walking down at the bottom of them.

Drew Preston seemed to know where she was going, she found what she said were old logging trails, so I followed her trustfully, and we passed into small sun meadows that I thought might do for a picnic but still she didn't stop but kept going in a generally uphill direction, and then I knew we were really in the hills some miles from the town because I heard the sound of water, and we came to the Onondaga River, which here was shallow and not much wider than a brook so that you could walk across it on the rocks imbedded in it, which we did, and I thought then she would want to stop but she kept going away from the river steeply uphill in a dark woods and I was thinking of beginning to complain, the socks in my new sneakers rubbing up blisters and the gnats itching my bare legs, for I was in my new Little Lord Fauntleroy summer shorts of linen and my short-sleeved polo shirt of blue-and-white stripes that she had chosen for me, but we came to a large flat natural park of brown woods, and here the sound of water became louder, and she was some yards ahead of me standing still now finally and silhouetted in a corona of dazzling light, and when I came up to her I saw we were at the edge of a great sunlit gorge of falling water, falling so thick it was white and thunderous breaking on tumblings of boulders all the way down. This was where she chose to have the picnic, seated with our legs hanging over the root-tangled and mossy banks into thin air, as if she had known all along this place was here and exactly where to find it.

We unwrapped our sandwiches from the wax paper, and laid the picnic out behind us on her skirt, which she had spread on the ground, she unscrewed the cap from the bottle of New York State red wine and had the tact or carelessness to assume I would naturally take my turn drinking from the bottle as she did, and so I did, but only after removing my glasses, and we sat in silence eating and drinking and staring into this very amazingly beautiful roaring gorge of washed white boulders streaming

with sun. At the very bottom there hovered a perpetually shimmering rainbow as if not water but light was pouring and shat-
tering into its colors. This had to be the most secret of places.
I had the feeling that if we just stayed here we would be free,
Mr. Schultz would never find us because he couldn't imagine
such a place existed. What new assumption was I making now
in this romantic setting? What could I have been about to declare when I turned to her only to realize this was not a shared
silence between us? She sat with her shoulders rounded in some
clearly deepening meditative privacy and forgot me and forgot
to eat and, holding the bottle in both hands between her knees,
forgot to give me any more swigs of wine. The advantage to me
in this was that I could stare at her without attracting her attention and first I looked at her thighs, you know the way thighs
broaden in the sitting position especially when they are not
overly muscular, and in this unsparing sun they were soft and
very milk-white girl's thighs with the thinnest bluest veins of
such tracing delicacy that it was with some shock I realized she
was younger than I had taken her to be, I didn't know her age
but the company she had kept and the fact that she was married
had made me think of her as an older woman, it had never
occurred to me she might be as precocious in her way as I was
in mine, she was a girl, clearly older than I but still a girl, maybe
twenty, maybe twenty-one, this Mrs. Preston with the gold band
on her finger. You could see that just looking at her skin in the
sun. Yet she lived a life so beyond mine in practiced knowledge
that I was a child beside her. I don't mean just her free access
as a great beauty to the most advanced realms of power and
depravity, she had chosen this life for herself when, perhaps for
her same reasons of staring meditation, she might have chosen
life in a convent, say, or to be an actress on the stage. I mean
rather how she knew this place would be here. How familiar
woods were to her. She knew about horses. I remembered her
invert husband, Harvey, had mumbled something about a
regatta. So she probably knew about sailing and oceans too, and
beaches to swim from with no crowds on them and skiing in the

European mountains of the Alps and in fact all the pleasures of the planet, all the free rides of the planet that you could have if you knew where they were and had the training to take them. This was what wealth was, the practiced knowledge of these things so you could appropriate them for yourself. So looking at her now I had revelation of the great expanse of my ambitions, I felt the first acute pain of this same knowledge, which was an appreciative inkling of how much I had so far missed and my mother had missed and would forever miss and how much the little dark-eyed Becky was doomed to miss if I didn't love her and take her with me through all the chain-link fences I had to get through.

I now found myself painfully conscious of Drew Preston, I was impatient of the solitude she made for herself, it seemed to me a slight. I found myself waiting upon her, waiting for her attention, which I wanted very badly but would not abase myself to demand. I was at this point up to her profile. The heat of the hike had matted her hair off her forehead and I saw the whole line of it, a bone-white curve smooth as sculpture. The sun's rays coming up off the boulders allowed me to see through the transparency of her eye to the green oval iris with its golden lights which blurred into radiance, and the whole orb seemed to magnify and I realized she was crying. She cried silently, staring through her tears, and she licked the tears at the corner of her mouth. I turned away as you do in intimate and uninvited witness of a terrible emotion. And only then did I hear her sniff and drink it in, like a normal sniveling human being, and she asked me in a choked voice to tell her how Bo Weinberg died.

I didn't want to talk about it any more than I do now but I did and so I will, this was the time I told it so now I have to tell it again.

"He sang 'Bye Bye Blackbird.' "

She stared at me with the water roaring and the rainbow shimmering below us. She didn't seem to understand.

" 'Pack up all my care and woe, here I go, singing low, bye bye

blackbird,' " I said. "It's a famous song." And then, as if I
thought I couldn't make it more clear, I sang to her:

> " 'Make my bed and light the light,
> I'll arrive
> Late tonight
> Blackbird, bye bye.' "

E L E V E N

He begins humming it early on while Mr. Schultz is down below with her, and I stand halfway between the upper decks hooked by my heels and my elbows on the bolted ladder, which rises vertically and falls vertically as the tugboat rides the waves or drops between them. And it is as if Bo has heard it in the throbbing of the engine or a phrase of the wind, in the way that mechanical or natural rhythms around us take on the character in our minds of a popular song. He raises his head and tries to square his shoulders, he seems to have found strength from the distraction of singing, the assumption of your control in song, as when you hum while you are busy with some work of quiet concentration, and his wits were somewhat recovered, he cleared his throat and sang a bit louder now but still wordlessly, and he only stopped in order to look as much behind him as he could, and not seeing but feeling I was there he called to me, hey kid, c'mere, talk to old Bo, humming again while he waited confidently for me to appear in front of him. And I didn't want to become any closer to this situation than I already was in the same deckhouse as this dying man, his state seemed to me contaminating, I did not want any part of his experience, neither its prayers nor appeals or plaints or last requests, I did not want to be in his eyes in his last hour as if then something of my being would go down with him into the sea, and that is not a pretty thing to confess but it was the way I felt, entirely estranged, being no saint, nor priest of absolution, nor rabbi of consolation, nor nurse of ministration, and not wanting to participate in any conceivable way with anything he was going through, not even as a looker-on. And so of course I had no alternative but to come down from the ladder and stand on the rolling deck where he could see me.

He nodded his head peering up at me from under his brow, he was uncharacteristically messy, everything awry, his dinner jacket, his pant legs, his shirt half pulled out, his jacket bunched up behind him as if he had a hunchback, his thick black shining hair fallen off to the side, he nodded and smiled and said, the word's good on you kid, they have high hopes for you, you know that, anyone tell you that? You're a runty little fucker aren't you, you'll never be fat your whole life, you grow another couple inches you can fight in the featherweight class. He smiled with his even white teeth from that swarthy face, the high cheekbones elongating his Siberian eyes. Little guys make good kills in my experience, they go up on it, you see, it's an upward stick, he said lifting his head sharply for a moment to represent the knife, you use a gun it kicks up so that's to your advantage too, but if you're as smart as they say you will get to where your nails are manicured and a pretty girl sits by your chair and cleans under them every day. Me I am six one but I always killed smartly, I did not torture and I did not miss, the guy has to go? *boom,* you put his lights out, tell me who it is Dutch, *boom,* it's done, that's all. I never liked anyone who enjoyed this work apart from the pride of doing something very difficult and very dangerous very well. I never liked the creeps, I'll give you some advice from the old Bo. This man of yours ain't gonna last long. You see his behavior, he is a very emotional man, an untrustworthy maniac fuck who doesn't give a shit for other people's feelings, I mean people who matter, people who are as tough as him, and have better organizations and I'll tell you just between us better ideas for the future than this wildass. He is obsolete kid, you know what that means? He's all finished and if you're as smart as they say you

are you'll listen to me and look out for yourself. This is Bo
Weinberg talking. Irving upstairs knows and he's worried but he
won't say anything, he's too far along he's ready for retirement
he's not going to change his colors now. But he has my respect
and I have his. What I've done in my life, my achievements, the
quality of my word, Irving respects these things and I bear no
brief against him. But he'll remember, you'll all remember, you
too kid, I want you to look on Bo Weinberg for your own sake
and understand the terrible usage of such a man, look him in the
eye if you can so you will never forget this as long as you live
because in a few minutes, in just a few minutes, he will be at
peace, he will be over it the ropes won't hurt he won't be hot
or cold or scared or humiliated or happy or sad or needful of
anything anymore, this is the way God makes up for the terrible
death, that it comes in time and the time goes on but the dying
is done and our persons are at peace. But you kid are a witness
and it's tough shit but that's the way it is, you'll remember and
the Dutchman will know you remember and you can never be
sure of anything again because you are doomed to live in remembrance of the foulness done to the man Bo Weinberg.

He looked away. And now I was startled to hear the song in
a strong baritone, hoarse with defiance: Pack up all my care and
woe, here I go, singing low, bye bye, blackbird. Dum de dum de
dumdedum, yah dah dee, yah dah dee, bye, bye, blackbird. No
one here can love or understand me, oh what hard-luck stories
they all hand me. Dum de dum, light the light, I'll arrive, late
tonight, blackbird, bye—and he shook his head with his eyes
squeezed shut to reach the high note at the end—byeeee.

Then his head slumped and he hummed the tune to himself
more softly, as if he was thinking again, almost not aware of
humming through his thoughts and when he left off and began
to talk again he was no longer talking to me but to some additional Bo sitting beside him perhaps in perfect elegance at the
Embassy Club, drinks in front of them, while they reminisced:
So I mean the guy is up there behind locked doors in the Grand
Central Building, what is it, the twelfth floor? people everywhere and you know he has to have a roomful of guns and an

outer office and an inner office, in this very legitimate well-cared-for building that straddles Park Avenue at Forty-sixth. So these are the conditions. But they know that and they know it is difficult, the man Maranzano has been in the business his whole life, it is not a sucker's proposition we are talking about and the Unione knows for this job they need the ace of spades. And Dutch comes to me and he says look Bo you don't have to do it this is their special Italian thing they like to clean out their generations every once in a while, but as a favor they have asked for you, and it wouldn't hurt us to be where they owe us a very big one so I say of course, I mean I was honored, of all the guns it's my gun they want, it was like I did this and I was in glory for the rest of my days, this one thing, like Sergeant York. You know I love to be reliable. I mean I like wining and dining and laying pretty women, I like the ponies I like the crap table, I like to come into a room cut an indolent swath, but under that I like best of all to be reliable, that is the purest pleasure, the pleasure of my purest being where someone will say not this one not that one, but Bo Weinberg, where someone will ask me and I will nod yes and it will be done as smoothly and quickly and easily as that nod, and they will know that and consider it done, as it will be, so when they read about it in the newspapers a day later, a week later, it's another unsolved mystery of a self-ordering world, another sweet tale of the tabloids. So I go to the meeting and I won't say his name but he's there and he says in that voice of a healed cut throat what do you need, and I say get me four police badges that's all. And his eyebrows go up but he says nothing and the next day they are in my hands, and I get my guys and take them to the haberdashery and we all dress ourselves like detectives in those raincoats and derbies and we walk right into the joint and flip open our wallets police you're under arrest, and they all go to the wall and I open the door the guy is behind his desk rising from his chair very slow on the uptake the man is seventy seventy-five he doesn't move too good I stand and brace myself on the front edge of the desk and I place the shot cleanly in the eye. But here is the funny part that building has marble halls and it sounds like no-man's-land it sounds through the open doors down the halls the stairwells the elevator shafts the shot heard round the world and everyone scrams, my guys, the hoods against the wall, everyone is running like hell and grabbing elevators and leaping down the stairs three at a time. And by the time I get out of there with this hot piece in my pocket doors are beginning to open up and down I hear those panics you know when people know something terrible has happened and they start shouting, and I lose my head I run down the stairs, I run up the stairs, and I get lost in this fucking building winding around corridors looking for exits walking into cleaning closets, I don't know I get lost, and somehow, somehow, when I get to the bottom I am not on the street I am in Grand Central Terminal and it is five six o'clock in the evening the place is like grand central, people in every direction making trains, standing waiting for the gates to open, the train announcements echoing in all that noisy mumble, and I attach myself to the crowd waiting for the five thirty-two and I slip the piece in some guy's pocket, I swear that's what I did, in his topcoat, he's holding his briefcase in his left hand he's got his *World-Telegram* folded for reading in his right hand and just as the gate opens and everyone presses forward in it goes so gently he doesn't even feel it and I saunter away as he gets through the gate and rushes down the ramp for his seat and, can't you see it, hello dear I'm home my God Alfred what's this in your pocket eek a gun!

And he is laughing now, tears of laughter in his eyes, one precious instant in the paradise of recollection, and even as I'm laughing with him I think how fast the mind can move us, the way the story is a span of light across space. I know he certainly got me off that boat that was heaving me up and down one foot at a time through an atmosphere rich in oil, I was there in Grand Central with my hand delivering the piece into Alfred's coat pocket but at the same time with my hands on the starched white tablecloth fiddling with the matchbook in the Embassy Club of the smart life, and the skinny girl singer doing "Bye Bye Blackbird" and outside in Manhattan the idling limousines at the curb sending their thin exhaust into the wintry night.

I became the object of his baleful stare. And what are you laughing at, he said, you think it's funny, wiseass? The story was clearly over, as in juggling when the ball you throw up finds the moment to come down, hesitates as if it might not, and then drops at the same speed of that celestial light. And life is no longer good but just what you happen to be holding.

You think it's funny, wiseass? He was a man who in his day took care of a great many people. May you last that long in your season till the last minute of your life at threescore years and ten. Then you may laugh. He was a greaser of consequence, Maranzano, not some piece of crazed slime like Coll who you couldn't ever put enough bullets in. Not like Coll that mick fuck of a child-killer for whom one death was not enough. But I killed Coll! he shouted. I turned him to spit and shit and blood in that phone booth. *Brrrrupp!* Up one window. *Brrrrup!* Down the other. I killed him! These are facts, you miserable wretch of a kid, but do you know what it is to do that, *do you know what it is to be able to do that*? You're in the Hall of Fame now! I killed Salvatore Maranzano! I killed Vincent Mad Dog Coll! I killed Jack Diamond! I killed Dopey Benny! I killed Maxie Stierman and Big Harry Schoenhaus, I killed Johnny Cooney! I killed Lulu Rosenkrantz! I killed Mickey the driver and Irving and Ab-badabba Berman, and I killed the Dutchman, Arthur. He stared at me his eyes bulging as if he was about to break the ropes that bound him. Then it was as if he could not look at me anymore. I have killed them all, he said bowing his head and closing his eyes.

Later he whispers to me take care of my girl don't let him do it to her get her away before he does her too, do I have your promise? I promise, I tell him in the first act of mercy in my life. For now the engine is idling and the tug rocks wildly in the wash of the ocean waves, I never knew they made a point of being out here too even bigger more ferocious with their own life in the middle of nowhere. Irving comes down the ladder and Bo and I both watch him in the economy of his movements swing open the double doors at the rear of the cabin and step outside and hook them fast. Suddenly the clean rage of air has blown out the smell of the oil and cigar, we are outdoors in here, I see the height of the heavy seas like gigantic black throats in the dim cast of our cabin light and Irving is at the stern rail, which he un-hooks and lifts and stows neatly to the side. The boat is yawing in such a wallow that I have gone back to my position on the side bench, which I affix myself to by bracing my heels against a steel deck plate and clutching the bulkheads on either side of me. Irving is a true sailor mindless of the rising and falling deck and no less of the splashing he has taken about the legs of his pants. He is back inside, his thin gaunt face is splotched with sea spittle, his thin hair glistens on his shining scalp, and methodically without asking my help he jimmies up one end of the galvanized tin tub and jams a dolly under it and shoves and bangs the dolly further and further under the tub to where he can use the lever-age of his whole weight to hold down the dolly with one foot and pull the tub up on it, an oddly dry scraping sound reminding me that if it were a sandpail and nobody's feet were in it, it could be turned over and tapped and leave whole a perfect cement sculpture of an overturned laundry tub perhaps even showing the embossed letters of the manufacturer. Bo's knees are now raised to a painful angle and his head is even lower, he is just about folded in half, but Irving fixes that next, after he jams wood shivs under the four rubber wheels of the dolly, he opens a steel tool kit and removes a fisherman's knife and cuts Bo's ropes, and lassoes them off and helps Bo up off the kitchen chair and stands him up in the tub on the dolly on the deck of the tugboat here at the very top of the Atlantic Ocean. Bo is shaky, he moans, his legs are buckling he lacks circulation and Irving calls to me, tells me to support Bo's other side, and oh this is just what I prefer not to do in my criminal training, exactly this, feeling Bo's palsy arm around me, smelling his hot breath, the sweat under his arm all the way through his black jacket on my neck, his hand fluttering grabbing my head like a claw, clutching my hair, his elbow drilling into the flesh of my shoulder, the man in his heat and animation resting his weight on me moaning over my head and his whole body in tremors. Here I am supporting the man I am helping to kill, we are his sole support, he holds on for dear life, and Irving says it's all right Bo, it's okay, and as calm and encouraging as a nurse, he kicks out the right stern shiv, we are facing the open deck you see, and commands me to do likewise with the shiv on my side, which I do quickly and accurately and we roll Bo on the dolly quite easily with the sea's help to the open hatch, where he lets go of us and grabs the framework standing now there alone his cement tub vehicle shooting back and forth like roller skates he can't quite manage yelling *ohh ohhoooooo,* his body twisting from the waist as he struggles to keep himself vertical and Irving and I stand back and watch this and all at once Bo learns the control, and manages to diminish the roll of the rubber wheels and with his legs locks his cement tub in some relatively governable slightness of motion and he trusts himself to look up and finds himself facing an open deck and a sea higher than he is and then lower than he is in a night of raging black wind, and his straining arms are being pulled out of the sockets and he takes great deep breaths of this awful wind and night and I see the back of his head moving and his shoulders and his head is up facing into this world of inexplicable terror and though I can't hear it for the wind I know he is singing and though I can't hear it I know the song, it is blown away by sea wind, his farewell chant, the song in his mind, all anybody ever has, and so Bo Weinberg was on his own in catastrophic solitude when the pilot engaged the engine and the boat suddenly shot forward and Mr. Schultz in his shirtsleeves and suspenders appeared and came up behind him and lifted one stockinged foot and shoved it in the small of Bo's back, and the hands broken from their grasp and the body's longing lunge for balance where there was none, careening leaning backward he went over into the sea and the last thing I saw were the arms which had gone up, and the shot white cuffs and the pale hands reaching for heaven.

T W E L V E

When I was through she didn't say anything. She handed me the wine bottle. I tilted my head up to drink from it and when I looked again she was no longer sitting beside me but had slid over the mossy bank and was by means of crevasses in the rocks and the small pine saplings growing from them lowering herself down the side of the gorge. I lay on my belly and watched. When she was two-thirds of the way down the mist enveloped her.

I wondered if she was going to do something really stupid. If I had told my story too well. I had not included everything, that for instance when Irving and the pilot were talking in the wheelhouse Bo Weinberg begged me to go below and see what was happening to her. I had done that and heard a little, not much, because the boat's engines were so loud down there. I listened for a few minutes outside the door of the cabin where Mr. Schultz had taken her and then I had gone back up to the deck and told Bo she was all right, that Mr. Schultz was pacing back and forth and explaining his point of view. But I had just wanted to make it easy for him.

"You wanted life?" I had heard Mr. Schultz shout. "Here, Miss Debutante, this is it, this is what it looks like!"

And then I couldn't hear anything for a while. I hunkered

down in the passageway and just before I was about to give up
I put my ear to the door and I heard his voice again: "You don't
care for what's dead, do you? I'm telling you aside from the
actual details he's dead. Can you understand that? You can
forget the dead, can't you? I think you've forgotten already,
haven't you? Well, I'm waiting, it's either a yes or a no. What?
I can't hear you!"

"Yes," she said, or must have. Because then Mr. Schultz said:
"Ahh, that's too bad. That's too too bad for Bo," and then he
laughed. "Because if I thought you loved him I might have
changed my mind."

I grabbed her skirt and shook it out and tossed it over the side
and watched it float into the mist and disappear. What was I
expecting? That she would find it, put it on, and climb back up?
I was not acting sensibly. I dropped over the side and turned my
back to the gorge and went after her. It was harder than it
looked, I found that out almost immediately with my head barely
below the edge when the root I put my foot on broke away and
I almost fell. I didn't like staring at rock face three inches from
my nose. The rocks were scratching the shit out of my elbows
and knees. I was in a panic of descent, I don't know what I
feared, that she would just leave me there forever, that someone
would find her, take her, do something bad to her. Some woods
maniac just waiting for the opportunity. But it was more than
that, that she would find him, that oblivious to the uses that
could be made of her she would somehow hone in on him
wherever he was skulking, in whatever foul den. Some of the
pine saplings had stickum on them which glued up my hands and
helped me to hold on. I felt the heat on my back, the farther I
descended the hotter it was becoming. In one place there was
a ledge and I stopped to rest: the sound of the water was moun-
tainous, like coal pouring down a chute. Getting off the ledge
was harder than getting on. Below it there were fewer and
smaller saplings to hold on to. Soon there were none and I held
on by sticking my sneakers in cracks and clutching outcroppings
with my fingers. Then all at once it clouded up, it was chilly, and
I realized there were boulders to stand on, and so, bit by bit I

climbed down these piled boulders to the bottom and stood in a white mist with the sun high above me diffuse and pale.

The waterfall was to my right about twenty or thirty yards, it was the last and longest fall of the water and had not been visible from the top. It came home to me that falling water is what makes gorges, I mean this could not have been news to anyone but it was practically the first bit of nature I had ever seen in operation. I have read about dinosaurs too but that would not be the same as finding the bones of one. The water coursed swiftly past where I stood on a steeply tilted bank of sand and rock, the channel couldn't have been more than six or eight feet wide but it was the widest here of any place that I could see right or left. Her skirt lay on the ground where I had flung it. I rolled it up under my arm and I headed to the left away from the waterfall, and soon I was on boulders again, jumping from one to another with the water boiling beneath and around them, this was all in a generally downhill direction, I felt as if I was descending into a pore of the planet, and then I came around a bend and was looking down at a cantilevered ledge shaped like an enormous arrowhead, and piled on it were her clothes and shoes and socks. I leapt down and ran to the edge, I saw below me a clear black pool of water entirely still except for a silver rim of spill off at the far side.

It seemed to me I looked at this water until anybody under it would have to surface or drown. I was terrified, I pulled off my sneakers and shirt and prepared to jump in, I don't swim very well but I felt I could dive down in the water if I had to and at this moment the water shook and she broke into the air, her head and shoulders rising, and shouted or drew a great gasping breath that was like a cry of pain as the water poured off her shoulders, and then she threw her arms behind her and settled and floated on her back with her arms outstretched and lay there in the water with her chest heaving and her legs seeming to attenuate and wither as they floated downward in the black water.

After a while she was upright, shaking her head and smoothing her hair. She swam sidestroke out of my sight and appeared

a minute later where I was not looking, climbing up onto the
ledge with her body pale and wet and her teeth chattering and
her lips blue. She looked at me without recognition. I rolled my
shirt into a wad and rubbed her as she stood with her knees
pressed together and her arms across her breasts, I rubbed her
shoulders and back, the backs of her legs and after a moment's
hesitation her backside and then the front of her legs while she
stood and held her hands at her mouth and shivered herself
warm. Then, for the second time in my life, I watched Mrs.
Preston get dressed.

She said little on the walk back. We followed the gorge to
where it went dry, and then widened on smaller rocks, and
finally flattened out with the land. I was overwhelmed and could
not speak on my own initiative and waited for her, and waited
upon her, I felt we had an alliance of sorts, but it was condi-
tional, as if I still had to grow up, I felt ignorant, I felt chastened
and foolish and like a child. We walked again through the brown
pine-needle forest and found the logging trail and came out into
the meadows. She said, "Did he really ask you to protect me?"
    "Yes."
    "How very strange," she said.
    I didn't answer.
    "I mean that he would think I couldn't take care of myself,"
she said by way of clarification. She stooped where the sun shone
through the trees to pick a small blue flower drooping over like
a bell. "And you promised him you would?"
    "Yes."
    She came up to me and hung the flower over my ear and I
found myself holding my breath till I no longer felt her touch.
She sent out a very secret and indiscriminate beaming attraction, Mrs. Preston, as if it was always there whether you were
or not.
    "Oh don't move it," she said. "You're such a pretty little devil,
do you know that?"
    "That's what they tell me," I said and a few minutes afterward
we scooted down a wooded embankment on our heels and came

out to the dirt road and so eventually to the paved road leading
down the hill to Onondaga. I walked backward to look at her in
the sun. Her hair had lost its wave and was dried sleek and off
the forehead with the tracks of her fingers showing her careless
attention to it. She had not a bit of makeup on her face but those
full lips were their natural color now and her skin had regained
the blush of her life. She was still not smiling though, and she
had reddened, swimmer's eyes. Before we got back to the hotel
she asked me if I had a girlfriend and I said I did, and she said
whoever that girl was was lucky, but the truth was when she
asked I felt guilty because I was no longer thinking of little
Becky, who seemed to me now no more interesting than a child,
but only of her. I was frightened by her, this woods guide, oh
what she had shown me, like some counselor with a whistle on
a lanyard, for the first time I understood what a match she made
with Mr. Schultz, she took her clothes off to gunmen, to water,
to the sun, life disrobed her, I understood why she went with
him, this was not like mothers and fathers of ordinary existence,
there was no consideration of love, it was not a universe of love
they lived in, fucking and killing as they did, it was a large, empty
resounding adulthood booming with terror.

I thought about her from the moment we went to our separate
rooms and I lay on my bed in the late afternoon as dull-witted
as the weather which hung hot and heavy in the Onondaga Hotel
with the gauzy white curtains motionless in the open windows.
The curtains grew gray, darkened, and were lit by a broad flashing and after an interval there was a muffled distant thunder. I
now liked her far more than I had and knew in fact I might even
be sweet on her, as how could a poor boy not after what she had
put me through. Of course I had not entirely lost my wits and
knew that whatever feelings I had I would suffer them in silence
if I wanted to live on Earth a little while longer. I closed my eyes
and watched her again climbing out of the pool at the bottom
of the gorge with her nipples all crimped and blue and her pale
pubic hair stringy with dripping water. I thought this time I
was seeing someone who had tried to die, though of course I
couldn't be sure because she lived an enlarged existence, it was

not her nature to be contained by judgments. I wondered what would happen if her intimacy with Mr. Schultz prevailed over my confidences and she told him the things I'd reported. But I had the feeling she would not, that she had the character of independence, that she lived alone in some sort of mystery of her own making and that it was her integrity to be self-driven and self-communicating only, however alluringly close she might drift toward anyone at any given moment. I told myself that she had finally expressed some appropriate human grief and thought maybe that was a large part of my new liking for her, or tried to persuade myself of that anyway, even though it didn't quite jibe with the heavy tool I found in my hand with its own made-up mind existing, as she did, in the demonstrated inadequacy of my thought. I was resolved by the time I had had a cold shower in the big white bathroom all my own and had dressed for the evening in my suit and tie and glasses that no matter what my feelings they would not deter me from the justice my life demanded. I really had promised Bo Weinberg I would look after her and protect her, and now that I had told her, I would have to, but I hoped for my sake as well as hers that it wouldn't ever come to that.

THIRTEEN

By now in our stay at the Onondaga Hotel, as in any billet occupied for any length of time, the troops had been provided with a supplemental bill of fare that was more like home. Mr. Schultz had established a supply line from New York and once a week a truck came up with steaks and chops, racks of lamb, fish on ice, delicatessen, good booze and beer, and every couple of days someone went down to Albany, where an airplane landed with fresh New York rolls and bagels and cakes and pies and all the newspapers. The hotel kitchen was kept hopping, but nobody in there seemed to mind, as I thought they would, the implied judgment in all of this seeming to have escaped them. Everyone was without undue pride or umbrage or sensitivity, only too willing to cook and serve Mr. Schultz everything he provided them with, and in fact seemed to pick up in their own qualifications just being proximate to the big time.

Dinner became a ritual occasion as if we were all a family gathering at the same hour, though at different tables, at the end of the day. The dinners tended to go on awhile and were often the occasion for extended reminiscences on Mr. Schultz's part. He seemed relaxed at these times unless he drank too much, in which case he became surly or depressed and glared at one or another of us if we seemed to be having too good a time despite

him, or eating too happily the food on our plates, which he liked
to ask us to pass over to him for spite so that he could spear this
or that morsel for himself before giving the plate back, he did
this to me several times, which never failed to enrage me or
cause me to lose my appetite, once he went over to the other
table and took a steak from their platter, it was as if he couldn't
be generous and hospitable without feeling at the same time that
people were getting the best of him, and on these nights dinner
was most unpleasant with Miss Drew excusing herself when she
didn't like what was going on, it really took the heart out of you
to think he begrudged the very food going into your mouth, it
was demeaning to have your portion violated, and these evenings were not good evenings at all.

But as I say for the most part if he stayed sober he was even-
tempered at dinner as if the days he spent showing Onondaga
New York his sunny disposition and altruistic nature somehow
actually made him feel right with the world. And on this particular evening I knew definitely I would get to eat everything I put
on my plate because we had two guests at our regular table,
Dixie Davis, who seemed to be staying past the hour of his
return to New York, and the priest from St. Barnabas Catholic
Church, Father Montaine. I like it that when the father arrived
he stopped first at the table by the door to greet Mickey and
Irving and Lulu, and Dixie Davis's driver who was seated with
them, and to chat for a few minutes with a lot of jovial priestly
banter. He was pretty lively for a man of God, he rubbed his
hands with enthusiasm when he talked as if only good things
could happen, he was brimming with ambitions for his small and
not terribly well-off parish, St. Barnabas being a modest neighborhood church down by the river, where the streets were narrowest and the houses small and close together, and it was made
of wood rather than stone like the Holy Spirit up on the hill,
although the inside was just about as large and even more decorative with its painted plaster Christ and attendant saints hooked
up along the walls.

On the menu was roast beef, served well-done the way I liked

it, and fresh asparagus I was not wild about, and homemade
french fries, big thick cuts of them, and salad greens, which I
don't touch on principle, and there was real French wine I was
learning to develop a taste for but did not indulge in for the
same reason that Drew Preston was seated as far away as possible across the table from Mr. Schultz. I sat on Mr. Schultz's left
and this Father Montaine on his right, and to my left was Dixie
Davis, and Drew Preston sat between him and Mr. Berman.
Dixie Davis chattered uncontrollably, perhaps he had been
worked over a bit during the afternoon meeting, perhaps he had
brought the wrong intelligence or his legal opinion had not met
with favor, but whatever it was he couldn't stop talking, maybe
it was just the fact of being seated next to the most beautiful
aristocratic woman he had ever seen, who wore a plain black
dress that set off her elegant neck, which was wound with a
single string of pearls in each of which glowed a pinpoint of the
light of the hotel chandelier, but he was telling Mrs. Preston how
he'd gotten started in the legal profession, from what humble
beginnings, reminiscing with hysterical self-satisfaction while
she nodded her lovely head to keep him going and resolutely
packed away everything in sight on her plate and downed several
glasses of wine, which he poured happily for her while he continued to bask in her presence and entreated to impress her with
the facts of his craven life. I know I wouldn't have boasted about
hanging around the greasy spoons near magistrates court suck-
ing up to bail bondsmen so that they would tip me off when
some poor slob was arraigned and needed a lawyer. That's the
way he'd got started, building up a practice from the daily court
traffic of numbers runners at twenty-five bucks per rap of the
gavel. "The rest is history," he said with his toothy, downturned
smile. I noticed too he sat with a hunch and his head pushed
forward toward its pompadour, so that all his grooming and fine
wardrobe was wasted on the posture of unctuousness. I don't
know why I had taken such a dislike to the man, I hardly knew
him, but I felt sitting next to him and watching him trying to look
down Drew Preston's dress that I should be sitting at the other

table with Irving and Lulu and the boys, not with this intellectual who did not once address a remark to me or even appear to notice that I was sitting there to his right.

And then he took a snapshot out of his wallet, it was of a woman in a halter and sun shorts squinting into the sun with her hands on her ample hips and her feet in their high-heeled shoes pointed outward, one before the other, and he placed it in front of Drew Preston, who peered down at it without touching it as if it was some object of natural curiosity, like a cricket or a praying mantis.

"That's my fiancée," he said, "the actress Fawn Bliss? Maybe you've heard of her."

"What?" Drew Preston said. "You don't mean it—*Fawn Bliss*?" she said enunciating the name in tones of such incredulity that the lawyer assumed she couldn't believe her good fortune in sitting next to him at the dinner table.

"That's the lady," Dixie Davis said, grinning and gazing at the snapshot with insipid adoration. Drew Preston caught my glance and her eyes glazed over and then crossed and I started to laugh, I didn't know she could do that, and it was at this moment I became aware of Mr. Berman, directly opposite, regarding me over the tops of his glasses, and he didn't have to say a word or even tilt his head, I knew that I had been listening to the wrong conversation. For all my resolve to stay alert I had been unable to take my eyes off Mrs. Preston, a truth I felt in the bones of my neck which actually creaked in their reluctance to swivel me around in the direction of Father Montaine and Mr. Schultz.

"Ah, but you must make the spiritual journey," the father was saying in his vigorous way, eating and drinking as he spoke so that the words were like what he was eating, "you must ask for the catechisme, you must hear the Gospel, you must purify yourself and prepare for election and undergo the scrutinies. Only then can you undergo baptisme and have the confirmahshun, only then can you receive the sacramahnt."

"How long does all that take, Father?"

"Oh well, this depends. A year. Five years, ten? How quickly you open your heart to the mysteries."

"I can move faster than that, Father," Mr. Schultz said.

I didn't dare look at Mr. Berman because he would immediately see that I had been caught unawares. Since meeting the father that time on the sidewalk in front of his church we had gone one Wednesday to St. Barnabas's Bingo Night, and Mr. Schultz actually ran a few games, calling out the magic numbers from the balls that popped into the cup, and making a big deal of it when someone won a dollar or two. Oh yes, and then he spoke into the ear of the father, who announced with great excitement Mr. Schultz's blessed generosity in putting up a special grand prize for the end of the evening of twenty-five dollars and there was a big round of applause, Mr. Schultz receiving it with a modest hand held in the air and a big sheepish smile, while all this time Mr. Berman and I sat in the back and thought about bingo cards, and he took a card and gave numerical values to each letter and showed me a possible way to handicap the lines after each number was called out, and then described to me several different ways an honest game could be rigged. But I didn't think how I could be faulted for not knowing the game of bingo was the first step in the conversion process.

The father put down his knife and fork and leaned back in his chair still chewing. He looked at Mr. Schultz, his heavy eyebrows raised in compassionate priestly skepticism. "From the Jewish to the Holy Church is a great revolution."

"Not so great, Father, not so great. We are in the same ballpark. Why else would all your big shots wear yarmulkes? I notice also you keep talking about our guys and reading our Bible. Not so great."

"Ah, but this is the point exactement, how we read, what we accept, this is the point, is it not?"

"I know guys, Catholic guys I grew up with, business associates, am I right, Otto?" Mr. Schultz said looking over to Mr. Berman, "Danny Iamascia, Joey Rao, guys like that. They think the way I think, they hold to the same virtues of right and wrong, they hold the same respect for their mothers, I have depended on Catholic businessmen all my life, Father, and how could I, and they on me, if we didn't understand one another like blood brothers."

With a deliberation matching these solemn sentiments he refilled the father's wineglass. Everyone had grown quiet.

Father Montaine gave Mr. Schultz a glance of Gallic reproach and then picked up the glass and drank it off. Then he patted his lips with his napkin. "Of course," he said very softly as if he was speaking of something better left unsaid, "there is in the special cases of the religious mature, another way."

"Now you're talking. The short form," Mr. Schultz said.

"In these case, I don't know, we must 'ave the confidahns that it is truly a beginning of the submisshun to the Lord Jesu Christe."

"I give you my word I couldn't be more sincere, Father. I brought it up, didn't I? I live a difficult life. I make important decisions all the time. I need strength. I see men I know take their strength from their faith and I have to think I need that strength too. I am just a man. I fear for my life like all men. I wonder what it's all for. I try to be generous, I try to be good. But I like the idea of that extra edge."

"I understan', ma son."

"How about Sunday," Mr. Schultz said.

After coffee Drew Preston excused herself and a few minutes later the party broke up and Mr. Schultz invited Father Montaine to the sixth floor in the hotel, where they sat in his suite and drank from a bottle of Canadian whiskey on the table and smoked cigars and enjoyed themselves like fast friends. I thought looking in on them they even looked alike, both of them stolid and neckless and sloppy with their ashes. Dixie Davis was in there with them. The rest of the gang was in Mr. Berman's office, sitting around looking glum and not saying much. Finally the father went home and everyone moved to Mr. Schultz's suite, no one called a meeting or anything like that we all just wandered in and sat down, and everyone was very quiet while our boss paced back and forth and gave us his thinking. "Mickey, you understand, don't you, Mickey would understand after all, I've got to be ready, I can't take chances, I need all the help I can get. Who knows? Who knows? Years ago I remember being very impressed by that Patrick Devlin, you remember the Devlin brothers they ran most of the Bronx beer at the time, so we was just getting started and I wanted to teach him a lesson, he was the tough one, we hung him up by the thumbs, you remember, Lulu? but he didn't know what we had in mind he thought we were killing him and he screamed for a priest. Well that impressed me. Not his mother, not his wife, not nobody but his priest when he thought he was dying. It gave me a pause for thought. I mean you look to your strength in moments like that, am I right? Actually alls we did was smear some guts and shit from a dead rat on his eyes and tape it down with adhesive tape and we left him hanging there in his own cellar so's they would find him, although by the time they did, the stupid fucks, he'd lost the use of his sight. But I never forgot he wanted the priest. Those things stay with you. I like that little french-fried Canuck, I like his church, I'm gonna put a new roof on it so it don't leak during the sacred moments, it gives me a good feeling, you know what I mean? I get a good feeling every time I walk in there, I don't understand Latin, but I don't understand Hebrew neither, so why not both, is there a law against both? Christ was both, for christsake, what's the big deal? They push confession, I can't pretend I'm wild about that, no offense, but I'll deal with it when the time comes. This mustn't get to my mother—Irving, your mother neither, the mothers shouldn't know this, they wouldn't understand. I never liked the old men davening in the synagogue, rocking swaying back and forth, everyone mumbling to himself at his own speed, the head going up and down the shoulders rocking, I like a little dignity, I like everyone singing something together, everyone doing the same thing at the same time, I like the order of that, it means something everyone goes down on their knees the same time, it puts a light on God, is this too deep for you, Lulu? Look at that, he is so unhappy, Otto, look at his expression he's gonna cry, tell him I'm still the Dutch-

man, tell him nothing is changed, nothing is changed, you dumb
Hebe!" And he gave his gunman a big bear hug, laughing and
pounding him on the back. "You know how it is with a trial,
don't you, you know we get a little nervous when we're on the
docket. That's all. That's all. It's not the last rites for christsake."

Nobody said anything by way of reply except Dixie Davis, who
kept nodding and smiling his vacuous uh-hums of encourage-
ment, everyone else was stunned, all in all it had been a stunning
day. Mr. Schultz kept talking, but when I judged the moment
proper I quietly slipped out and went to my room. Mr. Schultz
was excessive, anyone who worked for him should know that, he
couldn't stop, he took things to extremes, so that what might
have started out as business, like everything else up here, he
would want to do to the limit, he would go overboard in these
feelings just as he did in his angers. I hardly thought we were
in any danger of losing him to the priesthood, he just wanted a
little more coverage, like another insurance policy, he'd all but
said so, and unless you were a religious person yourself who
thought there was just one denomination of God, that God came
contained in one denomination and one only, he made a kind
of superstitious sense, he always wanted more of everything, and
if we were up here much longer he'd probably become a member of the Holy Spirit Protestant church too, God knows he
could afford it, this was his usual blithe everyday voracity, Mr.
Schultz's urge to appropriate was stronger than his cunning, it
was the central force of him, it operated all the time and wherever he happened to be, he'd appropriated speakeasies, beer
companies, unions, numbers games, nightclubs, me, Miss Drew,
and now he was appropriating Catholicism. That was all.

FOURTEEN

But now, not only was Mr. Schultz's trial due to start in the first week of September, his conversion was to precede it, in one blow he had doubled the critical ceremonies of his life for us all to think about. The following days were very busy, another lawyer appeared whom I had never seen before, a dignified portly white-haired gentleman clearly not a familiar of gangsters or their mouthpieces, as I could tell by his stately and solemn demeanor and his old-fashioned glasses, which were supported solely by his nose and were tied to a black ribbon, from which they dangled when not in use, and also the fact that he brought with him a young assistant, also a lawyer, who carried both their briefcases. These new arrivals entailed an all-day closed-door conference in Mr. Schultz's suite and a visit by everyone the next morning to the courthouse. The matter of preparations for Mr. Schultz's religious induction entailed meetings with Father Montaine at the church. In addition there was all the usual business, which seemed to send everyone off in every direction except Drew Preston and me.

So I found myself one morning on top of a living horse of the countryside holding very tightly to the reins, which seemed to me not enough in the way of structured support, and trying to communicate reasonably with this very tall and wide-backed

beast who pretended he didn't understand me. I had thought
horses were supposed to be dumb. When I said something to
slow him down he broke into a canter, and when I urged him to
go faster to keep up with Miss Drew on her gray filly, he stopped
and dipped his head and began to eat the sweet and luxuriant
grasses of the field. His back was my realm but it was his back.
I either bounced along hunched over him so that I wouldn't fall,
while Drew Preston beside me told me what I should be doing
with my knees and how my heels should be hooked into the
stirrups, fine points I wasn't quite ready for, or I sat there in the
sun looking past this grazer whose neck sloped down at a precip-
itous angle until his head disappeared entirely and listened to
him tear bunches of grass with his big teeth and grind the stuff
up in his molars while the field opened up between me and the
only other living human in sight. This horse was an ordinary-
enough-looking bay going to black between the eyes and across
the rump, but in perversity he was a champion. I thought it was
cruel of Mrs. Preston to arrange it for me to be humiliated by
a horse. I achieved a new respect for Gene Autry, who not only
rode so that it looked easy but managed to sing pretty much on
key at the same time. My only consolation was that nobody from
the gang was around to see me, and when we put the horses
away in the farmer's stable and walked back to town I loved the
feel of the earth under my own two feet and thanked God and
His sunny day for being alive, though slightly lame and sore-
assed.

We had a late breakfast in my tea shop. Nobody else was there
and the woman was back in her kitchen, so we could talk quite
freely, Mrs. Preston and I. I was awfully happy to be alone with
her again. She had not once laughed at my struggles atop the
horse, she had seemed seriously interested in my instruction
and thought I would be a good rider after a few more lessons.
I agreed. She looked very fine in her pale silk shirt with its big
collar and open neck, and with her blue velvet riding jacket with
the elbow patches of leather; we ate our cereal and eggs and
toast in leisure and drank two cups of coffee and smoked my
Wings while she asked me questions about myself and looked at

me with the most intense concentration and listened to my an-
swers as if nobody in all her life had ever interested her so much.
I knew she looked at and listened to Mr. Schultz in this same
manner but I didn't mind. I thought having her attention was a
great privilege and excitement, we were friends, intimates, and
I couldn't imagine anywhere else I'd rather be than with her at
this moment, in this shop out of sight of everyone, having breakfast together and talking in this natural way, although it wasn't
that natural since the situation impelled me to perform at my
brilliant best.

I told her I came from a criminal background.

"Does that mean your father is a gangster?"

"My father disappeared a long time ago. It means my neighborhood."

"Where is that?"

"Between Third Avenue and Bathgate Avenue in the Bronx.
And north of Claremont Avenue. It's the same section Mr.
Schultz comes from."

"I've never been to the Bronx."

"I didn't think you had," I said. "We live in a tenement. The
bathtub is in the kitchen."

"Who is we?"

"My mother and me. My mother works in a laundry. She has
long gray hair. I think she's an attractive woman or could be if
she took care of herself. She's very clean and neat, I don't mean
that. But she's a little bit crazy. Why am I telling you these
things? I've never talked about her to anybody and I feel bad
now saying this about my own mother. She's very kind to me.
She loves me."

"I would think so."

"But she's not quite right. She doesn't care about looking her
best, or having friends, or buying things or getting a boyfriend
or anything like that. She doesn't care what the neighbors think.
She sort of lives in her head. She's got the reputation of being
a nut."

"I think she has had a hard life. How long has your father been
gone?"

"I was very little. I don't even remember him. He was Jewish, I know that much."

"Isn't your mother Jewish?"

"She's an Irish Catholic. Her name is Mary Behan. But she'd rather go to temple than to church. That's the kind of thing I mean. She goes upstairs and sits with the women in the synagogue. She takes comfort from that."

"And what is the family name? Not Bathgate."

"Oh, you heard that."

"Yes, when you enrolled in Sunday school at the Holy Spirit. Now I know where you got it." She was smiling at me. I thought she meant where I got the name, from Bathgate Avenue, the street of plenty, the street of the fruits of the earth. But she meant the habit of ending up in the wrong church. It took me a moment. She was trying not to laugh at her own joke, looking at me askance, hoping I wouldn't take offense.

"You know that never occurred to me," I said. "That I was following in the crazy family footsteps." I laughed and then she did. We had a good laugh, I loved her laughter, it was low and melodious, like a voice under water.

Afterward, outside, with the sun burning down hot on the empty street, and without making a point of it, we naturally turned to stroll in the opposite direction from the hotel. She took off her jacket and slung it over her shoulder. I watched our reflections wavering in the empty store windows with their TO LET signs. Our reflections were black, very little color in them. Yet the street burned in light. I felt I knew Drew Preston this morning as she seemed to be in herself, without pretending anything or being afflicted with one of her large emotional wine-induced introspections, I felt I knew her under her brilliance of beauty, almost so that I forgot it, as she herself must looking out from it, and I thought I understood her as she must have understood herself, as someone maintaining her being while in the grasp of others. It was the kind of thing that would appear to the gang as slumming, which is why they had taken such offense, but was really more dangerous than that, more vulnerable of spirit, and I think what interested her about me was that I was in my way doing the same thing.

We walked for several blocks. She had fallen silent. Every once in a while she glanced at me. Then all at once she took my hand and held it as we strolled along. Just as I had been giving her credit for a kind of real basic sensibleness, she had to hold my hand in broad daylight like a girlfriend. It made me very nervous but I couldn't offend her by pulling away. I did look behind us to see if anyone we knew was on the street. I cleared my throat. "Maybe you don't appreciate the position you're in," I said.

"What position is that?"

"Well you're my governess."

"That's what I thought, but apparently all this while you've been looking after me."

"I have. But to tell you the truth," I said, "so far you seem to have done all right on your own." The minute I said this I thought it sounded snide. "But I guess I would keep my word if you got into a jam," I said by way of expiation.

"What kind of a jam."

"Well for instance it's not good if you aren't in this walk of life to have seen anything, to know anything," I said. "They don't like witnesses. They don't like it for people to have something on them."

"I have something on them," she said as if the idea was hard to understand.

"Just a little," I said. "On the other hand nobody outside the gang knows you do so that's a slightly better position than, say, if the D.A. knew you were on that boat and wanted to know what had happened on it. Then you might be in serious danger."

She was thoughtful. "You don't talk as if you're one of them," she said.

"Well I'm not. Not yet. I'm trying to catch on," I said.

"He has a high regard for you, he says only good things about you."

"What things?"

"Oh, that you're very smart. And that you have guts. That is not an expression I'm particularly fond of. He could have said you're bold, or feisty or fearless, he could have said you're stouthearted. Would you mind my asking how old you are?"

"Sixteen," I said exaggerating only slightly.

"Oh my. Oh my," she said as she glanced at me and lowered her eyes. She was silent for a moment. She removed her hand from mine, which was a great relief although I longed for her to put it back. She said, "Well you must have done something for them to have heard about you and chosen you above all the others."

"What others? It's not like getting into Harvard University, Mrs. Preston. I happened to catch their attention, that's all. I connected. This gang, they make things up as they go along. They use what's to hand."

"I see."

"I'm here the same way you are."

"I didn't understand. I thought you were even related in some way."

We went down the hill to the river and walked to the middle of the bridge and stood at the wood rail and looked down at the water coming down the wide shallows and breaking with rushing intent around all the rocks and boulders.

"If I have something on them," Mrs. Preston said, finally, "don't you?"

"If I don't catch on," I said, "yes, I will have something on them. If for some reason they decide against me. Yes. Nobody can tell what Mr. Schultz will do," I said. "I'll be a danger to them if he decides I am."

She turned to look at me. Her expression was troubled, there might even have been a glimmering fear in her though I could not be sure in this light that passed like waves of summer heat through those pale green eyes. If she was frightened for me I didn't want that, it was undermining, I thought if she had the reckless assurance of her own charmed life she should grant me mine. This may have been the dangerous moment of our alliance, when it was clear in its extent, that we actually cared for each other, I could not bear to be contemplated as overmatched, as a lamb among wolves, I wanted equality with her. I pretended to think she was in fear for herself.

"I don't really think you have to worry," I said, with a harsh peremptory edge to my voice. "So far as I can judge Mr. Schultz has every reason to believe you're trustworthy. And even if he didn't I think you can probably rely on the fact that he would do as little as he could to convince himself that you are."

"He would? Why?"

"Why, Miss Lola, I mean Miss Drew, I mean Mrs. Preston? Why?" I thought now I had hurt her and I felt bad. I was showing her I was a man with a man's crude judgments. But then I backed away from her on the wood bridge and she knew what I was up to and she was smiling again and I started to laugh, and now she lunged forward to grab my hand and as I tried to pull away she said, "Why, why, no tell me, tell me," like a little girl in her entreaties and she pulled me to her.

We stood there. I said feeling the heat of her on my face: "Because as everyone except you seems to know, Mr. Schultz is a pushover for blondes."

"How do they know?"

"Everyone knows," I said. "It was even in the papers."

"I don't read the papers," she whispered.

My throat had gone dry. "How can you know everything you need to know if you don't read the papers?" I said.

"What is it I need to know?" she said gazing into my eyes.

"Well maybe if you don't work for a living you don't need to know anything," I said. "But some of us trying to learn a trade have to be up on the developments."

I felt weak in the knees, overwhelmed, a little sick in the heat, I felt as if I was disappearing into her eyes. I wanted her in such totality of desire that it was diffuse, aching all through me, like my own blood heat, I wanted her in my fingertips and my knees and my brain and my face and in the little bones of my feet. Only the cock was not at this moment affected. I wanted her behind

the palate, where tears begin, in the throat, where words crum-
ble on the breaking voice.

"Here's the latest development," she said. And she kissed me
on the mouth.

On Sunday morning everyone was standing all turned out
clean and shining in front of the Church of St. Barnabas, even
Lulu, who wore a dark blue double-breasted suit that was tai-
lored to make as discreet as possible the bulge of the shoulder
holster and piece under his left arm. This would have to have
been the last week in August, a new weather was creeping up on
the days, like a different kind of light, on the hillside behind my
room some of the leafy trees had turned pale with little yellow-
ing patches, and here in front of the church a wind was blowing
along the street from the river so that as women of the parish
climbed the steps the hems of their Sunday dresses furled
around their legs. My own summer suit felt air-cooled and as we
stood waiting my careful haircomb ruffled up and began to break
the crust given it by my Vitalis.

Drew Preston held on to a big holiday hat that hid her eyes
from me. She had white lace gloves on her hands that just barely
came up to the wrist. She wore a dark conservative dress and
hose with the seams proper and straight down her calves and
low-heeled black pumps, which made her almost invisible in this
setting. At her side Mr. Schultz was nervous and kept picking at
the little carnation pinned to his lapel, he unbuttoned the jacket
of his gray pinstripe to yank up his trousers, and then he discovered the buttons of the vest were not in the right holes and tore
open the vest and rebuttoned it, and then he reset his jacket on
his shoulders and then brushed imaginary lint from the sleeves,
and then he discovered his shoelace was untied and was about
to bend down when Mr. Berman tapped him on the shoulder
and pointed to a car that had just come around the corner and
pulled up to the curb and sat there with its motor running. "He's
here," Mr. Schultz said and a moment later another car, a coupé,
came around the corner and drove past us and pulled up at the

end of the block, and then a third car appeared and it moved very slowly along the street and came to a stop where we were, a black Chrysler with the wheels hidden by the fenders, I think it must have been a custom-made model, I had never seen one like it. Mr. Schultz moved forward and we all stood in rank behind him as two unsmiling men got out and looked at all of us in that way that only cops and mob men consider people, with an officious but expertly quick assessment, and they gave curt nods to Mr. Schultz and Lulu and Irving, and one of them went up the steps and peered into the church and the other looked up and down the street with his hand on the rear car door and then the first one nodded from the top of the steps and the second opened the car door and a thin dapper man, quite short, got out and Mr. Schultz who had been standing by patiently, almost humbly, embraced him with joy, and he was someone whose name I will not give even here and now these many years later, a man I recognized immediately from his pictures in the *Mirror,* the scar under his jaw, the one droopy eyelid, the wavy hair, in the instant I saw him I found myself instinctively moving behind someone just out of his line of sight. He had a dusky sallow coloring that was almost lavender, he was shorter and slighter than I had imagined, he wore a well-tailored pearl gray single-breasted suit, and he politely shook hands with Abbadabba Berman and Lulu and Mickey and warmly embraced Irving and then was introduced to Drew Preston and he said in a whispery voice he was pleased to meet her and he said looking up at the blue sky, "What a nice day this is, Dutch, I think you must already have an in with Il Papa," and everyone laughed, especially Mr. Schultz, he was so happy, so honored that a man of this position would agree to come all the way up from New York to speak for him as his godparent and present him formally to the priest for admission to the Church.

   That's the way it works, a Catholic in good standing has to testify as a kind of character witness, I had thought it would be someone from inside the gang, like John Cooney or even Mickey if nobody else was convenient, because the gang was self-sufficient and whatever it needed it always arranged from its own resources, and I had no reason to believe it would not do the same in this circumstance. But I looked at Lulu Rosenkrantz, who stood behind Mr. Schultz with a beaming content, all of the gang were at peace in this moment, everything made sense now, they had worried about this conversion as they had worried about the girl, as if the Dutchman was going off half-cocked in every direction, but he had surprised them again, of course it figured that he would want the most eminent of men to get him in, not only so that that way there would be no hitch but because it was a political honor, it signified a certain recognition. I saw it was an obeisance on his part, perhaps, but also a degree of acknowledgment from a peer, I was gratified, I thought this is what Mr. Berman must have meant when he talked about the time coming when everyone would read the numbers, they were working on it already with this ritual of amity. In fact it was an imprimatur of a kind, in the stately morning shadow of the church, good faith was arraying itself in procession, these were the first representations of the new world coming, the guys had thought it was religion he was doing but it was the rackets after all, and all in all I thought it was a cunning move by Mr. Schultz, although probably not without Mr. Berman's help, to make such use of his own blind impulses, a man no more sophisticated than superstitious, and who had been using his unaccustomed time in the country learning to ride horseback from a blue blood with that same all-around three-hundred-and-sixty-degree enterprise.

I wanted very badly on this morning to believe in Mr. Schultz's powers. I wanted order in his sway, I wanted everything in its place where it belonged, it was a working tyranny he ran and I wanted him to run it well, without wavering. I didn't want him to make an error just as I didn't want myself to lose the harmonies of gang life, if a distortion of his vision was dangerous to the ruling order, so was my brazen sin of thought, my madness of usurpation stirring at the root. In my mind as I stood there I checked myself for weaknesses, unconscious revelations, errors of demeanor, losses of circumspection, and I found none.

My patrolling mind found only the quiet, the peace of the unsuspecting.

At this moment the St. Barnabas Church bells began to ring as if confirming me in my hopes. My heart lifted and I experienced a rush of fierce well-being. While it is true I detest church organs I have always liked the bells that peal out over the streets, they are never quite on key but that may be why they suggest the ancestry of music, they have that bold and happy ginggonging that makes me think of a convocation of peasants for some primitive festivity such as mass fucking in the haystacks. Anyway not many emotions can be sustained, but self-satisfaction is one of them, and as I stood there with the air ringing I could review my overall position and feel confident that it was stronger now at this point of the summer than it had been at the beginning, that I was in the gang more firmly and seemed to have secured myself with varying degrees of respect from the others, or if not respect, acquiescence. I had a gift for handling myself with grown-ups, I knew which ones to talk to, and which ones to be clever with, and which ones to shut up in front of, and I almost astonished myself that I did it all with such ease, without knowing in advance what I was doing, and having it come out right most of the time. I could be a Bible student, and I could shoot a gun. Whatever they had asked me to do I had done it. But more than that, I knew now I could discern Mr. Schultz's inarticulate genius and give it language, which is to say avoid its wrath. Abbadabba Berman was uncannily perceptive, he had surprised me with my Automatic in that same manner of advanced thinking that allowed him to know exactly where I lived when he used the Bronx precinct cop to summon me. But I was no longer awed. Besides, he was so clearly given over to my education, how could I have gotten this far if he knew everything about me and could scan my mind, awake or dreaming, and know what inherited empowerment was looped in there, like my fate? Even if he knew about me exactly what I feared most, and I was still here, and not only here but growing and filling out to his hopes, then he had his own purposes for me, and my secret was good anyway. But I didn't really believe that he knew, I believe that

in the most important knowledge I was now ahead of him, and
that his inadequacy, finally, was that he would know everything
except the crucial thing.

So I felt that things couldn't be better, I was elated just to be
in the company I was in, there seemed to me no limit to the
heights of which I was capable, Drew was right, I was a pretty
little devil, as the eminent guest went up the steps and into the
church with Mr. Schultz I even wished that someone had introduced me, or that I might have at least been noticed, though I
had made a point not to be, but I was not put out, I knew that
in the excitement of historic moments the niceties are sometimes scanted, I was directly behind these great men looking up
at their haircuts, I was in a line of ascension with these famous
gangsters of my yearnings, I was feeling generous and eager to
give everyone the benefit of every doubt, even at the back of the
line, at the bottom of the front steps, and the last in the procession that stopped now in the church entrance and waited while
the regular service went on until it was time for Father Montaine
to come off the altar and greet Mr. Schultz and usher him in to
the church building as a symbol of his entrance to Catholicism.

As it happened this would take longer than anyone expected.
Abbadabba Berman came back down the stairs to have himself
a smoke on the sidewalk, I cupped the match for him against the
wind, and then Irving came out to join us, and the three of us
leaned with our backs against the visitors' glamorous streamlined Chrysler parked at the curb, and ignoring the other cars
at each end of the block, we faced the edifice of St. Barnabas with
its clapboard siding and wooden steeple. The bells now ceased
with a little sequence of tapping afterthoughts, softer and softer,
and I could hear faintly the different sound from inside the
church of its organ. At this moment Irving came as close to a
criticism of Dutch Schultz as I was ever to hear him utter.

"Of course," he said, as if he was continuing a conversation,
"the Dutchman is wrong about one thing, he has no idea why
the old Jews pray that way. Maybe if he knew he wouldn't say
those things. Kid, you know the explanation of that?"

"I'm not big on religion," I said.

"I am not a religious man myself," Irving said, "but the way they nod and bow and don't keep still a minute, there's a very reasonable explanation for that. It's the way it is with candles, the old men praying in the synagogue are the flames of candles that sway back and forth leaning one way and another way, every one of them nodding and bowing like a little candle flame. That's the little light of the soul, which of course is always in danger of blowing out. So that's what that is all about," Irving said.

"That's very interesting, Irving," Mr. Berman said.

"But Dutch wouldn't know that. All he knows is it bothers him," Irving said in his quiet voice.

Mr. Berman held his elbow so that the hand holding the cigarette was up around his ear, which was his favorite position for thinking: "But when he says the Christians do everything in unison, he's right about that. They got a central authority. They sing together and they chant and they sit down and they stand up and they kneel and they do things in an orderly manner, everything under control. So he's right about that," Mr. Berman said.

When things finally got going I found myself sitting in a pew up front next to Drew Preston, which is where I wanted to be. I reminded myself that it was all right, that nothing had happened yet except that I had been admitted into the secret mysterious realm of her afflictions. That was all. She did not acknowledge me, which I both appreciated and agonized over at the same time. I blindly turned the pages of the missal. Her face in the church under her hat glowed in the soft colors of stained glass and suggested for me the more appropriate and ennobling role as her boy protector. But I wanted to fuck her so badly I could hardly stand. I didn't know if I would survive the service. Mr. Schultz had called this the short form and that made me wonder what the long form was like, in fact I understood for the first time the meaning of the word *eternal.*

I remember just a few things from the entire excruciatingly eternal service. The first was that Mr. Schultz went through it all, he was nominated, baptized, confirmed, and partook of the Eucharist, with his shoelace untied. The second was that when his honored godparent, standing just behind him, was directed by Father Montaine to place his hand on his shoulder, Mr. Schultz nearly jumped out of his skin. Maybe I fixed on these odd things because most everything else was going on in Latin and only when something actually happened did I really pay attention. I think Father Montaine was the only man in the world who would be allowed to pour a pitcher of water over Dutch Schultz's head not once but three times without suffering the consequences. He did this in a way I thought was lusty and full of liturgical enthusiasm as Mr. Schultz each time came up sputtering, with his eyes red and glaring while he tried to smooth his hair back without seeming to.

But the last thing I remember about that morning was the enigmatic presence at my side of my beautiful and amazing Drew, who became more innocent in my view the more devilishly I thought about her. She seemed to drink up the church music and become enameled in sanctity like one of the nun saints up in a niche on the wall. In the way my spinning world revolved now like some fiendishly juggled ball of God, her failure to acknowledge my presence beside her confirmed our conspiracy in my heart. I knew I could no longer deceive myself that I didn't adore her, and wouldn't destroy myself in submission to her, the moment, with the organ blasting away and the congregation singing at its most sacred pitch, she raised her white-gloved fingers to her lips and yawned.

PART
THREE

FIFTEEN

The trial was almost upon us. I pulled my pistol practice and ran errands for Dixie Davis, who was by now in residence on the sixth floor. One morning when I had to deliver a letter for him to the courthouse clerk I stopped afterward to look through the little porthole windows of the doors to the court-rooms. None were occupied. Nobody said not to so I went into Part One and sat down. It was an open uncluttered kind of place, as opposed, say, to a precinct station: wood-paneled walls and big windows that were raised for the breeze and light globes hanging by chains from the ceiling. All the furniture in place for judge, jury, prosecution, defense, and audience. It was very quiet. I heard the ticking of the wall clock behind the bench. The courtroom sat there waiting was the impression I had. I had the impression that behind the waiting was a limitless patience. I understood the law had a prophetic utility.

I found myself entertaining a guilty conviction. I pictured Mr. Schultz being led off by the guards with the gang of all of us standing by not doing anything. I imagined him led away in an apoplectic rage, my last glimpse of his murderous being seg-mented by the diamond crisscross chain link welded across the rear windows of the Black Maria. I felt very bad.

Here I will say about Dutch Schultz that wherever he went he created betrayals of himself, he produced them perpetually from the seasons of his life, he brought betrayers forth from his nature, each in our own manner shape and size but having the common face of betrayal, and then he went murdering after us. Not that I didn't know, not that I didn't know. I took the elevator each night to the Schultz family dinner table and sat there aching in love or terror, it was hard to tell which.

A couple of nights before the trial a man named Julie Martin appeared who everyone in the gang knew except me. He was a stout man with jowls that shook as he talked, he was very much taller than Mr. Schultz or Dixie Davis, but he walked with a cane and wore a slipper on one foot. His eyes were very tiny and of indeterminate color and he needed a shave, he was gruff, with a voice even deeper than the Dutchman's, and he was not at all well groomed, dark hairs curled off the back of his neck and his enormous hands had blackened fingernails as if he spent his time working on automobiles.

Drew Preston excused herself from dinner almost immediately and I was relieved she did. The fellow was trouble. Mr. Schultz treated him with a sardonic respect and addressed him as Mr. President. I didn't know why until I remembered Mr. Schultz's restaurant shakedown business in Manhattan, the Metropolitan Restaurant and Cafeteria Owners Association. Julie Martin had to be the man who ran it, that's what he was president of, and because most of the fashionable restaurants in the midtown area had joined the association, including Lindy's and the Brass Rail, Steuben's Tavern and even Jack Dempsey's, he was a pretty important man about town. He wouldn't be the one who actually threw the stink bomb through the window when the owner was reluctant to join the association, so I didn't understand why his fingernails were dirty or why he needed a haircut or why generally he didn't exude the confidence of a successful man of the rackets.

Apart from the occasional stink bomb, restaurant extortion was an invisible business, even more invisible than policy and almost as profitable. While diners were dining in the fine Broadway steakhouses, or while the old men were sitting in the cafe-

terias over their cups of coffee or sliding their trays past the hot
table with its perpetual steam rising from the cooked carrots and
cauliflower, the business went invisibly and brilliantly forward
on the discreet conversation of men who were not ever, at the
moment of their visits to any establishment, hungry.

Mr. Schultz was telling Julie Martin about his day of entry into
the Catholic Church and bragging about who it was who had
sponsored him. Julie Martin was not terribly impressed. He was
a rude man and acted as if he had more important matters to
attend to elsewhere. A bottle of whiskey was on the table, as
there was now every night, and he kept pouring himself half
tumblers of rye and drinking them down like table water. At one
point he dropped his fork on the floor and called to the waitress,
"Hey you!" as she was going past carrying a tray full of dirty
dishes. She nearly dropped them. Mr. Schultz was by now fond
of this girl, she was the one whom no generosity of tip or banter-
ing small talk could persuade that she was not each night at
dinner in danger of losing her life. Mr. Schultz had told me it
was his ambition to lure her to New York to work in the Embassy
Club, a great joke considering her all-consuming dread of
him. "For shame, Mr. President," he said now. "This ain't one
of your union help. You're in the country now, watch your
manners."

"Yeah, I'm in the country all right," the big man said in his
basso. Then he delivered himself of a prodigious belch. I knew
boys who had this ability, I had never trained in it myself, it was
a weapon of the boor and implied a similar aptitude at the
opposite end of the digestive system. "And if I can get through
this lousy dinner and you can get around to telling me what's
on your mind that's so important I had to come all the way up
here I'll be able to get the fuck out of your goddamn country and
not too soon to suit me."

Dixie Davis sent a fearful glance in Mr. Schultz's direction.
"Julie's a true New Yorker," he said with his down-at-the-mouth
smile. "Take them out of Manhattan they go bananas."

"You've got a big mouth, you know that, Mr. President?" said
Dutch Schultz looking at the man over his wineglass.

I didn't wait for dessert, even though it was apple cobbler, but went up to my room and locked the door and turned on the radio. Eventually I heard them all come out of the elevator and go into Mr. Schultz's suite. For a moment all their voices were talking at the same time in a kind of part song of diverse intent. Then the door slammed. In my peculiar state of mind I had an idea that seemed to me quite rational, that somehow I had invoked the argument, that my secret transgression had fired the metaphysical Dutchmanic rage, and that it happened only for the moment to be directed inaccurately at another of his men, and a valuable one too, as Bo was valuable. Not that I had any sympathy for the huge boor with the bad foot. I didn't know exactly what the fight was about except that it was serious enough and loud enough for me to hear the sound of it, if not the exact words, when I sneaked down the corridor and stood in front of the door. The exchange of angers terrified me because it was so close, like the loud close thunderclap of a lightning storm still some distance away, and I kept going back and forth from my room to the corridor to see if Drew's door was closed, to make sure she was not involved, and whenever the radio static crackled with extra snap I imagined I had heard a gunshot and ran out again.

This all went on over an hour or more, and then, it must have been about eleven o'clock, I did hear the real gunshot, there is no question what it is when it is that, the report is definitive, it caroms through the chambers of the ear, and when its echoes died away I heard the silence of the sudden subtraction from the universe of a life, and this time in the quaking reality of what I knew I sat on the side of my bed too paralyzed even to stand up and lock my room door. I sat there with my Automatic fully loaded and held it under a pillow on my lap.

What did I mean to have come with these men to their ferocious business in upstate hotels, was it to understand, only to understand? I had known nothing of their lives a few short months ago. I tried to believe they could have been doing all this without me. But it was too late, and they were so strange, they were all so strange. They all roiled up out of the same idea because they seemed to understand each other and make their measured responses accordingly, but I kept losing my fix on it, I was still to know what it was, this idea.

I can't say how many minutes passed. The door flew open and Lulu was standing there beckoning with his finger. I left my gun and hurried after him down the corridor into Mr. Schultz's suite. The furnishings were awry, the chairs were pushed back, this Julie Martin lay in his bulk across the coffee table in the living room, he was not yet dead but lay gasping on his stomach with his head turned sideways and a rolled-up hotel towel under his cheek and another towel rolled up neatly behind his head to take the blood, and both towels were reddening quickly, and he was gasping, and blood was trickling out of his mouth and nose and his arms hanging over the table were trying to find something to hold on to and his knees were on the floor and he was pushing back, pushing the tips of his feet with their one shoe off and one shoe on against the floor as if he was trying to get up, as if he thought he could still get away, or swim away, it was kind of a slow-motion breaststroke he was doing, whereas he was only lifting his broad back in the air and then slumping down again under its weight, and Irving was bringing more towels from the bathroom to put beside the coffee table where blood was dripping to the floor and Mr. Schultz was standing there looking down at this immense tortoiselike body, with its waving arms and eyes glazed blind like eyes from the sea, and he said to me, very calmly, quietly, "Kid, you got good vision, we none of us can locate the shell, would you be so good as to find it for me?"

I scrambled around on the floor and found under the couch the brass casing still warm of the thirty-eight-caliber round from his gun, which showed now under his belt with his jacket open, his tie was pulled down from his collar but somehow in this moment he glittered with a calm orderliness in all this mess of blood and unfinished death, he was still and thoughtful, and he thanked me courteously for the shell, which he dropped in his pants pocket.

Dixie Davis was sitting in a corner holding his arms around himself, he was groaning as if he was the one who had been shot.

There was a soft knock on the door and Lulu opened it to admit Mr. Berman. Jumping to his feet Dixie Davis said, "Otto! Look what he's done, look what he's done to me!"

Mr. Schultz and Mr. Berman exchanged glances. "Dick," Mr. Schultz said to the lawyer, "I am very very sorry."

"To subject me to this!" Dixie Davis said, wringing his hands. He was pale and trembling.

"I am sorry, Counselor," Mr. Schultz said. "The son of a bitch stole fifty thousand of my dollars."

"A member of the bar!" Dixie Davis said to Mr. Berman, who was looking now at the agonized aimlessly repetitious movements of the sprawled body. "And he does this thing with me standing there? Takes out his gun in the middle of a sentence and shoots into the man's mouth?"

"Just calm down, Counselor," Mr. Berman said. "Just calm down. Nobody heard a thing. Everyone is asleep. They go to bed early in Onondaga. We will take care of this. All you have to do is go to your room and close the door and forget about it."

"I was seen at dinner with him!"

"He left right after dinner," Mr. Berman said looking at the dying man. "He went away. Mickey drove him. Mickey won't be back till tomorrow. We have witnesses."

Mr. Berman went to the window, looked out from behind the curtain, and pulled the shade down. He went to the other window and did the same thing.

"Arthur," Dixie Davis said, "do you realize in a matter of hours there will be federal lawyers from New York checking into this hotel? Do you realize in two days your trial starts? In two days?"

Mr. Schultz poured himself a drink from a decanter on the sideboard. "Kid, take Mr. Davis to his room. Put him to bed. Give him a glass of warm milk or something."

Dixie Davis's room was at the far end of the hall, near the window. I had to physically help him, he shook so badly, I had to hold his arm as if he were an old man who could not walk by himself. He was gray with fear. "Migod, migod," he kept muttering. His pompadour haircomb had collapsed over his forehead.

He was soaking with perspiration, he emitted an unpleasant smell of onions. I sat him down in the armchair by his bed. Stacks of legal papers in folders were piled on the room desk. He looked at them and started to chew on his fingernails. "I, a member of the bar of New York State," he muttered. "An officer of the court. In front of my very eyes. In front of my very eyes."

I thought perhaps Mr. Berman was right, there wasn't a sound from anywhere in the hotel as there would have been by now if the shot had been heard beyond our floor. I looked out of the corridor window and the street was empty, the streetlamps shone on stillness. I heard a door open and when I turned, there down the hall with the light behind her stood Drew Preston barefooted in her night shift of white silk, she was scratching her head and had a half-dopey smile on her lips, I will not speak here of the derangement of my senses, I pushed her back in her room and closed the door behind us and told her in urgent whispers to be quiet and go back to sleep, and I led her into her bedroom. In her bare feet she was about my height. "What happened, has something happened?" she said in her smoked-up voice full of sleep. I told her nothing and not to ask Mr. Schultz or anyone about it in the morning, just to forget it, forget it, and sealed my instruction with a kiss on her swollen mouth of sleep, and laid her down, smelling the lovely essence of her being gathered on her sheets and pillow like the meadows we had walked through, and put my hand on her small high breasts as she stretched and smiled in her moment, as always in her moment, and then I was gone and out the door, closing it quietly just as the elevator door opened at the other end of the corridor.

Mickey backed out of the elevator pulling a heavy wood-and-pipe-metal dolly, he did this as quietly as it could be done, I thought about the elevator boy and ducked behind the window drapes but Mickey had run it up himself and when he had maneuvered the dolly into the hall he turned out the light in the elevator and closed the brass gate not quite all the way.

The gang was in its element, the thing is when you're mob you move in the presence of violent death quickly and efficiently as a normal ordinary human being could not, even I, an apprentice, half-ill with dread and distraction, was able to follow orders and think and move in constructive response to the emergency. I don't know what they did to the body to make it still but it lay now quite dead across the coffee table and Irving was spreading editions of the New York dailies and the *Onondaga Signal* on the dolly, someone said one two three and the men rolled the immense cadaver of Julie Martin off the coffee table onto the newspapers, death is dirt, death is garbage, and that is the attitude they had toward it, Lulu wrinkling his nose and Mickey even averting his head as they handled this sack of human offal. Mr. Schultz sat in an armchair with his arms on the armrests like Napoleon and he didn't even bother looking, he was thinking ahead, planning what? convinced in his instinctive genius that however abrupt and sudden his murderous act had been, it had chosen the moment well, which is why the great gangsters don't get caught except by numbers and tally sheets and tax laws and bankbooks and other such amoral abstractions whereas the murders rarely stick to them. It was Abbadabba Berman who supervised the cleanup, pacing up and down in that sideways scuttle of his, his hat pushed back on his head, the cigarette in his mouth, it was Mr. Berman who thought to retrieve the cane and put it beside the body. He said to me, "Kid, go to the lobby and cover it so nobody notices the arrow."

I ran down the fire stairs three at a time, flight after flight, swinging around the landing posts, and got to the lobby, where the elevator boy sat dozing on the side chair next to the big snake plant with his arms folded across his tunic and his head on his chest. The clerk was similarly occupied behind his desk under the mailboxes. The lobby was empty and the street as well. I watched the indicator and in a minute the arrow began to swing around the circle, it came down around the one and kept going, to stop at the basement.

Out behind the hotel I knew they would have the car and that details I couldn't even anticipate would have already been thought through, there was a kind of comfort in that, I was an accessory after the fact, among my other problems, and when the elevator came back up to the lobby and the door opened

Mickey put his finger to his lips and left the elevator as he had found it, lit, but with the brass folding gate pulled across, and he sneaked right back out to the fire stairs and after a minute I coughed loudly and woke the elevator boy, who was a Negro man with gray hair, and he took me up to the sixth floor and bid me goodnight. I might have congratulated myself for my essay in coldblood cunning except for what happened next. In Mr. Schultz's suite, Lulu had remained to put the furniture back in position and Mr. Berman came in the door with a set of keys and a pile of fresh white towels from the chambermaids' closet, I admired all the details of their professionalism, I thought of the crime as committed on one of those writing tablets for kids where the drawing disappears when you lift the page. Finally roused, as if from a slumber, Mr. Schultz stood and walked around the room to see that everything looked as it should, and then he stared at the carpet near the coffee table where there soaked in a dark black stain, with several drops beside like moons around a planet, the blood of the former president of the Metropolitan Restaurant and Cafeteria Owners Association, and then he went to the phone and woke up the desk clerk and said, "This is Mr. Schultz. We have an accident here and I need a doctor. Yes," he said. "As soon as you can. Thank you."

I was puzzled and somewhat alarmed, my mind struggled to understand what it knew only as something so enigmatic that it could not be good for me. Everyone else in the room was now deadly casual. Mr. Schultz stood looking out the window for several minutes and just as I heard the sputter of a car coming down the street he turned back to the room and told me to stand over by the coffee table. Mr. Berman sat down and lit a new cigarette from the old one, and then Lulu came over to me as if to adjust my position, because it was apparently not quite right, he positioned me and continued to hold my shoulders and just at the moment of my revelation but a moment too late I thought I saw him grin with a flash of one gold tooth, although maybe the slowness of my mind on this occasion was a blessing because actually as he swung I did not have the opportunity to reveal anything less than total sacrificial loyalty, it would not have done in this hierarchy of men to say why me why me, a blinding pain struck me dumb, my knees buckled, and a starlike flash exploded in my eyes, just the way prizefighters say it does, and an instant later I was crouched over, groaning and dribbling in my shock, holding both my hands over my poor nose, my best feature, bleeding profusely now through my fingers to the stained rug, and so I contributed the final detail of the Schultz gang's brilliant representations in matters of applied death, mixing my blood with the dead gangster's and suffering my rage of injustice as I heard the businesslike rap of our country doctor knocking on the door.

I remember what that whack across the face did to the passage of time, in the instant I felt it, it became an old injury and the rage it engendered in me was an ancient resolve to somehow pay them back, to get even—all this in the space of a moment's obliterating pain. While I had thought when I heard the gunshot that it could have been meant as appropriately for me, I thought the broken nose was uncalled-for. I was really upset and felt badly used, my courage flowed back with my anger and I was renewed in the heedless righteousness of my appetites. All night I kept an ice bag on my face so that the swelling would not disfigure me and make Drew Preston think I was no longer pretty. In the morning it was not as bad as I had expected, a certain puffiness, and a blueness under the eyes that might be attributed as well to debauchery as to a good sock.

I went out for breakfast as usual, I found that the act of chewing was painful, my lip was a little sore too, but I swore I would be as hardened and casual about the awful night that had just passed as anyone else. I put the image of that rising and slumping dead man out of my head. When I got back Mr. Berman's office door was open across the hall and I caught his eye and he motioned me to come in and close the door. He was on the phone, holding it under his chin with a raised shoulder and going over some adding-machine tapes with the person on the other end. When he had hung up he indicated a chair beside the desk, and I sat down like a client in his office.

"We are moving shop," he said. "We're moving out tonight and only Mr. Schultz and the lawyers will be in residence. The day after tomorrow begins the jury selection. It would not look good for the boys to be hanging around during a trial what with the press descended."

"The press will be here?"

"What do *you* think? It's gonna be like a hive of hornets has got loose in Onondaga. They'll crawl all over everything."

"The *Mirror* too?"

"What do you mean, of course, all of them. Newspapermen are the creeps of the earth, they have no sense of honor or decency and they are totally lacking in the ethics of behavior. If he was just Arthur Flegenheimer do you think they would find him worth the attention? But Dutch Schultz is a name that fits in the headline."

Mr. Berman shook his head and made a gesture, lifting his hand and letting it fall into his lap. I had never seen him so disconcerted. He was not his usual dapper self this morning, he was in working trousers and shirtsleeves and suspenders and bedroom slippers and he hadn't yet shaved that pointed chin. "Where was I?" he said.

"We are moving out."

He studied my face. "It's not too bad," he said. "A bump adds character. Does it hurt?"

I shook my head.

"Lulu got carried away. He was supposed to bloody your nose, not break it. Everyone is under a strain."

"It's okay," I said.

"Needless to say the whole thing was unfortunate." He looked around on his desk for his cigarettes, found a pack with one cigarette left, lit it, and leaned back in his swivel chair crossing his legs and holding the cigarette up around his ear. "It sometimes happens that there is more life than you can keep book on, and that is certainly true of up here, this is an unnatural existence, and why we got to get through this trial as quickly as possible and get back home where we belong. Which brings me to what I want to say. Mr. Schultz will be very busy from now on, he'll be in the spotlight, in court and out of it, and we don't want him to have anything on his mind except the problem to hand. Does that make good sense to you?"

I nodded.

"Well then why can't she understand that? This is a serious business, we can't afford any more mistakes, we've got to keep our wits about us. All I want is for her to take a powder for a few days. Go to Saratoga, see the races, is that too much to ask?"

"You mean Mrs. Preston?"

"She wants to see the trial. You know what will happen if she walks into that courtroom. I mean won't it bother her to have her picture taken as a mystery woman or some other goddamn cockamamie thing that they will cook up? That her husband will know? To say nothing of Mr. Schultz is a married man."

"Mr. Schultz is married?"

"To a lovely lady waiting for him and worrying about him in New York City. Yes. What do you keep asking all these questions for? We are all married men, kid, we got mouths to feed, families to support. Onondaga has been a tough son of a bitch for every one of us and it will all be for naught if love conquers all."

He was looking at me very intently now, not being sly in his study of my reactions or the thoughts that might be visible on my face. He said: "I know you been spending more time with Mrs. Preston than I or the boys, even from that first night when you walked her back to her apartment and kept an eye on her. Is that fair to say?"

"Yes," I said, my throat going dry. I could not swallow or he would see the rise and fall of my Adam's apple.

"I want you to talk to her, explain to her why laying low for a while is in the Dutchman's interests. Will you do that?"

"Does Mr. Schultz want her to go?"

"He does and he doesn't. He's leaving it up to her. You know, there are women," he said almost as if to himself. He paused. "There always is. But in all our years I have never seen him like this. What is it, he won't let himself admit he knows better, that she takes men down like bowling pins, what is it?"

At that moment the phone rang. "You haven't failed me so far," he said, turning in his chair and leaning forward to pick up the receiver. He gave me his look over the tops of his eyeglasses. "Don't fuck up now."

I went in my room to think. It couldn't have been more perfect, like an affirmation of my wish for release from the life and task I had chosen for myself, and I knew exactly what I would do from the moment he told me to talk to her. Not that I didn't appreciate the danger. Were these my own thoughts of freedom or was I acting under his influence? This was really dangerous, they were all married people, willful and unpredictable mad passionate adults with God knows what depths of depravity, they lived hard and struck suddenly. And Mr. Berman hadn't told me everything, regardless of what he said, I didn't know if he was speaking for himself only or for Mr. Schultz as well. I didn't know if I was supposed to be working for Mr. Schultz in this matter, or conspiring to do what was in Mr. Schultz's best interests.

If Mr. Berman was shooting straight with me I could be gratified that he appreciated my utility as a superior brain in the outfit, he was handing me an assignment nobody else could handle as well, including himself. But if he knew what was going on between Mrs. Preston and me he could be telling me just the same things he had told me. If we were going to be murdered would it not be somewhere else than Onondaga? If Mr. Schultz could not afford her anymore? If he found me expendable? He murdered people who acted on his behalf at a distance from him. I knew for a possibility that if I left I was going away to die because either he knew my heart's secret in which case he would kill me, or my being gone from his sight would create the betrayal in his imagination that would amount to the same thing.

Yet what was any of this speculation but the symptom of my own state of mind? I would think of nothing like this if my conscience was clear and I was intent only to advance myself. I found myself starting to pack. I had a lot of clothes now and a fine soft leather suitcase with brass snaps and two cinch belts,

I folded my things neatly, a new habit, and tried to think of the first moment when I would have the chance to talk to Drew Preston. I was feeling the first yawning intimations of the nausea I recognized as pure dread, but there was no question that I was going to make the best of the opportunity Mr. Berman had presented me. I knew what Drew would say. She would say she hadn't wanted to leave me. She would say she had big plans for her darling devil. She would say I was to tell Mr. Berman she was ready to go to Saratoga but wanted me to go with her.

That night, while Drew accompanied Mr. Schultz to the district school gymnasium, where he was throwing his big end-of-summer party for everyone in Onondaga, I moved out of the hotel with the rest of the gang, I didn't even know where we were going, only that we were going there, bag and baggage, in two cars, with an open truck following with Lulu Rosenkrantz sitting in the back with the steel safe and a stack of mattresses. The whole time in the country I had never gotten used to the night because it was so black, I didn't even like to look out of my window because the night was so implacably black, in Onondaga the streetlights made the stores and buildings into shapes of night, and out past the edges of town the endless night was like a vast and terrible loss of knowledge, you couldn't see into it, it did not have volume and transparency like the nights of New York, it did not suggest day was coming if you waited and were patient, and even when the moon was full it only showed you the black shapes of the mountains and the milky black absences of the fields. The worst part was that country nights were the real ones, once you rolled across the Onondaga Bridge and your headlights picked up the white line of the country road, you knew what a thin glimmering trail we make in that unmappable blackness, how the heat of your heart and your motor is as sufficient in all that dimensionless darkness as someone still not quite dead in his grave for whom it makes no difference if his eyes are opened or closed.

I was frightened to belong so devoutly to Mr. Schultz. I was made bleak in my mind by his rule. You can live in other people's decisions and make a seemingly reasonable life for yourself, until the first light of rebellion shows you the character of all of them, which is their tyranny. I didn't like for Drew to be back there with him while I was driven like the baggage. The distance would not be that great, only twelve miles or so as I was surprised to see from a surreptitious check of the mileage when we arrived, but I felt each mile attenuated my connection with Drew Preston, I was not confident her feelings could endure.

We pulled up to this house, who had found it, rented it or bought it, I was never to know, it was a farmhouse but there was no farm, just this run-down clapboard house with the leaning porch situated atop a dirt ramp rising suddenly up from the road, so that the porch looked over the road east and west from this bluff that was really not set back from the road but more like on top of it. Behind the house was a steeper hill of woods blacker than the night, if that was possible.

This was the new headquarters, which we were to see first by flashlight. Inside smelled very bad, the polite word is "close," which is the smell of an old unlived-in wood house, and the windows were rotted shut, and animals had lived here and left their droppings now dried to dust, and there was a narrow stairs going up from the entryway and what I supposed was a living room through a door on one side of the entryway, and a short hall going straight back under the stairs to a kitchen with an astonishing thing in the sink, a hand pump for water, which came up in a trickle and then a loud crashing rush of rust and muck that brought Lulu running. "Stop fucking around and pull your weight," he told me. I went outside to the truck and helped bring in mattresses and cardboard cartons filled with groceries and utensils. We were doing everything by flashlight until Irving got a fire going in the living-room fireplace, which improved matters not that much, there was a stiff dead bird on the floor who must have come in through the chimney, oh this was terrific, no question about it, I asked myself who would choose the carpeted life of hotels when he could have this historic mansion of the American Founding Fathers.

Late that night Mr. Schultz appeared, in his arms were two big

brown bags full of containers of chow mein and chop suey that
someone had brought up from Albany, and while it was not the
same thing as good Chinese food from the Bronx it was much
appreciated by all of us. Irving found some pots to warm the
stuff up and I got a fair share of everything, the chicken chow
mein over a mound of steaming rice and crisp roasted noodles,
the chop suey for the second course, litchi nuts for dessert, the
paper plates got a bit soggy but that was all right, it was a good
satisfying meal, except that it lacked tea, all I had to drink with
it was well water, while Mr. Schultz and the others washed it
down with whiskey, which they did not seem to mind at all. A
fire was going in the front room and Mr. Schultz lit a cigar and
loosened his tie, I could tell he was feeling better, and might
even be feeling good here in this hideout where he was not on
display as he had been for many weeks in Onondaga and would
be as soon again as the morning, I think there was something
bitterly comforting to him about being holed up again because
it matched his sense of his situation as someone surrounded on
all sides.

  "You boys don't have to worry about the Dutchman," he said
as we all sat around against the walls, "the Dutchman takes care
of his own. Don't think twice about Big Julie, he wasn't anyone
you should concern yourselves. Or Bo. They were no better
than Vincent Coll. They were the bad apples. You guys I love.
You guys I would do anything for. What I said long ago, my
policy still stands. You get hurt, you get sent up, or God forbid
you lose it all, you never have to worry, your families will be
taken care of as if you was still on the payroll. You know that.
All the way down to the kid here. My word is my bond. It's better
with the Dutchman than with the Prudential Life Assurance.
Now this trial, in a few days we will be clear. While the Feds have
been fucking away the summer on the beach we been up here
sowing our oats. Public opinion is on our side. You shoulda seen
that party tonight. I mean it wasn't your or my idea of a party,
when we get back to town that will be a party, but this, the rubes
loved it. In the high school gymnasium with the crepe paper and
the balloons. I had one of them back-hill fiddle-and-banjo bands

playing their doughsee doughs and all the hands right. Hell I danced myself. I danced with my babe in all that crowd of washed and laundered hardship. I have become very attached to them. Not a wiseass will you find in the countryside, just hardworking slobs, work till they keel over. But they got one or two cards in their hand. The law is not majestic. The law is what public opinion says it is. I could tell you a lot about the law. Mr. Hines could tell you more. When we had the important precincts, when we had the magistrates court, when we had the Manhattan D.A.? Wasn't that the law? We got a man to argue for me tomorrow who wouldn't have me to dinner in his house. He talks on the phone with the president. But I have paid his price and he will be at my side for as long as it takes. So that's what I mean. The law is the vigorish I pay, the law is my overhead. The hondlers, they make this legal, they make that illegal, judges, lawyers, politicians, who are they but guys who have their own angle into the rackets except they like to do it without getting their hands dirty? You gonna respect that? Respect will kill you. Save your respect for yourselves."

He was speaking softly, modulating his resonant rasp even here twelve miles out of Onondaga in this house that could barely be noticed from the road in the daytime. Maybe it was the darkness of firelight that did it, the expression of the private mind in the intimacy of a fire, when you hear only your own thoughts in the night and see only shadows.

"But you know, it's a kind of honor, isn't it," he said. "After all, people have been counting out the Dutchman for quite a while now. And yet the whole world has followed me here, it's almost like Onondaga is another borough. Starting the other day with my new best friend from the downtown mobs. So I must be all right. See? I got my rosary. I carry it all the time. I will take it into court with me. This is a nice evening, this is good booze. I feel good now. I feel at peace."

Upstairs were two small bedrooms and after Mr. Schultz drove back to town I went to sleep in one of them in my clothes on a mattress on the floor with my head in the gable where I tried to believe I could see through the opaque windowpane to stars in the night sky. I did not question why with only two small bedrooms one was mine, perhaps I assumed it was my due as a boy with a governess. In the morning when I awoke two other guests whom I didn't recognize were asleep on their mattresses in their clothes except that they had hung their guns in their shoulder holsters from hooks on the wood door. I stood up, stiff and cold, and went downstairs and outside, it was barely dawn, there was some question in this moment as to whether the world would actually come back, it seemed in some sort of wet wavering drift as if it was not up to the task, but from this whitish blackness something detached itself, twenty yards down the road and at my eye level a man I recognized as Irving was at the top of a telephone pole and splicing a wire which was the same black wire that came up the dirt ramp and went past my feet into the front door. And then I looked across the road and saw down there a white house with green trim and an American flag hanging from a big pole in the front yard, and in a pine grove behind the house sprinkled among the trees were several tiny cabins of the same white with green trim and beside one of them the black Packard was parked pointed to the road with its windshield covered with frost.

I went around to the back of our hillside manse and found an ideal spot for a lengthy and meditative urination. I imagined that if I had to live here I could create a gorge as monumentally geographical as the one Drew Preston had found on our walk. Mr. Schultz seemed to have beefed up the firepower, if I understood correctly the two snoring strangers upstairs. I noted too of this ramshackle house on its bluff that it provided a good prospect of the road in both directions. And someone sticking a tommy gun out the window of his car couldn't just tear on past and shoot it up. All this was of technical interest to me.

But in a matter of hours I was leaving, although I didn't know for how long and to what end. My life was estranged from me, whatever my resolve I no longer was childish enough to feel it was commanding. Last night as we had sat in the firelight I had felt I was one of them in a way not just my own, not just of my

own thinking, but in the common assumption of our meal
shared in the empty hideout house, disguised by the bad light
as a grown-up, a man in the rackets, once in never out, and
perhaps this more than church bells ringing was the true quiet
signal of the end of my provisional determination, the snuffing-
out of my unconscious conviction that I could escape Mr.
Schultz anytime I wished. Now I thought this layout was more
truly theirs, more like the real habitat of their lives, than any
other place I had seen. I was impatient for people to get up. I
wandered about, I was hungry. I missed my tea shop breakfast
and I missed my *Onondaga Signal,* which I liked to read over
breakfast, and I missed my big white bathroom with the hot
water shower. You would think I'd lived in fine hotels all my life.
I stood on the porch and looked in the living-room window. On
a wood table was Mr. Berman's adding machine and the hot
phone Irving was in the process of hooking up, there was an old
kitchen chair with a tall back, and prominently in the middle of
the floor, the Schultz company safe. The safe seemed to glow for
me as the indisputable center of the upheaval of the past twenty-
four hours. I thought of it not only as the repository of Mr.
Schultz's cash deposits but as the strongbox for Abbadabba's
world of numbers.

Irving saw me and put me to work, I had to sweep the floors
and go around to all the windows and wipe them down so you
could see out of them, I chopped wood by hand for the kitchen
stove, which made my tender nose throb with pain, I hiked to
a general store about a mile away and bought paper plates and
bottles of Nehi for everyone's breakfast, I was as deep in nature
as you could get, like a damn Boy Scout at a jamboree. Irving
left in the Packard with Mickey and so Lulu was in charge then
and he put me to work out in back digging a latrine, there was
an outhouse there that looked perfectly usable to me though it
tilted a bit, but Lulu found it offended his sensibilities to use a
strange outhouse and so I had to take a shovel and dig this hole
in a clear and level place in the woods above the house going
into the soft earth around and around deeper and deeper with
my hands getting blistered and sore before one of the men took

over, I had thought I had imagined all the possible dangers attached to a life in crime, but death by excrement had escaped me. Only when Irving came back and resolutely built a small throne of pine boards for the hole did I remember what dignity lay in labor that was done with style, whatever the purpose, he was a model for us all, Irving.

I got myself into as clean and presentable shape as I could manage under primitive conditions and at about nine that morning I drove with Mr. Berman and Mickey into Onondaga and sat in the parked car across the public square from the courthouse. Almost every parking space was taken as the Model T's and A's and the chain-drive flatbeds came in from the countryside, and the farmers in their clean and pressed overalls and the farmers' wives in their unfashionable flowered dresses and sunbonnets climbed the steps and went through the doors for their impaneling. I saw the government lawyers with their briefcases walking up the hill from the hotel, I saw Dixie Davis looking very solemn beside the older portly lawyer with his rimless glasses dangling from their black ribbon, and then, slouching along in twos and threes, the fellows with the writing pads sticking out of their jacket pockets and the morning paper rolled under their arms and their little press cards like decorative feathers in the headbands of their fedoras. I studied the reporters very carefully, I wished I knew which of them was the *Mirror,* whether he was the one with horn-rim glasses who bounded up the steps two at a time or the one with his tie knot pulled down and his collar open at the neck, you could only guess about reporters, they never wrote about themselves, they were just these bodiless words of witness composing for you the sights you would see and the opinions you would have without giving themselves away, like magicians whose tricks were words.

Up at the top of the stairs news photographers with big Speed-Graphics in their hands stood around not taking pictures of the people going past them into the building.

"Where's Mr. Schultz?" I said.

"He snuck inside a half hour ago, while those jokers was still eating their breakfast."

"He's famous," I said.

"That's the tragedy in a nutshell," Mr. Berman said. He took out a wad of one-hundred-dollar bills and counted out ten of them. "When you're in Saratoga don't let her out of your sight. Whatever she wants, pay for it. This one has got a mind of her own, which could be inconvenient. There's a place called the Brook Club. It's ours. You have any problems you speak to the man there. You understand?"

"Yes," I said.

He handed me the bills. "Not for your personal betting," he said. "If you want to make a few bucks for yourself, you'll be calling me every morning anyway. I know something, I'll tell you. You understand?"

"Yes."

He handed me a torn piece of paper with his secret phone number on it. "Horses or women alone is bad enough. Together they can kill you. You handle Saratoga, kid, I'll believe you can handle anything." He sat back in the seat and lit a cigarette. I got out of the car and took my suitcase from the trunk and waved goodbye. I thought in this moment I understood the limits of Mr. Berman, he was sitting in this car because it was the closest he could get to the courtroom, he couldn't go where he wanted to go and that made him plaintive, a little humpbacked man with over-colorful clothes and Old Gold cigarettes the two indulgences of his arithmetized life, I felt looking back at him watching me from the car window that he was someone who could not function without Dutch Schultz, as if he were only an aspect of him, reflected into brilliance by him, and as dependent as he was needed. I thought Mr. Berman was the curious governor of this amazing genius of force, who if he one moment lost his spin would lose it forever.

SIXTEEN

A moment later a beautiful dark green four-door convertible came into the square, and it took me a moment to realize Drew was driving it, she didn't quite stop but drifted past me in low gear, I heaved my valise into the back, stepped on the running board, and as she put the car into second and picked up speed I vaulted over the door into the seat beside her and we were away.

I didn't look back. We went down the main street past the hotel, to which I said my secret goodbyes, and headed for the river. I had no idea where she had gotten this baby. She could do whatever she wanted to do. The seats were light brown leather. The tan canvas top was folded back on chrome stanchions so that most of it was recessed in a kind of well. The dashboard was made of burled wood. I sat with my arms on the door and the back of the seat and enjoyed the luxury of the sun shining as she turned to me and smiled.

I will say here how Drew Preston drove, it was so girlish, when she shifted she sort of leaned forward with her white hand on the gearshift knob, her slender leg draped in her dress rode down the clutch and she put her shoulders down and bit her lip in the concentration of her effort and shoved her arm straight ahead from the elbow. She wore a silk kerchief tied under her chin, she was happy to have me in her new car, we rattled across the wood bridge and came to the intersection where the road went east and west and she turned east and Onondaga was a church spire and some rooftops in a nest of trees, and then we went around a hill and it was gone.

We drove that morning down among the mountains and between lakes that lapped both sides of the road, we passed under canopies of pine and through little white villages where the general store was also the post office, she drove hard, with both hands on the wheel, and it looked like such pleasure that I wanted very badly to take a turn driving, to feel this great eight-cylinder machine moving under my hands. But one thing I hadn't yet had in my gang training was auto-driving instruction and I preferred to act to myself as if I knew how to drive and didn't care to than actually have her broach the subject, I wanted equality, the last and most absurd wish of this affection, I think now what an outrageous boy I was, with what insatiable ambition, but I had to have known it on this morning on our drive through the beautiful state of our wilderness, I had to have realized how far I had come from the streets of the East Bronx where the natural world was visible only in globules of horse manure pressed flat by passing tires, with dried seeds pecked at by the flittering flocks of street sparrows, I had to have known what it was to breathe the air of these sun-warmed mountains alive and well and well-fed with a thousand dollars in my pocket and the heinous murders of the modern world the inuring events of my brain. I was a tougher kid now, I had a real gun stuck in my belt, and I knew in my mind I must not be grateful but take what I was given as if it was my due, I felt there would be a price for all this and since the price would be in a currency too dear for life, I wanted to make it worth my while, I found myself angry at her, I kept looking at her imagining what I would do to her, I admit I entertained some mean and sadistic pictures born of my bitter boy's resignation.

Yet of course when we stopped it was because she stopped, she glanced at me and gave a bel canto sigh of capitulation and suddenly pulled off the road, bouncing along between trees and over tree roots, and jerked the car to a stop barely out of sight of any passing cars in a grove of tall high trees through which the sun flashed dappling us in moments of heat, moments of shade, moments of brilliant light, moments of dark green darkness, as we sat there looking at each other in our isolation.

The thing about Drew was she was not genitally direct, she wanted to kiss my ribs and my white boyish chest, she held my legs and ran her hands up and down the backs of my thighs, she caressed my ass and sucked my earlobes and my mouth, and she did all these things as if they were all that she wanted, she made small editorial sounds of approval or delectation, as a commentator to the action, little single high notes, whispers without words like remarks to herself, it was as if she was consuming me as an act of eating and drinking, and it wasn't designed to arouse me, what boy in that situation needed arousal? from the moment she stopped the car I was tumescent, and I waited for some acknowledgment from her that this was in fact part of me too but it didn't come and it didn't come and I flared through my need into an exquisite pain, I thought I would go mad, I became agitated and discovered only then her availability, that in all of this she was only waiting for me to find her absolute willingness to be still and listen to me for a change. This was so girlish of her, so surprisingly restrained and submissive, I was not artful but simply myself and this brought forth from her a conspiratorial laughter, it gave her the pleasure of generosity to have me in her, it was not an excitement but more like a happiness of having this boy in her, she wrapped her legs around my back and I rocked us up and down in the back seat of the car with my feet sticking out of the open door, and when I came she held her arms around me tight enough to stop my breath and she sobbed and kissed my face as if something terrible had happened to me, as if I had been wounded and she was, in an act of desperate compassion, trying to make it as if it had not happened.

Then I was following her stark naked through the brush into this noplace of such great green presence she had chosen arbi-

trarily or by happenstance, with her gift for centering the world
around herself, so that it was all very beautifully central in my
mind, the place to be, following her flashing white form around
trees, under tangles, avoiding the whip of branches, with a brilliant chatter of communities of unseen birds telling me how late
I was to have found it. And then we were going generally downward, and the ground became swampy and the air close and I
found myself slapping at stings in my skin, I had wanted to catch
her, tackle her and fuck her again, and she was doing this to me,
taking me into furies of mosquitoes. But I came upon her squat-
ting and ladling handfuls of mud over herself and we applied
this cold mud to each other and then we walked like children
into the sinking darkness of forest, hand in hand like fairy-tale
children in deep and terrible trouble, as indeed we were, and
then we found ourselves at this still pond as black as I had ever
seen water to be and of course she waded in and bid me to follow
and my God it was fetid, it was warm and scummy, my feet were
in wet mats of pond weed, I treaded water to keep my feet from
sinking and couldn't crawl back out fast enough, but she swam
on her back a few yards and then came crawling out on all fours,
and she was covered with this invisible slime, her body was
slimed as mine was and we lay in this mud and I punched into
her and held her blond head back in the mud and pumped slime
up her and we lay there rutting in this foul fen and I came and
held her down and wouldn't let her move, but lay in her with her
breath loud in my ear, and when I lifted my head and looked into
her alarmed green eyes in their panic of loss, I grew hard again
right in her and she began to move, and this time we had the
time, by the third time it takes its time, and I found the primeval
voice in her, like a death rattle, a shrill sexless bark, over and
over again as I jammed into her, and it became tremulous a
terrible crying despair, and then she screamed so shriekingly I
thought something was wrong and reared to look at her, her lips
were pulled back over her teeth and her green eyes dimmed as
I looked in them, they had lost sight, gone flat, as if her mind
had collapsed, as if time had turned in her and she had passed

back into infancy and reverted through birth into nothingness, and for an instant they were no longer eyes, for an instant they were about to be eyes, the eyes of soullessness.

Yet a few moments later she was smiling and kissing me and hugging me as if I had done something dear, brought her a flower or something.

When we staggered upright globs of mud fell from us, she laughed and turned to show me the back of her, absent in darkness, as if she had been cleaved in half, with the front of her shiny and swollen into sculpture. Even her golden head seemed halved. There was nothing for it but to go back into the pond, and then she swam further out and insisted I come after her, and the water grew cooler, it was deeper and it went on behind a bend, I swam with her stroke for stroke, giving her my best YMCA crawl, and we came out on the bank on the far side, washed clean of mud and somewhat less slick.

By the time we got back to the car we were dry, but putting clothes on was uncomfortable, as if we were covering extreme sunburns, we smelled of pond scum, we smelled like frogs, we drove off trying not to lean back in the seats and several miles down the road we came to this motor court and rented a cabin and we stood together in the shower and washed each other with a big cake of white soap and stood holding each other under the water, and then we lay on the top of the bed and she curled herself along my side with my arm around her, and perhaps created with that nuzzling gesture the moment of our truest intimacy, when by some shuddering retrenchment of her being she matched me in age and yearning for sophistication, like a boy's girlfriend, only two bodies between us and a long life ahead of terrible surprises. So I felt a kind of fearful pride. I knew I could never have the woman Mr. Schultz had had, just as he hadn't known the woman Bo Weinberg had known, because she covered her tracks, she trailed no history, suiting herself to the moment, getting her gangsters or her boys in transformative stunts of the spirit, she would never write her memoirs, this one, not even if she ever lived to an old age, she would never tell her life because she needed no one's admiration or sympathy or wonder, and because all judgments, including love, came of a language of complacency she had never wasted her time to master. So it all worked out, how protective I felt there in that cabin, I let her doze on my arm and studied a fly drifting into its caroming angles under the roof and understood that Drew Preston granted absolution, it was what you got instead of a future with her. Clearly she would not be interested in the enterprise of keeping us alive, so I would have to do that for both of us.

The rest of that day we drove down through the Adirondacks until the hills softened, the land took on a groomed look, and in the early evening we rolled into Saratoga Springs and came down a street that had the insolence to call itself Broadway. Yet as I looked there was something appropriate too, the place looked like old New York, or as I imagined it must have looked in the old days, there were very civilized shops with New York names and striped awnings lowered against the evening sun, the people strolling in the street didn't look like Onondagans at all, there was not one farmer among them, there were lots of fine cars in the traffic, some of them with uniformed chauffeurs, and people clearly of the monied classes sat on the long porches of the hotels reading newspapers. I thought it odd at the height of the evening that nobody had anything better to do than read newspapers, until we checked into our own hotel, the Grand Union, the finest of them all with the longest broadest porch, a boy took our bags, another drove off to park the car, and I saw that the newspaper of choice was the *Racing Form,* at the front desk there was a stack of them with the next day's date at the top and the next day's card for the handicappers to go to work on. And there was no news in it except horse news, in the month of August in Saratoga nobody was interested in anything but horses, and so even the newspapers conformed, giving only horse headlines and horse weather and horse horoscopes, as if the world was populated only by horses except for the scattered few numbers of eccentric humans who gathered to read about their important doings.

As I scanned the lobby I did detect one or two persons whose interest in horses might not be sincere, a couple of badly dressed men sitting in adjoining armchairs and only glancing at their papers when I noticed them. The clerk recognized Miss Drew and was pleased she had finally arrived, they were getting worried about her, he said, smiling, and I realized she had rooms for the whole month of racing whether she used them or not, it was a place she would come to at this time of year whether Mr. Schultz said to or not. We got upstairs into this grand suite of rooms that immediately made me realize what small and modest resources the Onondaga Hotel had offered, a great basket of fruit lay on a coffee table with a card from the hotel management, and there was a side bar with a tray of thin-stemmed glasses and decanters of white and red wine and a bucket with ice and a cut-glass square-cornered bottle with a little chain hanging over it with a nameplate that said BOURBON, and another that said SCOTCH, and a big seltzer bottle of blue glass, and light streamed through these long paned windows that came practically down to the floor, and big slow-turning fans hanging from the ceiling kept the air cool and the beds were immense and the carpets thick and soft. Oddly enough all of this made me think not too highly of Mr. Schultz because none of it depended on him.

Drew took delight in my reactions to this luxury especially as I tested the bedsprings with a backward lateral body fling, and she fell on top of me and we rolled one way and then the other in a playful wrestle in the guise of which we really tested each other's strength. She was no slouch, though I pinned her by the arms soon enough so that she had to say, "Oh no, not now please. I've planned this evening, I want to take you to see something marvelous."

So we dressed for the evening in our summer whites, I in my slightly wrinkled linen double-breasted suit she had ordered for me from her store in Boston, and she in a smart blue linen blazer and white pleated skirt. I loved it that we dressed in our adjoining rooms with the doors opened between us, I loved the assumption of advanced relationship in our preparations to be seen together. We came down through the hotel lobby of evening idlers including my two shabby friends, and when we stepped outside the evening was warm with the heat rising from the pavement into the cool sky, so she suggested we walk.

We crossed the avenue and I noticed that the policeman directing traffic wore a white short-sleeved shirt. I couldn't take a police department seriously that dressed like that. I didn't know what it was, this marvelous place she wanted me to see, but I thought I had better stop drowsing in dreamland. It would have been lovely to be with her still in the deep woods, but we were going past stately lawns and in the shadows of big black shade trees with enormous homes behind them, this was a well-developed and serious resort, it was tempting not to look beyond her, so dazzled by her brilliant offering as to forget the circumstances, and not one person we passed on the street failed to notice her and to react to her, which made me foolishly proud, but we were holding hands and the warmth of her hand alarmed me, it suggested her pumping blood, it created in my mind visions of terrible retribution.

"I don't mean to be coarse," I said, "but I think we'd better remember what our situation is. I'm going to let go of your hand now."

"But I like to."

"We will again. Please let go. I'm trying to tell you something. My professional opinion is we are being shadowed."

"Whatever for? Are you sure? That's so dramatic," she said, looking behind us. "Where? I don't see anyone."

"Will you please not turn around? You won't see anything, just take my word for it. Where is this place we're going? The cops in this town, when the money comes up from New York, they can't be relied on."

"For what?"

"For the protection of law-abiding citizens, which you and I are pretending to be."

"What do we have to be protected from?"

"From the likes of us. From mob."

"Am I mob?" she said.

"Only in a manner of speaking. At the most you are a moll."

"I am your moll," she said, considering it.

"You are Mr. Schultz's moll," I said.

We strode through the quiet evening. "Mr. Schultz is a very ordinary man," she said.

"Did you know he owns the Brook Club? He's well connected in this town. You get the feeling he doesn't trust you out of his sight?"

"But that's why you're here. You're my shadow."

"You asked for me," I said. "That means they would watch both of us for good measure. He's married. Did you know that?"

After a moment she said: "Yes, I think I did."

"Well where does that leave you? Do you have any idea? I want to remind you he made a mortal mistake when he took Bo out of the restaurant with you there."

"Wait," she said. She touched my arm and we stood facing each other in the dark beside a tall hedge.

"You think he's ordinary? Everyone who's dead now thought he was ordinary. The night you came out of your room. Do you remember me putting you back to bed?"

"Yes?"

"They were getting rid of a body. That fat guy with the cane. He stole some money. Not exactly your salt of the earth. I mean I'm not suggesting it's a loss to the world. But it happened."

"You poor boy. So that's what that was all about."

"This nose: Mr. Schultz had Lulu slug me to explain the spots on the rug."

"You were protecting me." I felt her cool soft lips on my cheek. "Billy Bathgate. I love that name you chose for yourself. Do you know how much I love Billy Bathgate?"

"Mrs. Preston, I'm so nuts about you I can't see straight. But I'm not even talking about that, I'm not even beginning to think about that. It was not a good idea to come here. I think maybe we ought to get out of this town. The man kills regularly."

"We should talk about it," she said and she took my hand and we came around a corner past some tall shrubbery to a brilliantly lit pavilion with people streaming into it and cars pulling up as if to a concert.

We stood under a tent lit by bare bulbs and watched these horses being walked around a dirt ring, each horse had a small velvet blanket across his back with a number on it, and people standing with printed programs in their hands were able to read about its lines and specifications. They were young horses, they had never been raced, and they were up for sale. Drew explained things in a soft voice, as if we were in church. I was extremely agitated and almost hated her for bringing us here. She couldn't concentrate on what was important. Her mind didn't work properly. I noticed of the horses their coats were glossy, their tails combed, and some of them lifted their heads up against the leash or halter or whatever it was their handlers held them by, and others walked with their heads looking at the ground, but they were all incredibly thin-legged and rhythmically beautiful. They got led around by the nose, and were bred for business and trained and raced, their lives weren't their own but they had a natural grace that was like wisdom and I found myself respecting them. They produced a nice strawy tang in the air, the smell of them amplified their great animal being. Drew gazed at them with a kind of stunned attention, she didn't say anything but merely pointed when a particular horse attracted her as even more powerfully breathtaking than the others. For some weird reason this made me jealous.

I noticed of the people examining the horses that they were very nattily got up in horse-theme sporting wear, the men with silk cravats, more than one with a long cigarette holder like President Roosevelt's, and they all had a certain nose-in-the-air carriage that made me square my shoulders. No one was as beautiful as Drew but they were her long-necked people, all very straight and thin, with an assurance bred into them, and I thought it would be nice to have a program showing their lines and specifications. At any rate I began to relax somewhat. I

calmed down. This was an impregnable kingdom of the privi-
leged. If anyone from the rackets was here he would be highly
visible. I felt from the one or two discreet glances given me that
though I wore clothes of Drew's rich good taste and had taken
the trouble to put my studious fake eyeglasses on, I just about
pushed them to the limits of their sniffing tolerance. The
thought passed my mind that Drew knew what she was doing in
her own way of making the world, just as Mr. Schultz did, without sufficient thought.

After a turn or two around the ring, the horses were led out
through a passageway into what appeared to be an amphitheater, as far as I could see from my angle of vision, with an audience in tiered seats and an announcer. Drew motioned to me
and we went outside and around to the lighted front entrance,
where the chauffeurs stood beside their cars, and came into the
amphitheater and saw the same horses from a height under the
stagey lights of the auction ring while the announcer or auction-
eer proclaimed their virtues. And then they were held by the
bridle in front of his podium while he directed the bidding,
which came not as far as I could see from any of the people in
their tiered seats but from employees like himself stationed here
and there in the crowd who communicated the bids offered
invisibly and in silence by the patrons on whose behalf they
acted. It was all very mysterious and the sums were astonishing,
going up in leaps and bounds to thirty, forty, fifty thousand
dollars. These numbers frightened even the horses, many of
whom saw fit to drop manure behind them as they were walked
into the ring. When this happened a Negro man in a tuxedo
appeared with a rake and shovel and quickly removed the offense from sight.

That was the whole show. I saw as much as I wanted to see
in about three minutes but Drew couldn't get enough of it. Up
behind the stands where we were, there was a constant traffic of
people wandering around and looking each other over in a kind
of unconscious imitation of the horses circling the ring below.
Drew met a couple she knew. Then a man came over and soon
she was in a small group of chatting friends and she made no

reference to me whatsoever. This put me in the frame of mind of the shadow I was supposed to be. I was full of scorn, the women greeting one another appeared to kiss cheeks but in fact laid them together for a moment side by side and kissed the air beside each other's ear. People were glad to see Drew. I had a sense of an adenoidal group resonance. There was some giggling I imagined was directed at me, an entirely unreasonable assumption, which I also realized, but it made me turn away and lean on a railing and look down at the horses. I didn't know what I was doing here. I felt all alone. Mr. Schultz had held Drew for some weeks, clearly I was a strong enough novelty only for a couple of days or so. I had made a mistake to reveal my fears. Fears did not hold her interest. I had told her about Julie Martin's death and it was as if I had said I had stubbed my toe.

Then she appeared at my side and gave me a sideways hug and we looked together down at a new horse being led into the ring and in thirty seconds I was back in abject love. All my resentment dissolved and I reproached myself for questioning her constancy. She said we ought to have some supper and suggested we go to the Brook Club.

"You think that's smart?" I said.

"We will be what we're supposed to be," she said. "The moll and her shadow. I'm starving, aren't you?"

So we took a cab to the Brook Club and it was really an elegant place, with an awning all the way to the curb and beveled-glass doors and leather-padded walls, a horsey kind of place in dark green with little shaded lamps on the tables and prints of famous racehorses on the walls. It was somewhat larger than the Embassy. The host looked at Drew and wasted no time in showing us to a table right up front near a small dance floor. This was the man I was supposed to contact if I had to but he looked right through me and Drew did all the ordering. We had shrimp cocktails and aged sirloin steaks and hash browns, and chopped salad with anchovies, I hadn't realized how hungry I was. She ordered a bottle of red French wine, which I shared with her, though she had most of it. It was so dark in the club that even if friends of hers from her horsey set were there they couldn't have seen far enough in that low and heavily shadowed light to recognize her. I began to feel good again. There she was across the table from me, we were cocooned in our own light, and I had to remind myself I had had intercourse with her, that I had had carnal knowledge of her, that I had made her come, because I wanted to do this all over again, but with the same yearning as if it had never happened, with the same questions about her, and wonderings and imaginings of her physical quality, as if I was looking at an actress in a movie. This was the moment I began to understand that you can't remember sex. You can remember the fact of it, and recall the setting, and even the details, but the sex of the sex cannot be remembered, the substantive truth of it, it is by nature self-erasing, you can remember its anatomy and be left with a judgment as to the degree of your liking of it, but whatever it is as a splurge of being, as a loss, as a charge of the conviction of love stopping your heart like your execution, there is no memory of it in the brain, only the deduction that it happened and that time passed, leaving you with a silhouette that you want to fill in again.

And then musicians came out on the bandstand and they were my friends from the Embassy Club, the same group, with the same skinny lackadaisical girl singer who pulled at the top of her strapless evening dress. She sat on a chair to the side and nodded in time to the first number, an instrumental, and I caught her eye and she smiled and gave me a little wave, bobbing her head in time to the music all the while, and I felt very proud to be recognized by her. Somehow she communicated my presence to the other members of the band, the saxophonist turned to me and dipped his horn and the drummer laughed to see the company I was keeping and he twirled his sticks at me and I felt right at home. "They're old friends," I said to Drew, over the music, I was happy to be able to reveal the dimension in me of Man About Town, I felt in my pocket to make sure I hadn't lost Mr. Berman's thousand dollars, I thought it would be appropriate to buy the band drinks when they finished the set.

Drew toward the end of the dinner was a little bit looped, she sat with her elbow on the table and her chin propped in her hand and gazed at me with an aimless smiling affection. I was very comfortable now, the darkness of a nightclub is sustaining, it is a kind of shelter of controlled darkness as opposed to the open darkness of the real night with the weight of the whole sky of unfathomable possibilities, the music seemed so clear and figurative, they were playing standards, one after another, and every lyric seemed meaningful and appropriate and every melodic line of the solos had the clarity of a sweet truth. And as it happened one of the songs was "Me and My Shadow," which made us laugh—*Me and my shad-ow, strolling down the aven-ue* was its sly lyric, and it came to me that a kind of message was being sent of the conspiracy we all made together, I half expected Abbadabba Berman to scuttledance into the room, it was the old thing, as usual I never felt safe from Mr. Schultz when I was separated from him, Drew's idea to come here was a good one, if we were being watched we were doing the right thing having dinner in his club, getting the money back to him as loyalists would, this was his realm and because it made me feel closer to him to be here I wasn't afraid anymore.

I decided to worry no longer and make no decisions but trust our fate to Drew's impulses, to put myself at her disposal like a real companion in Mr. Schultz's interest, she knew more than I did, she had to, and what I perceived as her impracticality had the power of her nature. She really did know her way around, and for all her recklessness she was still alive. She was, in fact, quite safe in Saratoga. I was, in fact, looking after her for Mr. Schultz. I didn't know whose idea it had been that she come here, but I felt now that she could as easily have initiated this trip by claiming not to want to leave Onondaga as Mr. Berman could have by insisting that she should.

But then people began dancing on the little dance floor in front of our table and when she wanted to dance with me I strongly suggested that it was time to go home. I paid the bill but got her advice on the tips, and on the way out I left money with the bartender for the band's drinks. We took a cab back to the Grand Union Hotel and went prominently to the separate doors of our adjoining rooms and, once inside, met giggling at the open door between them.

But we slept in our own beds and when I woke in the morning I found a note on my pillow: She had gone to have breakfast with some friends. She said I should buy a clubhouse admission and meet her for lunch at the track. She gave me her box number. I loved her handwriting, she wrote a very even line with round letters that were almost like printing and she dotted her *i*'s with little circles.

I showered and dressed and ran downstairs. The two men were not there. I found real morning papers in the lobby news-stand and took them with me to the front porch and sat and read them all in a big wicker chair. The jury had been chosen. The defense had used none of its peremptory challenges. The actual trial would begin today, and the prosecutor was quoted as saying he thought it would take a week at the most. The *Daily News* had a picture of Mr. Schultz and Dixie Davis conferring with their heads together in a corridor outside the courtroom. The *Mirror* showed Mr. Schultz coming down the courthouse steps with a big fake smile on his face.

I left the hotel and went along Broadway till I found a drug-store with a phone booth. I got a handful of change and asked the operator for the number Mr. Berman had given me. To this day I don't know how he was able to secure a number for a phone the phone company didn't know anything about, but he answered on the first ring. I told him we had gotten into town as scheduled, gone to the yearling sales, and were going to have a day at the races. I told him Mrs. Preston had met some of her friends here, silly people with whom she had nothing but silly conversation. I said we had had dinner at the Brook Club but that I hadn't felt the need to identify myself to the man there because everything was going fine. I told him the truth about these things, knowing that he would know it already.

"Good for you, kid," he said. "You want to parlay some of your expense money?"

"Sure," I said.

"There is a horse who will be the number-three position in the seventh race. That will be a good bet with handsome odds."

"What's his name?"

"How do I know, look at your program, just remember the number three, you can remember a three can't you?" He sounded testy. "Whatever you earn you can keep. You take it with you to New York."

"New York?"

"Yeah, get yourself on a train. We'll need you to do some things. Go home and wait there."

"What about Mrs. Preston?" I said.

At that moment the operator cut in and asked for another fifteen cents. Mr. Berman had me give him the phone number I was calling from and told me to hang up. I did and almost immediately the phone rang.

I could hear a match striking and then the exhaling of a lungful of smoke. "That's twice now you mentioned people by name."

"I'm sorry," I said. "But what do I do about her?"

"Where is the tomato at this moment?" he said.

"She's at breakfast."

"A couple of friends of yours are on the way. You'll probably see them at the track. Maybe one of them will even give you a lift to the train station you ask him nicely."

This is what I thought as I strode the streets of Saratoga, around the block and then around again, as if I was going somewhere, as if I had a purposeful destination: They had given me all that money, clearly more than I could use up in a day or even two, it was a week's big-time spending, hotel bills, restaurants, and paying for the play bets Drew Preston might want to make. Something was different. Either they really did need me in New York, a kind of advance man of the return to town, or they wanted me where I would not be in the way, but something had changed. Perhaps with Drew out of sight, Mr. Schultz had been persuaded of the danger she represented, perhaps his alienation was merely a reflection of hers, Mr. Berman seemed to think Mr.

Schultz was perilously in love, but as I thought about it, after the first week or so when they were together in my company, Mr. Schultz ignored Drew more often than not, she became more like his display, an embellishment that added to his presence rather than someone he doted upon or squeezed the hand of, or seemed to deeply care about in the fond and foolish way people in love comport themselves. Whatever decision had been made, it seemed to me only expedient to assume it was of the nature of nightmare. I am proud of this boy I was, thinking through his cold dread, and you know the quickest thinking is the thinking of the body, and the body thinks surely, errorlessly, because it is not soaked in character as the brain is, and my best guess was of the worst that could happen, because I didn't remember coming in from the street or going through the lobby, but I found myself becoming aware that I was in my room and I was holding my loaded Automatic in my hand, I was holding my gun. So that was what I thought. The worst was he had turned against her, he needed more death, he was using up his deaths so quickly now he needed them faster and faster. What would she say, what would she do to him, if he wasn't able to protect himself, pinned down by the law, with the gang flying apart like a bomb had hit, and he abandoned and alone like one of those bombed screaming children of China, with the rubble falling down around him?

It was peculiar that Mr. Schultz knew everything about betrayal but the way it worked, in the freedom of the joyfully voracious spirit of all of us, or else why would his Abbadabba take the trouble to give me a horse? Mr. Schultz lacked imagination, he had a conventional mind, Drew was right, he was ordinary. Nevertheless I now faced enormous executive responsibilities, I had to bring things to pass, I had to engage people to do things I thought they ought to do and from a position of no authority whatsoever. As I thought about it, men in movies who got things done had assistants and secretaries. On a card right in front of me was the Grand Union Hotel's list of services, including a masseur, a barber, a florist, a Western Union office, and so on. I had an entire hotel at my disposal. I steeled myself and picked up the phone and in my lowest, softest voice, affecting the kind of nasality of speech of Drew Preston's friends, I informed the hotel operator that I wanted to reach Mr. Harvey Preston at the Savoy-Plaza in New York, and if he was not in residence to find out from the operator there his forwarding number, which might, perhaps, be Newport. When I hung up my hand was shaking, I, the juggler extraordinaire. I assumed it would take some time to locate Harvey, undoubtedly in bed somewhere with the company of his taste, so I called Room Service and they very respectfully took my order, which was honeydew melon and corn flakes and cream, scrambled eggs and bacon and sausages and toast and jelly and danish pastry and milk and coffee, I just went right down the menu. I sat in a wing chair by the open windows and tucked my Automatic behind the cushion and waited for my breakfast. It seemed to me very important to remain quite still, as one does in a very hot bath, so as to be able to endure it. Mickey would be driving and probably it was Irving with him because whatever they wanted to do would require precision in Saratoga, and perhaps patience, and something deft and sad in its effect rather than outrageous. I liked them both. They were quiet men and bore no ill will toward anyone. They didn't like to complain. They might inwardly demur but they would do their job.

I thought of what I would say to the elegant Harvey. I hoped he would be near a phone. It could even be white. He would hear me out having had the most perfunctory concern for Drew's safety over the summer because of the steady flow of charge account bills or canceled bank checks that had undoubtedly come to him in the mail. I would represent myself as transmitting his wife's wishes. I would be very businesslike. In my mind at the moment I had no personal interest at all in Mrs. Preston, certainly nothing that would tinge my voice with love or guilt. Not that I could ever feel guilty toward Harvey. But apart from that, I had lost in this situation any capacity at all for the eroticized affection, it wanes pathetically in terror, I not only could not remember making love with Drew, I could not even imagine it. She didn't interest me. There was a knock on the door and

my breakfast was wheeled in and the very cart it came on was
gatelegged out under its white linen cloth into a dining table. All
the food was served in or under heavy silver. The melon was set
in a silver bowl of ice. I had learned last night from Drew not
to overtip and got the bellboy out of the room with aplomb. I
sat feeling my gun in the small of my back and stared at this
enormous breakfast as if I carried Bathgate Avenue where I
went, with all the sweet fruits of the earth spilled on my plate.
I missed my mother. I wanted to be wearing my black-and-white
Shadows jacket. I wanted to steal from the pushcarts and hang
around the beer drops and catch a glimpse of the great Dutch
Schultz.

At noon, after I packed my bag and left it downstairs with the
bell captain, I asked directions to the racecourse and made my
way there on foot. It was about a mile from the hotel down a
broad boulevard of dark three-story, deep-porched houses, one
after another. In the front yards were signs that said PARK HERE
and the residents stood in the street and tried to wave the passing cars into their driveways. Everyone in Saratoga was trying to
make a little money, even the owners of these grand gabled
houses. Most of the traffic was heading for the track's own parking lot, at every intersection cops in their short-sleeved shirts
were waving it on. Nobody seemed to be in much of a hurry, the
black cars moved at a stately pace and nobody blew their horns
or tried to improve their position, it was the most mannerly
traffic I had ever seen. I looked for the Packard even though I
knew I wouldn't find it. If they set out in the early morning, even
with Mickey driving it would take them to midafternoon to get
here. All at once I saw the green roof of the grandstand, like
some pennanted castle in the trees, and then I was on the
grounds, and the day was festive with people streaming to the
gates under their panama hats and sun parasols, they carried
field glasses, men were hawking programs, the place was not as
big as Yankee Stadium but grand of scale nonetheless, it was a
wooden structure painted green and white, it had the air of a
distinguished old amusement park with flower beds lining the

paths. I stood on line for a clubhouse ticket and was told they would not let me in as an unaccompanied minor, I wanted to take out my Automatic and shove it up the guy's nose, but instead I asked an elderly couple to buy my ticket for me and walk me through the turnstile, which they were gracious enough to do, but it was a humiliating recourse for the trusted associate of one of the most deadly gangsters in the country.

Then when I climbed the stairs to the stands and came out to my first glimpse of the great oval track I felt immediately at home, it was that delicious shock of looking down from a deep shade to a green field in the sun, you got it from a baseball diamond or from a football gridiron, and now I saw the racecourse had it too, that sense before the sport begins of the glory of the day to come, the palapable anticipation of a formal struggle on a course as yet unmarked, with phantom horses racing to the finish line in a pristine brilliance of air and light. I felt I could handle myself here, I enjoyed the unexpected confidence that comes of recognition.

So there I was burdened with my deadly serious reponsibilities on this fine day when it seemed as if the whole society was coming to gamble, and the common people would do their betting on the grounds and stand in the sun by the rail to see what they could of the actual race, which was the homestretch, while the well-to-do bettors sat in the shade of the raked wooden stands so they could see somewhat more of the course, there were the boxes right at the front edge of the stands which had been bought for the season by politicians and men of wealth and fame, but if unoccupied on any particular day could be bought with a bribe to the usher to be used on a contingency basis, and finally, set back on a separate tier above the grandstand, was the expensive clubhouse where the truly sporting came to sit at tables and have their luncheon before the start of the day's races. I found Drew up there alone at a table for two with a glass of white wine in front of her.

I knew of course no matter what I told her she would not dream of leaving before she'd had her fill of the horses. I knew too that if I spoke of the danger she was in or acknowledged my

fear her eyes would wander, her mind would wander, she'd drift
away in her mind and spirit and the light I held in her eye would
dim. She liked my precocity. She liked my street-tough self, she
liked her boys gallant and bold. So I told her I had a sure thing
in the seventh race and I was going to bet everything I had and
make enough dough to keep her in bonbons and silk underwear
for the rest of her life. It was supposed to be a joke but somehow
it came out in a constricted voice, with more fervor than I intended, like a declaration of my childish love, and the effect on
her depthless green eyes was to set them brimming. And now
we both sat there in silence and great sadness, it was as if she
knew from her own system of reckoning everything I didn't dare
tell her. I couldn't look at her but turned my gaze to the track
out there in the sun, a long wide beautifully kept raked-dirt oval
track with white fencing, inside of which was an inner oval track
of grass with obstacles for the steeplechase races, and inside that
were plantings of red and white flowers and a pond with real
swans paddling around, and all of it set in a vast verdant countryside with the foothills of the Berkshires far to the east, but I only
saw oval, and ran my eyes around the closed track as if it were
an endless bulkhead, as if I had not all the air of the world to
breathe but the stifling diesel fumes in a tugboat deckhouse, and
every moment that we had lived since that night was my halluci-
nation, a moment's reprieve from the great heaving sea lunging
up from itself to gulp at the night's prey, and people of my
barest acquaintance who were dead had not yet died.

Little by little the tables filled up, though neither of us was
hungry we lunched on cold salmon and potato salad, and finally
the mounted men in red hunt coats came onto the track and the
trumpet blew and the horses with their jockeys paraded at a slow
pace past us to the far turn where the starting gate had been set
up, and the first of the day's races went off, as they were to do
thereafter every half hour, every thirty minutes or so a race went
off, a mile or more or sometimes less around the broad raked-
dirt track, you saw them perhaps for a few moments out of the
starting gate and then unless you had glasses they became a
rolling blur, as if one undulant individual animal was rippling

around the far stretch of the track, and it was moving not all that quickly and only when it came into detailed view as horses again, in urgent and walloping whipped exertion, did you understand what a great distance they had run in what little time, and they were swift as devils as they galloped past you and crossed the finish line in front of the stands with the jockeys standing up then in their stirrups. And there was much excitement and importuning and shouting and screaming during the race, but it was not the kind of noise and cheering you got at a baseball game when Lou Gehrig hit a home run, it was not a joyous life sound and did not continue past the moment of the first horse's finish, but died off suddenly as if someone had thrown a switch, with everyone turning back to their charts to give the next half hour to the new bets, and only the winners still buzzing with happiness or gloating over their winnings, the flesh of the horse the least of anyone's concern, except perhaps the owner stepping into the winner's circle in front of the stands to pose for pictures with the jockey and the horse in its garland of carnations.

And I knew what Mr. Berman meant, what mattered were the numbers each animal carried around the track, the numbers on the big boards facing the stands that showed the odds at post time. The horses were running numbers, animated odds, even to the very wealthy squires who bred them and bought them at the yearling sales and owned them and raced them and won purses with them.

But all these impressions came to me through the corners of my eyes, as it were, and on the edges of my attention, as I left Drew and came back to her, and then took her down to her box and left her there, and went looking everywhere on all the levels for the hoods I knew and the hoods I didn't know, because this was not the exclusive horse show of the night before, this was a grand convention of all the idlers of the world, I saw people pushing their two dollars under the grate who clearly were busted, people in the sun by the rail in their undershirts clutching their tickets that were the one way they could get out, whatever it was, to get out of it, I had never seen such pale faces come to enjoy a day, and everywhere on every tier, in every aisle, were the men who knew what others didn't and talked from the sides of their mouths and nodded the knowing nods of commerce, this was such a seedy stand of life, such a grubby elegance of occupation, with the drinkers of tall iced drinks or shots of neat all wanting too much from life and losing too much to it as they stood on the betting lines to try again in their democratic ceremonies of gain and loss on the creaking tiers of these old wooden stands.

All I asked of Drew was that she not go down to the paddock to see the horses before they came onto the track, that she sit in her box, which was numbered and known, just near the governor's box at the finish line, and content herself looking at them through her binoculars.

"You don't want me to bet?"

"Bet what you want. I'll go to the window for you."

"It doesn't matter."

She was very thoughtful and still and made a quietness around herself that I felt as a kind of mourning.

Then she said, "You remember that man?"

"Which man?"

"The one with the bad skin. The one he respects so."

"Bad skin?"

"Yes, in the car, with the bodyguards. Who came to the church."

"That man. Of course. How could I forget such skin."

"He looked at me. I don't mean he was forward or anything like that. But he looked at me and he knew who I was. So I must have met him before." She pursed her lips and shook her head with her eyes cast down.

"You don't remember?"

"No. It must have been at night."

"Why?"

"Because every night of my life I am a damn drunk."

I pondered this: "Were you with Bo?"

"I think I must have been."

"Did you ever tell Mr. Schultz?"

"No. Do you think I should have?"

"I think it's important."

"Is it? Is it important?"

"Yes, I think it might be."

"You tell him. Would you?" she said and raised her binoculars as the horses of the next race came at a walk onto the track.

A few minutes later a uniformed messenger came up to the
box with an enormous bouquet of flowers in his hand and they
were for Drew, a great armload of long-stemmed flowers, and
she took them and her face colored, she read the card and it said
From An Admirer, just as I had dictated, and she laughed and
looked around her, up into the stands behind her, as if to find
whoever it was who had sent them. I called to an usher and put
a folded five-dollar bill in his hand and told him to bring a
pitcher of water, which he did, and Drew placed the flowers in
the pitcher and put them on the empty chair beside her. She was
cheerier now, some people in the next box smiled and made
appropriate remarks, and then another uniformed messenger
arrived, this time with a floral arrangement so large it came with
its own wicker stand, like a little tree with flowers like stalks of
popcorn, and big green fan leaves mixed in and bell flowers of
blue and yellow with little tails, and the card said *Ever Yours,* and
now Drew was laughing with that shocked happiness of people
who get Valentine's Day greetings or surprise birthday parties.
I can't imagine, she answered when a gentleman leaned over
and asked her what the occasion was. And when the third and
fourth even larger deliveries were made, the last a display with
dozens of long-stemmed roses, the whole box was transformed
with flowers, she was surrounded by them, and there was considerable amusement and interest in the boxes around her and
people stood up in their seats to see what was going on and
there was a flurry of interest that spread through the stands
and people started to come over from all directions to ask questions, to make remarks, some people thought she was a movie
star, a young man asked her if he ought to be asking for her
autograph, she had now more flowers around her than the win-

ner of a cup race, she held them and was surrounded by them, and even more important, she was surrounded by the people who came up to see what all the excitement was about. Some of them were her friends from the horse set, and they sat with her and made jokes, and one woman had her two children with her, two little blond girls with bowl haircuts who were dressed in white dresses and bows and white anklets and polished white shoes, nice shy little girls, and Drew improvised little corsages for them to hold, and a photographer appeared from the local newspaper and took flash pictures, everything was going so well, I wanted those children to stay there, I asked the mother if they would like some ice cream and ran off to get some, and while I was at it I ordered from the clubhouse bar a couple of bottles of champagne and several glasses, flashing my roll and dropping Drew's name so that the bartender wouldn't give me a hard time, and soon she was entertaining right there in the box amid her flowers, and I stood back a step and saw that even some of the race officials on their horses glanced up from the track to where she was, it was as if the queen was present in her flower-be-decked box with little girl attendants and people lifting their glasses in her honor.

So all that was as good as it could be, still to come were deliveries of boxes of candy from the hotel chocolatier, I just didn't want her alone, I had other things up my sleeve if I needed them, I stood back and looked on my work and it was good, all I had to do was make it go on, how long I didn't know, another race's worth, another two, I thought it unlikely that members of the profession would want to perform at a crowded racetrack, that they would want to add to the history of a great track the story of an inexplicable assassination, and it would be clear to them if they checked the hotel first that her things were not packed, that she was not running, but how could I be sure of anything if I didn't know everything, I wanted a moving shield around her, like a fountain of juggled balls, like a thousand whirring jump ropes, like fireworks of flowers and the lives of innocent rich children.

So that was the situation, and I suppose it was during the fifth race, the horses were in the far stretch and all the glasses were raised, and how could I not know that among thousands of people one pair of binoculars down along the rail in the sun was turned the wrong way, how can you not know in the instant's deflected ray that you are looking down a tunnel into the eyes of your examiner, that through the great schism of sun and shade and over the cupidinous howl of the masses, you are quietly under the most intimate study? I turned and raced down the wooden staircase to the ground level and made my way past the tellers' cages, where a surprising number of bettors waited, listening to the public-address announcer's account of the race even though all they had to do was walk a few steps outside to see it for themselves. Everywhere on the ground was a litter of cast-off pari-mutuel tickets, and if I had been a few years younger I would probably have gone around and picked them up just because there were so many like things on the ground that could be collected, but the people who were hunkering here and there, turning the tickets over and picking them up and throwing them down again, were grown-ups, wretched pathetic losers scrounging around for that mystical event, the winning ticket mistakenly cast aside.

Out in front of the stands I immediately felt the heat of the afternoon, the light was blinding, and over the shoulders of shouting people I saw a blur of horses thundering past. You really heard them too, you heard the footfalls, you heard the whips in their sibilance. Did the horses run to win or to get away? I found Irving and Mickey at the rail looking for all the world like citizens of sport, with checked jackets and binocular cases hanging from their shoulders, and in Mickey's case a panama covering his bald skull and a pair of sunglasses masking his eyes.

"Faded badly in the stretch," Irving said. "All legs, no heart. You run a speed horse like that no more than six furlongs, if you're kind," he said and tore several tickets in half and put them in a nearby receptacle.

Mickey trained his glasses on the stands.

"Her box is just short of the finish line," I said.

"We can see that. All it lacks is the Stars and Stripes," Irving said in his whispery voice. "What is going on up there?"

"He's very happy to see her."

"Who is?"

"Mr. Preston. Mr. Harvey Preston, her husband."

Irving looked through his glasses. "What does he look like?"

"A tall man? Older."

"I don't spot him. What is he wearing?"

"Let me look a minute," I said and I tapped Mickey on the shoulder. He gave me his glasses and when I focused them she came into view so close in her anxious glance behind her that I wanted to call out I was here, I was down here, but the charm of my life held because as she stared, there indeed was Harvey coming down the stairs waving at her and a moment later he was in the box with his arms around her and she was hugging him, and they held each other at arm's length and smiled, he was saying something, she was genuinely happy to see him, she said something and then they both looked around them at all the flowers and he was shaking his head and holding his palms up, and she was laughing, and there was this milling crowd around them and one man was applauding as if in appreciation of the large gesture.

"Ain't love grand," I said. "In the madras jacket with the maroon silk foulard."

"The what?"

"That's what they call those handkerchiefs where the tie ought to be."

"I see him," Irving said. "You should have told us."

"How was I to know?" I said. "He showed up at lunch. This is their season here. How was I to know they practically own the damn town."

A few minutes later the whole box seemed to rise, a levitation of people and flowers, as Drew and Harvey proceeded toward the exit. He was waving at people like a politician and ushers hurried toward him to make themselves useful. I kept my eyes on Drew with her flowers in her arms, I don't know why but she

seemed to move through the crowd with such care that I thought
of a woman with child, that was my impression from this distance
without the benefit of binoculars, that was my blurring impression. When they had disappeared down the passageway I moved
with Irving and Mickey through the field crowd back under the
stands past the betting cages and stood on the far side of a
hotdog counter and we watched the party come down the staircase and Harvey had a car waiting right there, they had let it in
through the gates where no cars were supposed to come, Drew
turned and stood on her toes to look around, she was trying to
find me, which was the last thing I wanted, but Harvey got her
into that car fast, and jumped in after her, I had told him no
cops, but a couple of state troopers stood there in jodhpurs and
gun belts crisscrossed on their chests and those smart olive-drab
felt scout hats complete with leather thong ties under their
chins, these guys were on duty mostly for decoration, in case the
governor showed up or someone like that, but they were large
and incorruptible, I mean what could they give you in return, a
highway? and the situation was ambiguous, I didn't like the
frown I saw on Irving's face, if they had the idea that she was
scared and running we were both in terrible trouble.

"What's this all about?" Irving said.

"Big-shot stuff," I said. "These guys have nothing better to
do, that's all."

Moving quickly without running, Irving and Mickey left the
park through a side entrance and moved to their own car. They
insisted I come with them and I didn't feel I was in a position
to argue. When we got to the Packard, I opened the door to get
in the back and was shocked to see Mr. Berman sitting there. He
was still up to his tricks. I said nothing and neither did he, but
I knew now it was his passion I was dealing with. Irving said:
"The husband showed up." Mickey got us into the traffic, and
he picked up the car within a block and we followed it at a
discreet distance. I was as surprised as anyone when it gathered
speed and headed south out of town. They weren't even stopping for her things at the hotel.

Quite suddenly Saratoga ended and we were in the country.

We drove behind them ten or fifteen minutes. Then I looked through the side window and realized we were abreast of an airfield, planes, single and double wings, were lined up parked like cars. Harvey's driver turned in there and we went past the entrance and pulled off the road under some trees where we could see the hangar and the runway beyond it. A wind sock at the end of the runway hung limp, just the way I felt.

There was a terrible silence in the car, the motor was left running, I could feel Mr. Berman calculating the odds. They had driven up to a single-engine plane whose door was open just under the wing. Someone already inside was extending his arms to help them climb in. Again Drew turned to look behind her and again Harvey stepped into her line of vision. She still had flowers in her arms.

"Looks like the little lady has pulled a fast one," Mr. Berman said. "You didn't see this coming?"

"Sure," I said. "Like I knew Lulu was going to bust me in the nose."

"What could she be thinking?"

"She's not scared, if that's what you mean," I said. "This is the way they travel in this league. The truth is she's been ready to move on for a while now."

"How do you know? Did she tell you that?"

"Not in so many words. But I could tell."

"Well that's interesting." He thought a moment. "If you were right that would certainly change the picture. Did she say anything about Dutch, was she angry at him or anything?"

"No."

"How do you know?"

"I just know. She doesn't care, it doesn't matter to her."

"What doesn't matter?"

"Nothing. Like she left a brand-new car at the hotel. We can take it, it won't matter to her. She's not after anything, she's not naturally afraid like most girls you'd meet or jealous or any of that. She does whatever she wants, and then she gets bored and then she does something else. That's all."

"Bored?"

I nodded.

He cleared his throat. "Obviously," he said, "this is a conversation that must never again be spoken of." The cabin door closed. "What about the husband. Is he someone who we should expect to give us trouble?"

"He's a cream puff," I said. "And in the meantime I have missed the seventh race and I didn't get to put a bet down on that sure thing you gave me. That was my paycheck, that was my big chance to make a killing."

A man came out of the hangar and grabbed one end of the propellor with two hands and spun it and jumped back when the engine turned over. Then he ducked under the wings and pulled the chocks from under the wheels and the plane taxied onto the runway. It was a lovely silver plane. It paused for a moment with its ailerons flapping and its rudder waggling from side to side, and then it took off. After a moment it lifted into the air. You could see how light and fragile it was rising and sliding and shuddering through the volume of the sky. It banked and flashed in the sun and then rose on its new course and began to be hard to see. As I watched it, its outlines wavered, like something swimming. Then I felt as if it was one of those threadlike things drifting across the ball of my eye. Then it disappeared into a cloud but I was still left with the feeling of something in my eye.

"They'll be other races," Mr. Berman said.

PART
FOUR

SEVENTEEN

The moment I returned I realized the country had damaged my senses, all I could smell was burning cinder, my eyes smarted, and the clamor was deafening. Everything was broken down and falling apart, the tenements looked worn out by history, the empty lots were rubble, but what was most serious of all, what was clearly a sign to me of my brain damage, was how small my street looked, how miserably humble and wretchedly squeezed in among the other streets. And I came along in my rumpled white linen suit with the points of my collar curling up in the heat and my tie knot loosened, and I had thought I had wanted to look good for my mother, so that she would see how well I had done for myself over the summer, but I was instead wilted from the long trip, it was a hot Saturday in New York and I felt weak and washed out, with the leather valise a heavy weight on the socket of my arm, but the way the people looked at me I realized I was deranged in this sense of things too, I looked too good, I was not someone returning home but an absolute foreigner, nobody in the East Bronx had clothes like this, nobody owned a leather valise with two cinch straps, they all looked at me, the kids diverted from their games of skelly and box ball, the adults on the stoops forgetting their conversation, and I walked past them, stepping by in the damaged sense of my hearing, everything now hushed, as if the bitter acrid and stifling air had steeped me in silence.

But all of this was as nothing when I climbed the dark stairs. The door of our apartment was not entirely closed because the lock was broken, the first of a series of infinitesimal changes the universe had made in the downward direction while I was away, and when I pushed the door it swung open to a dismal low-ceilinged flat that was at the same time familiar and arbitrarily insane with slanting linoleum floors and furniture whose stuffing was hanging out, and a dead plant on the fire escape, and in the kitchen a whole wall and ceiling blackened where my mother's lights must have flared too hot. The kitchen table of burning drinking glasses was not now in operation, the tabletop was covered with hardened spires and globs and pools of white wax with small black craters and pits that made me think of a planetarium model of the moon. And there was no sign of my mother though she still lived here, I could tell that, her jar with the long jeweled hairpins was not moved, the photograph of her as a young woman standing next to my father, whose figure had been X'd out with a crayon and face carefully excised, that was still there, her few clothes hanging from the back of the bedroom closet door, and up on the shelf the hatbox I had sent from Onondaga, the hat still inside and wrapped in tissue just the way it had come from the store.

In the icebox were some eggs and a stale half a rye bread in a paper bag, and a bottle of milk that was curdled on top.

I turned on a light sat down on the floor in the middle of this domain of a lost woman and her lost son and from each of my pockets removed the folded bills of our wealth and smoothed them out and arranged them by denomination and straightened them into a stack, tapping them on all four sides with my stiffened palms: I had come down from the country with a little over six hundred and fifty dollars, the remains of my Saratoga expense account which Mr. Berman told me I could keep. It was an immense amount of money but it was not enough, nothing was enough to pay the bill for this high holy life of rectitude, faith, and bathing in the kitchen sink. I put the cash in my bag and the bag in the closet and found a pair of old knickers that were torn in the knees and a ribbed undershirt and my old Nat Holman lace-up sneakers with the soles worn away, and I changed into these things and felt a little better, I sat on the fire escape and smoked a cigarette and began to remember who I was, whose son I was, except that the prospect across the street of the brick-and-limestone Max and Dora Diamond Home for Children presented itself first to my eyes and then to my mind, I stuck the cigarette in the corner of my mouth, swung over the side of the fire escape, handed myself down the ladder, and hanging there from my hands dropped the last ten feet to the sidewalk, only realizing as I landed that I was not quite the flowing phantom of grace I had been, there was more of a shock to the knees in this hanging drop and to the little bones of the feet, I had eaten well in the country and perhaps filled out a bit, I looked up and down to see who was watching and walked across the street as slowly as I needed to in order to mask my inclination to limp, and went down the steps to the basement of the Diamond Home for Children, where my friend Arnold Garbage who had sold me my Automatic sat in his ashen kingdom and collected everything as it made its way down to us from the higher realms of purposefulness.

Oh my stolid friend, "Where was you," he said, as if I had been under a misapprehension all these years that he was dumb, the verbosity of the fellow, and he had grown too, he was going to be a giant fat man, like Julie Martin, he stood to greet me and tin pots fell from him clattering to the cement basement floor and he stood in his full height, this glandular genius, and he smiled.

So that was good, coming to the basement again, and sitting around smoking and telling lies to Arnold Garbage while he examined one mysterious unidentifiable inorganic item after another in order to make a determination as to which bin to throw it in, and the footfalls overhead of the Diamond orphans at their games thrupped and pounded the foundations and made me think of the sweet gurgling exertions of children as water springing from the earth. I actually wondered if perhaps

I ought to return to school, I would be in the tenth grade if I did, Mr. Berman's favorite number, containing the one and the zero and capping all the numbers you needed to express any number, it was just a passing thought, the sort of idea you have when you're hurt and in a weakened condition.

But when I went upstairs to look in the old gym and see if I saw there anyone else I knew, a small black-haired girl acrobat, for example, I caused consternation, the rhythm of their games broke and that same silence came over them as when I walked into the block with my suitcase, the children, who now looked awfully young, stared at me in the sudden gymnastic hush, a volleyball rolled across the shiny wood floor, and a counselor I didn't recognize who was holding her whistle attached to a woven lanyard around her neck approached me and said this was not a public place and visitors were not allowed.

This was the first bulletin of the news that my assumptions were expired, that I could not reinsert myself, as if there were two kinds of travel and while I was moving upstate on roads over mountains, the people of my street were advancing in the cellular time of their being. I found out Becky was gone, she had been taken by a foster family in New Jersey, one of the girls on her floor told me this, how lucky Becky was because she had her own room now, and then she told me to leave, that I shouldn't come to the girls' floor, that it wasn't right, and I went to the roof where before I knew I loved her I had paid that dear little girl for her fucks, and the super was up there painting green lines for a shuffleboard court, and he stood up and rubbed the back of his hand that was holding the brush across his face where the sweat was itching, and he told me I was street trash and that he'd give me *three* to get off the property and that if he ever saw me here again he'd beat the shit out of me and then call the cops so that they could do it again.

Well all this as you can imagine was indeed an interesting homecoming, but really what angered me was how vulnerable I was, and stupid, to expect something, I didn't know what, from this neighborhood I hadn't been able to leave fast enough. In the days following I realized that wherever I had been, whatever

I had done, the people knew about it not in its detail but in its fulfillment of their myth-knowledge of the rackets. My reputation had advanced. In the candy store on the corner where I bought the papers every morning and evening, on the stoops of hot twilight, and all the way over to Bathgate, I was known by sight, and who I was and what I did made this light around me as I walked, I understood I was illuminated as one *in their midst,* it was a kind of infamy. I had known those neighborhood feelings myself, there had always been someone like me to know about from the other kids, to hear mentioned only after he had turned the corner, to be feared, to be told to stay away from. Under the circumstances it was pretentious for me to wear my old kid juggler's rags, I would go back to wearing the wardrobe of my success. Besides, I didn't want to disappoint anybody. Once you're in the rackets you can never get out, Mr. Schultz had told me, and he had said it not in any menacing way but with a voice of self-pity, so that I thought, as a proposition, it was suspect. But not now, not now.

Of course I am summarizing the rueful conclusions of some days, at first there was only bewilderment, the worst shock was my mother, whom I saw just a few hours after my arrival, she was coming down the street pushing her brown wicker baby carriage and I knew immediately even from a distance her lovely distraction had gone awry. Her gray hair was uncombed and flowing, and the closer she got the more terribly sure I was that unless I stepped in front of her and spoke to her she would pass me by without a glimmer of recognition. Even at that it was touch-and-go, the first emotion that registered on her face was anger, because the carriage had met an impediment, then her eyes lifted and for a moment I felt as if I was out of focus in her mind, that she saw me and knew just enough to know it was important to make sense of me, and only then, after an unendurable stop in my heart's beat, did I live again in the recognition of stately, mad Mary Behan.

"Billy, is this you?"

"Yes, Ma."

"You've grown out."

"Yes, Ma."

"He's a big lad," she said to whoever it was who was listening. She was staring at me now with such intensity that I had to move toward her to get out of the glare, I hugged her and kissed her cheek, she was not fresh and clean as I'd always known her to be, but had about her the acrid, cindery redolence of the street. I looked down in the baby carriage and saw there browning leaves of lettuce flattened neatly and spread like lily pads over the inside, and corncobs, and the spilled insides of cantaloupe seeds still attached in their mucusy webs. I didn't want to know what she imagined she had there. She was unsmiling and not to be consoled.

Oh Mama, Mama, but once the carriage was in the house she overturned it and dumped the detritus on newspaper and rolled it up in a paper bag and put it in the kitchen trash can, which waited as always for the super's buzzer to signal when it was to be loaded onto the dumbwaiter. So that was reassuring. I was to learn that she went in and out of her states as if she suffered her own passing weather conditions, and every time she cleared up I decided she would be all right for good now, that the problem was over. Then she would storm over again. On Sunday I showed her all the money I had, which seemed to please her, and then I went out and brought back the materials for a proper breakfast and she cooked everything up in the old way, remembering how we liked our sunny-sides up, and she had bathed and dressed herself nicely and combed and pinned her hair so that we were able to have a morning stroll to Claremont Avenue and up the steep stairs to Claremont Park and to sit in the park on the bench under a big tree and read the Sunday papers. But she would not ask me anything about the summer, where I had been or what I had done, not from any lack of curiosity, but from a knowledgeable silence, as if she had heard it all, as if there was nothing I could tell her that she didn't already know.

I felt by this time terribly guilty of neglect, she seemed so to enjoy being out of the immediate neighborhood, sitting in the peacefulness of the green park, and the possibility that she had been affected by my actions, that she had been made to feel estranged, as I was, in the general community misgiving of a bad family, a crazy woman who had of course raised a bad boy, was enough to make me want to weep.

"Ma," I said. "We have enough money to move. How would you like a new apartment somewhere around here, right near the park, maybe we could find a building with an elevator and we could look down into the park from every window. See, like those houses over there."

She gazed in the direction I pointed and then shook her head no over and over, and then sat and stared at her hands folded on her pocketbook in her lap and shook her head again as if she had to rethink the question and answer it again as if it kept popping up again and again and wouldn't stay answered.

I was so blue, I insisted we have lunch out, I was ready to do anything, take her to the movies, the thought of going back to our street was insupportable, I was so lost I could only think of living in public places, where something was happening, where I might be able to reanimate my mother, get her to smile, get her to talk, get her to be my mother again. At the edge of the park I flagged a taxi and had him take us all the way up to Fordham Road, to the same Schrafft's where we had had our tea that day she had come with me to buy clothes. We had to wait for a table but when we sat down I could see it pleased her to be back there, and that she remembered it and enjoyed its dainty pretensions, its suggestion of the dignity given to people from their patronage, though now of course I found it a dull place with very bland food in mincy portions, and thought to myself with a laugh of those heavily taken meals with the gang at the Onondaga Hotel and how they would all look right now if they were eating here at Schrafft's with the churchgoers from East Fordham Road, the expression on Lulu Rosenkrantz's face when the waitress served him his little cucumber-and-butter sandwich with the crust removed and the tall ice-cream glass of iced tea without enough ice. And then I made the mistake of thinking about my steak dinner at the Brook Club with Drew Preston and the way she looked across the table leaning on her elbow and drinking me in with her smiling tipsy dreaminess of expression and I felt my ears grow hot and looked up and there was my mother smiling at me in just the same way, in terrifying resemblance, so that for an instant I didn't know where I was, or who I was with, and it seemed to me they knew each other, Drew and my mother, by some imposition of one on the other that made them old friends, and that their full mouths matched and their eyes passed like rings through each other's eyes, and that I was cursed with an undifferentiated love that made them inseparable. This was all in the space of an instant but I cannot remember now when I have felt as catastrophically self-informed, I had molted and muscled out, skin and mind and wit, molted and muscled out again and again, except in the heart, except in the heart. I was all at once enraged, at what, at whom, I didn't know, at God for not moving as quickly, as adeptly, as I could, at the food on my plate, I was bored by my mother, I loathed the pathetic existence to which she had consigned herself, it was not fair to be dragged back into the hopeless boredom of family life, to be taken down this way after all the hard work of my criminal intentions, I was doing it, didn't she realize? She'd better not try to stop me. Let anyone try to stop me.

But you know, the waitress comes over and says will that be all and then you ask for the check and pay it.

On that first Monday morning after my return my mother went off to her laundry job as she always had, which suggested to me her madness was self-governed, which meant it was not madness at all but just a passing version of the distraction I had always known. Then I happened to look into the wicker carriage and saw there arranged as in a nest the eggshells from our Sunday breakfast. So for the first time but not the last, I went from confidence to despair in the space of a second. I wondered, as I would wonder over and over as part of the whole irresolute cycle, if perhaps I should stop fooling myself and come to grips with the truth that something had to be done, that I had better get her to a doctor, have her examined and treated, before she got so bad she would need to be put in an asylum. I didn't exactly know how to go about this, or whom to consult, but it seemed to me Mr. Schultz had an old widowed mother he took care of, perhaps he could help, perhaps the gang even had its doctors the way it had its lawyers. Anyway, who else could I turn to? I didn't belong here anymore, I didn't belong with the orphans or the people in the neighborhood, all I had was the gang, whatever my ultimate intentions and passing disloyalties, I was theirs and they were mine. Whatever desires I had—to abandon my mother, to save my mother—they all convened on Mr. Schultz.

But I wasn't hearing from him and I wasn't hearing from them and all I knew was what I got from the papers. I would not go out now except to get the papers or my packs of Wings, I read every paper I could get my hands on. I bought them all, all day and all night, it began late at night when I went up to the kiosk under the Third Avenue El and bought the early editions of the next morning's papers, and then in the morning I went to the candy store on the corner for the late editions, and then at noon I'd go over to the kiosk for the the early editions of the evening papers, and then in the evening I'd go to the corner and pick up the final editions. The government's case seemed to me inarguable. They had evidence on paper, they had accountants from the Internal Revenue Bureau explaining the income tax law, they were really laying it out. I was very nervous. When Mr. Schultz took the stand it seemed to me he was not persuasive. He explained that he had been given the wrong advice by his lawyer, that his lawyer had simply made a mistake, and that once another lawyer had explained the mistake he, Mr. Schultz, had endeavored to pay every penny he owed as a patriotic citizen, but this was not good enough for the government, which decided it would rather prosecute him. I didn't know if even a farmer would believe that lame story.

As I waited for the news I tried to see the good in either verdict as it might be handed down so as to try to prepare myself whatever happened. If Mr. Schultz went to jail we would all be safe from him for as long as he was put away. That was an undeniable good. Oh to think of being freed of him! But at the same time my faith in the quietly working clockwork of my given destiny would be shattered. If something as ordinary and mundane as government justice could tilt my life awry, then my secret oiled connections to the real justice of a sanctified universe were nonexistent. If Mr. Schultz's crimes were only earthly crimes with earthly punishments, then there was nothing else in the world but what I could see, and whereas I had been humming in the conviction of invisible empowerments, it was my own mind only making them up. That was unendurable. But if he beat the rap, if he beat the rap, I was back in my lines of danger and trusting with a boy's pure and shaking trust I would get through to the just conclusion of my chosen perils. So which did I want? Which verdict, which future?

In the way I waited I realized my answer, I looked every morning in the back of the *Times* at the passenger ship sailings, I just wanted to know which ships they were and where they were going and that there were lots of them to choose from. I trusted Harvey Preston had worked things out, I was beginning to like him, he'd certainly come through in Saratoga and I saw no reason why he wouldn't now. In my mind I watched her leaning on the railing with the moon out and staring at the silvery ocean and thinking of me. I imagined her in shorts and halter playing shuffleboard on the rear deck in the sun just the way the kids played it on the roof of the orphan home. If I had been wrong, if Mr. Berman and Irving and Mickey had only come to Saratoga to take her back or to talk to her on behalf of Mr. Schultz, well then what, after all, had been lost except Drew to me, except my Drew to me?

In the Wednesday evening papers, the lawyers presented their summations, and on Thursday the judge gave his instructions to the jury, by Thursday evening the jury was still out and late Thursday night I went to Third Avenue and Mr. Schultz was the headline in Extras put out by both the evening and the morning papers: He was innocent of all charges.

I whooped and hollered and jumped up and down and danced around the kiosk while a train rumbled overhead. You wouldn't know from looking at me that I believed this was the man who just a week before had been intending to kill me. He was shown close up, broadly smiling at the camera in the *Mirror,* kissing his rosary in the *American,* and holding Dixie Davis's head in the crook of his arm and planting a big kiss on the top of it in the *Evening Post.* The *News* and the *Telegram* showed him with his arm around the foreman of the jury, a man in overalls. And all of the papers carried the remarks of the judge on hearing the jury's verdict: "Ladies and gentlemen, in all my years on the bench I have never witnessed such disdain of truth and evidence as you have manifested this day. That you could on hearing the meticulous case presented by the United States Government find the defendant not guilty on all charges so staggers my faith in the judicial process that I can only wonder about the future of this Republic. You are dismissed with no thanks from the court for your service. You are a disgrace."

My mother saved the front page of the *Mirror* with Mr. Schultz's smiling face and folded it so that just the picture showed, she laid it down in the carriage and brought a threadbare blanket up to its chin.

And now I will tell of the revels that went on for three nights and two days in the brothel on West Seventy-sixth Street between Columbus and Amsterdam avenues. Not that I knew at any given time whether it was night or day because the red velour drapes were pulled across every window and the lights were always on, the lamps with their tasseled shades, the cutglass chandeliers, and the particular hour was not something very important after a while. It was a brownstone and one of the sights I remember is of a trembling slightly aged whore's puckered behind as she ran up the stairs shrieking in mock fear while this hood tried to catch her but fell on his face instead and slid down the flight of stairs face down and feet first and arms up. Most of the women were young and pretty and slender, and some of them got tired and left and were replaced by others. Also there were a lot of men I didn't recognize, this was sup-

posed to be for the top gang members but word had gotten
around and the unshaven faces kept changing, and on the second night or day I even saw a cop in his undershirt with his
suspenders holding his blue pants up and a whore with his braid
cap set awry on the back of her head kissing his bare feet, toe
by toe.

Women were laughing and getting playfully pinched and tick-
led by fearsome men, but showing no fear and in fact going off
with them up the stairs, like multiples of Drew in their fearless-
ness of taking killers into themselves. I was stunned by this
transformation of the value of feeling into numbers, in a corner
of a room I saw Mr. Berman's sly laughing face appearing
through his cigarette smoke, and in the big downstairs parlor
three or four women were draped all over Mr. Schultz, on the
arms of his chair, in his lap, nibbling on his ears, begging him
to dance, he laughed and fondled them and pinched them and
handled them, there was a profusion of flesh and as I looked it
didn't seem to be organized according to individual persons but
was all jumbled together, profusions of breasts and constella-
tions of nipples, cornucopic bellies and asses and tangles of long
legs. Mr. Schultz saw me looking and appointed a woman to take
me to bed, she reluctantly disentangled herself and led me upstairs, and there was a good deal of attendant merriment on the
part of my colleagues, which turned the occasion into something
unpleasant for me and for the woman too, who was seething
with anger because she felt demeaned by my age and unimpor-
tance. Both of us could hardly wait to be finished, this was not
the party, the party was elsewhere, it was appalling to me how
unsexy sex could be humped up with such scorn and impatiently
delivered, I had an actual Manhattan to drink afterward, it at
least was sweet with a crunchy cherry at the bottom of it.

The madam who ran things stayed in the kitchen on the
ground floor in the back, a very nervous woman whom I sat with
and talked to for a while, I felt sorry for her because Mr. Schultz
when drunk had slugged her for some imagined offense and had
given her a black eye. Then he'd apologized and given her a new

hundred-dollar bill. She was a tiny woman he called Mugsy maybe because she so resembled the little Pekingese she held in her lap, she had a little pug-nosed button-eyed face with highly curled but very thin red hair and a small skinny body dressed in a black dress and stockings which drooped a little at the knees. She had a low voice, like a man's. I talked to her while she held a slice of raw steak over her eye. In the oven of the stove were all the guns people had to turn over when they arrived. She would not leave the kitchen I think because she didn't want anyone to come in and get a gun and start shooting up her house, although what she could have done to prevent it, this little tiny lady, I can't say. She had a staff of Negro maids who kept things going, changing linens, emptying ashtrays, collecting empty bottles, and she had delivery boys, also colored, coming in the back door with cases of mixer and beer and booze, and cartons of cigarettes and hot dinners in metal containers from steakhouses and hot breakfasts in cardboard cartons from neighborhood diners, she was tense but had things very well organized, like a general who had planned well and deployed all his troops and had only to hear them report from time to time how the battle was going. I juggled some hard-boiled eggs in their shell and she was so sure I was going to drop them that she laughed with appreciation when I didn't, she took a liking to me, she wanted to know all about me, what my name was, where I lived, and I said yes, and how had a nice boy like me come to this sordid profession, which made her laugh again. She pinched my cheek and offered me chocolates from a fancy painted metal box which she kept by her side, it showed scenes of men in knee britches and white wigs bowing to ladies in big hoop skirts.

But this Madam Mugsy understood my inclination to linger in the kitchen for what it was, and with great delicacy and tact she suggested that she had something special for me, that most desirable item, a fresh girl, by which she meant a young one fairly new to the trade, and she made a phone call and within an hour I was up in a small quiet bedroom on the top floor with what indeed was a young girl, light-haired round-faced high-

waisted and somewhat shy and rubbery to the touch, who lay
with me through the night, or the quiet hours that passed for
night, and fortunately needed as much sleep in her youth as I
needed in mine.

I was too self-conscious and unsure of myself and sad to really
enjoy these revels. Up in the Bronx as I'd waited for the trial to
end I had the avid desire to reconnect with the gang, I felt love
for every one of them, there was a kind of consistency to their
behavior that made me feel grateful for their existence, but now
that I was reunited with them the other side of that gratitude was
guilt, I looked to the faces of Mr. Schultz and the others to see
how I fared there, in a smile of gold teeth I read exoneration one
moment, retribution the next.

But then, I suppose it was by the second night, I realized I
wasn't the only one in a less than ecstatic state, Mr. Berman had
entrenched himself in the front parlor and sat reading the papers and smoking and sipping brandy, he went out a lot to use
public pay phones, and while Lulu was still exercising his un-
couth being upon a selection of ladies not one of whom failed
to complain to the management, Irving absented himself rarely,
and only gave way to the joy of the occasion by taking off his
jacket, loosening his tie, and rolling up his sleeves and serving
as bartender to all the close and casual freeloaders of the criminal trades. I finally realized that Mr. Schultz's chief lieutenants
were waiting, that is all they were doing, and that the celebration
was by the second day not a joyful party of men who had been
through something together but a sort of statement to the profession, a business announcement that the Dutchman had
returned, and all the true merriment and joy and relief of vic-
tory had given way to the hollow gaiety of a public-relations
event.

Even Mr. Schultz sought now the places in the house for the
quieter pleasures of reflection, and I happened to pass one of
the bathrooms where he was sitting in a hot soapy tub puffing
a cigar into the steamy air and enjoying a back wash from the
madam, Mugsy, who sat on a wooden stool beside the tub and

talked and joked with him as if he hadn't slugged her the day before.

He glanced up and saw me. "Come in, kid, don't be shy," he said. I sat down on the lid of the toilet bowl. "Mugsy this here is my pro-to-jay, Billy, you two met yet?" We said we had. "You know who Mugsy is, kid? You know how far we go back? I'll tell you," he said, "when Vince Coll was on the rampage, gunning for me all over the Bronx, and going crazy looking for me where do you think I was all the time?"

"Here?"

"Except then I had my house on Riverside Drive," the madam said.

"Coll was so dumb," Mr. Schultz said, "he wouldn't know about the finer things of life, he didn't know what a high-class whorehouse looked like, and while he's going around shooting everything that moves, hitting bars and drops and clubhouses, the dumb fuck, I am snug like a bug in a rug at my Mugsy's taking pleasure and biding my time. Sitting in the bathtub and getting my back washed."

"That's right," the woman said.

"Mugsy's as square as they come."

"I better be," she said.

"Get me a beer, would you, doll?" Mr. Schultz said lying back in the tub.

"I'll be back," she said and dried her hands on a towel and left the room, closing the door.

"You having a good time, kid?"

"Yes, sir."

"It's important to get that clean country air out of your lungs," he said grinning. He closed his eyes. "Also to get your heart back in your balls, where it belongs. Where it's safe. Did she say anything?"

"Who?"

"Who, who," he said.

"Mrs. Preston?"

"I think that was the lady's name."

"Well she did tell me she liked you very much."

"She said that?"

"That you have class."

"Yeah? Comin' from her," he said and a pleased smile came over his face. He kept his eyes closed. "In a better world," he said. "If this were a better world." He paused. "I like the idea of women, I like that you can pick them up like shells on the beach, they are all over the place, little pink ones and ones with whorls you can hear the ocean. The trouble is, the trouble is . . ." He shook his head.

The steamy water and the tile did something to his voice, so that even as he spoke softly it hollowed out as if we were in a cavern. He was now staring at the ceiling. "I think you only fall for someone, what I mean is the only time it's possible is when you're a kid, like you, when you don't know the world is a whorehouse. You get the idea in your mind and that's it. And for the rest of your life you're stuck on her, and you think every time you turn around she's this one or that one who comes along and smiles like her and fills her in. We have that first one when we're stupid and don't know any better. And we walk away, and she becomes the one we look for for the rest of your life, you know?"

"Yes," I said.

"Hell, she was a dignified girl, Drew. Not ordinary ginch at all, nothing cheap about her. She had this lovely mouth," he said pulling on his cigar. "But you know the expression 'summer romance'? Sad to say it was no more than that. We both have our lives we had to go back to." He glanced at me to see my response. "I have a business to run," he said. "And I have survived in this business because of my attention to business."

He sat up in the tub, bubbles of soapy water caught in the black hairs of his shoulders and chest. "When you think who I have outlasted, what I have had to contend with. Every day in the week. The thieves, the rats. Everything you build up, everything you work for, they try to steal it from you. Big Julie. My dear Bo, my dear dear Bo. And like Coll, who I have mentioned. You know what loyalty is worth? You know what a loyal man is

worth these days? His weight in gold. I was good to Vincent
Coll. And he goes and skips bail I put up for him. Did you know
that? I never start these things. I'm just this good-natured slob
people think they can walk all over. And before you know it, I'm
in a fucking war with this madman and having to hide out in a
whorehouse. To tell you the truth I felt very bad about that, it
was not the manly thing to do. But I had to bide my time. One
day in the middle of everything Vincent is picked up and de-
tained, he goes into temporary detention on some rap, and I
figure this is my chance, so we lay in wait for him when he comes
out except he knows we're there so he gets his sister to meet him
and walks out holding his sister's kid in his arms. You see what
I'm saying? We back off, we are not barbarians, he has us and
we go away to fight another day. Just to show you. But the Mick
he doesn't play by any rules of civilization, not a week later he
comes rolling around the corner of Bathgate Avenue looking for
me with the windows down as I happen to be in the neighborhood to visit my old mother and bring her some nice flowers.
When I go see Mama I go alone, maybe that is stupid, I mean
I know it is, but it is another life she leads and I don't want to
offend it, so I am by myself with a nice bouquet of flowers I have
just bought and I am on this crowded street nodding to this one
or that who happens to know me, and I have that sixth sense,
you know? or maybe I see something in the eyes of someone
walking toward me, that he would look past me? I dive behind
a fruit stall, the slugs fly and the oranges go up in the air and
the peaches and watermelon busting like skulls spraying, and I
am lying there under falling crates of grapefruits and plums and
pears and all this juice, so I think I've been hit, it feels wet, it
would be funny, I'm lying there with all this fruit juice leaking
over me, except the screaming of the women and children, it is
a family street for christsake, you know with all the pushcarts and
the balabustas out doing their marketing, and then the car is
gone and I get up and I see over the top of the stall people
running the mother screaming in Italian and there is a baby
carriage on its side with a baby spilled out, the baby nightie
soaked in blood, blood all over his bonnet, the fuckers have

killed the kid in its carriage, God help us all. And then someone
starts pointing at me, cursing me, you know? like I have shot the
kid! and I have to run for it with people shouting after me! Well
when that happened I knew I would kill Vincent Coll if it was the
last thing I did, I felt honor bound, I made a sacred vow. But
the press gives me the rap, me, the Dutchman, because I am at
war with this maniac madman, that is the joke of it, I am getting
the blame for Vincent Coll, as if I didn't warn everyone, as if I
didn't try to tell everyone to watch out for him, I get the blame
for being the missing target, for not being shot instead of that
murdered infant when the fact it was the Mick who did wrong
from the beginning, jumping the bail of ten grand I put up for
him, ten grand! and then hitting on my trucks and drops, it was
a remorseful error of judgment I ever hired him in the first
place, I had to get him, I swore to myself I would take him down,
it was a matter of restoring the moral world in its rightful position. You know how I did it?''

There was a knock on the door and the little madam came in
with a tray with two bottles of beer and a couple of tall glasses
and set it down on the stool. "I'm telling about Vince," he said
to her. "It was very simple, a simple idea, like the simple things
are always the best. I remembered he and Owney Madden talked
a lot, that was all.''

"A gentleman, Owney," the madam said, lighting herself a
cigarette.

"Exactly so," Mr. Schultz said. "Exactly the point, so I don't
know, he must have had something on Owney because why else
would a class guy like Owney have anything to do with him? So
it wasn't that difficult. I send Abe Landau to Owney's office and
he sits there with him all night in his office till the phone rings
and Abe puts the gun in Owney's side, and he says just keep
talking, Mr. Madden, keep him on the line, and we got this cop
outside who gets the call traced, and the Mick is in a phone
booth in the Excelsior drugstore on Twenty-third Street and
Eighth Avenue. In five minutes I have a car there and he's got
two guys sitting at the fountain to watch out for him but they

look at the Thompson and out they go, running up the street as fast as their legs can carry them, no one has seen them since, and my guy, he stitches the rounds up one side of the phone booth and down the other, and Vincent he couldn't even get the doors open, he falls out only when they come off the hinges, and back in Owney's office Abe listens on the phone and hears it all and then there is silence on the line and he hangs up and says, Thank you, Mr. Madden, sorry to have been of inconvenience, and that was how we did in the Mick, may his gizzards boil in hell till the end of time."

Mr. Schultz fell silent and I heard him breathing hard in the exertion of his memory. He took a beer from the tray and guzzled it down. It gave me some comfort to see from his example that people can sustain any loss as long as they can go on being themselves.

The next morning I came down the stairs and it was immediately clear to me something had happened. There were no women in sight, the doors to the rooms were open. I heard a vacuum cleaner, I found Irving in the kitchen pouring mugs of coffee and I followed him to the front parlor and before he closed the door on me I saw that a meeting was going on, maybe a dozen or more men sitting around all dressed and every one of them sober.

I had been told to take a walk, which I did, I walked back and forth on the side streets of the Seventies from Columbus to Broadway, the town houses of brownstone and limestone, with their high stoops and basement doorways under the stairs, all stuck to one another from one end of the block to the other, not an alley in sight, no spaces, no views or vistas, no empty lots, just this continuous wall of residence. I felt closed out by these stone façades and shaded windows, and it was chilly too, I had not been out of doors for two days and three nights and it seemed to me true autumn had come in, a brisk breeze scuttled up the litter in the street, and the plane trees in their little fenced-in sidewalk plots were turning yellow, as if a tree blight of the north country had followed me, as if the cold was coming down after me no matter where I went. I felt at this moment as if I should never have left the city, I didn't feel at home in it anymore, from every crack in the sidewalk a weed grew, every corner had its cluster of puttering pigeons, squirrels ran the wires between the telephone poles like portents of lurking Nature, little spies of the encroachment.

Of course I was hurt to be shut out of what was clearly a serious business council, I wanted to know what I had to do to have my worth recognized, no matter what I did and how well, there were always these setbacks. I said fuck it and went back and I found that the meeting was over, the visitors were gone, and it was just Mr. Schultz and Mr. Berman in the front room, they were dressed for business in shirts and ties. Mr. Schultz paced while he twirled his rosary around his hand, not a good sign. When the phone in the front hall rang he ran out himself and took the call, and a moment later he was putting on his suit jacket and setting his fedora on his head and he stood in the hall inside the front door absolutely pale in his fury. I was standing in the doorway to the parlor. "What does a man have to do?" he said to me. "Tell me. To be deserving of a break, to be able to begin to reap the fruits of his labor. When does that happen?" Mr. Berman at the window in the parlor called "Okay" and Mr. Schultz opened the front door and closed it behind him. I ran to the window and parted the drapes and saw him ducking into a car, Lulu Rosenkrantz was on the running board on the street side, and he looked up and down the street before he swung in next to the driver, and the car moved off smartly and was gone, leaving only the exhaust rising in the air.

The little madam, Mugsy, came in and she had under her arm a shoebox which she placed on the coffee table. It held all her receipts and invoices, and she and Mr. Berman went over them together like a stunty little couple in a fairy tale, an old woodcutter and his ancient wife puffing their magic white weeds of smoke and child mystification and having a conversation in their language of numbers. I picked some newspapers off the floor:

Mayor La Guardia had warned Dutch Schultz that if he was seen anywhere in the five boroughs of New York he would be arrested, and Special Prosecuting Attorney Thomas Dewey had announced he was preparing an indictment of Dutch Schultz for state income tax evasion. So that's what it was. It all had to do with that verdict upstate, the editorial writers were outraged, I never read editorials but Mr. Schultz's name was all over them, everyone was calling for his scalp, and every politician who could be found and quoted was likewise outraged, borough presidents were outraged, controllers, members of the Board of Estimate, attorney generals, police commissioners, deputy commissioners, even a lieutenant in the Department of Sanitation was outraged, even the man in the street in the *News*'s Man in the Street feature. It was interesting, in the context of all this outrage, how Mr. Schultz's happy smiling face of exoneration looked so brazen and sneering and sinister.

"That is for damage," the madam was saying as Mr. Berman held up a slip of paper in query. "Your boys broke a dozen fine dinner plates, you didn't hear that I suppose, when they was throwing my Wedgwood at each other."

"And this?" Mr. Berman said.

"General overhead."

"I don't like estimates. I like factual numbers."

"This overhead is factual wear and tear. Look, right there, the very couch you're sitting on, you see the stains? That don't come out, wine doesn't come out, I'll need new slipcovers, and that's an example. How shall I say this, Otto, it is not a YMCA crowd you run through here."

"You wouldn't perchance be taking advantage, Mugsy."

"I resent that remark. You know why Dutch comes to me? Because I am the best. This is a high-class establishment and it don't come cheap. You like the girls? You should, they are show girls, they are not whores from the street. You like the service and the furnishings? How do you think I supply them, by chintzing on everything? I get what I pay for and so do you. It'll take me a week to get this place to where I can reopen. That is time

lost, but I still got to pay rent and the payoffs and the doctors'
fees and the electric company. I'll tell you what, the black eye
I give to you. On the house."

Mr. Berman took out a thick bankroll and removed the rubber
band. He counted out hundred-dollar bills. "This and not a
penny more," he said, pushing the money across the coffee
table.

When we left the woman was sitting there on the couch holding her hand over her eyes and crying. A car was at the curb. Mr.
Berman told me to get in and he got in after me. I didn't recognize the driver. "Nice and easy," Mr. Berman said to him. We
drove down Broadway and then over to Eighth Avenue and
down Eighth past Madison Square Garden and then west to the
river and down past the docks, which frightened me for a moment until I realized what we were doing, we passed the landing
of the Hudson River Day Line, where a paddle steamer was
taking on passengers for an excursion, and then we headed east
on Forty-second Street and then north up Eighth again, and so
on, marking a big rectangle around the area known as Hell's
Kitchen uptown and down, east and west, three or four times,
until we finally came to a stop on a block in the West Forties not
far from the stockyards. I saw Mr. Schultz's car parked maybe a
half a block ahead of us on the south side of the street, right in
front of a big brownstone church with an attached rectory and
schoolyard.

The driver did not turn off the engine. Mr. Berman lit a
cigarette and he said to me the following: "We cannot call the
Chairman on the telephone. Nor will he speak to any of us on
sight, not even Dixie Davis, who anyway is in Utica testifying at
an inquest having to do with the lamentable death of a dear
colleague of ours. My judgment is you are the only one who can
get in the door. But you must dress nice. Wash your face and
wear a clean shirt. You are going to have to see him for us."

All at once I was consoled. The crisis included me. "Is that Mr.
Hines?" I said.

He took out a notepad and wrote down an address and tore

off the page and handed it to me. "You will wait till Sunday. On Sunday he receives people in his home. You may tell him where we are in the event he has news for us."

"Where?"

"If I am any judge we will be residing at the Soundview Hotel in the city of Bridgeport Connecticut."

"What do I say to him?"

"You will find him charming and easy to talk to. But you don't have to say anything." Mr. Berman had removed his bankroll again. This time when he took off the rubber band, he unfolded the money the other way, where the thousand-dollar bills were, and he counted off ten and gave them to me. "Put these in a white envelope before you go. He loves clean white envelopes."

I folded the ten thousand dollars flat and shoved them deep in my breast pocket. But they felt very bulky, I kept pressing my side to make sure they were flat. We sat there in the car looking down the street at the black Packard.

I said: "I don't suppose this is a good time to bring up a personal problem."

"No, not too good," Mr. Berman agreed. "Maybe it's something you can take it up with the padre after he's through with Mr. Schultz. Maybe you will have better luck."

"What is Mr. Schultz doing in there?"

"He's asking for a safe harbor. He wants to be left in peace. But if I am any judge, although I'm not a religious man myself, they will give him confession and communion and all the things they give, but providing a hideout is not one of their sacraments."

We stared through the windshield at the empty street. "What is your problem?" he said.

"My mother is sick and I don't know what to do," I said.

"What's wrong with her?"

"Her mind is wrong, she acts crazy."

"What does she do?"

"She does crazy things."

"Does she comb her hair?"

"What?"

"I said does she comb her hair? As long a woman combs her hair you don't have to worry."

"Since I have come home she combs her hair," I said.

"Well then maybe it's not so bad," he said.

EIGHTEEN

Of course I would be lying if I said I didn't think about that ten thousand dollars in my pocket, and what I could do if I just went away with it, packed our bags and took my mother to the train station and got us on a train to go somewhere far away, migod, ten thousand dollars! I remembered the Business Opportunities section of the *Onondaga Signal,* how you could buy farms of hundreds of acres for a third of that, surely what was true of one part of the country would be true everywhere. Or we could buy a store, a little tea shop, something reliable, where we could work and keep ourselves decently and in my off hours I could scheme for the future. Ten thousand dollars was a fortune. Even if you just left it in a savings bank you made money.

At the same time I knew I would do nothing of the kind, I didn't know what I would do but I sensed that the nature of my own business opportunity was still to make itself known, life held no grandeur for a simple thief, I had not gotten this far and whoever had hung this charm over my life had not chosen me because I was a cowardly double-crosser. I tried to imagine what Drew Preston would think. She wouldn't even understand such small-mindedness, and it would have nothing to do with morality, she would just not understand backing off to the furtive edges of life like that because it was going in the wrong direction. What was the right direction? Toward trouble. To the agony of circumstance. It was the same direction I had been traveling since that first ride on the back of the trolley car to Mr. Schultz's policy business on 149th Street.

So while I had my larcenous thoughts I did not seriously consider them, my real problem was to keep this incredible amount of money safe, I had stashed my truly earned six hundred dollars in my suitcase on the top shelf of the bedroom closet, but that clearly wouldn't do, so I got down on the floor and stuck my hand up into the hole under the couch where the stuffing was falling out, and made a little cottony shelf in there and rolled the bills into a tube and wrapped a rubber band around them and shoved them in. Then for three days I hardly left the apartment, I thought that I might unwittingly betray my secret by the expression on my face, that people could read money in my eyes, but mostly I didn't want to leave the house unattended, I bought our groceries and ran home, if I wanted air I sat on the fire escape, and in the evening after my mother cooked dinner, I watched her very carefully when she lit one of her memory glasses because since my return she had taken to doing that again, one each evening, she was getting her lights going so she could understand what there was to understand.

On the second day I went to the candy store and bought a white business envelope for a penny, and early the next morning, bathed and combed and wearing a clean shirt, but not willing to risk a trip to Manhattan looking like a swell with money in his pocket, I wore only the trousers of my linen suit and topped everything with the black side of my Shadows jacket, and I took the Third Avenue El downtown. I would have given whatever odds you asked that nobody else on the train was carrying ten thousand dollars in his pants, not the stolid working men bobbing in unison on the cane seats, not the conductor opening the doors, nor the motorman in the front cab, or for that matter the people in the windows of the tenements we passed. I would have given odds that unless there was some smartass school kid in one of the cars nobody on the train would even know whose face was on a thousand-dollar bill. If I got up and announced that I was carrying that amount of money people would move away from me as from a crazy man. But these callow reflections finally had the effect of making me nervous, and rather than continue by train, I got out at the 116th Street station and invested my own money in a cab crosstown to Eighth Avenue and 116th, where the Chairman, James J. Hines, maintained an apartment.

It was interesting how slummy, run-down, and squalid his neighborhood was at the foot of Morningside Heights, with overflowing garbage cans and Negro men standing around on the corners and pitching pennies, but how grand and finely kept his apartment house, as if it was on Park Avenue. A doorman in a uniform politely answered my inquiries and a shiny brass modern self-service elevator took me to the third floor. But the squalid life had preceded me: I found myself at the end of a corridor of waiting men, they were standing in the dim light as if on a breadline. Men on a breadline stand close upon one another with their feet spread somewhat apart and their attention directed to the head of the line, as if only absolute concentration could move it along. But the line moved very slowly and when someone, having concluded his business, made his exit everyone stared at him as if to see in his face the success or failure he had had. It took me thirty or forty minutes to reach the open door of the great man's apartment. In that time I imagined myself living my whole life in destitution. Year after year, standing on lines and looking for a handout, shrinking in my clothes, my mind slowly polishing itself into the mind of a beggar. I carried money for the man, I was there to give him something, yet I had to stand there in that sweltering hallway and wait my beggar's turn.

Then I was in a foyer, or anteroom, where a few disconsolate men sat with their hats in their hands like patients in a doctor's office and I joined them, moving along chair by chair as I got closer to the inner sanctum, until finally I was admitted through double doors to a hallway where a man at a desk and another man standing behind him looked me over, I recognized them as of the same ilk I had been living among for some months, the kind you can hear thinking. Mr. Berman had felt no need to instruct me. I was not old enough to be a voter looking for a job, I was not a familiar of the neighborhood, I was a scrubbed boy trying to look his threadbare best. "I am the son of Mary Kathryn Behan," I said truthfully. "Since my father deserted us we have fallen on hard times. My mother works in the laundry but she is too ill to hold her job much longer. She says I must tell Mr. Hines she has always voted the Democratic ticket." The gorgons exchanged a glance and the standing one went off down a hallway. Maybe a minute went by and he came back and escorted me the same way, past a dining room with glass-doored china cabinets, and a living room filled with massive furniture, and some sort of game room with framed citations and a billiards table, and then I was shown into a carpeted heavily draped bedroom that smelled of apples and wine and shaving lotion, a very atmospheric habitat that did not appear to include any open windows. And there propped atop the covers on a grand bank of pillows, in a dark red silk robe, with the hairless legs of an old man protruding, was James J. Hines himself, the Tammany district leader.

"Good morning, lad," he said, looking up from his morning paper. He covered the whole length of the bed. His feet were large and knobbed and had thick callus on the bottoms, but other than that he was a handsome man, with silver hair combed down flat, a ruddy squarish face set with small features, and very clear light blue eyes, which looked at me amiably enough, as if he was reasonably disposed to hear whatever story I was about to tell, considering the stories he had already heard this morning and the stories still waiting in the corridor all the way to the elevator. I said nothing. He waited, and then grew puzzled. "Do you want to speak your piece?" he said.

"Yes sir," I said, "but I can't with this gentleman breathing down my neck. He reminds me of my truant officer."

That drew a smile until he saw the deadly serious expression on my face. He was not a stupid man. He dismissed the henchman with a wave and I heard the door close behind me. I stepped boldly to the side of his bed and removing the envelope from my pocket placed it on the coverlet beside his large meaty hand. His blue eyes fixed on me with alarm. I stepped back and watched the hand. First the index finger tapped in thought. Then the whole hand slid into the envelope, which was not sealed, and the fingers, spatulate though they were, deftly withdrew the crisp bills and fanned them out like cards, in what was, all in all, an impressive exhibition of an old man's dexterity of joints.

When I looked up, Mr. Hines leaned back on his pillow and sighed as if the burden of his life was suddenly too much to be borne. "So he has such cunning, still, as to use a lad to get through to me, the dirty bastard?"

"Yes sir."

"Where would he find such a trustworthy child?"

I shrugged.

"Then there is no Mary Behan after all?"

"Oh yes, she is my mother."

"I am relieved to hear that. Years and years ago I placed a fine young Irish woman in service who came to America by that name. She was the age of my youngest daughter. Where do you live?"

"In the Claremont section of the Bronx."

"That's right. I wonder if it's not the same person. She was a tall girl with a lovely carriage, and a quiet and modest way about her, the kind of girl the Sisters adore, I knew she would find a husband in no time at all, Mary Behan. And who is the scoundrel who would desert a woman like that?"

I didn't answer.

"What is your father's name, lad."

"I don't know, sir."

"Oh, I see. I see. I am sorry." He nodded several times and pressed his lips together. Then his expression lightened. "But she has you, has she not. She has raised a capable son with a bold spirit and a clear inclination to live dangerously."

"She has indeed," I said, slipping right into a mimicry of his lilting rhythms, it was hard not to, his speech was powerfully a part of him, he was a politician, the first I'd ever met, but I could tell by the way he made you translate yourself into his language that he was a good one.

"I was an adept fellow too, at your age. Perhaps a bit bigger in the bones, coming of a line of smiths. But with the same little man's gift for trouble." He paused. "You do not need my assistance, do you, to take your mother out of that laundry and see to her ease and comfort in the sadness of her life?"

"No sir."

"I thought as much but I wanted to be sure. You're a clever boy. Maybe you have some black Irish in you. Or Jew. Maybe that accounts for the company you keep." He grew silent and stared at me.

"Well if that is all, sir," I said, "I know you have people waiting."

As if he had not heard, he indicated a chair next to the bed where I should sit. I watched the big hand snap closed the fan of bills and insert them in the envelope. "Nothing makes me sadder I assure you than to turn back such a generous warrant of heartfelt feeling," he said. He pushed the envelope toward me. "They are fine crisp bills in the noblest of denominations. You understand I could accept them and he would be none the wiser. You understand? But I won't do that. Will you explain that to him? Will you explain that James J. Hines does not perform miracles? It's all too far along, Master Behan. There is that little Republican with the mustache. And he with not a touch of the poet in him."

The blue eyes regarded me until I realized I was to pick up the envelope. I did and slipped it into my pocket. "Where did he discover the son of Mary Behan, on the street?"

"Yes."

"Well you tell him for me I am impressed, at least, with that. And as for you personally you know I wish you only a long and prosperous life. But I'm through with him. To hell with him. I thought he understood after that unpleasantness upstate. I thought I had made myself clear. You don't know what I'm referring to, do you?"

"No sir."

"Never mind, I don't have to give him chapter and verse. Just tell him I can have nothing to do with him. The business between us is over. Will you tell him that for me?"

"I will."

I rose and went to the door. "It is a momentous thing when the money won't flow," Mr. Hines said. "I had hoped never to see the day." He picked up his newspaper. "Not that our friend is a man given to introspection, but he had a highly regarded associate in Mr. Weinberg. Who knows if that was the beginning. Who knows, perhaps the day he found you was the beginning."

"The beginning of what?"

He lifted his hand. "Give my fondest regards to your dear mother and tell her I asked after her," he said, and he had resumed his reading by the time I shut the door.

When I got back to the Bronx I went into the cigar store on Third Avenue under the El and bought a pack of Wings and got a handful of nickels for the pay phone and put in a long-distance call to the Soundview Hotel in Bridgeport Connecticut. There was no Mr. Schultz registered, no Mr. Flegenheimer, no Mr. Berman. I went home and when I got upstairs the door was open and a man from the telephone company was there with that belt they wear with all the tools hanging from it, he was considerately installing a telephone just beside the couch in the living room. I looked out the window and, just as I had thought, there was no green phone company truck anywhere on the street, I hadn't remembered seeing one. He left as considerately as he had worked, without a word, and the front door ajar only slightly. The white hub of the dial where the number was supposed to be printed was blank.

I put the envelope with the Hines money back up inside the couch stuffing and sat over it and waited. It seemed to me that ever since catching on with Mr. Schultz I had been assailed by these advanced beings who were there before I was and knew more than I knew, they'd invented telephones and taxicabs and elevated trains and nightclubs and churches, and courtrooms and newspapers and banks, it was all quite dazzling to be inserted by birth into their world, to slide out raw through the birth canal to be christened with a great clop, as if from a champagne bottle upside the head, so that life was forever after dazzling, with nothing quite making sense. What was I now supposed to do with them all and their arcane dealings, what was I supposed to do?

Not more than fifteen minutes passed before the phone rang. It was a strange sound in our little apartment, it was loud as a school bell, I could hear it ringing up and down the hall stairs. "You got a pencil?" Mr. Berman said. "I'll give you your number. You can call your mama now from anywhere in the United States."

"Thank you."

He gave me the number. He sounded almost jovial. "Of course you can't call out, but on the other hand you won't get a bill neither. So? How did it go?"

I told him the result of my interview with Mr. Hines. "I tried to reach you," I said. "They said you weren't there."

"We're in Union City New Jersey, just across the river," he said. "I can see the Empire State Building. Tell it again with the details this time."

"He says it's more than he can handle. He says you can blame the man with the mustache. He says not to contact him anymore."

"What mustache?" It was Mr. Schultz's voice. He had been listening on an extension.

"A Republican mustache."

"Dewey? The prosecutor?"

"I guess that's who."

"That son of a bitch!" he said. It was amazing, most people's voices are skinned down by the phone, but I could hear Mr. Schultz's in all its rich tonality. "Do I need him to tell us Thomas E. fucking Dewey is on my back? The son of a bitch. The goddamn shiteating son of a bitch. Won't take the money? Suddenly after all these years my money's not good enough? Oh, I'm going after that cocksucker, I'll take that money and shove it in his teeth, I'll make him eat it, he'll choke on it, I'll cut him open and paper his insides with it, he'll shit money I get through with him."

"Please, Arthur. Just a moment."

Mr. Schultz slammed his receiver and my ear rang all the way to New Jersey and back.

"Are you there, kid?" Mr. Berman said.

"Mr. Berman, meanwhile I'm holding this envelope and it makes me nervous."

"Just put it in a safe place for the time being," he said.

I could hear Mr. Schultz yelling in the background.

"We'll have things organized in a couple of days," Mr. Berman said. "Don't go anywhere. We need you I don't want to have to start looking."

So that was my situation for those hot Bronx days of Indian summer and the Diamond Home sprinkler fixing a rainbow every morning like a halo over the wet street and the children running under it and shrieking. I was mournful. My mother every day got up and went calmly enough off to work, and there was a wobbly balance to our lives, but she didn't like the phone on the end table next to the couch and dealt with it by putting the framed photograph of her and my defaced father in front of it. I bought us an electric fan that swiveled back and forth through a hundred-and-eighty-degree arc, flaring up the candles in their tumblers in the kitchen, but bringing a cool blow periodically to my shirtless back as I sat and read the papers in the living room. I had a lot of time to think about what Mr. Hines had said. He was a very wise man, it truly was a momentous thing when the money wouldn't flow. I had counted off my time with Mr. Schultz by the killings, the gunshots and sobs and cracking skulls resounded in my memory like tolling bells, but something else had been going on all that while, which was the movement of money, it had come in and it had gone out all that time, as uninterrupted as a tide in its incoming and outgoing, as steady and unceasing as the quiet celestial system of the turning earth. I had naturally fixed on the coming in, it had always been the matter of most vociferous concern as Mr. Schultz struggled to maintain his control despite his being on the lam and his legal

problems, despite the difficulties of running his business interests at a distance, and the thievery of lieutenants and the treachery of trusted associates, but the money that went out was just
as important, it bought arms and food, it bought lawyers and
cops and the goodwill of poor people, it paid for properties, it
paid for salaries and the good times that assured the men he
depended upon that he was of the magnitude of incandescence
they expected of a bright burning star. As far as I knew Mr.
Schultz didn't use the fortune he had undoubtedly made over
the years, he surely had amassed it but there was no sign of it
in his life, I supposed he must have a house or fancy apartment
somewhere where his wife lived, I knew they must have nice
things, but none of it sat on him like the mantle of their wealth
on those people in the boxes at Saratoga. He did not live rich,
he did not look it or act it or, from any evidence I had, feel it,
up in the country he had an entourage whose daily living ex-
penses he took care of, he went for the occasional horseback ride
and flung his money about like he was expected to, but it was
all for survival, there was no relaxed indolence of his right to it,
ever since I had first seen him he had been on the run, he was
a vagabond, he lived in hotel rooms and hideouts, he spent his
money to make more of it, he had to make it in order to keep
making it, because only if he kept making it would he live to
make more of it.

So that was why Mr. Hines's refusal to take the ten thousand
was such a monumental reverse: It didn't matter how the money
stopped flowing, in or out, the result was equally disastrous, the
whole system was in jeopardy, just as, if the earth stopped turning, according to what a teacher explained to us once in the
planetarium, it would shake itself to pieces.

Now I found myself pacing the floor the way he did, I was truly
excited, I knew now what Hines meant by the beginning, he
meant the end, the fact of the matter was that I had never seen
Mr. Schultz at the height of his powers, I didn't know him when
he had a handle on things and everything was as he wanted it
to be, I had come into his life when it had begun not to function
in his interest, all I had ever seen him do was defend himself,

I didn't remember a time when he wasn't embattled, everything we did, any of us, came of his concern to survive, everything he'd asked me to do that I had done was in the interest of his survival, collecting policy, going to Sunday school, even having my nose busted, even sleeping with Drew Preston and taking her to Saratoga and getting her out of his clutches was finally in the interest of his survival.

I couldn't have understood it that day on the cobblestones in front of the beer drop, when the third of the three silent cars pulled up to the curb, and all the boys came in awe to their feet and I juggled two Spaldeens, an orange, an egg, and a stone in adoration of our great gangster of the Bronx: He had risen and he was falling. And the Dutchman's life with me was his downfall.

After a silence of a day or two the phone began to ring regularly. Sometimes Mr. Berman was my dispatcher, sometimes Mr. Schultz, and I went off to do errands the nature of which I didn't usually understand. The press was following the story, so every day going downtown on the subway I found myself trying to figure out what I was doing by reading in the newspapers what the Special Prosecutor's Office was doing. One morning I went to the Embassy Club, which looked in the daytime down on its luck with its faded canopy and tarnished brasswork, and a man I didn't know opened the door and shoved a Dewar's White Label box into my arms and told me to get moving. In the box were ledgers and loose adding-machine tapes and business letters and invoices and so on. As I had been instructed I went to Pennsylvania Station and put the box in a coin-operated locker and I mailed the key to a Mr. Andrew Feigen at a hotel in Newark New Jersey. Then I read in the *Mirror* that the special prosecutor had subpoenaed the records of the Metropolitan Restaurant and Cafeteria Owners Association upon the mysterious death of its late president, Julius Mogolowsky, alias Julie Martin.

On another day I ran up a dank creaking stairs off Eighth Avenue to seek out the boxing trades of Stillman's at their work. This is the famous gymnasium, and I am thrilled to pay my admission, but I don't know what I'm supposed to do here except to give one of the thousand-dollar bills to someone I don't know the name of or what he looks like. I notice in the ring a shining black man with beautiful muscles and wearing leather armor about the head, punching punching while five or six men stand around shouting out advice, the same proportion as in the WPA pothole crews. Trow der right, Nate, dat's it, one two, give it toom. This is the race of men Mickey the driver comes from, the race of the raised ear, the flattened nose, the blind eye, they hulk about and skip and nod and spit in pails, and oh the whoppering bags and the resined sneakers squeaking, I understand the sweetness of this life, it is held in a small space, like a religion, it is all suspended in the thick smell of men's sweat, sweat is the medium of existence, like righteousness, they breathe one another's faith, it is in the old leather, it is in the walls, I can't resist, I grab a jump rope and give it a half a hundred turns. And as it happens I don't have to look for my man, it is very simple, he is the one who notices I am here. One of the men instructing the boxer in the ring, he comes over in his sweatshirt that doesn't quite cover all of his hairy white belly and gives me the big long-time-no-see greeting, putting one stinking arm around my shoulder, which brings me in tight to the open palm he holds in front of me as he walks me to the exit.

There was nothing in the papers to help me with that one, only the feeling that it all went together, all the sweating exertions of the killer spirit.

Another thousand goes to a bail bondsman at magistrates court where Dixie Davis got his start, he is a little bald guy with a cigar stub that works its way from one side of his mouth to the other as he watches me remove the bill from my wallet. I reflect that John D. Rockefeller only gave away dimes. On Broadway and Forty-ninth at the august offices of Local 3 of the Window Washers and Building Maintenance Workers, a man who is to take another of the one-thousand-dollar bills does not happen at the moment to be in, and so I wait, sitting in a wooden chair by a railing across the desk from a woman with a black mole over her lip, and she is frowning about something, perhaps her loss of privacy, because I might see how little she has to do, the window behind her is tall and wide and entirely unwashed and stepping down through its plane of dirt are the legs of the monocled top-hatted Johnny Walker whiskey sign on the roof of the building across the street, these enormous rising and falling black boots walking in air over Broadway.

To tell the truth I loved this time, I sensed my time was coming, and it had to do with the autumn, the city in its final serious turn toward the winter, the light was different, brilliant, hard, it tensed the air, burnished the top deck of the Number Six double-decker bus with a cold brilliant light, I made a stately ride in anticipation of death, crowds welled at the corners under the bronze streetlamps with the little Mercuries, police whistles blew, horns blew, the tall bus lurched from gear to gear, flags flew from the stores and hotels, and it was all for me, my triumphal procession, I reveled in the city he couldn't enter, for a minute or two it was mine to do with what I would.

I wondered how long he could resist, how long he could control himself and not test their resolve, because they knew his haunts, they knew where his wife lived, they knew his cars and his men, and now without Hines there was no fix, not in the precincts, not in the courts, he could board the Weehawken ferry, he could come through the Holland Tunnel, he could cross the George Washington Bridge, there were a lot of things he could do, but they knew by now where he was and would know when he left, and that made New York a fortress, a walled city with locked gates.

After a week or so I had dispensed half of the ten one-thousand-dollar bills. As far as I could understand these were not payoffs I was making, for the most part they were warrants of continuity, little organizational stanchings because Thomas E. Dewey was drawing blood, he had found some Dutch Schultz bank deposits under false names and had had them frozen, he had subpoenaed records of the brewery the Dutchman owned, his assistants were interviewing police officers and others whose names they would not divulge to the press. But if there was money for this aspect of things, there had to be money to rebuild from the bottom, payoff by payoff, someone had to be doing it, there were ways after all, you're telling me Mickey couldn't shake a tail? Irving couldn't turn invisible? There were twenty, twenty-five men at the morning meeting in the whorehouse parlor, not all of them were in Jersey, the organization was functioning, twenty-five was not a hundred or two hundred but business was going on, stripped down, on hard times, its reach diminished, but mean and murderous and with plenty of money for lawyers.

So that's how I figured it to be, or how it would be if I was running things, I would be patient and bide my time and take no chances, and for a couple of weeks, maybe even into early October, that's the way it was. But I was not Mr. Schultz, he surprised you, he surprised himself, I mean why suddenly do I read that an entire floor in the Savoy-Plaza has been wrecked, that an unknown thief or thieves have broken into one of the residential apartments and done tens of thousands of dollars' worth of damage, cut up paintings, ripped down tapestries, smashed pottery, defaced books, and presumably stolen property of a value not known because the residents of the apartment, Mr. and Mrs. Harvey Preston—he is the heir to the railroad fortune—are abroad and cannot be reached?

Then one night, following my instructions, I took the Third Avenue El to Manhattan, and the streetcar all the way crosstown to the West Twenty-third Street ferry slip, and then I stood on the deck of the beamiest bargiest boat in the world, a boat that carried thousands of people every day in such unnautical stability as to suggest a floating building, a piece of the island of New York separated for the convenience of its citizens and let out on a line across the river, I stood on this boat that smelled like a bus or a subway car with chewing-gum wads pressed into its decks and candy wrappers under the cane seats and looped straps for standees to hang on to, and the same wire trash baskets you found on street corners, and I felt under my feet the tremors of the dark harbor, the lappings of the alive and hungry ocean, I looked back on New York and watched it drift away and I thought I was going for a dead man's ride.

I will say here too, at the risk of offending, that my arrival at the industrial landing on the Jersey shore, with ranks of coal barges lying at anchor and brick factories spewing smoke and the whole western horizon filled with the pipes and tanks and catwalks of hellish refineries, did not give me the assurances I sought from having land under my feet. A yellow cab was waiting outside the terminal and the cabby waved and as I approached he reached back and opened the passenger door, and when I got in it was Mickey who greeted me with an uncharacteristically effusive nod and a smart takeoff that threw me against the back of the seat.

You had to go through Jersey City to get to Newark, there was apparently some governmental distinction to be made between them, but I could see no difference, both cities together being just a continuous dreary afterthought of New York, a kind of shadow on the wrong side of the river, you could tell they thought they were the Bronx or Brooklyn, and they had the bars and the streetcars and the machine shops and warehouses, but the air stank in a different way, and the stores were old-fashioned and the width of the streets was wrong and the people all had that look of being noplace, they looked at up at the signs on the corners to remember where they were, it was a most depressing flatland, a monument to displacement, and I could tell Mr. Schultz would go out of his mind here trying to get comfortable prowling from Union City to Jersey City to Newark to find the best window where he could look out and see the Empire State Building.

It was a cemetery, no question about that, it was too ugly to live in. Mickey pulled up in front of this bar on a street paved not with asphalt but in whitish cement and with the telephone and streetcar wires hanging like a loose net over everything and let me off and drove away. The name of the place was the Palace Chophouse and Tavern. Now I will admit I had come to a tentative conclusion—that if Mr. Schultz was to all intents and pur-

poses locked out of doing business in New York, and none of
the trusted associates could take a chance either on going in for
any prolonged length of time, I mean as the only one who had
free rein, my value to the gang was increased and I thought I
should be made a full-fledged member. I was doing more and
more responsible work and I wondered why I had to depend on
the odd handout that was thrown my way, no matter how
munificent it happened to be. They were making advanced assumptions about me, counting on me in a really brazen fashion
when you thought that I was not even being paid. I wanted a real
wage and I thought if Mr. Schultz didn't happen to murder me
I might be in a position to ask for it. But when I walked down
the bar, turned a corner, and passed through a short corridor
into the windowless back room where Mr. Schultz and Mr. Berman and Irving and Lulu Rosenkrantz were sitting at a table by
the wall, the only diners, I knew I would not bring up the matter,
it was peculiar, it was not a question of fear, which I was reck-
lessly prepared to deal with, but of a loss of faith, I don't know
why but I looked at them and I felt it was too late to ask for
anything.

The room they were in had pale green walls, with decorative
mirrors of tarnished metal, and the overhead light made them
all look sallow. They were eating steaks and there were bottles
of red wine on the table that looked black in this light. "Pull up
a chair, kid," Mr. Schultz said. "Are you hungry or anything?"

I said I wasn't. He looked thin, peaked, his mouth was primed
to its most undulant pout, he was sorely oppressed, and I noticed the collar of his shirt was curled at the corners, and he
needed a shave.

He pushed his plate away with his dinner hardly eaten and he
lit a cigarette, which was another thing because when he was
feeling in control of things he smoked cigars. The others went
on eating till it became apparent he had not the patience to wait
for them to finish. One by one they put their knives and forks
down. "Hey, Sam," Mr. Schultz called, and a Chinese man came
out of the kitchen and took the plates away and brought cups of
coffee and a pint bottle of cream. Mr. Schultz turned and

watched him go back to the kitchen. Then he said, "Kid, there is a son of a bitch named Thomas Dewey, you know that, don't you?"

"Yes sir."

"You seen his picture," Mr. Schultz said, and he removed from his wallet a photo that had been torn out of a newspaper. He slapped it down on the table. The special prosecutor, Dewey, had nice black hair parted in the middle, a turned-up nose, and the mustache to which Mr. Hines had alluded, a little brush-style mustache. Mr. Dewey's dark and intelligent eyes gazed at me with a resolute conviction of the way the world ought to be run.

"All right?" Mr. Schultz said.

I nodded.

"Mr. Dewey lives on Fifth Avenue, one of those buildings that face the park?"

I nodded.

"I will give you the number. I want you to be there when he comes out in the morning and I want you to watch where he goes, and who is with him, and I want to know what time that is, and I want to know when he comes home from work and what time that is and who is with him then. He runs his show from the Woolworth Building on Broadway. You don't have to worry about that. It is only the comings and the goings from home to office and back. The comings and the goings is what interests me. You think you can handle it?"

I glanced around the table. Everyone, even Mr. Berman, was looking down. Their hands were folded on the table, all three of them like children at their school desks. None of them besides Mr. Schultz had said a word since I had walked in.

"I guess."

"You guess! Is that the attitude I come to expect from you, I *guess*? You been talking to these guys?" he said pointing his thumb to the table.

"Me? No."

"Because I was hoping someone in this organization still had guts. I could still rely on somebody."

"Aw boss," Lulu Rosenkrantz said.

"Shut the fuck up, Lulu. You're ugly and you're dumb. That is the truth of you, Lulu."

"Arthur, this is not right," Mr. Berman said.

"Fuck you, Otto. I am being punched out and you are telling me what is not right? Is it right my getting my ass handed to me?"

"This was not the understanding."

"How do you know? How can you tell?"

"The decision was to take it under advisement, they're looking into it."

"I'm looking into it. I'm looking into it because I'm gonna do it."

"We have a compact with these people."

"Fuck compacts."

"You don't remember he came hundreds of miles to stand for you in church?"

"Oh I remember. He came up showing me this attitude like he and the pope together was doing me this big fucking favor. Then he sits and eats my food and drinks my wine and says nothing. Nothing! I remember all right."

"Maybe not nothing," Mr. Berman said. "Maybe just the fact of his being there."

"You can't hear him half the time, like he has no voice box. You gotta lean over and put your face in that garlic mouth and then it still doesn't matter because you don't know what anything means, he likes something he don't like something, it's all the same, you don't know what he's thinking, you don't know where you stand with him. He's taking what under advisement! How do you know? Can you tell me what anything means with the son of a bitch? Me, if I like something I tell you, I don't like something I tell you that, I don't like someone he fucking well knows it, that's the way I am and that's the way it should be, not this secrecy of feelings each and every moment that keeps you guessing what the truth is."

Mr. Berman lit a cigarette and cupped it in his palm with his thumb and forefinger. "These are matters of style, Arthur. You got to look past these things into the philosophy. The philosophy is that their organization is intact. It is available to us. We have the use of it, the protection of it. We combine with it and together we make a board and we sit on the board with our vote. That is the philosophy."

"Yeah, it's a great philosophy all right, but have you noticed? I'm the one this dog-fucker Dewey is after. Who do you think sicced the Feds on me! It's my leg he has in his teeth."

"You have to understand they have an interest in our problem. It is their problem too. They know he knocks down the Dutchman it's their turn next. Please, Arthur, give them a little credit. They are businessmen. Maybe you're right, maybe this is the way. He said they would study it to see how it could be done but in the meantime they want to think about it a little while. Because you know as well as they do even when it's a lousy cop on the beat who is hit the city goes wild. And this is a major prosecutor in the newspapers every day. A hero of the people. You could win the battle and lose the war."

Mr. Berman kept talking, he wanted to calm Mr. Schultz down. As he went on to make each point of his argument, Lulu kept nodding and furrowing his brow as if he had been just about to say the same thing. Irving sat with his arms folded and his eyes lowered, whatever decision was made he would go along with it, as he always had, as he would to the day he died. "The modern businessman looks to combination for strength and for streamlining," Mr. Berman said. "He joins a trade association. Because he is part of something bigger he achieves strength. Practices are agreed upon, prices, territories, the markets are controlled. He achieves streamlining. And lo and behold the numbers rise. Nobody is fighting anybody. And what he has a share of now is more profitable than the whole kit and caboodle of yore."

I could see Mr. Schultz gradually relaxing, he had been leaning forward and holding the edge of the table as if he was about to turn it over, but after a while he sagged back in his chair and then he put his hand on top of his head, as if it hurt, a peculiar gesture of irresolution that as much as anything compelled me to pipe up as I did: "Excuse me. This man you mentioned, the one who came to the church. Mrs. Preston told me something about him."

I will talk about this moment, what I thought I was doing, or what I think now I thought I was doing, because it is the moment the determination was made, I think about all their deaths and the manners of dying, but more about this moment of the determination, where it came from, not the heart or the head, but the mouth, the wordmaker, the linguist of grunts and moans and whimpers and shrieks.

"She knew him. Well not that she knew him but that she'd met him. Well not that she entirely remembered meeting him," I said, "or she would have mentioned it herself. But she drank," I said looking a moment at Irving, "she herself told me that and when you drink you don't remember that much, do you? But what she felt on the street in front of St. Barnabas," I said to Mr. Schultz, "is that when you introduced them, she thought he looked at her as if he recognized her. She thought perhaps she must have met him before."

It was so still now in the Palace Chophouse and Tavern that I heard Mr. Schultz's breathing, the magnitude of his respiration was as familiar to me as his voice, his thought, his character, it came in slowly and went out quickly in a kind of one two rhythm that left a silence between breaths that seemed like a consideration of whether to breathe at all.

"Where did she meet him?" he said, very calm.

"She thought it must have been with Bo."

He swiveled in his chair and faced Mr. Berman and sat back and stuck his thumbs in his vest pockets and a big broad smile came over his face. "Otto, you hear this? You grope around and you grope around and all the time the child is there to lead you."

The next moment he had jumped out of his chair and smashed me on the side of the head, I think he must have used his forearm, I didn't know what had happened, the room wheeled, I was suddenly confused, I thought there had been an explosion, that the room was falling in on me, I saw the ceiling lift and the floor jump toward me, I was flying backward over the chair, going down backward in the chair I'd been sitting in and when I hit the floor I lay there stunned, I wanted to hold on to the floor because I thought it was moving. Then I felt terrible pounding pains in the side, one after another, and as it turned out he was kicking me, I tried to roll away, I was crying out and I heard chairs scraping, everyone talking at once, and they pulled him off me, Irving and Lulu actually pulled him away from me, I realized that later when I began to hear in my mind what they had been saying, *it's the kid for christsake, oh Christ, leave off, boss, leave off,* all that urgent straining talk in the pinioning of violence.

Then as I rolled on my back I saw him shrug loose of them and hold his hands in the air. "It's all right," he said. "It's okay. I am all right."

He yanked on his collar and pulled at his vest and sat back down in his chair. Irving and Lulu took me under the arms and put me instantaneously on my feet. I felt ill. They righted my chair and sat me in it and Mr. Berman pushed a glass of wine toward me and I took it with both hands and managed to swallow some of it. My ears were ringing and I felt a sharp pain on the left side every time I took a breath. I sat up straight, in that way your body instantly accepts what has happened to it, though your mind does not, I knew that if I sat straight and took only shallow breaths through the nose the pain was relieved somewhat.

Mr. Schultz said: "Now kid, that was for not telling me before. You heard what she said, that cunt, you should have come to me right away."

I started to cough, little hacking coughs that were excruciatingly painful. I swallowed more wine. "This was the first chance," I said, lying, I had to clear my throat to get my voice back, I didn't want to sound like I was sniveling, I wanted to sound offended. "I been busy doing everything you asked me, is all."

"Let me finish, please. How much of that ten grand is left that you been holding."

With trembling hands I took five thousand dollars out of my wallet and put it on the white tablecloth. "All right," he said. He took up all the bills but one. "That is for you," he said pushing it toward me. "A month's advance. You are now on the payroll at two hundred and fifty a week. This is what justice is, you see? The same thing you deserved a licking for you deserve this." He looked around the table. "I didn't hear nobody else give me the word on our downtown comparey."

Nobody said anything. Mr. Schultz poured wine in all the glasses and drank his own with a loud smacking of the lips. "I feel better now. It didn't feel right in that meeting, I knew it didn't feel right. I don't know how to combine. I wouldn't know how to begin. I was never a joiner, Otto. I never asked anybody for anything. Everything I got I got for myself. I have worked hard. And how I got where I got is I do what I want, not what other people want. You put me with those goombahs and suddenly I have to worry about their interests? Their interests? I don't give a shit for their interests. So what is all this crap. I'm not about to give it away, I don't care how many D.A.s come after me. That is what I was trying to tell you. I didn't have the words. Now I got them."

"It doesn't have to mean anything, Arthur. Bo liked a good time. It could have been at the track. It could have been in a club. It don't have to mean anything."

Mr. Schultz shook his head and smiled. "My Abbadabba. I never knew the numbers were for dreaming. A man gives me his word and it's not his word, a man works for me all those years and the minute I turn my back he conspires against me, I don't know, who has gotten to him? Who in Cleveland gets such an idea?"

Mr. Berman was very agitated. "Arthur, he's not stupid, he's a businessman, he looks at the choices and he takes the path of least resistance, that is the whole philosophy of the combination. He didn't have to see the girl to know where Bo was. He showed you a mark of respect."

Mr. Schultz pushed back from the table. He took his rosary out of his pocket and began to twirl it, around went the rosary in a tightening circle, it dangled for a pendulous moment and then spun the other way, looping out before snapping up tight again. "So who turned Bo? I see your precious combination, Otto. I see the whole fucking world ganging up on me. I see the man who takes me into his church, the man who makes me his brother and embraces me and kisses me on the cheek. Is this love? These people have no more love for me than I have for them. Is this the Sicilian death kiss? You tell me."

NINETEEN

And that's how I came to shadow Thomas E. Dewey, the special public prosecutor appointed to clean up the rackets, and future district attorney, governor of New York, and Republican candidate for president of the United States. He lived in one of those limestone-cliff Fifth Avenue apartment buildings that look over Central Park, it wasn't that far north of the Savoy-Plaza, in one week I became very familiar with the neighborhood, I idled lurked and strolled usually on the park side, across the street, along the park wall in the shade of the plane trees, sometimes diverting myself by trying not to step on the lines of the hexagonal paving blocks. In the early morning the sun came up through the side streets filling them from the east with light and shooting out like Buck Rogers ray guns across the intersections, I kept thinking of shots, I heard them in the backfirings of trucks, I saw them in the rays, I read them in the chalk lines made by the kids on the sidewalks, everything was shots in my mind as I shadowed the public prosecutor with a view toward setting him up for assassination. In the evening the sun went down over the West Side and the limestone buildings of Fifth Avenue glowed gold in their windows and white on their faces, and all up and down the stories maids in their uniforms pulled the drapes closed or let down the awnings.

In these days I felt very close to Mr. Schultz, I was the only one cooperating in the deepest spirit with him, his most trusted adviser deplored his intentions, his two most loyal personal attendants and bodyguards suffered grave misgivings, I was alone with the man in his heart, was what I felt, and I have to confess I was excited to be there alone with him in his cavernous transgression, he had slugged me and kicked my ribs in and now I felt a real love for him, I forgave him, I wanted him to love me, I realized he was able to get away with something no other person could get away with, for example I still did not forgive Lulu Rosenkrantz my broken nose, and in fact when I thought about it I didn't like the way Mr. Berman had lifted twenty-seven cents from me with one of his cheap math tricks that time in the policy office on 149th Street when I had barely caught on with the organization, Mr. Berman had been my mentor ever since, generously bringing me along, nurturing me, and yet I still did not forgive him that loss of a boy's few pennies.

You can't expect to shadow someone effectively unless you are an unremarkable figure appropriate to the landscape. I bought a scooter and wore my good pants and a polo shirt and I did that for a day or so, then I got a puppy from a pet shop and walked him along on a leash except people who were out early walking their own dogs kept stopping to say how cute he was while their dogs sniffed his wagging little ass, and that was no good, so I gave him back, it was only when I borrowed the wicker carriage from my mother for a couple of days and took it downtown by taxicab to stroll along with it like an older child watching his mother's new baby that I felt I had the right camouflage. I bought a doll from Arnold Garbage for two bits with a cotton bonnet to keep its face in shadow, people liked to get their babies out in the early morning, sometimes nurses in white stockings and blue capes pushed these elaborate heavily sprung lacquered perambulators along with netting to keep the bugs off of the little darlings, so I bought netting and draped it over the carriage so that even if some old lady got really nosey she couldn't see inside, and sometimes I walked and sometimes I sat on the bench just across the street from where he lived and pushed the carriage out and pulled it back and bounced it gently on its broken-down springs and in this manner learned that the early morning was the time with the fewest people and the most inflexible routine, without a doubt the morning appearance of Mr. Dewey was the preferred time to dispatch him.

And my mother liked that doll, she was pleased to have me enter her imagination with her, she rummaged through her old cedar chest to find the baby clothes there, my baby clothes, and to dress the doll in the musty little gowns and scalp caps she had dressed me in fifteen years before. But all this you see was the innocence of murder, I loved my mother for being innocent of the murders around her, as worried prophets are, I loved her very much for the stately madness she had chosen to suffer the murders in her life of love, and if I had any qualms for the work I was doing I had only to think of her to know that I was on the nerve of my innate resolve and so I could trust that it was all going to work out, that everything would end as I dreamed it would.

In fact I will declare right now that I knew while I held something of these events in my hands, I would not have them bloodied. I realize this assurance sounds self-serving and I hereby apologize to all of Mr. Dewey's relatives, heirs, and assignees for the revulsion they may feel, but these are confessions of a wild and desolate boyhood and I would have no reason to lie about any one of them.

Oddly enough the person I felt bad about was Mr. Berman, the moment I had chosen at the Palace Chophouse to reveal what Drew Preston had told me he must have perceived as an act of treachery, the moment of his ruination, it was the end of all his plans, when his man would not finally be brought along into the new realm he foresaw, where the numbers ruled, where they became the language and rewrote the book. He said to me once, apropos of this idea, this dapper little humpbacked man with the clawlike fingers: "What the book says, well let me put it this way, you can take all the numbers and stir them around and toss them up in the air and let them fall where they may and remake them back into letters and you have a whole new book, new words, new ideas, a new language you've got to understand with new meanings and new things happening, a new book entirely." Well that was a dangerous proposition, if you thought about it, was the proposition of X, the value he couldn't abide, the number not known.

But in his last glance for me over his glasses, the brown eyes widening to their blue rims, he saw everything instantly, with a kind of despairing reproach. What a tidy little thing the mind is, how affronted by the outlying chaos, he was game, this little guy, he'd made a brilliant life out of one faculty, and he'd always been kind to me, if deviously instructive. I ask myself now if my small word to the wise made that much difference, if it wasn't better for Mr. Schultz to go down knowing what his situation was, as Bo Weinberg had, if that honor wasn't due him; whereas he might never have known what hit him. And anyway I think now he knew all along, it was why perhaps he publicized his desire to assassinate the prosecutor, a suicidal act in any event, real or proposed, and it was as he said, I had just given him the words he was looking for all along for the feeling he had, that at the age of what, thirty-three? thirty-five? he'd run out of reprieves, the moment had long since passed when all the elements for his destruction had combined, and his life was attenuated, in the manner of a fuse.

But what I thought I was doing was delivering a message between intimates, a necessary message that could not be left undelivered, though I had tried, and he had understood that I had tried and so had thrashed me. I knew them both so well. She made me a boy again in the humming space between them: You tell him, would you? she had said, and lifted her binoculars so that I could see the parade of small horses curving around the lens.

And then it is time for my report, and it is late one night in the same back room of the Palace, with the pale green walls and the regularly spaced tarnished mirrors in frames suggesting with a few lines of hollowed-up tin the streamlined modernity of the skyscraper, their hierarchy of arches like a platformed chorus of

pretty girls with raised knees, and we all sit sallow at the same
back table with the impeccably clean cloth and it is so late by the
time I get there, dinner is over, they have before them now not
the thick plates and cups and saucers but the thinnest of adding-
machine tapes, their eternal fascination, the time is midnight, I
saw that on the neon-blue clock over the bar as I walked in,
midnight, the moment of justice cleaved to the moment of
mercy, Midnight, the best name for God.

And this is the moment I am finally with them, one of them,
their confidant, their colleague. There is first of all the sense of
craft that suffuses me, the sweetness of knowing one thing well.
There is second of all the malign pleasure of conspiracy, the
power you feel from just planning to kill someone who may at
that moment be kissing his wife or brushing his teeth or reading
himself to sleep. You are the raised fist in his darkness, you will
fell him from his ignorance, it will cost him his life to know what
you know.

Every morning he comes out exactly the same time.

What time?

Ten minutes to eight. There is a car there, but the two plain-
clothes get out of the car to meet him at the door and they walk
with him while the car follows. They walk together to Seventy-
second, where he goes into the Claridge Drugstore and makes
a call from the phone booth.

Every day?

Every day. There are two phone booths to the left just inside
the door. The car follows and it waits by the curb and the
bodyguards stand outside while he makes his call.

They wait outside? Mr. Schultz wants to know.

Yes.

What's inside?

On the right as you walk in is the fountain. You can get
breakfast at the counter. Every day is a different special.

Is it crowded?

I never saw more than one or two people at that hour.

And then what does he do?

He comes out of the booth and waves to the counterman and he leaves.

And how long is he in there altogether?

Never more than three or four minutes. He makes that one phone call to his office.

How do you know to his office?

I've heard. I went in to look at magazines. He tells them what to do. Things he's thought of during the night. He has a little pad and he reads from his notes. He asks questions.

Why would he leave his house to make a phone call? Mr. Berman says. And then on the way to work where he's going to see them in fifteen twenty minutes anyway?

I don't know. To get more done.

Maybe he's afraid of a tap? Lulu Rosenkrantz says.

The D.A.?

I know, but he knows from taps, maybe he just don't want to take the chance calling from his own house.

He's seeing witnesses all the time, Mr. Schultz says. He is very secretive, he gets them in there the back way or something so nobody knows who's squealing. I know that about the son of a bitch. Lulu's right. He doesn't miss a trick.

What about the return journey? says Mr. Berman.

He works late. It could be anytime, sometimes as late as ten. The car pulls up, he gets out and he's in the lobby in a second.

No, the kid's got it figured, Mr. Schultz says, the morning is when. You put two guys with silencers at the counter with their coffee. Is there a way out of there?

There's a back door leading into the lobby of the building. You can go down to the basement and come out on Seventy-third Street.

Well then, he says, putting his hand on my shoulder. Well then. And I feel the warmth of the hand, and the weight of it, like a father's hand, familiar, burdensome in its pride, and he is beaming his appreciation in my face, I see the mouth open in laughter, the large teeth. We will show them what is not allowed, won't we, we will show them how far you can't go. And I will be in Jersey all the time and will pull a long face and say I had no personal grief against the man. Am I right? He squeezes my shoulder and rises. They will thank me, he says to Mr. Berman, they will end up thanking the Dutchman for the caution I have instilled, you mark my words. This is what streamlining means, Otto. This.

He tugs on the points of his vest and goes off to the bathroom. Our table is in the corner in a right angle of pale green walls. I am facing the walls with my back to the doorway leading to the bar, but I have an advantage because the tarnished mirror allows me to see farther down the transverse corridor into the bar than someone sitting under the mirror and looking straight out. It is the peculiar power of mirrors to show you what is not otherwise there. I see the blue neon cast of the clock tube above the bar as it encroaches on the floor of the passageway to the dark tavern. It is like a kind of moonlight on black water. And then the water seems to ripple. At the same time I hear the bartender's rag suspended in its swipe over the zinc bar beneath the draft beer taps. I hear now that I heard the front doors to the street open and close with unnatural tact.

How did I know? How did I know? With the first wisp rising from the crossed wires of murderous intent? Had I believed of our conspiring that we had invoked images too powerful for the moment, as in some black prayer, so that they had inverted, and were flashing back on us to blow us sky-high? There is that earliest notion of leaning forward in the chair, the body getting ready from the base of the spine up.

Silencers, Lulu says, thinking of his life to come. Mr. Berman is just twisting around to look to the entrance and Irving's eyes rise with me as I rise to my feet. I notice how well-combed Irving's thin hairs are, how neatly in place. Then I am in the short passage leading to the kitchen at the rear. I find the men's room door. I am hit by the salt stink of a public bathroom. Mr. Schultz stands at the urinal with his legs apart and his hands on his hips so that the back of his jacket wings out, and his water arcs from him directly into the urinal drain, thus making the rich foaming sound of a proud man at his micturation. I try to tell

him how, as an action, this is terribly obsolete. And when I hear
the guns I think he has been electrocuted through the penis, that
he made the mistake I have read about in the novelty books, of
urinating in a thunderstorm when the lightning can hiss up from
the ground in an instantaneous golden rainbow and flash you
out like a bomb.

But he is not electrocuted, he is jammed with me in the small
stall, I am standing on the toilet seat and his shoulder bangs into
me as he fumblingly removes the pistol from his belt, I don't
even know if he knows I'm there, he holds the gun cocked,
pointed at the ceiling, and with his other hand he is doing an
amazing thing, he is trying to button his fly, we don't listen to
the explosions, we are rocked by them, they ring in the ears, they
become a continuous erupting disaster in the ears, and I dig in
the pocket of my Shadows jacket for my Automatic and it is
twisted in the material of the lining, and I have to struggle with
it, I am as graceless as Mr. Schultz, and now I smell the powder,
the bitter sulfurous aftermath coming under the door like a
poison gas, and at this moment Mr. Schultz must realize that he
has no real protection in here, he will be killed in a toilet stall,
he slams the door open with the heel of his hand and pulls open
the bathroom door and I understand he is shouting, a great
wordless scream of rage issues from him as he springs out and
raises his arms to shoot, and through the two doors as they are
held open by the wind of fire I see the black ovoid stain of sweat
under his arm, I see him stumble forward and disappear, I see
the pale green corridor wall, and I hear the deeper roar of the
new caliber even as he spins back into view, and totters out again
leaving sensational maps of the holes in him on the wall of the
passageway as the doors slowly swing closed.

You don't know urgent life if you haven't heard a gun in your
ears, it is the state of being able to do anything, defy all laws,
a small window, like a transom, is at the back of the stall, just
under the ceiling, I use the chain of the holding tank to haul
myself to where I can reach it, it opens down into the room on
a pair of elbow hinges, the window is much too small to get
through, so I do it feet first, swinging them up and hooking them

one at a time, and then twisting sideways and getting my legs
through and then my hips then my painful ribs, and then I let
go with my arms over my head like Bo going into the drink, I
give myself a good crack as I slide out and fall to the ground,
it is a ground of crushed cinders, like the bed of a railroad track,
and it compacts my legs, I feel sharp pain, I have twisted my
ankle, cinders are imbedded in my palms. And my heart seems
to have gone awry, it pounds in furious broken rhythms as if it
has gone off its shocks, it's sliding around my chest, lodging in
my throat. It is the only thing I hear. I limp I scurry down the
alley, holding my gun in my jacket pocket just like a real gangster
in action, I peek around the corner of the Palace Chophouse and
Tavern into the street and a speeding car without lights a half
a block away fishtails and wavers a moment and in another
moment it is lost in the shadows of the street, and I watch and
wait but I don't see it anymore. I didn't see it turn, I step off the
curb and stand in the gutter and the long back street is empty
under its streetcar wires as far as I can see.

And what I hear now are my own streaming sobs. I open the
door to the bar and look in. The smoke lingers in the blue light
and bottleshine. The bartender's head rises above the bar, sees
me and appears to decapitate itself, and that is funny, fear is
funny, I gimp my way to the back, turn, come down the short
corridor of the visitation, and before I look into the room oh the
air is bad burned air and humid with blood, I don't want to see
this vealy disaster, I don't want to be contaminated by this terrible sudden attack of the plague. And I am so disappointed in
them, I peek in, I almost trip on Irving, face down, a gun still
in his hand, one leg drawn up as if he is still in the act of chasing
them, and I step over him and Lulu Rosenkrantz sits blasted
back against the wall, he never got out of his chair, it is tilted
precipitously, like a barber's chair, and held fast against the wall
by his head, Lulu's hair sticks up ready for the haircut and his
forty-five caliber is in his open hand on his lap as if it was his
penis and he stares at the ceiling as in the intense sightless effort
of masturbation, my disappointment is acute, I do not feel grief

but that they have died so easily, as if their lives were so care-
lessly held, this is what disappoints me, and Mr. Berman slumps
forward on the table, his pointed back stressing the material of
his plaid jacket in a widening hole of blood, his arms are flung
forward and his cheek rests against the table and his glasses are
pressed under his cheek on one leg the other standing away
from his temple, Mr. Berman has failed me too, I am resentful,
I feel fatherless again, a whole new wave of fatherlessness, that
they have gone so suddenly, as if there was no history of our life
together in the gang, as if discourse is an illusion, and the sequence of this happened and then that happened and I said and
he said was only Death's momentary incredulity, Death staying
his hand a moment in incredulity of our arrogance, that we
actually believed ourselves to consequentially exist, as if we were
something that did not snuff out from one instant to the next,
leaving nothing of ourselves as considerable as a thread of
smoke, or the resolved silence at the end of a song.

Mr. Schultz lying flat on his back on the floor was still alive,
his feet were turned slightly outward he looked at me quite
calmly as I stood over him. His expression was solemn and his
face was shining with sweat, he had his hand inside his bloodied
vest like Napoleon standing for his portrait and he seemed to be
in such imperial control of the moment that I hunkered down
and spoke to him in the assumption that he was quite rationally
aware of his situation, which he was not. I asked him what I
should do, should I call the cops, should I get him to a hospital,
I was ready for his orders, not mistaking the seriousness of his
condition, but half expecting him to ask me to help him up, or
to get him out of here, but in any event to be the one who
decided what should be done and how. He gazed at me as calmly
as before but simply did not answer, he was so extendedly suffering the shock of what had happened to him that he wasn't
even in pain.
But there was a voice in the room, I heard it now like the
wording of the acrid smoke, a whispering it was, too faint to
understand, yet Mr. Schultz's lips did not move but he only

stared at me as if, given the character of my feeling, his impassive gaze was commanding me to listen, and I tried to locate the sound, it was terrifying, fragmentary, where it came from, I thought for a moment it was my own breathy intake of stringed snot, I wiped my nose on my sleeve, I dried my eyes with the heels of my hands, I held my breath, but I heard it again and terror made my knees buckle as I realized, swiveling on my heels, that it was Abbadabba talking from his grimace alongside the tabletop, I cried out I didn't think he was alive I thought he was giving utterance from his death.

And then it seemed to me quite natural that their division would be expressed at this moment too, between the brain and the body, and that as long as Mr. Schultz was still alive, Mr. Berman would still be thinking for him and saying what Mr. Schultz wanted said, however corporeally dead Mr. Berman might be. Of course Mr. Berman was still himself alive, however faintly, but it was this other idea that presented itself as the logical explanation to my mind. It was perhaps some comfort for the thought that I had myself sundered them. I laid my head on the table alongside his and I will say here now what he said though I cannot suggest the time it took his voice to round itself for each word, with long rests between them as he sought for additional breath like a man searching his pockets for the money he cannot find. While waiting I stared at the blurred columns of numbers on his adding machine tapes that were strewn on the table. There were lots of numbers. Then, to make sure I was hearing correctly, I watched the words form in his teeth before I heard them. It is difficult for me to suggest the sense of ultimate innocence conveyed by his statement. Before he got through it I was hearing the distant sound of police sirens, and it was so arduous for him to speak it that he died of the effort: "Right," he said. "Three three. Left twice. Two seven. Right twice. Three three."

When I realized Mr. Berman was dead, or again dead, I went over to Mr. Schultz. His eyes were closed now, and he moaned, it was as if he was regaining consciousness of what had happened, I didn't want to touch him, he was wet, he was too alive

to touch, but I put my fingers in his vest pocket and felt a key
and I removed it, and wiped the blood on his jacket, and then
I found his rosary in his pants pocket and I put it in his hand,
and then, since the police cars were pulling up to a stop outside,
I went back into the bathroom and went through the window
again, again torturing my ribs and my ankle, and at the head of
the alley the street was filling in with lights and people running
and cars pulling to a stop, I waited a minute or two and slipped
out quite easily into the crowd and stood for a while across the
street in the doorway of a radio store and watched them bring
out the bodies on stretchers covered with sheets, the bartender
came out talking with police detectives and then they brought
Mr. Schultz out strapped in a stretcher and with a blood plasma
bottle held alongside by the ambulance attendant, and the
Speed-Graphics flashed, and when the photographers dropped
their used bulbs in the street they went off like gunshots, which
made the neighborhood people jump back nervously who had
come out to watch in their bathrobes and housecoats, and everyone laughed, and the ambulance with Mr. Schultz moved off
slowly, its siren wailing, and men ran alongside a few steps to
look in the rear window, murders are exciting and lift people
into a heart-beating awe as religion is supposed to do, after
seeing one in the street young couples will go back to bed and
make love, people will cross themselves and thank God for the
gift of their stuporous lives, old folks will talk to each other over
cups of hot water with lemon because murders are enlivened
sermons to be analyzed and considered and relished, they speak
to the timid of the dangers of rebellion, murders are perceived
as momentary descents of God and so provide joy and hope and
righteous satisfaction to parishioners, who will talk about them
for years afterward to anyone who will listen. I drifted to the
corner, and then walked quickly down a side street away from
the scene, and then made a two-block-wide circuit of the Palace
Chophouse and Tavern, and when that yielded nothing, I went
out two more blocks and made a bigger square, and by this
means found the Robert Adams on Trenton Street, a four-story
hotel of pale brick hung with rusted fire escapes. I sneaked easily

past the clerk sleeping behind his reception desk and hobbled up the stairs to the fourth floor, and after reading the number on the key I had taken from Mr. Schultz's pocket I let myself into his room.

The light was on. In the closet, behind his hanging clothes, was a smaller safe than the one I remembered from the hideout in the house outside Onondaga. I was not able to open it right away. I could smell his clothes, they smelled of him, of his cigars and his rages, and my hands were shaking, I was not well, I was in pain that made me sick to my stomach, and so it took me a few minutes to work the combination, right to thirty-three, twice around left to twenty-seven, and two twirls to the right back to thirty-three. Inside the little safe were packs of bills in rubber bands, the real actual facts of all those numbers on the tapes. I shoveled them out and stacked them in an elegant alligator valise chosen for Mr. Schultz by Drew Preston in the early days of their happiness in the north country. The bills filled it full, it was very satisfying to build this solid geometry of numbers. A great solemn joy filled my breast, in the nature of gratitude to God, as I realized I had made no mistakes to offend Him. I snapped the hasps shut just as I heard the footsteps of several people running up the stairs of the old hotel. I relocked the safe, drew Mr. Schultz's clothes across the bar in front of it, let myself out the window and climbed up the fire escape, and I spent that night, it was October 23, 1935, on the roof of the Robert Adams hotel in Newark New Jersey, sobbing and sniffling like a wretched orphan, and falling asleep finally in the paling dawn, where to the east, I could see in the distance the reassuring conformations of the Empire State Building.

T W E N T Y

Mr. Schultz had been mortally wounded and he died at New-ark City Hospital a little after six the next evening. Just before he died a nurse's aide brought his dinner tray into the room and left it there, having had no instructions to the contrary. I came out from behind the screen where I'd been hiding and I ate everything, consommé and roast pork and cooked carrots, a slice of white bread, tea, and a trembling cube of lime Jell-O for dessert. Afterward I held his hand. He was by then in a coma and lay quietly with his broad, bare and badly sewn chest rising and falling, but for hours, all afternoon, in fact, he'd been delirious and talked constantly, he shouted and wept and issued orders and sang songs, and because the police were trying to find out who shot him they sent in a stenographer to put his ravings on record.

I found to hand behind my screen a nurse's clipboard with some pages of medical record forms attached, and in the top drawer of a white metal table, which I slid out very slowly, the stub of a pencil. And I wrote down what he said as well. The police were interested to know who killed him. I knew that, so I listened for the wisdom of a lifetime. I thought at the end a man would make the best statement of which he was capable, delirious or not. I figured delirium was only a kind of code. My version doesn't always match the official transcript, it is more selective, being in longhand, there are words misheard, mistakes of my own emotion, I was also constrained not to be noticed by anyone who came at various times into the room, it was busy in there at times what with the stenographer, police officers, the doctor, the priest, and Mr. Schultz's real wife and family.

The stenographer's transcript made its way into the newspapers and so Dutch Schultz is remembered today for his protracted and highly verbal death, coming of a culture where it tends to happen abruptly to men who never had that much to say in the first place. But he was a monologist all his life, he was never as silent as he thought he was or as ill-equipped in speech. I think now, as one who linked my life to his, that whatever he did was of a piece, the murdering and the language for it, he was never at a loss for words, whatever he pretended. And while this monologue of his own murder is a cryptic passion, it is not poetry, the fact is he lived as a gangster and spoke as a gangster, and when he died bleeding from the sutured holes in his chest he died of the gangsterdom of his mind as it flowed from him, he died dispensing himself in utterance, as if death is chattered-out being, or as if all we are made of is words and when we die the soul of speech decants itself into the universe.

No wonder I got hungry. He went on for over two hours. I sat there and got to know that screen well, I think the material was muslin and it was laced taut on a green metal frame that could be rolled about on four little rubber casters, and his words seemed to paint themselves there on the translucent light of the cloth, or perhaps it was on my own unwritten mind, and I wrote them down, interrupted only by the wearing-down of the lead of the pencil, which I then had to reexpose by picking at the wood with my fingernails. Anyway I'll enter this here as I heard it delivered between the hours of four and six P.M. of October 24, until the moment before he finally but not for all time fell silent.

"Oh mama, mama," he said. "Oh stop it stop it stop it. Please make it quick, fast and furious. Please, fast and furious. I am getting my wind back. You do all right with the dot dash system.

Whose number is that in your pocketbook, Otto: 13780? Oh oh,
dog biscuit. And when he is happy he doesn't get snappy. Please,
you didn't even meet me. The glove will fit what I say. Oh Kay
Oh Kaioh, oh cocoa, I know. Who shot me? The boss himself.
Who shot me? No one. Please, Lulu, and then he clips me? I am
not shouting, I am a pretty good pretzel. Ask Winifred in the
department of justice. I don't know why they shot me, honestly
I don't. Honestly. I am an honest man. I went to the toilet. I was
in the toilet and when I reached—the boy came at me. Yes, he
gave it to me. Come on, he cuts me off, the beneficiary of his will,
is that right? A father's son? Please pull for me. Will you pull?
How many good, how many bad? Please, I had nothing with him.
He was a cowboy in one of the seven days a week fights. No
business, no hangout, no friends, nothing, just what you pick up
and what you need. Please give me a shot. It is from the factory.
I don't want harmony. I want harmony. There is none so fair,
beyond compare, they call Marie. I'll marry you in church,
please, let me just put it in a little way. Let me into the district
fire factory. No no, there are only ten of us, and there are ten
million somewhere of you so get your onions up and we will
throw in the trucc towel. Oh please let me up, please shift me,
police, that is communistic strike baloney! I still don't want him
in the path, it is no use to stage a riot. The sidewalk was in
trouble and the bears were in trouble and I broke it up. Put me
in control, I'll throw him out the window, I'll grate his eyes. My
gilt edged stuff, and those dirty rats have tuned in! Please
mother, don't tear, don't rip. That is something that shouldn't
be spoken about. Please get me up, my friends. Look out, the
shooting is a bit wild, and that kind of shooting saved a man's
life. Pardon me I forgot I am plaintiff and not defendant. Why
can't he just pull out and give me control? Please mother, pick
me up now. Don't drop me. We'll have the blues on the run.
They are Englishmen and they are a type I don't know who is
best, they or us. Oh sir, get the doll a roofing. For God's sake!
You can play jacks and girls do that with a soft ball and play
tricks with it. She showed me, we were children. No no and it
is no. It is confused and it says no. A boy has never wept nor

dashed a thousand kim. And you hear me? Get some money in
that treasury we need it. Look at the past performances, that is
not what you have in the book. I love the boxes of fresh vegetables. Oh please warden, please put me up on my feet at once.
Did you hear me? Please crack down on the Chinamen's friends
and Hitler's commander. Mother is the best bet and don't let
Satan draw you too fast. What did the big fellow shoot me for?
Please get me up. If you do this you can go and jump right here
in the lake. I know who they are they are Frenchy's people all
right look out look out. Oh my memory is all gone. My fortunes
have changed and come back and went back since that. I am
wobbly. You ain't got nothing on him and we got it on his hello.
I am dying. Come on Missy, pull me out I am half crazy about
you. Where is she, where is she? They won't let me get up, they
dyed my shoes. Open those shoes. I am so sick, give me some
water. Open this up and break it so I can touch you. Mickey
please get me in the car. I don't know who could have done it.
Anybody. Kindly take my shoes off there is a handcuff on them.
The pope says these things and I believe him. I know what I am
doing here with my collection of papers. It isn't worth a nickel
to two guys like you and me, but to a collector it is worth a
fortune. It is priceless. Money is paper too and you stash it in
the shithouse! Look, the dark woods. I am going to turn—turn
your back to me please, Billy I am so sick. Look out for Jimmy
Valentine for he's a pal of mine. Look out for your mama, look
out for her. I tell you you can't beat him. Police, please take me
out. I will settle the indictment. Come on, open the soap duck-
ets. The chimney sweeps. You want to talk, talk to the sword.
Here is French Canadian bean soup on the altar. I want to pay.
I am ready. All my life I have been waiting. You hear me? Let
them leave me alone."

Simultaneous with the shootings in the Palace Chophouse
there had been attacks on known Schultz gang members in
Manhattan and the Bronx, two were dead, including Mickey the
driver, whose real name was Michael O'Hanley, three were seriously wounded, and the rest of the gang was presumed scat-

tered. I had read about it in the morning papers while waiting
for a train to Manhattan in the Newark station of the Pennsylvania Railroad. I was not mentioned in any of the accounts, the
bartender's statement had not included reference to a kid in a
Shadows jacket, which was good, but I put the valise in a pay
locker and rolled up my jacket and disposed of it in a trash
basket on the theory that not everything the bartender told the
police might have found its way into the newspapers, and then
I went out and got a taxicab to take me to Newark Hospital,
having persuaded myself that Mr. Schultz's room was at that
moment the safest place to be.

But now that he was dead, I was on my own. I looked at his
face, it was the deep red color of a plum, the mouth was slightly
open and the eyes staring up as if he had something else to say.
For a moment I was fooled into thinking he did. Then I realized
my own mouth was open as if I had something to say too, so that
my mind flashed with an entire normal conversation between us,
the one it was too late for, his confession and my forgiveness,
or perhaps the other way around, but in either case the conversation you only have with the dead.

I limped away before the nurses came in and discovered him.
I reclaimed my suitcase at the station and rode the train into
Manhattan. It was a chilly night for a boy having no jacket. I took
the crosstown trolley to the El, and I got back to the Bronx by
about nine at night and did not go home directly but came
around through the backyard of the Diamond Home for Children, and made my way into the basement where Arnold Garbage was listening to "The Make-Believe Ballroom" on the
radio while looking through old *Collier's* magazines. Without
going into details I told him I had to stash something and he
found me a small space in the back of his deepest darkest bin.
I gave him a dollar. Then I went back the way I had come, circled
around to Third Avenue, and walked home the front way.

For weeks afterward I sat in the apartment, I couldn't seem to
move, it was not that I was sore and aching, I could take aspirins
for that, I felt as if I weighed a thousand pounds, everything was

an enormous effort, even sitting in a chair, even breathing. I found myself looking at that black phone, waiting for it to ring, I even picked it up from time to time to see if anyone was on the other end. I sat with my Automatic stuck inside my belt, it was just the way Mr. Schultz had carried his gun. I was fearful that when I went to bed I would have nightmares but I slept the sleep of the innocent. Meanwhile the autumn began flying through the Bronx, winds rattled the windows and the leaves from God knows what distant trees came wheeling down our street on their crisp edges. And he was still dead, they were all still dead.

I kept thinking about Mr. Berman's last words to me and whether they meant anything more than the numbers of a combination lock. They were words to keep going, I could say that much, he was preserving something, he was passing it on. So they were trustful words. But trust could mean either of two things, not knowing any better or knowing full well, knowing all the time and never having let on, with those little looks over the tops of his glasses, the teacher, every act a teaching.

It was a strong powerful ghost they made in me, my dead gang. What happened to the skills of a man when he died, that he knew how to play the piano, for instance, or in Irving's case to tie knots, to roll up pant legs, to walk easily over a heaving sea? What had happened to Irving's great gift of precision, his just competence in everything, that I so admired? Where did that go, that abstraction?

My mother didn't seem to notice my state but she began to cook things for me that I liked, and she began to really clean the apartment. She snuffed the candles and threw out all her tumblers of lights, it was almost funny—now with someone really dead she was no longer in mourning. But I was only half aware of all of this. I was trying to figure out what to do with myself. I thought about going back to school and sitting in a classroom and learning whatever it was you learned in classrooms. Then I took it as a commentary on my sad state of mind that I would even consider such a thing.

I would from time to time take my transcript out of my pocket and unfold the pages and read again what Mr. Schultz had said.

It was a disheartening babble. There was no truth of history in it, no message for me.

My mother found a store on Bathgate Avenue that sold seashells, and she brought home a brown paper bag full of these tiny ridged shells, some were no bigger than a pinky nail, and she began another one of her mad projects, which was to paste them to the phone using airplane cement she had found from an old balsa model I had never finished constructing. She dipped a toothpick in the bottle of dope and spread a glistening drop around the rim of the tiny shell and glued it to the phone. Eventually the entire phone, receiver and base, was covered in shells. It was rather beautiful, generally white and pink and tan, and rippled and gnarled, as if it was losing its form, as if the form of all things is lost in our attentions. She even attached shells to the cord, so that it seemed like a string of underwater lights. I found myself crying for my crazy mother when I thought of her as James J. Hines recalled her, a young and stately and thoughtful and brave young immigrant. I thought she must for a time have ennobled my father and that he had enlightened her in their undeniable love for each other before he had taken a powder. I had the money now never to have to send her away. I swore she would stay with me and I would take care of her for as long as she lived. But I couldn't seem to get going on anything, not even to the point of persuading her to quit her job. I suppose it was not a very gladdening prospect I saw before us. I was made very lonely by her strange use of objects, candles or pictures or remnants of clothing, broken dolls, and shells. One evening she came home with a fish tank, it was very heavy and she had trouble carrying it up the stairs, but her face was flushed and her expression happy as she put it on the end table beside the couch and filled it with water and then gently submerged the phone. How I loved my mad mother, how beautiful she was, I felt so bad, I felt I had failed her, I thought she had not changed because I had not gotten the final justice for us. The money in the valise across the street in the basement wasn't enough, I couldn't believe all the efforts of my intuitive scheming were fulfilled by it, of course, though I didn't know how much there

was, even one month's weakened earnings of Schultz enter-
prises was enough to live on for several years, good God if I just
drew from it twice my mother's salary from the laundry we
would have everything we could possibly need, but I was terribly
worried by it, we wouldn't be able to take it to a bank, I would
have to think about it how to protect it all the time and use it
in such dribs and drabs that it wouldn't draw attention to us and
this seemed to me part of its skimpy insufficiency. I thought if
it was going to change anything then it should have already, just
the possession of it. But it hadn't. Then I realized that even
though he was dead I felt about the money that it was still Mr.
Schultz's. I had picked it up on instructions from Mr. Berman
and now I found myself waiting for further instructions. I did not
feel the calm I knew should come to me from the resolution of
all my dreaming. I had nobody to talk to, nobody to know, in any
event, to tell me I had done well. In fact only the dead men of
my gang could ever appreciate as much as I had done.

And then late one night I was buying the papers at the kiosk
on Third Avenue under the El when a De Soto pulled up and
the door opened, and I was surrounded by men, two had come
out of the cigar store at the same time as two came out of the
car, and they had the impassive expressions on their faces of the
criminal trades. All one of them had to do was nod toward
the open door of the car and I folded my papers under my arm
and got right in. They drove me all the way downtown to the
Lower East Side. I knew it was important not to panic, or to
imagine what might be happening to me. I thought back to all
my movements of the past year and couldn't understand how he
could know about me, I hadn't even let him get a good look at
me in front of the church steps. I saw now that I had made one
terrible mistake in not writing a letter to my mother with instructions to her only to open it if I didn't come home and didn't
come home and died of not coming home to my mother.

They pulled up in a narrow tenement street, though naturally
they didn't give me a clear look at it. I felt across my face the
barred shadows of fire escapes in the dimly lit street. We
climbed a stoop. We walked up five flights.

All at once I was in a kitchen under a bare ceiling-bulb and facing, as he sat at a little table covered with oilcloth like a rich visiting relative, the man who had won the gang wars. Here is what I saw: two mildly inquisitive eyes of no great intelligence and one of them drooped under a heavy hanging eyelid. And he really did have bad skin, I saw that now, and the scar under his jaw was whiter than everywhere else. All told he had a kind of lizardy look. His best feature was a good head of slicked-back wavy black hair. He was wearing a well-tailored topcoat over his businessman's ensemble. His hat was on the table. His nails were manicured. I smelled an eau de cologne. His was altogether a different style of malignity from Mr. Schultz's. I felt as you feel when you walk a few blocks into another neighborhood though it is not that far from your own. He gestured with an open hand very politely so that I would sit down opposite him.

"First of all, Billy," he said in a very soft voice, as if all conversation was regrettable, "you know how bad we feel what happened to the Dutchman."

"Yes sir," I said. I was appalled that he knew my name, I didn't want to be in his registry of names.

"I had the greatest respect. For all of them. I knew them how many years? A man like Irving, you don't find his quality."

"No sir."

"We are trying to find out the cause of this thing. We are trying to get his boys back and put something together, you know, for the widows and children."

"Yes sir."

"But it is turning out to have difficulties."

The tiny room was crowded with the men standing behind me and behind him. Only now did I see, off to the side, Dixie Davis, the mouthpiece, slumped in a wooden chair with his knees pressed together and holding his hands locked between them to keep them from shaking. The underarms of Mr. Davis's expensive pinstripe suit had big dark sweat stains and his face was covered by a film of sweat. I knew these as signs of the extreme unction. I acknowledged him with the briefest of glances because I understood now who had identified me, which meant all

I was giving away was the truth they already knew and I thought it might suggest I wasn't smart or devious enough to try to hide anything.

Then I turned back to my interrogator. It seemed important to me to sit straight and look at him clear-eyed. He would learn as much from my attitude as from anything I said.

"You were coming along nicely in their eyes is my understanding."

"Yes sir."

"We might have a job for a bright kid. Did you get out of it at least with something to show?" he said as casually as if my life wasn't in the balance.

"Well," I said, "I was just catching on. I was put on salary the week before and he gave me a month's advance because my mother's been sick. Two hundred dollars. I don't have it with me, but I can get it from the savings bank first thing in the morning."

He smiled, the corners of his mouth turned up for an instant, and he raised his hand. "We don't want your wages, kid. I'm talking about business affairs. They managed their business not always in a business way. I was asking if you could help us figure out about assets."

"Gee whiz," I said, scratching my head, "that is more in Mr. Davis's department. All I did was run out for coffee or if someone needed a pack of cigarettes. They never let me in meetings or where anything was going on."

He sat there nodding. I could feel Dixie Davis's eyes on me, I could feel the intensity of his stare.

"You never saw any money?"

I thought a moment. "Yes, once, on a Hundred Forty-ninth Street," I said. "I saw them counting the day's collection while I was sweeping. I was impressed."

"You were impressed?"

"Yes. It was something to dream about."

"Have you dreamed?"

"Every night," I said looking him in the drooped eye. "Mr. Berman told me the business is changing. That they will need smart quiet people with good manners who have been to school. I am going back into school and then I'm going to go to City College. And then we'll see."

He nodded, and grew very still and gazed into my eyes for a moment as he made up his mind. "School is a good idea," he said. "We may look in on you from time to time, see how you're doing." He lifted his hand, palm up, and I rose with it. Dixie Davis had put his hand over his face.

"Thank you, sir," I said to the man who had ordered the killings of Mr. Schultz, Mr. Berman, Irving, and Lulu. "It is an honor to meet you."

I was returned safely to Third Avenue, driven right back and dropped off in front of the cigar store. Only then did I become terrified. I sat down on the curb. My hands were black where they had moistly picked up the newsprint of the papers I had been holding. I read fragments of headlines in my palms, pieces of words. I had no idea what might be going to happen to me. Either I was free or my days were numbered. I just didn't know. I jumped up and began to walk the streets. I found myself shaking, but not with fear, with anger at myself for my fear. I thought: Let them kill me. I waited for the sound of the engine of the specific killing car screeching around the corner with the windows rolling down. And then I tried to figure out what they would think I had done to make them kill me. They wouldn't kill me, they would watch me. That's what I would do if I didn't know where the money was.

The fact was I had learned something very interesting: The newspapers had estimated Mr. Schultz's fortune as anywhere between six and nine million dollars. Very little of it had been put in banks. The Combination hadn't found it, they were looking for it, they had the business but they wanted the money too, they wanted the business from its beginnings.

And it was odd but from one moment to the next I was exhilarated by the attentions of another great man, dangerous as they were, I thought it was indeed possible my days were numbered but my competitive spirit was reawakened, I realized I had been sharing the defeat of the gang in a morbid way, I had been dwelling on their deaths. But nothing was over, it was all still going on, the money was deathless, the money was eternal and the love of it was infinite. I waited a few days and then went down to Arnold Garbage's basement while he was out foraging, and I made a private space for myself in case anyone came in, and in the ashen air, with the footfalls of children over my head, I counted the cash in the alligator suitcase. I was a long time counting, it was far more than I had thought, I will mention the precise amount, it took me several hours to count it, it was three hundred and sixty-two thousand and one hundred and twelve dollars I had taken for my portion and stashed there under carriage parts and old newspapers and broken toys and bed slats and stovepipes, and paper bags of shoes, and clothing in bales, and pots and pans and panes of glass and machine gears and acetylene torches and screwdrivers without handles and hammers and saws without teeth and shoeboxes of bubble-gum cards, and bottles and jars and baby bottles and cigar boxes of rubber nipples and typewriters and parts of saxophones and the bells of trumpets and the torn skins of drums and bent kazoos and broken ocarinas, and baseball bats and ships in cracked bottles and bathing caps and Boy Scout hats and badges and campaign buttons and piggy banks and bent tricycles and molding stamp collections and tiny flags on toothpicks from all the nations of the world.

And then of course I went back to my handwritten statements of what he had said and studied them and found there my vision of living in flowering reward, I had been too impatient, a great charmed fate unfolds, unfolds, unfurls in waves, and floops out to the sun like the planet in flower, I heard Mr. Schultz's voice say *a capable boy, a capable boy* and oh I was! because I found stashes of money in his sentences, the money of his delirious passion locked away there like an insane man's riddle, I studied that transcript in my own handwriting and I learned from it what he had told me, he told me there would be money for Mrs.

Schultz and his children somewhere they would know about, but the meaning of his life and his genius, why he would salt it about as his years went on so that you could find it in the periods of his criminal career as in his neighborhoods. And to test this proposition I went one night with Arnold Garbage after I had sat for weeks in schoolrooms to prove myself not worth watching, and we broke open a lock in the old abandoned beer drop on Park Avenue where I used to stand around and juggle, and in the shudder of a passing train we went down into a darkness black as if the fires had gone out in hell, and with rats brushing against our ankles and in the dankness of the history of the old beer runs, found there in the shit and refuse of Arnold's dreams, by his faint flashlight, an unbunged barrel stuffed to the coops with the currency of the United States, and Arnold lugged it and rolled it home on a pushcart over the cobblestones while I went ahead of him and stood in the shadows of doorways, and from that midnight hour we became partners in a corporate enterprise that goes on to this very day.

But I don't mean to suggest I was satisfied that was all there was, the more he was beset the more he would gather it to himself, didn't I know him? I studied that transcript of his ghost's voice and I learned from it what he had told me, he had told me that as the world closed in he would pull his fortune to him, that the worse things got the more he would gather himself unto himself, he would call it in, like stocks like bonds like chips from the gambling table, keep more and more of it near him from day to day as he made the ever more perilous journey. And at the end he would stash it where no one ever dreamed he had been and if he never got back to it it would die with him if no one was smart enough to find it.

So now I knew everything, and everything brings with it an exacting discretion, I went back to school to stay, hadn't I been told it was a good idea? and though it was ordeal enough to quash the most resolute heart, I sat there in those classrooms alone with my education and for good measure worked prominently in a fish store after school for five dollars a week, and wore a white apron ornamented with normal daily splashings of blood, and managed to bide my time simply by assuming that all of it was being watched.

Within a year of Mr. Schultz's death the man with bad skin was himself indicted and tried by Thomas E. Dewey and sent away to prison. I knew enough of gang rule that as it accommodated itself to change, priorities shifted, problems were redefined, and there arose new issues of criminally urgent importance. So it would have been possible right then to go upcountry in safety. But I was in no rush. Only I knew what I knew. And something like a revelation had come to me through my school lessons: I was living in even greater circles of gangsterdom than I had dreamed, latitudes and longitudes of gangsterdom. The truth of this was to be borne out in a few years when the Second World War began, but in the meantime I was inspired to excel at my studies as I had at marksmanship and betrayal, and so made the leap to Townsend Harris High School in Manhattan for exceptional students, whose number I was scornfully unastonished to be among, and then the even higher leap to an Ivy League college I would be wise not to name, where I paid my own tuition in reasonably meted-out cash installments and from which I was eventually graduated with honors and an officers' training commission as a second lieutenant in the United States Army.

In 1942, the man with bad skin was pardoned by Governor Thomas E. Dewey, who as district attorney had sent him up, and deported to Italy in thanks for the assistance he was thought to have provided in making the New York City waterfront secure against Nazi saboteurs. But by then I was myself patriotically employed overseas, and so, what with one thing and another, I was not able to claim the treasure until I got home from the war in 1945. That is almost all I will say of this matter although the larcenous reader will be able figure things out for himself, for herself, in fact anyone can put two and two together, it's all right with me, because of course I did go and collect it, it was just where I knew it would be, Mr. Schultz's whole missing fortune which to this day and until now people have believed was never recovered. It was in the form of bundled Treasury certificates and crisp bills in the noble denominations of Mr. Hines's love and it was stuffed in a safe, packed in mail sacks. My veteran's self was moved by the prewar quaintness of it, it was like pirate swag, monument to an ancient lust, and I had the same feelings looking at it that I get from old portraits or the recordings of dead though still fervent singers. But none of these feelings discouraged me from taking it.

And here I realize I have come almost to the end of this story of a boy's adventures. Who I am in my majority and what I do, and whether I am in the criminal trades or not, and where and how I live must remain my secret because I have a certain re-nown. I will confess that I have many times since my investiture sought to toss all the numbers up in the air and let them fall back into letters, so that a new book would emerge, in a new language of being. It was what Mr. Berman said might someday come to pass, the perverse proposition of a numbers man, to throw them away and all their imagery, the cuneiform, the hieroglyphic, the calculus, and the speed of light, the whole numbers and frac-tions, the rational and irrational numbers, the numbers for the infinite and the numbers of nothing. But I have done it and done it and always it falls into the same Billy Bathgate I made of myself and must seemingly always be, and I am losing the faith it is a trick that can be done.

I find some consolation, however, in having told here the truth about everything of my life with Dutch Schultz, although in some respects my account differs from what you will read if you look up the old newspaper files. I have told the truth of what I have told in the words and the truth of what I have not told which resides in the words.

And I have now just one more thing to tell, and I have saved it for last because it is the fount of all my memory, the event that doesn't exonerate the boy I was but may delay for a moment reading him out of heaven. I drop to my knees in reverence to think of it, I thank God for the life He has given me and the joy of my consciousness, I praise Him and give all reverent thanks

for my life of crime and the terror of my existence. In the spring
following Mr. Schultz's death my mother and I were living in a
top-floor five-room apartment with a southern exposure overlooking the beautiful trees and paths and lawns and playgrounds
of Claremont Park. And one Saturday morning in May there was
a knock on the door and a man in a chauffeur's uniform of light
gray stood there holding a straw basket by the handles, and I
didn't know what I thought it was, laundry or something, but my
mother came past me and took the basket as if she had been
expecting it, she had great authority and confidence now, so that
the chauffeur was very relieved, he'd had on his face an expression of the utmost anxiety, she was dressed in a real black dress
that was appropriate to her figure and in fashionable shoes that
fit her, and hose, and her hair was cut and combed in a comely
manner to frame her serene lovely face, and she just took the
baby, because that's of course who it was, my son with Drew, I
knew the minute I looked at him, and she brought him into our
apartment of morning sun and laid him in the holey brown
wicker carriage that she had brought with her from the old
apartment. At that moment I felt a small correction in the just
universe and my life as a boy was over.

There was some confusion after that, of course, we had to go
out and buy bottles and diapers, he didn't come with any instructions, and my mother was a little slow remembering some
of the things that had to be done when he cried and waved his
arms about, but we adjusted to him soon enough and what I
think of now is how we used to like to go back to the East Bronx
with him and walk him in his carriage on a sunny day along
Bathgate Avenue, with all the peddlers calling out their prices
and the stalls stacked with pyramids of oranges and grapes and
peaches and melons, and the fresh bread in the windows of the
bakeries with the electric fans in their transoms sending hot
bread smells into the air, and the dairy with its tubs of butter and
wood packs of farmer's cheese, and the butcher wearing his thick
sweater under his apron walking out of his ice room with a stack
of chops on oiled paper, and the florist on the corner wetting
down the vases of clustered cut flowers, and the children run-

ning past, and the gabbling old women carrying their shopping bags of greens and chickens, and the teenage girls holding white dresses on hangers to their shoulders, and the truckmen in their undershirts unloading their produce, and the horns honking and all the life of the city turning out to greet us just as in the old days of our happiness, before my father fled, when the family used to go walking in this market, this bazaar of life, Bathgate, in the age of Dutch Schultz.

E. L. DOCTOROW is the author of *Welcome to Hard Times* (1960), *Big as Life* (1966), *The Book of Daniel* (1971), *Ragtime* (1975), *Loon Lake* (1980), *Lives of the Poets* (1984), and *World's Fair* (1985). His play, *Drinks Before Dinner* (1978), was originally produced by the New York Shakespeare Festival. Mr. Doctorow is the recipient of the National Book Critics Circle Award, the National Book Award, the John Simon Guggenheim Fellowship, and the Arts and Letters award of the American Academy and National Institute of Arts and Letters. He lives and works in New York.